High Praise for Jill Shalvis

"Count on Jill Shalvis for a witty, steamy, unputdownable love story."

—Robyn Carr, *New York Times* bestselling author

"Fall in love with Jill Shalvis! She's my go-to read for humor and heart."

—Susan Mallery, *New York Times* bestselling author

"I always enjoy reading a Jill Shalvis book. She's a consistently elegant, bold, clever writer."

—All About Romance

"Shalvis [has a] knack for creating witty, humorous, warmhearted characters dealing with complex emotional situations."

—*Library Journal*

"Shalvis writes with humor, heart, and sizzling heat!"

—Carly Phillips, *New York Times* bestselling author

Lucky in Love

"Shalvis pens a tale rife with the three 'H's of romance: heat, heart and humor. *Lucky in Love* is a down-to-the-toes charmer..."

—*RT Book Reviews*

"Another touching, funny, delectably sexy treat."

—*Library Journal*

"*Lucky in Love* hits all the right notes—funny yet sweet, a light romance that was made all the more unforgettable by its witty heroine and *Mysterious Cute Guy* hero."

—TheRomanceReviews.com

Head Over Heels

"[A] touching, character-rich, laughter-laced, knockout sizzler."

—*Library Journal*, starred review

"Healthy doses of humor, lust, and love work their magic…a big winner."

—*Publishers Weekly*

"A Perfect Ten! A truly fun and engaging tale from beginning to end."

—RomanceReviewsToday.com

One
Lucky
Day

One Lucky Day

2-in-1 Edition with
Head Over Heels and *Lucky in Love*

JILL SHALVIS

FOREVER

NEW YORK   BOSTON

Head Over Heels copyright © 2011 by Jill Shalvis
Lucky in Love copyright © 2012 by Jill Shalvis

Cover design by Daniela Medina. Cover copyright © 2021 by Hachette Book Group, Inc.

Forever
Hachette Book Group
1290 Avenue of the Americas, New York, NY 10104
read-forever.com
twitter.com/readforeverpub

Head Over Heels originally published in 2011 and *Lucky in Love* originally published in 2012 by Forever.
First 2-in-1 edition: February 2021

Forever is an imprint of Grand Central Publishing. The Forever name and logo are trademarks of Hachette Book Group, Inc.

The publisher is not responsible for websites (or their content) that are not owned by the publisher.

The Hachette Speakers Bureau provides a wide range of authors for speaking events. To find out more, go to www.hachettespeakersbureau.com or call (866) 376-6591.

ISBN: 978-1-5387-5405-4 (mass market 2-in-1)

Printed in the United States of America

CW

10 9 8 7 6 5 4 3 2 1

One
Lucky
Day

Head Over Heels

*To another youngest sister. To my
youngest, Courtney, whose heart
is the biggest of all.*

*And also to Lance Tyler, my real life
inspiration for the Lance in my story,
who I know is sitting on a cloud
somewhere, amused at my attempt at
giving him a Happy Ever After. For
additional information on cystic
fibrosis, go to www.cff.org.*

Acknowledgments

To Melinda, who read the rough draft and lent me her husband Todd's expertise on being a cop. And to Todd, for answering the endless questions. All mistakes are mine.

To Gena, who asked for a big, tough, stoic hero. Sawyer's all for you.

And last but definitely not least, to Jolie and Debbi, because without you two, this book would still be on the floor in little bits and pieces, and me alongside it. :)

Chapter 1

"If at first you don't succeed, destroy
all evidence that you tried."
—*Chloe Traeger*

It wasn't often that Chloe Traeger beat her sisters into the kitchen in the morning, but with Tara and Maddie currently sleeping with the town's two hottest hotties, it'd been only a matter of time.

And in the name of fairness, Chloe hadn't actually gotten to bed yet, but that was just a technicality. With a wide yawn, she started the coffee. Then, gathering what she needed, she hopped up onto the counter—hissing in pain from her throbbing legs. The quiet in the kitchen soothed her as she mixed ingredients together for her natural antibacterial cream. Given how loudly she lived her life, the silence was a nice start to the day.

Especially today, which promised to get crazy quickly, though not much could out-crazy last night. Later in the afternoon, she'd be doing her esthetician thing at a high-end spa in Seattle, but first she had to put in some time here in Lucky Harbor at the B&B that she ran with her sisters.

The fact that her days were centering around work instead of play had her shaking her head with a rueful smile. Oh, how things change. Only a year ago, she'd been free as a bird, roaming happily from spa to spa at will, with no real ties. Then she and the half-sisters she'd never really known had inherited a dilapidated, falling-down-on-its-axis beach inn. With absolutely no knowledge of what to do with it.

Hard to believe how far they'd come. They'd renovated, turned the place into a thriving B&B, and now Chloe, Tara, and Maddie were real sisters instead of strangers. Friends, even.

Well, okay, so they were still working on the friends part, but they hadn't fought all week. Progress, right? And the fact that Chloe had been gone for four of the past seven days working at a five-star-hotel spa in Arizona instead of here in Washington didn't count.

Chloe looked down at the organic lavender oil she'd just "borrowed" from Tara's stash for her cream and winced.

Probably she could work harder on the friend thing...

Out the window, waves pounded the rocky shore in the purple light of dawn as she yawned again and stirred the softened beeswax and lanolin together with the lavender oil. When she was done, she carefully poured the cream into a sterile bottle. Then, still sitting on the counter, she tugged the legs of her sweat bottoms up to her knees, cringing in pain as she began to apply the antiseptic to the two long gashes on each of her calves. She was still sucking in a pained breath when the back door opened.

Sheriff Sawyer Thompson.

He practically had to duck to come in. He was in uniform, gun at his hip, expression dialed to Dirty Harry, and just looking at him had something pinging low in Chloe's belly.

He didn't appear to have the same reaction to her, of course.

Nothing rippled Sawyer's implacable calm or got past that tough exterior. And he did have a hell of an exterior. At six feet three inches, he was built like a linebacker. But in a stunning defiance of physics, he usually had a way of moving all those mouth-watering muscles with an easy, male, fluid grace that would make an extreme fighter jealous.

Stupid muscles, Chloe thought as something deep within her tightened again from just looking at him. Some complicated combination of annoyance and reluctant lust. Last she'd checked, they had developed a sort of uneasy truce, meaning he lived by his rules and she lived by hers. Mostly this meant two different roads to the same conclusion, but there'd been some... misunderstandings.

Not wanting to explain last night—which would undoubtedly lead to another misunderstanding—she quickly yanked her sweatpants legs down to hide her injuries, shooting him the most professional smile in her repertoire. "Sheriff," she said smoothly.

The guarded expression that he wore as purposefully as he did the gun at his hip slipped for a single beat as he looked around. "Just you this morning?"

"Yep." Her smile turned genuine as Chloe enjoyed achieving what few could. She'd knocked that blank expression right off his face. She knew that was because he hadn't been expecting her. It was usually Tara who made the coffee every morning, coffee so amazing that Sawyer routinely stopped by on his way to work for a cup instead of facing the station's crap.

"Tara's not out of Ford's bed yet," she informed him.

The mention of his best friend and Chloe's sister in bed together made him grimace. Or more likely, it was Chloe's bluntness. In either case, he recovered and strode to the coffeemaker, his gait oddly measured, as if he was as tired-to-the-bone as she.

The county police and sheriff departments played weekly

baseball games against the firefighters and paramedics, and they'd had one last night. Maybe Sawyer had played too hard. Maybe he'd had a hot date after. Given how women tried to get pulled over by him just to get face time, it was possible. After all, according to Lucky Harbor's Facebook page, phone calls to the county dispatch made by females between the ages of twenty-one and forty went up substantially whenever Sawyer was on duty.

His utility belt gleamed in the bright overhead light. His uniform shirt was wrinkled in the back and damp with sweat. She was wondering about that when he turned to her, gesturing to the coffeepot questioningly.

Heaven forbid the man waste a single word. "Help yourself," she said. "I just made it."

That made him pause. "You poison it?"

From her perch on the counter, she smiled. "Maybe."

With a small head shake, Sawyer reached into the cupboard for the to-go mugs Tara kept there for him.

"You're feeling brave, then," she noted.

He lifted a broad-as-a-mountain shoulder as he poured, then pointed to her own mug steaming on the counter at her side. "You're drinking it. You're a lot of things, Chloe, but crazy isn't one of them."

She suspected one of those "things" was a big pain in his very fine ass, but she shrugged.

Sawyer leaned his big frame against the counter to study her. Quiet. Speculative.

Undoubtedly, people caved when he did this, rushing to fill the silence. But silence had never bothered Chloe. No, what bothered her was the way she felt when he looked at her like that. For one thing, his eyes were mesmerizing. They were the color of melting milk chocolate but sometimes, like now, the tiny gold flecks in them sparked like fire. His hair was brown, too, the sort that contained every hue under the sun and could never be replicated in a salon. At the moment, it was on the wrong side of his last cut and in a state of dishevelment, falling over his forehead in front and nearly to his collar in back. The lines in his face were drawn tight with exhaustion, and she realized that he probably hadn't been headed in for his shift as she'd assumed, but just finishing one. Which meant that he'd been out all night, too, fighting crime like a superhero.

And yet somehow, he still managed to smell good. Guy good. She didn't understand it, but everything about him reminded her that she was a woman.

And that she hadn't had sex in far too long. "Seems a little early, even for you," she noted.

"Could say the same to you."

Something in his voice caused the first little niggle of suspicion in her brain and put her on alert. "Got a lot of things to mix up for the day spa I'm running later," she said.

His eyes never wavered from hers. "Or?"

Crap. Crap, she'd underestimated him. He was onto her, and the nerves quivered in her belly. "Or what?" she asked casually, shifting to get down off the counter, not looking forward to the pain at the contact. But Sawyer moved before she could, blocking her escape. His hips wedged between her legs, one hand on her thigh, the other on her opposite ankle, holding her in place.

"Romantic," she said dryly, even as her heart began to pound. "But I should get breakfast first, don't you think?"

"You're bleeding through your sweatpants." He shoved the sweats back up her legs to her knees, careful to avoid the wounds. As his eyes fixed on the deep gashes, the only sign he gave that he felt anything was the bunching of his jaw.

Chloe tried to pull free, but he was twice her size and tightened his grip on her thigh. "Hold still." He looked over the injuries, expression grim. "Explain."

"Um, I fell getting out of bed?"

He lifted his head and pinned her with his sharp gaze. "Try again, without the question mark."

"I fell hiking."

"Yeah," he said. "And I have some swamp land to sell you."

"Hey, I could be telling the truth."

"You don't hike, Chloe. It aggravates your asthma."

Actually, as it was turning out, *living* aggravated her asthma.

Sawyer bent to look more closely, pushing her hand away when she tried to block his view. "Steel," he said. "Steel fencing, I'm guessing. Probably rusted."

Her heart stopped. He knew. It seemed impossible—she'd been so careful—but *he knew*.

"You need a tetanus shot." He straightened his big frame but didn't move or let her go. "And a keeper, too," he added tightly. "Where are the dogs, Chloe?"

"I don't know what you're talking about." Except that she did. She knew because she'd spent the long hours of the night with her best friend, Lance, procuring the very six dogs he'd just mentioned.

AKA stealing them.

But in her defense, it had been a matter of life and death. The young pit bulls belonged to a guy named Nick Raybo, who'd planned on fighting them for sport. What Chloe and Lance had done had undoubtedly saved the dogs' lives, but had also been good old-fashioned breaking and entering. And since B&E wasn't exactly legal . . .

Sawyer waited her out, and for the record, he was good at it. As big and bad as he was, he had more patience than Job, a result, no doubt, of his years behind the badge and hearing every outrageous story under the sun. And like probably thousands before her, Chloe caved like a cheap suitcase. "The dogs are with Lance," she said on a sigh.

He stared at her for one stunned beat. "Jesus, Chloe."

"They were going to die!"

His expression still said one-hundred-percent cop, but there was a very slight softening in his tone. "You should have called me," he said.

Maybe, she thought. "And you would have done what? They hadn't begun the fighting yet so you couldn't have taken the dogs off the property. And they were going to fight them tonight, Sawyer." Even now it made her feel sick. "They were going to pit them against each other. To the death." Her voice cracked a little on that, but he didn't comment as he once again bent his head and studied the gouges on her legs.

He was right about how she'd gotten them. It'd happened when she'd crawled beneath the fence behind Lance as they'd made their escape. She held her breath, not knowing what Sawyer might do. He could arrest her, certainly. But he didn't reach for his cuffs or cite her Miranda rights, both good signs in her book.

"These are deep," was all he said.

She let out a breath. "They're not so bad."

"You clean them out?" He ran a long, callused finger down her calf alongside one particularly nasty gash, and she shivered. Not from pain. Maybe it was her exhaustion, or hell, maybe it was just from having him stand so close, but the stoic, tough-guy thing was sort of doing it for her this morning. He was a little on edge and sweaty, and a whole lot hot and sexy, and utterly without her permission, her brain rolled out a "Stern Cop and the Bad Girl" fantasy...

"Chloe."

She blinked away the image of him frisking her. "Yeah?"

His expression a little wary now, he repeated himself. "Did you clean these out?"

"Yes, sir."

He slid her a look, and she smiled innocently, but clearly she needed to have her hormone levels checked when she got her tetanus booster for this injury because she was *way* too aware of the heat and strength of him emanating through his uniform. Not to mention the matching heat washing through *her*, which was especially annoying because she had a personal decree that she never dated uptight, unbending men—particularly ones with badges.

The back door opened and Chloe jumped. Not Sawyer. Nothing ruffled him. Hell, he probably had sex without getting ruffled.

No, she thought, glancing up into his eyes. That wasn't true. Sawyer would have no qualms about getting ruffled, and a little shiver racked her body just as her sister Maddie walked into the kitchen, followed by her fiancé, Jax.

Not too long ago, both Tara and Chloe had nicknamed Maddie "the mouse," but she'd outgrown that moniker in spades since coming to Lucky Harbor. Now Maddie took one look at Sawyer wedged between Chloe's thighs and stopped short so fast that Jax plowed into her back. "What's this?" she demanded.

Chloe couldn't blame anyone for the shock, as typically she and Sawyer didn't share space well. In fact, usually when forced into close proximity, they resembled two tigers circling each other, teeth bared.

"Whatever it is," Jax said, taking in the scene, "it looks like fun." Jax was tall, lean, and on a mission as he poured himself a coffee and came directly toward Chloe, reaching for the drawer beneath her right thigh. "Can you move her leg?" he asked Sawyer. "I need a spoon, man."

Mouth still agog, Maddie plopped down into a chair. She waggled a finger between Chloe and Sawyer. "So you two are . . . ?"

"No!" Chloe said and shoved at Sawyer, who still didn't budge, damn him. The two-hundred-plus lug was bent over her left calf again—the worst one—his hair brushing the insides of her thighs. She told herself *not* to think about how the silky strands would feel on her bare skin, but she totally did, and shivered again.

Sawyer looked up at her and she did her best to look cold instead of turned on. "You might actually need stitches," he said.

With a horrified gasp, Maddie hopped up to come look. Seconds later, Chloe had her sister, her sister's fiancé, and the man she didn't quite know how to categorize at all, standing far too close, staring at her injuries. She tried to close her legs but couldn't and tossed up her hands. "They're just scratches!"

"Oh, Chloe," Maddie murmured, concern creasing her brow. "Honey, you should have called me. What happened, and where else are you hurt?"

Sawyer's gaze ran over Chloe's entire body now, as if he could see through her sweats. A very naughty part of her brain considered telling him that the scratches went all the way up just so he'd demand a more thorough inspection.

Bad, *bad* brain. Because at just the thought, her chest tightened, and she had to reach for her inhaler, thanks to the asthma that always kept her slightly breathless.

And sexless. "It's nothing," she said. "I'm fine, all right? Back up."

Sawyer gave Jax a light shove away from her. "She and Lance rescued six dogs from the McCarthy place last night," he said to Maddie, ratting Chloe out without qualm.

Maddie shook her head, clearly horrified. "Chloe. God. That was…crazy dangerous."

Hearing the worry in her voice had guilt tugging at Chloe. She couldn't believe how much she'd grown to care about the two strangers that were her half-sisters, or for that matter, about Lucky Harbor and the people in it. The fact that she'd let down her guard enough to care at all was new.

For most of her childhood, it had been just Chloe and her

mom, and the lessons had been clear: Connections weren't meant to last past the overnight camping pass. Only traditionalists let themselves get trapped by things like boring relationships or full-time jobs. The special people were destined to spread their wings and live life fully and freely.

Like Chloe and Phoebe.

"Raybo is crazy," Maddie said, moving to get coffee. "It could have gotten ugly."

Chloe wished Sawyer would move, too, and gave him a nudge with her foot. Actually, it might have been more like a kick. Didn't matter, he was a mountain and didn't move.

"It's awfully hot in here," Maddie said, and opened the window.

"It's called sexual tension." Jax sent an eyebrow wiggle in Sawyer and Chloe's direction.

Humor from the peanut gallery.

Sawyer sent Jax the sort of long, level look that undoubtedly had bad guys losing control of their bowels, but Jax just smiled. "If *I* was going to make that move on a woman, I'd at least have bought her breakfast first."

Chloe nodded. "That's what I said."

Maddie plopped into Jax's lap to cuddle up to him. "You made *plenty* of moves on me before you ever bought me breakfast."

"I'm not making moves," Sawyer said. Maddie and Jax stared pointedly at his position between Chloe's thighs. He lifted his hands from her as if he'd been burned, backing up with his hands in the air. "Okay, I'm going to bed now. Alone."

"You know what your problem is?" Jax asked. "You don't know how to have fun. Haven't for a long time."

"Does this"—Sawyer pointed in the general vicinity of Chloe's lower body—"look anything like *fun* to you?"

Jax choked back a snort, and even Maddie bit her lower lip to hide a smile.

"Jesus," Sawyer said with a small head shake. "You know what I mean."

Yeah. He'd meant the sorry mess Chloe had made of her legs, as well as the risks she'd taken last night, but she said "*hey*" anyway in token protest. Because dammit, her lower half could be lots of fun.

If she ever got to use it, that is.

Chapter 2

"If things don't seem right, try going left."
—*Chloe Traeger*

One week later, Sawyer Thompson walked into his bedroom, dropped his gun and cell phone onto the nightstand, and glanced at his bed. It'd been a hell of a day, and the only thing that could have saved it would have been a woman waiting for him.

Naked.

With nefarious intentions in mind.

He should have thought ahead when he'd broken it off with Cindy a few months back. But after four dates, the sweet, quiet, unassuming middle school teacher had already been unhappy going out with a guy who was on call just about 24-7.

He couldn't blame her. But nor could he change for her.

Needing a hot shower, he stripped and stood beneath the spray. Pressing his palms to the tile wall, he dropped his head and let the water bead over his aching neck and shoulders. Today should have been a day off, but the county was perpetually understaffed, and fellow sheriff Tony Sanchez had taken a personal day to help his wife take their newborn twins for a checkup. This left Sawyer covering not just Lucky Harbor but two neighboring small towns as well.

By midmorning, he'd faced a dead homeless guy slumped on a park bench—natural causes, according to the ME—and delivered a newborn out on Highway 37 from a woman in labor who somehow thought it was a good idea to drive herself to the hospital with contractions only one and a half minutes apart.

After that, there was still time left in his day to break up a barroom brawl, deal with a domestic dispute call, and his favorite, rescue a five-year-old and his puppy from a muddy storm drain.

The shower removed the residual dirt clinging to him from that last call, but it didn't revive him or numb the unrest coiling in his gut. A pizza and a beer might make a dent, but he didn't have time for that. Earlier he'd heard a rumor that Nick Raybo had procured more dogs and was planning a midnight event. Sawyer was going to make sure that didn't happen. Maybe he'd get pizza and beer afterward with Ford and Jax. Either of his best friends would join him no matter the time, but Sawyer knew he'd be shitty company tonight.

And in any case, what he really craved was a woman to bury himself in, and it wasn't sweet Cindy who came to mind as he soaped up. Nope, against all the reason and logic that he prided himself on, he wanted the one woman whose favorite pastime seemed to be pushing his buttons.

The thought of it, of having Chloe, was about as crazy as his week had been. She was obstinate, impulsive, trouble with a capital T...and damn. *Hot*. She was also a walking-talking reminder of a part of his life he'd given up—the wild part. There was a lot of sexual attraction, but no future. Because while he was a permanent fixture in this town, Chloe was just a sexy little tumbleweed blowing through.

The day after the dog-nabbing incident, there'd been an article in the opinion section of the local paper about recent vandalisms and petty theft in the area. The anonymous writer had gone on to include a list of people in town known for trouble seeking, and Chloe had been on it.

Not a big surprise.

He wondered if she'd been disturbed or upset by it. It wasn't in her nature to worry about what people thought of her. But he bet her sisters had been. They were trying to generate *good* press for the B&B, not negative.

Of course, if he'd arrested her for trespassing, B&E, and theft, *that* would have been negative press. And a personal hell for him since Tara and Maddie would have skinned him alive. Which was not why he hadn't arrested her, he told himself. He hadn't arrested her because . . . shit. Because for the first time in his adult life, he'd chosen to look the other way, and it didn't sit well.

He'd seen her several times this week. Once when she'd been coming out of the urgent care with a Band-Aid on her arm from her tetanus shot, and then again riding her Vespa on the highway, her long, wild red hair billowing out behind her, her helmet and Hollywood-style sunglasses hiding most of her face.

And yesterday he'd run into her at the grocery store just as she was pulling a bottle of vodka from the shelf, which she'd assured him was for work.

He'd laughed. He'd only been in the store to grab a sports drink on the way to his weekly baseball game, but he'd immediately forgotten about that, standing there in the aisle feeling . . . alive. "Work," he said. "The vodka's for work."

"It cleans glass like nobody's business. And if applied topically, it works as a great preservative. And did you know that used as a *non*-topical application, it's the perfect man cure?"

"How's that?"

"A few shots, and you're cured of wanting one."

He shook his head now at the memory. How in the hell she managed to make him want to both kiss her and run like hell was beyond him. He stepped out of the shower, dropped his towel, and pulled on fresh clothes before going back out. When he was on duty, he drove a department marked SUV. His personal vehicle was a truck. Both were equipped for whatever came his way, and tonight, going low profile, he took the truck. Lucky Harbor was basically a tiny little bowl sitting on the rocky Washington State coast, walled in by majestic peaks and lush forest. It was all an inky shadow now.

Nick Raybo had ten acres of land out at Eagle's Bluff, deep into the forest. It was rugged and isolated out there, perfect for all sorts of illegal dealings and a favorite place for partiers.

But that's not where Sawyer headed first.

At this time of night, his truck was the only vehicle on the road as he headed down the hill into town. The moon peeked through the clouds, hanging low and wan. It cast a pale glow over the Pacific Ocean churning against the rocky terrain off to his left. The pier was dark, the town was dark, and his thoughts were darker still.

He'd been raised here, though he used the term "raised" loosely. It'd been just him and his father, Nolan Thompson, a blue-collar union man who believed in hard work, Jim Beam, and ruling with an iron fist.

Or in Sawyer's case, a wicked long leather belt.

It hadn't helped much. Sawyer had been just about as wild as they came, which made it all the more amusing to those who knew him best that he now wielded a badge.

He drove through town and onto the narrow road that led to the Lucky Harbor Beach B&B. The inn was a Victorian, freshly painted and renovated, lit up warm and welcoming for guests.

Pulling around to the back of the property, he idled in front of the small owner's cottage where Chloe lived.

The lights were off.

Sawyer hoped like hell that meant she was sleeping and *not* up at Eagle's Bluff with Lance in the middle of another Two Stooges act that could get them killed this time, but his luck wasn't running that way. A quick swipe of his flashlight didn't reveal her Vespa.

Shit.

Exhausted and doing a slow burn at the thought of what Chloe might be up to, he got out of his truck to check around. To his relief, he found her Vespa parked on the side of the cottage.

On the way back to his truck, he flicked his light to the front door, taking in the potted plants thriving there and the yoga mat leaning against the wall. When she was in Lucky Harbor and not working at a spa somewhere around the country, Chloe liked to do yoga on the beach at sunrise. He'd seen her on that very mat, lit by the morning sun glinting off the waves, her tanned, toned limbs bent in impossible ways that made him think of other, better ways to bend them. Chloe on her mat was not only a huge turn-on, but an anomaly. She was blithe and breathless, literally, both from her free-spirited nature and from her severe asthma— the one exception being when she was doing yoga, the sole thing in her life that required a deep, calm stillness. Most likely that was what drew her to it.

He had no idea what drew him to her.

Okay, not true. She had a sharp mind, an even sharper wit, and used both to drive him up a wall as often as she could.

She was good at it.

He was good at letting her.

Shaking his head at himself, Sawyer turned to go just as someone cried out, the sound cutting through the night. He was at the front door, gun in hand, when the cry came again.

Not a pain-filled scream, he realized. Not one of terror either, but of passion. *Loud* passion, he corrected as she did it again.

Chloe.

Jesus. Closing his eyes, Sawyer dropped his head to the door, wishing like hell he wasn't here, listening to Chloe in the throes of what sounded like wild animal sex.

When the scream came a third time, a ridiculously over-the-top porn-star wail of epic proportions, it was accompanied by a low, husky, unmistakably male voice.

Definitely time to get the hell out of there. Sawyer turned on his heel to do just that, but the porch light suddenly flickered on, fully illuminating him to whoever was peeking out the peephole. A second later, the bolt clicked and the front door whipped open.

"*Sawyer?*"

Grimacing, he turned back. Chloe stood in the doorway, her best friend, Lance, at her side, both fully dressed, thank Christ.

Lance ran the ice cream shop on the pier with his brother, Tucker. He was in his mid-twenties like Chloe, but painfully thin and pale from the cystic fibrosis that had been ravaging his body all his life.

Next to him, Chloe seemed to glow, the embodiment of health and exuberance. Her shiny, dark red hair was in wild waves tonight, loosely flying past her shoulders except for the few long bangs that framed her face. She was beautiful enough to be a model, but missing the compliant gene. Chloe had never met a direction or a command that suited her.

She wore a soft, black hoodie sweater that clung to her breasts and dark, hip-hugging jeans tucked into high-heeled boots that gave off a don't-fuck-with-me air but made him ache to do just that. There was a wildness to her tonight, hell, every night, and an inner darkness that he was drawn to in spite of himself.

It called to his true inner nature, the matching wildness and darkness within *him*, which he'd tried to bury a long time ago. Ridiculously relieved that she wasn't having sex, Sawyer backed up to go. She was home, safe and sound, and that was all he cared about.

"Sawyer? What are you doing here?"

Good question. He opened his mouth with absolutely no idea exactly what he planned to say, but Lance suddenly staggered and put his hand to his head.

Chloe instantly slid an arm around Lance's narrow waist to steady him. "What's the matter?"

"Nothing," Lance said, pushing free. "Got up too fast, is all."

"Here, sit." Ignoring his resistance, Chloe gently pushed Lance back inside, to the couch in the small living room. With a hand on his shoulder, she lifted her face to Sawyer, leveling him with her dark green eyes.

A jolt went through him, a zap of something he didn't care to name.

"What can I do for you, Sheriff?" she asked.

Yeah, Sawyer, what can she do for you? He searched his brain. "You can explain breaking the noise ordinance."

Lance laughed softly.

"Noise ordinance?" Chloe asked. "I broke the *noise ordinance* with my pretend orgasm?"

"You did sound like a mule stuck in a tar pit," Lance said helpfully.

"A mule—" Chloe choked on a laugh. "Okay, no one who's heard the real thing would ever even *think* of comparing me to a mule."

This information didn't help Sawyer *at all*. "Is that right?"

Chloe's gaze locked on his. In the sudden charged silence, Lance cleared his throat. "This is weird. I'm going to the kitchen now, while the two of you finish... whatever the hell this is. Call for me if you're going to need bailing out, Chloe."

"Sure," she said, her gaze never leaving Sawyer's. "I'll let you know if I end up in cuffs."

Lance grimaced. "Okay, never mind. *Don't* call me."

Chloe laughed, but Sawyer was stuck on the mental image of her in his cuffs. If he'd been half the cop he liked to think he was, it wouldn't, *couldn't*, cause such an erotic rush.

Something came into Chloe's eyes that told him she knew exactly where his mind had just gone—and that just maybe hers had gone there, too. The temperature in the room seemed to shoot up, but the sound of a harsh coughing in the kitchen, hard and relentless, like someone was dying, sent a chill down Sawyer's back.

Chloe rushed into the kitchen, instantly all soft, warm, caring woman, in a way that Sawyer had never seen directed at him. When he followed, he found her murmuring something for Lance's ears only, reaching for him.

Lance, clearly not willing to be babied, held her off, pounding a fist to his own chest to try to catch some desperately needed air. When he'd finally recovered, he looked over Chloe's head at Sawyer. "If you're here to make sure she's not going to Eagle's Bluff tonight, the coast's clear. She's *not* going."

"Wait— What?" Chloe said, dividing a look between both men. "Nick has more dogs?"

Lance's face went blank. "*Had*."

Sawyer sighed. "You took them already."

"That would be breaking and entering, and stealing," Lance said.

Ah, Christ. Sawyer didn't know whether to be relieved that Lance hadn't dragged Chloe into it again, or be pissed off that he'd once again taken matters into his own hands instead of letting Sawyer handle it. He settled on pissed off because it was easier. "It has to go through proper channels to get it stopped permanently. You know that."

"Proper channels are too slow for the dogs," Lance said unapologetically.

"If you get caught with them, Raybo will press charges."

Lance shrugged. He didn't care. And why should he? The guy was already facing a virtual death sentence with the CF, which left him hell bent and determined to say "fuck you" to karma whenever possible.

Chloe was giving Lance a dark look. She was pissed. But Lance just shook his head. "Like you needed another mention in the paper as a troublemaker."

"I don't care what people think, Lance. I care about you. And those dogs."

"You care what people think of the inn. You care that people whispering about you might keep the inn from getting good word of mouth. You care that it could hurt your sisters."

Chloe let out a breath. "Yeah. I do."

The sudden scent of acrid smoke had Sawyer frowning, and turning on his heel, he headed back outside. Beyond the inn and the cottage was the ocean. He couldn't see it in the dark, but he could hear it pounding the shore. Off to the left was the marina building and dock, and beyond that, woods. The trees were thick as feathers, growing right up to the waterline in some spots. He couldn't see a fire, but he could sure as hell smell it. It was illegal to have a campfire without a permit, not to mention they were in the middle of high fire season, but suddenly from somewhere beyond the tree line came an undeniable glow.

Sawyer turned back to the door, nearly plowing over Chloe, who'd come out after him. It was automatic to reach for her, to grip her arms until balance was restored, but for a beat, they were plastered to each other. Her hair brushed his jaw, her soft breasts pressed against his chest, and as tended to happen with her, he felt something stir inside him other than a frustrated indifference.

She murmured a soft, nearly inaudible apology but didn't pull away.

"My fault," he said, looking down in her face. "Who's in your woods?"

"Tucker and some of his friends," Lance said from behind her.

Tucker was Lance's older brother, which meant the friends with him were Jamie and Todd, and aside from the fact that Todd and Sawyer went way back, to a time Sawyer preferred not to think about, the combo of those four guys usually spelled mayhem. "They have a permit?"

Lance laughed.

Right. No permit. "They doing anything illegal out there besides the campfire?" Sawyer asked.

"Maybe drinking beer."

Perfect. When Todd drank, he became the King of the Terminally Stupid. The others were never far behind. Sawyer stepped off the porch, stopping when Chloe followed him. He grabbed her wrist, his thumb brushing the very small tattoo she had there at her pulse point, an Asian symbol he didn't know the meaning of.

"I want to come with—"

"No," he said, knowing the smoke would bring on her asthma. "Wait here."

At the command, her face closed, and for a moment he wished . . .

Hell. He had no idea what he wished when it came to her. She twisted him in fucking knots. It used to be they just rubbed each other the wrong way, but lately he'd been extremely caught up in rubbing her the right way. Which actually, when it came right down to it, made *him* the King of the Terminally Stupid.

Chapter 3

*"It's always darkest before dawn. So if
you're going to steal your neighbor's
newspaper, that's the time to do it."*
—Chloe Traeger

Chloe held Sawyer's steely gaze with one of her own, though
she got a crick in her neck doing it. He was big, armed to the
teeth, and if the flash in his eyes meant anything, his irritation
level was on the rise.

Nothing new when it came to her.

To be fair, she'd certainly earned his wrath on several
occasions, back when she'd first arrived in Lucky Harbor. But
she'd grown up over the past year and was learning—or trying
anyway—to curb her impulsive, reckless behavior. Having
grown up with a mother whose only consistent passion had been
following the Grateful Dead, Chloe hadn't learned a whole lot
about roots or long-lasting relationships. Or long-lasting *anything* for that matter. But she was working on it, on becoming

more aware of both herself and how her actions affected others. And also what it meant to care. There was no doubt that she was still a work in progress, but then again, she'd never claimed to be anything but.

And slightly tamed though she might be, she could still dig in her heels with the best of them. So when Sawyer commanded her to "wait here," the urge to do the opposite was strong.

It would appear that she wasn't quite as grown up as she thought.

In response to her unspoken reaction, the very corners of Sawyer's lips twitched. Not quite a smile. More like a grimace to go with the faint lines of stress around his eyes and mouth and the tension in his shoulders.

He was tired. From the look of it, he'd already had a hell of a long day, which only added to the ruffian edge to him. He wore a button-down untucked over the gun at his hip, and jeans that fit him perfectly across the butt. Yes, she'd checked.

And let's not forget the testosterone and pheromones and all around general air of badassness. He was a man always ready for anything, anytime, and he wasn't someone to tangle with. Something she knew all too well. He was intense, hard, unyielding, and—

"The smoke, Chloe. Stay back because of the smoke."

—and uncompromisingly fair. With a sigh, she nodded.

He gave her one last long look and walked toward the woods. She'd never been drawn to ridiculous displays of naked courage or sheer brawn, but Sawyer really brought it to a whole new level.

"You're drooling," Lance said dryly, having stepped up to her side.

She ignored him, not taking her eyes off the spot where Sawyer had vanished. No, she wasn't drooling, but something just as bad. She was tingling. It's okay, she told herself. A woman would have to be dead not to feel anything when she looked at Sawyer Thompson, and Chloe wasn't close to dead.

Yet, she thought wryly, feeling the smoke begin to invade her lungs. Twice a day, she took meds to control her asthma, but she also carried a fast-acting inhaler for the in-between times when she hit trouble—like now. She pulled it out of her pocket and took a puff. Then she looked over at Lance. "Where's your sweatshirt? Your lips are blue."

They both knew his lips weren't blue because he was cold, but Lance obligingly went back inside for his sweatshirt. "You're so predictable, Chloe."

Chloe was many things. She was a sister, a friend, an esthetician. She was a wanderer and an adventurer. She was also hard-willed, stubborn as an ox, and quick to temper. But one thing she wasn't, was predictable. "Take that back," she said.

"*Predictable*," he repeated. "Among other things."

"Such as?" She stepped off the porch but stopped when Lance grabbed her wrist.

"You're staying," he said. "I don't want to get arrested tonight for aggravating an officer."

"He won't arrest you for that." But he was right, there was no reason to piss Sawyer off. And yet, dammit, staying went against the grain. Like so many other things in her life. It was her asthma's fault. It held her back, and because of it, she tended to push the envelope too far in other ways. She understood that, from the outside looking in, it might seem like she had a secret death wish, but she didn't. It was just that when she was in the midst of an asthma attack, she often felt so close to death that she, well, *dared* it. But she just wanted to run or dance or laugh hard, or have sex without needing an inhaler and possibly an ambulance.

Not exactly a common problem, but one that often left her straddling a fine line between socially acceptable behavior and the wild yearnings her mother had always encouraged. Her sisters wanted her to stop pushing those boundaries and settle down a little. And it was that which bothered Chloe more than anything. The message was simple: If she wanted to be accepted, even loved, by those she'd come to care about, she'd need to change. But dammit, she wanted to be accepted just as she was, imperfections and all. "Predictable," she said like it was a dirty word.

Lance sighed and put a hand over hers. "Okay, maybe not predictable so much as…"

"Crazy?"

He laughed softly.

He got her, and always had. So it really sucked that they had no chemistry together. "Lance?"

"Yeah?"

She squeezed his fingers. "I'm really annoyed that you aren't sexy."

"Gee, thanks," he said dryly.

"To me, I mean." She nudged her shoulder against his. "I want to want you. You know?"

Lance slid a hand to her ass. "Give me ten minutes and I'll change your mind— *Oof*," he said when she elbowed him, but he laughed good-naturedly. He knew. They both knew. First of all, he was like her brother and had been since the day they'd met. And second, he was totally, completely, pathetically hung-up on one of the cute nurses at the medical center where he spent far too much of his time.

Not that he'd ever do anything about it.

"What woman would be attracted to a sick guy with a looming expiration date?" he'd asked her once.

Which left it just the two of them against the world.

Not having sex.

A low-lying fog was rolling in off the water, slipping through the night toward them like silvery fingers. Through it, several shadows appeared, materializing into the outlines of men. Todd, Tucker, and Jamie, with bad attitude in every line of their bodies.

Sawyer was behind them.

As they came closer, Chloe saw that Todd was holding a piece of paper. Normally he was also one of those easy charmers who could convince a nun to give up her habit. He'd certainly turned it on her as often as possible—not that it'd ever gotten him anywhere. But now he displayed none of that charm, passing by the porch without a word, heading around to the side of the marina where they'd parked. Jamie went with him.

Not Tucker. He stopped and looked up the porch steps at his brother, an odd tension simmering between the siblings. "You okay?" Tucker finally asked, and when Lance nodded, he gestured the way Todd and Jamie had gone. "Then let's go, we're out of here."

Lance's gaze slid to the retreating stiff shoulders of Todd and Jamie with unease, and Chloe grabbed his hand. "You promised to stay and try out my chest rub to see if it helps you breathe easier, remember? I'll drive you home after."

When Tucker left without another word, Lance squeezed her hand, then dropped it. "I'll be inside," he said, and with one last look at the still silent Sawyer, vanished into the cottage.

Chloe turned to the sheriff. The shimmering tension between them certainly wasn't sibling-like. Nor was it going to disappear anytime soon, which meant she had two choices: Get used to it or fight it.

Because Sawyer was the last man on earth that she should ever get involved with, option number two was the smart route.

Returning her gaze evenly, he waited. He never spoke more words than absolutely necessary, and this drove her batshit crazy. "What happened out there?"

"I ticketed Todd for the illegal bonfire."

"Just Todd?"

"He was the one who started it."

She paused. Todd was one of those guys who could talk his way into a bank vault with nothing but a smile, and then walk out with all the money, leaving the bank manager happy to have been ripped off. He was also a native Lucky Harbor guy, and the residents were very fond of their own, troubled son or no.

Sawyer was native too, and just as well liked, if not more so. "You ticketed him even though everyone lights illegal bonfires out there?"

"Not in a high fire hazard season, they don't," he said.

"It's almost October."

"Fire season," Sawyer repeated.

"So...if I lit a campfire, you'd arrest me?"

"Ticket," he corrected. "Not arrest. Not for a first offense."

What was wrong with her that the stern cop thing he had going on was doing it for her? Huh. Maybe she didn't want to fight this attraction so much as test its boundaries. "What if it was my second offense? Would you frisk and cuff me then?"

His eyes darkened. "What is it with you and my cuffs?"

"Well, if you don't know," Chloe said as demurely as she could, "I don't want to corrupt you." She made to go inside, but Sawyer snagged her sweater and tugged her back.

"Not so fast," he said and studied her, giving nothing of his thoughts away. "You're playing with me," he finally decided.

"Trying."

"I don't like games, Chloe."

No shit. She'd known him for nearly a year now, and yet she didn't know him at all. He kept everything extremely close to the vest, which she could admit made her quite envious, as she was completely incapable of doing the same.

"What were you and Lance up to earlier?" he wanted to know.

"Popcorn. Chatting. Stuff."

"I mean with the Meg Ryan orgasm impersonation."

She hesitated. This was going to be embarrassing. "I'm not sure you're going to understand."

"Try me."

"Okay, well, sometimes the cottage creaks at night, you know?"

"It's probably the wood and joints settling."

"Yes, but it's the 'probably' part that gets me. At night, it's...loud."

"And you sleep here alone now."

"Yes." Maddie had moved in with Jax, and in fact, was marrying him in two months. Tara had moved out as well to live with her boyfriend, Ford. The three sisters worked out shifts when they had overnight guests, but for the most part, Chloe took care of anything that came up because she was the one without a life. "Sometimes it sounds like there's a...ghost." She waited for him to laugh, and even gave some thought to all the ways she might hurt him if he did, but he didn't.

He just looked at her meditatively. "You could tell your sisters you don't like sleeping here alone."

Hell, no. She'd already managed to stir up negative press; she wasn't going to bring more chaos. "They have more on their plates than I do. I'm not going to add worry or grief to it by telling them I'm afraid." And she wished like hell that she wasn't telling him either. "It's no big deal. It's just that I read one Stephen King too many, and sometimes, I get a little freaked is all. Lance knows that and comes over, and we make up funny stories to go with my ghost."

"Stories."

"Tonight we decided the ghost died here at age ninety-nine. A virgin."

"A ninety-nine-year-old-virgin ghost."

"Hey, it's not as unlikely as you might think. Anyway, she can't go on to her afterlife until she has an orgasm. So she stays here, granting wishes. Tonight Lance wished for a long, normal life, and..." Her throat tightened because Lance could wish all he wanted but it wasn't going to happen for him. And God, how she hated that, hated it so damn much that sometimes she couldn't breathe just thinking about it. "So assuming the ghost grants his wish," she said softly, "in return, we were trying to give her the orgasm she'd never had."

His mouth twitched. "A *fake* orgasm."

"Yes, well, it's the best we had." She didn't know how she felt about Sawyer catching her silly show, or what the hell he could have possibly thought when he'd heard her screaming.

Or why she cared...

But she did. And in return, he nodded in understanding. It didn't exactly go with the tough, unflappable cop image she'd always had of him, a guy who followed the rules and a set path for life like a map, no veering. Black and white, always.

He certainly wasn't someone who would get her need to live saturated in color.

Lance poked his head out and showed her that he was holding the chest rub. "Ready to take me home?"

Nodding, Chloe turned from Sawyer.

"Chloe," he said. "You're staying away from Eagle's Bluff tonight."

She glanced back, not surprised he'd bring it up again, and even less surprised that it was a command and not a question. "Sure."

"I mean it, Chloe."

He was back to being all cop. It defined him. It suited him. It must be nice to know what defined you, what suited you. "I know you do, Sheriff."

He let her go, and she got on the Vespa, putting on her

helmet. Lance got on behind her and slid his arms around her waist. Chloe revved the engine and hit the gas, glancing into her side mirror.

As they pulled away, she could see Sawyer standing there watching them go in the growing fog.

Chapter 4

*"Why was man created before woman?
Because you always need a rough draft
before the final copy."*
—Chloe Traeger

Chloe got up before dawn, when the sky was still inky black. Every October was fire season but this October, drier than any in recent history, made it all the more dangerous. Still, there were some benefits to a dry fall, and taking advantage of it, she dressed in yoga pants and a long-sleeved tee and took her mat to the beach to work out. When she was on the road, she did yoga in some of the fanciest hotels in the world, but here, with the rhythmic pulsing of the waves crashing onto the rocks, the seagulls squawking, the sand crunching beneath her mat—this was her favorite.

Afterward, she walked. She didn't usually do that, couldn't if her chest was too tight, but she had the time this morning and needed to burn some energy.

Everything was quiet, not a single soul stirring except the

seagulls and the pounding surf, but she knew her way well enough by now to get along in the predawn. Lucky Harbor was a picturesque little beach town, nestled in a rocky cove with an eclectic mix of the old and new. The main drag was lined with Victorian-style buildings, most painted in a variety of bright colors. There was a long pier that jutted out into the water, lined with a café, a few shops, an arcade, and a Ferris wheel. Since Chloe wasn't ready to face her day, she walked the pier to the end, standing in one of the far corners between two benches so that she could feel surrounded by the ocean below.

She gave herself a *Titanic* moment, closing her eyes, raising her face to the salty, still chilly air. To the east, the dark sky was tinged slightly purple with the coming day.

It was hard to believe that she was still here in Lucky Harbor. A year ago, she, Tara, and Maddie had been living their own lives, rarely connecting, so different. Whether that was due to the mysteries of genetics from their three different fathers or simply the fact that they'd been raised separately, Chloe didn't know. Their mom, Phoebe Traeger, had been the embodiment of a true, free spirit. She'd kept to the road, found love—often—then had moved along. Nothing had stuck to Phoebe, not even her two eldest daughters. Nothing except Chloe. Chloe had been her one concession to a traditional life, if you could consider being schooled in the back of a VW bus and eating most of their meals in soup kitchens traditional.

Tara's father had taken Tara with him when he and Phoebe's relationship had deteriorated. Maddie's father had done the same when she'd come along a few years later. Chloe couldn't say what her own father had done or felt, as she'd never known him. Phoebe hadn't talked about him and had always dodged Chloe's questions by claiming Chloe was a gift from a life well lived.

Ahead of Chloe, the Pacific Ocean was a deep, choppy sea of black, meeting the metallic sky. The entire vista was framed by rocky bluffs, misty and breathtaking. She stood there and wondered at her fondness for this place, which seemed to anchor her like no other. She'd been fond of places before, lots of them, but she'd never had a connection like the one she'd had with Lucky Harbor.

When she heard footsteps come up behind her, she instinctively grabbed her inhaler like it was Mace and whirled around.

Sawyer stood there all rugged and damp from exertion and looking damn gorgeous. He took in her ready stance and then the inhaler, held out like a gun. "Going to shoot me with that?"

Chloe shoved the inhaler back into her waistband. "What are you doing?" It was a stupid question, born of nerves. He was dressed in sweatpants and a T-shirt, breathing heavy but not overly labored. Clearly he'd been running, which caused a yearning to well up within her to do the same. But running would be like stepping out in front of a speeding car—deadly.

"You okay?" he asked.

"Of course." It was easier to think of Sawyer as a badge. A sanctimonious authority figure, and an irritating one at that. But whether she liked it or not, there *was* more to the man, much more. Yeah, he was tough, stoic, and impenetrable, but once in a while he'd reveal more, like the way his eyes filled with concern when he'd seen her injuries after rescuing the dogs, not to mention how he'd let her stretch the letter of the law that night. "I'm always okay," she said. "Tell me what happened last night at Eagle's Bluff."

He gave her one of his patented "yeah right" looks.

Okay, so he was still more irritating than intriguing. Good to know. "Come on, Sheriff. It'll be on Facebook if anything went down, so you might as well spill."

The threat was legit. Lucille ran the local art gallery and Lucky Harbor's Facebook page with equal enthusiasm. In fact, her updates were practically required reading for Lucky Harbor residents. She reported on the happenings in town, each detail joyfully chronicled, the juicier the better.

"We found no dogs on the premises," he said.

He shifted to go, but she asked the question that was tweaking her curiosity. "So why did you stop?"

"Excuse me?"

"Why didn't you just keep running when you saw me out here?"

Not a blink. Not even a shrug.

"Sheriff Sawyer Thompson," she murmured. "Communication master."

The very corner of his mouth turned up slightly. It knocked her off balance a little.

A lot.

"Let me guess," she said. "You couldn't resist me." She couldn't say why she was poking the bear, but maybe it was her version of running...with scissors. "You saw me, and you couldn't resist me, and so you stopped to..."

"To...?"

"Well, that's the question, isn't it?" she asked. "I mean, we don't like each other. We don't have anything in common. Whatever would we do with each other?"

His eyes heated at that, and in reaction, her nipples contracted to two tight beads. Hmmm. Apparently they could do plenty. But before she could process that, he took a step back as if to go.

"I scare you," Chloe said.

"Hell, yeah," he admitted, shocking a laugh from her. He wasn't afraid. Nothing scared him. But she'd learned not to tangle with the good sheriff unless she was on her A-game, and that wasn't the case at the moment. Being in Sawyer's presence took all of her concentration so that she didn't accidentally give herself away. Because the truth was, in spite of the overwhelming odds of the two of them being a major train wreck if they ever got together, she wanted him.

It was the most ridiculous thing she'd ever wanted.

After all, he was rigid where she was flexible. He was black and white, and she was all the rainbow in between, and they didn't go together.

Not that her body cared about logic. He was the most virile, potent, testosterone-filled guy she'd ever met. Sex with him would be fireworks, thunderstorms.

Magic.

But even she knew that she wasn't ready for prime time with Sawyer Thompson. "I have to go."

"Now who's scared?"

"No, I have to get back to the inn." It was nearly seven, and she needed to beat her sisters there. They hadn't had any guests last night, but Tara was adamant that someone always be available, even at the ass crack of dawn.

Someone being Chloe, naturally.

"Know what I think?" Sawyer asked.

"I have no idea. I never do."

He was leaning against the back of the bench, all six feet three inches of brawn at rest. "I make you nervous."

"You don't make me nervous." Okay, he *so* made her nervous. She turned to the water and tried to take a deep, relaxing breath. With the ocean in front of her—a much more relaxing view than the one of the gorgeous, smug bastard behind her—it should have been no problem. But it took a few tries, and she had to close her eyes. When that didn't work, she added a stretch, rolling her shoulders, then lifting her arms high.

A low sound of male appreciation came from behind her in mid-stretch, and she turned to face him.

Sawyer's eyes lifted from the vicinity of her ass. "What are you playing at now?" he asked softly.

And wasn't that just the thing. "I don't think I'm playing," she said back, just as softly.

He studied her carefully, clearly searching for half truths.

But she never dealt in half truths. Or lies for that matter. Too much to remember. Nope, she liked her life dealt straight up. Possibly the one thing they had in common.

Sawyer stepped toward her, something in his stance making her feel like Little Red Riding Hood facing down the Big Bad Wolf. With the pier rail at her back, she tilted her head up to meet his gaze. "What?" she whispered.

"Is there something going on with you and Lance that I should know about?"

"No. Why?"

"Just trying to figure out if last night's fake caterwauling was a warm-up."

"For the real thing? No." She paused. "Caterwauling?" He was giving her a complex. "It happens, you know. Screaming during sex." Although not to her, dammit.

"Does it?" he wondered. "Moaning, I get." He stepped even closer. Since she had nowhere to retreat to, his body touched hers. "Panting? Definitely." His voice dropped an octave. "Some dirty talk? Oh hell, yeah. But not that horrendous sound you were making, no."

He was warm, so deliciously warm. "It happens," Chloe repeated, having to lock her knees so they didn't wobble. She put a hand on his chest because he'd moved into her personal space and suddenly there wasn't nearly enough air.

"When?" he asked, his hand circling her wrist, and as he'd done once before, he let his thumb brush over the tiny tattoo there. "When does it happen?"

"Well . . . in books."

His eyes softened slightly at this and so did his mouth. "What kind of books are you reading, Chloe?"

"Er . . ." Okay, so *maybe* she'd been reading a lot of romances lately, so what? And maybe some erotica, too. There was nothing wrong with that, or daydreaming about being those women in the stories, the women who had enough breath in their lungs to scream in passion. "Not the point," she said, no longer certain what the point was.

And why the hell was he standing here teasing her instead of running? And... "Why did you ask about Lance?"

Sawyer stared into her face for a long, speculative moment. "So that I could do this." He cupped her jaw, then lowered his head until their lips nearly met. Not hesitant, not uncertain.

The opposite, in fact.

There was a beat of stillness, during which his gaze held hers prisoner while all her parts came alive and her eyes drifted shut. Their mouths brushed lightly, then not so lightly, and when his tongue touched hers, she moaned. At the sound, he threaded his hands in her hair and deepened the kiss.

She melted into him. There was no other word for what happened. One minute her bones were there and then in the next they were gone. Then as quickly as it'd started, it was over, and she was blinking up at him, her breathing nowhere close to under control. "Okay, what... what was that?"

Sawyer shoved a hand through his hair, leaving it tousled. "I don't know. You drive me crazy."

Just what a girl wanted to hear. She used her inhaler, and he frowned. "Come on," he said. "I'll walk you back."

"I can walk myself."

Her phone vibrated. She pulled the cell from her pocket and stared down at the ID. Todd. Because she hung out with Lance so much, she ran into Todd often. Occasionally he called her to see if she wanted to go out—his euphemism for hooking up.

Chloe might have earned the moniker the "wild child" here in Lucky Harbor, but she wasn't the "stupid child." Everyone knew there was simmering tension between Sawyer and Todd, and she wasn't going to be the cause of seeing it burst into flame. She hit ignore and shoved her phone back in her pocket.

"Problem?" Sawyer asked.

"Nope."

Their gazes met and held. He didn't say anything more but stubbornly stuck by her side all the way back to the inn. He waited at the bottom of the steps while she climbed them and reached for the front door, making the mistake of looking back at him.

He was quite a sight standing there, muscles tense and gleaming from his run, sweats riding low on his hips. He looked dangerous, alluring, and hotter than sin. "I'm going to pretend that didn't happen. The kiss," she clarified.

"Can you?"

Her nipples were still hard so she sort of doubted it. It'd been a hell of a kiss. "It doesn't matter. The fact is that we experimented, got it out of our system. We're done with that now." She paused. "Right?"

"Yeah."

Not even a nanosecond of a hesitation. *Ouch.* "Okay, good," she said, lifting her chin. "Good, then."

Sawyer turned and began jogging back the way they'd just come. She watched him until he'd vanished from sight, then let herself drop to the top step, completely unsettled. Because for two people who valued the truth over all else, they'd both just lied their asses off.

Chapter 5

*"When you don't know what you're
doing, fake it."*
—*Chloe Traeger*

Chloe stepped inside the inn and came face-to-face with a pissed-off Tara. "What?" Chloe asked, still a little off her game from kissing Sawyer. *Sawyer*. Holy smokes.

"Where were you?"

"On a walk." Making out with the sheriff. "Why?"

"Because you were supposed to be here."

"I was gone for an hour before sunrise. We didn't have any guests."

"No, but when a family of four stopped by, who'd been driving all night, you weren't here. They were just leaving when I drove up."

"So you caught them in time."

"They didn't stay," Tara said. "They said they didn't feel comfortable staying in a deserted inn."

"Shit. I'm sorry, I—"

Tara held up a hand. "If it's too much, sugar, just say so. You can't fake your way through this."

"It's not too much." Goddammit. She swallowed the urge to get defensive. "I'll do better."

Tara nodded and went into the kitchen, leaving Chloe alone to wrestle with that promise.

* * *

A few days later, Sawyer was off duty and running errands, which rated right up there with paperwork on his hate-to-do list. It didn't help that he'd spent the last twelve hours on a special task force working for the DEA. Under Agent Reed Morris, they'd tracked and rooted out a known drug dealer who'd holed up in Alder Flats, a particularly isolated, rugged area on the edge of the county. Ric Alfonso had been just one piece of a bigger puzzle they were working on, but despite their best efforts, it had ended badly.

Ric was now on a slab in the morgue, and Sawyer was questioning the sanity of his chosen profession. It wasn't the first time he'd been present at a death shot, and it probably wouldn't be the last, but Christ.

Ric had been nineteen years old.

At nineteen, Sawyer hadn't been dealing drugs, but he had been on the fast track to becoming a criminal. Which begged the question—what made the fragile difference between a life lost and a life won? Was it sheer guts and determination? Hard work? Karma? The question was too deep for him at the moment, stuck at a red light when he'd rather be flying over the water on Ford's boat, or lying on a warm beach with a woman, skimpy bikini optional.

Neither was in the cards for him, not today. He got some

food, picked up his mail, and then drove to the heart of town, to a square block of small, ranch-style homes built back in the 1970s. Most had been repaired and renovated. Sawyer pulled into the driveway of one that hadn't. The garage door's springs were broken. The owner said he was having a guy take care of it, and though the owner's only living relative, a son, had offered to fix it numerous times, the offer had been firmly rebuked.

Tough. Sawyer spent the next half hour doing it himself in spite of the fact that he wouldn't be thanked. The grass needed mowing again as well. He stretched the kink out of his neck as he went for the ancient lawn mower on the side of the house. It was a stall tactic, and he usually wasn't much for stalling, but he mowed the entire lawn and side yard, and finally, with nothing left to do, turned to the front door.

Nolan Thompson stood in the doorway. Sawyer's father was dressed today, which was an improvement over last week, when he'd faced Sawyer in his underwear. It was hard as hell to take the old man's righteous anger seriously when it was delivered with plaid cotton boxers sagging over a body ravaged by alcohol and fifty-plus years of physical labor.

"I told you I'd hired a kid to do this shit," his dad growled in the same low, gruff voice that once upon a time had struck terror to the depths of Sawyer's troublemaking soul.

It'd been that way until the day he'd realized he was bigger and badder than his father. Instead of taking his punishment for whatever stupid thing Sawyer had done that day—and Sawyer had no doubt it *had* been stupid—he'd shoved back.

He'd been sixteen. After that, the two of them had resorted to stony silence for Sawyer's last year in the house. Contact had remained rare and estranged until Sawyer's twenty-fifth birthday, which he'd spent in the hospital at his father's side after Nolan's first heart attack. That had been ten years ago. Now their visits were still spent in silence, but there'd been two more heart attacks and a new frailty in his father that Sawyer hated.

Because it meant that every time Sawyer looked at him, he had no choice but to feel. Compassion, regret, guilt, whatever emotion bombarded him, he hated every minute of it. He looked around his father's yard. "So where is this paragon of virtue you've hired?"

"He'll be here."

"Uh-huh."

"Look, if he said he'd come, he'll come. He shows up on time, doesn't give me attitude, and doesn't rip me off."

Sawyer had stolen a twenty off his father's dresser exactly once. He'd been twelve and an idiot, but he'd been *twelve*, for God's sake. His father had never forgotten about it. But at least that infraction had been real.

Yeah, Sawyer had been a rotten-to-the-core kid and an even worse teenager. But Jesus, he'd been working his ass off ever since trying to make up for it, which should count for something.

It didn't.

Time had stopped for Nolan as far as Sawyer was concerned. "The garage door is fixed, so you can park in there again. And the grass needs watering."

Another gruff sound, maybe one of grudging appreciation, but that was probably wishful thinking on Sawyer's part. He took a peek inside the house. It was a mess again. Odds were the housekeeper that Sawyer had hired was chased off by Nolan's bad temper. Since the woman had also brought in the groceries, this meant his father was undoubtedly eating crap, not good with his restricted diet. "Didn't Sally come this week?"

"She's out of town."

Bullshit. Sawyer brushed by his father into the house and was bombarded with unhappy memories. He checked the fridge—

nearly empty. Pulling some money out of his wallet, he set it on the kitchen table and turned to leave.

His father was blocking his way, eyes bright with anger and something else. Shame.

Shit. "I'll be back tomorrow with groceries and someone else to clean up," Sawyer said.

"Don't bother. I have the kid."

"Fine."

"Fine," Nolan snapped, then paused uncomfortably. "I, uh, have to get another angioplasty."

Sawyer's own heart skipped a beat. "When?"

"Friday."

"I'll be there."

"It's just a routine thing, no big deal."

"I'll be there, dammit."

Sawyer left feeling like shit. Nothing new there. Needing a caffeine kick, he parked at the convenience store, and for just a moment, leaned back and closed his eyes. He needed something, and caffeine wasn't it.

Balls-to-the-wall sex had a nice ring to it.

A shout interrupted the thought. Glass shattered, followed by running footsteps, which was never good. Sawyer straightened just as a guy came barreling out of the convenience store, hugging his sweatshirt close to his body as if protecting something.

A piece of paper fluttered from the sweatshirt.

Aw, Christ on a stick, Sawyer thought, catching a flash of green. Not paper.

Money.

The guy hopped into a banged-up Celica and sped away with a show of squealing tires and smoke.

Goddammit. Sawyer hit the gas to follow as he called dispatch to report that he'd caught a robbery in progress. The piece-of-shit sedan in front of him turned right at the end of town, obviously headed toward the open highway. At the freeway entrance, there were two delivery vans, moving slow as molasses. The car swerved around them, heading directly into a small, quiet neighborhood filled with midsized houses, hard-working people, and kids. Lots of kids.

Sawyer swore again and kept on the car's bumper while simultaneously keeping dispatch abreast of their coordinates. Thankfully it was midday, both a work and school day, and the streets were relatively empty.

At the corner, the sedan went up and over the sidewalk and popped the two right tires. By the middle of the next street, the car was slowing, then drifting to a complete stop.

"Don't run," Sawyer said under his breath, pulling up behind him. "Don't fucking run." He *hated* foot chases. But, of course, in the next second, the suspect had abandoned his car and was hauling ass down the street.

"*Fuck*." Grabbing a spare set of cuffs, Sawyer shoved them into the back of his jeans and hit the pavement. "Stop," he yelled. "Police."

The suspect didn't stop. Of course not. Goddammit. Sawyer shook his head and followed with the ease that running five miles every day afforded him. He didn't run for pleasure. Hell no. He ran every day, rain or snow or shine, so he didn't lose assholes like this one. He chased the guy through a yard, over a fence, and into some bushes, yelling at the few curious people poking their heads out to "get back inside!" Closing the distance, Sawyer made a swipe for the guy's sweatshirt and hauled him to the ground.

They landed hard, the suspect on the bottom, limp as a rag doll. Great, Sawyer thought. He'd killed him.

But then the guy groaned, and Sawyer was glad for it. He put a knee in the guy's back and reached for his cuffs. "What the hell was that?"

The suspect shook his head. "*No Ingles.*"

No problemo. Sawyer had some Spanish. He could say "give me a beer," "throw down your weapon, asshole," and lucky for this idiot, he could also recite the Miranda rights.

* * *

It took another two hours and more paperwork before Sawyer could go. He had aching knees from the takedown and a mother of a headache brewing, but it was the adrenaline flowing through him that sent him straight to the gym.

Working out wasn't his first choice for letting down the adrenaline. That honor would still go to the balls-to-the-wall sex he'd wished for earlier, but that wasn't in the cards for him today.

The gym he went to was small but new, and state of the art. A friend of his met him here several times a week. Matt Bowers was a district supervisor forest ranger, and Sawyer's sparring partner.

Sawyer changed and found Matt beating the hell out of a punching bag. "Why don't you try someone who'll fight back?" Sawyer asked.

Matt turned and looked Sawyer over. "I'll get more action out of the bag. You're looking soft, Thompson."

Sawyer smiled. They both knew Sawyer was in top fighting shape himself; he made sure of it. He let out a sound mimicking a chicken clucking.

Matt smiled, one of the few people in Lucky Harbor not intimidated by Sawyer's size. With good reason, since Matt was an ex-cop from Chicago, and deceptively laid-back. "Having a bad day?"

"Yeah, I broke a nail."

Matt grinned. "Pussy."

They beat the shit out of each other for the next thirty minutes before finally dropping to their backs on the mat, gasping for breath.

"You going to tell me what crawled up your ass?" Matt managed to ask.

"No." Wheezing, Sawyer studied the ceiling while he waited for his heart to stop drumming in his ears.

"I know it's not a woman," Matt said. "You don't have one. You've scared them all off."

"Fuck you."

Matt chuckled. "Not my type, man. I like 'em soft and pretty." He paused. "Is it work?"

It was his life, Sawyer thought wearily.

"I'd try to beat it out of you some more, but I can't feel my legs," Matt said.

"So *who's* the pussy exactly?"

Matt snorted and managed to get to his feet. "I'm hitting the shower."

Sawyer lay there for another moment. He'd definitely gotten rid of the excess energy and adrenaline. His body was letting down now, or so the level of pain indicated anyway. Dripping sweat and holding his sore ribs, he staggered to his feet and came face-to-face with Chloe.

She was dressed for a workout in black, cropped yoga pants and a yellow sports bra that he needed sunglasses to look at. Not that *that* stopped him.

"You got your ass kicked, Sheriff."

"Fuck if I did."

"I don't know." She cocked her head to look him over. "Your hot friend got to his feet much easier than you."

"Hot?"

"Mmm-hmm. Your lip's bleeding, Sheriff."

Sawyer swiped at his lip and resisted the urge to grab a ridiculous amount of weights and do an arm curl. "I'm fine."

"Okay," she said doubtfully. "If you're sure..."

Jesus. A minute ago he'd doubted that he could drag himself to the shower, but now he sat heavily on a weight bench and reached for the weights.

Chloe raised a brow but said nothing more as she put in her earphones and sat on a weight bench facing away from him.

"What about your asthma?"

"This isn't cardio. I'm good as long as I go slow." Then she began to work her arms, moving that taut, curvy body to some mysterious beat.

Sawyer watched her. He couldn't help himself. She'd piled her glorious mass of red hair into a ponytail that swung back and forth with her every arm curl. Her shoulders were straight, the lean muscles in her back sleek and feminine. She had the best ass he'd ever seen. Sure there were other cute butts in the gym, but Chloe's was right there in front of him, drawing his gaze. He was very busy attempting to see as much of it as he could when she turned her head and caught him.

He hurriedly pushed up the weights and was relieved when his arms obeyed and he didn't totally humiliate himself.

Chloe was watching him, something new in her eyes now, something hot and lethal and dark.

And just like that, as if she'd let out a mating call, the matching hot, lethal, dark place inside *him* reared its head. Good thing he'd long ago beaten that part of him back, trading it in for a different kind of life. One he could depend on, no matter what obstacles he faced. Which, of course, didn't stop him from pushing the weights up again. He would have decapitated himself for sure if two big hands hadn't appeared to stop him.

Matt.

Hair wet from his shower, he looked down at Sawyer and smirked as he pulled all but twenty-five pounds of the weights off. "There," he said patronizingly. "*Now* you can go ahead and show off for the pretty lady." He shot a warm smile and a quick wink Chloe's way.

Chloe smiled back.

And Sawyer wished he'd pounded Matt into the floor when he'd had the chance.

Chapter 6

*"It may be that your sole purpose in life is
simply to serve as a warning to others."*
—Chloe Traeger

Chloe had always loved traveling for her work, meeting new
people, going from place to place. It was reminiscent of the
wanderlust gypsy life she'd had growing up with Phoebe, and in
its own odd way, was comforting.

But now there was Lucky Harbor and her sisters, and against
all odds, these things gave her comfort, too. It'd taken months
to figure out exactly why, but sitting on the counter in the
B&B's large, homey kitchen, stirring up a bowl of avocado and
mayonnaise, she finally got it.

It was because for the first time in her entire life, she had a
sort of home base. It was extremely new, and if she was being
honest, not as claustrophobic as she'd imagined. She was at war
with herself over it.

Luckily she didn't have much time to dwell on it. Later

today, she'd be giving spa treatments at an upscale Portland boutique hotel, and since her products were all made up of fresh ingredients, she had a hell of a lot of work to do to prepare. "That smells…interesting," Tara said. She was at the center island, cooking away. As the oldest, she'd gotten the lion's share of imperturbability. Neatness, too. Despite getting ready to cook breakfast for the three guests they'd had show up last night, there wasn't a hair out of place or a crumb or speck on her pretty black wool trousers and crisp white blouse. And how she cooked and served in those heels was beyond Chloe.

Chloe eyed her own feet, comfy in ballet flats. Everything she wore was built for comfort: leggings, long cami top with a cropped sweater open over it. "How do you stay so neat all the time?"

Tara smiled. She was doing a lot more of that now that she was getting laid regularly by Ford, one of the sexiest guys Chloe had ever met.

"Well, I'm not mixing up a batch of"—Tara peered into Chloe's bowl—"stinky green stuff for spa clients."

"It's avocado and mayonnaise hair conditioner, and it's not stinky. It works better than your fifty-dollar conditioner."

"Avocado and mayo?" Tara's Southern accent was faint and charming when she was amused. "Your fancy clients are going to put that in their hair?"

"It's 'au natural.' Back to basics and all that. Plus, it's loaded with all sorts of good fats and oils. People love it."

"You know what I'd love, sugar? Help with the dishes."

Better than cleaning toilets, Chloe told herself, and she did plenty of those as well. "I really miss Mia."

At the mention of Tara's teenage daughter—whom Tara had when she was a teen herself—Tara smiled. "I miss her, too."

Last summer, Mia had worked here at the inn, helping with the cleaning and whatever was needed, giving Chloe a welcome break. But Mia was in Spain now, spending her senior year of high school as an exchange student.

Setting her bowl down, Chloe ran hot water in the sink and was halfway through the pile of pots and pans when Maddie came into the kitchen. She was carrying an armful of dishes that she must have collected out of the guest rooms, all of which she set into the sink with a sweet smile.

Dammit. Chloe added more hot water to the sink.

"Oh, and hey," Maddie said, turning back to her. "I'm nearly out of that face mask you made me, the one with strawberries, oatmeal, and honey. Can I get some more?"

"Sure." Chloe would be making up a batch today anyway. "Did you like the scent? Because I can switch the strawberries with—"

"No, don't change a single thing. Jax says it makes me glow."

Tara and Chloe exchanged a look. Good as Chloe's mask was, and it *was* good, it wasn't the ingredients making Maddie glow.

That would be the sex.

Maddie looked into the bowl of avocado conditioner, swirling the spoon around, sniffing curiously. "Dip?" She grabbed a bread stick from the counter and scooped up a dollop of the hair treatment.

"Chloe, don't you dare let your sister eat hair conditioner," Tara said, not looking up as she expertly flipped her omelet.

"Hair conditioner?" Maddie narrowed her eyes at Chloe and threw the bread stick at her.

Chloe ducked and grinned. "It's just avocado and mayo. And you need it, too. It'd fix your frizz problem."

Maddie's hand flew to her hair. She had a mass of brown curls, rarely tamed unless it was tied back. Today was no different. It fell in curls to her shoulders, looking full and thick, and, well, frizzy.

"And your shirt's inside out again," Chloe noted.

"It is not." But Maddie stretched out the collar of her tee to see it and eyed the stitching on the outside. "*Crap*."

"You still dressing in the dark, or what?" Chloe asked.

That was what Maddie had tried to tell them last week when she'd shown up at the inn all flushed, mussed, and wearing her shirt inside out.

Maddie whipped her shirt off to turn it right side out. She was wearing a pink bra and a hickey on her collarbone.

Chloe burst out laughing. "Go, Jax."

"He didn't— We weren't—" Maddie sagged. "Oh, forget it." She clapped her hands to her cheeks. "I jumped him on the way over here."

"While *driving*?" Tara asked in horror.

Maddie was beet red now. "We...pulled over." A ridiculous grin escaped. "I just always want to eat him up. Does it ever stop?"

"I don't know," Chloe admitted. "But for your sake, I hope not." If anyone deserved happiness, it was Maddie. Before coming to Lucky Harbor, a bad experience with an ex had put Maddie off men entirely. Then she'd met Jax. With a little bit of patience, along with his easy, outgoing personality, Jax had woman-whispered Maddie right out of her shell. Now they were getting married.

Given the long-enduring and heated love that Tara and Ford also shared, Chloe had no doubt that they'd soon be following suit down the aisle as well.

It was wonderful for them. And exciting, too. But Chloe wasn't quite sure what it all meant for her. What her plan would be, or what kind of future she'd have...

"You'll find it, too," Maddie said softly, watching Chloe. "Love."

"Oh," Chloe said, shaking her head. "No. I don't need—"

"You will," Maddie promised and hugged her. "Maybe after you settle down a little."

Ah, there it was. The problem. The *real* problem. In order to find that elusive acceptance that she craved, Chloe had to "settle down," had to stop being who she was. Grow up. No more letting her sister eat hair conditioner...

But dammit, hadn't she taken on her share of the responsibility for this place? Hadn't she cut back drastically on the constant traveling to help with the inn? Shifted her schedule so that most of the trips she took were only day trips now, and doing so only when she could, between guests?

Chloe had done everything asked of her. And yet it still wasn't enough. Feeling a tightening in her chest that might have been anxiety or an oncoming asthma attack, she pulled out her inhaler and took a puff.

"Already?" Maddie asked with some concern. "You're having trouble breathing today already?"

Chloe shrugged. In times of stress, they all had their ways of coping. Maddie mainlined potato chips. Tara cooked. Chloe used her inhaler. "Maybe I don't want to settle down."

"Everyone does eventually," Maddie said.

"I don't think it's for me." Not looking at either sister, Chloe added more soap to the hot water and dug into the pile of dishes, searching for happy thoughts. Chocolate. Puppies. Rainbows.

Guys.

Yeah, guys always worked as a nice distraction. She thought of Matt Bowers, the sexy forest ranger she'd seen at the gym. Then there was Dr. Josh Scott, the ER doc. She'd met him during a particularly rough asthma attack when she'd landed in the ER on his shift, and they'd since run into each other several times. He'd asked Chloe out but she'd been too busy balancing her travels with the inn. Maybe it was time to sync their schedules and play doctor together.

And then there was Cute Guy. She didn't know his name. He was a new Lucky Harbor resident and a real mystery. He'd moved into a house on the bluffs, an expensive one. Even the Facebook mavens had been caught by surprise. No one knew what Cute Guy did or who he was, but Chloe had seen him at the grocery store, and he was H-O-T.

And yet as she washed the last pot, it was a different man entirely who popped into her head and made her breath catch— the one who wore both a gun and a bad attitude with such wild sexiness that he'd begun to haunt her dreams.

As had their kiss. Yowza, that kiss. She'd been ignoring him just fine before that. "Damn sheriff," she muttered, scrubbing hard at the reticent pot.

"Sawyer?" Tara asked.

Chloe closed her eyes. "No, that's my point. *Not* Sawyer. I want Matt. Or Josh. Or Cute Guy. Hell, even Anderson at the hardware store. *Not* the sheriff, thank you very much."

What followed was such an awkward silence that Chloe could feel it blister her back. With her stomach knotting on itself, she turned to face the room.

Sawyer stood in the back doorway, in uniform, armed, silent, filling up the entire room with his presence.

There was a long beat during which nobody breathed.

"Nothing personal," Chloe said to Sawyer with as much dignity as she could muster, which wasn't much. But hell, she had to be the last woman on the planet that he'd pick, too, so no harm no foul, she figured. Except their gazes were locked now, reminding her of how his mouth had felt slanted over hers, hot and hungry, and a sudden, rather powerful longing filled her.

Okay, time to get the hell out of Dodge. She needed to think. Preferably alone, on top of a mountain somewhere. As for what Sawyer needed, it was hard to tell. He was a rock when he wanted to be.

Tara handed him a mug of coffee to go. "Guess you're wishing you'd stopped at Starbucks this morning, huh?" she quipped, clearly trying to lighten the tension.

"Can't go into places like that in uniform," Sawyer told her.

"Why not?"

"Sometimes people spit in the food or drinks when they see a cop."

"Well, in all my born days," Tara murmured, her accent thickening with her temper as she spoke into the horrified silence.

Chloe shut off the water and stared at Sawyer, her unhappy awkwardness replaced with something that felt like possessive protectiveness. "Why would you do it then, be a cop, just to be treated like that?"

"You mean besides the glory?" he asked dryly, then shrugged. "I'm good at it."

She knew he was. He was doggedly determined and aggressive behind that calm veneer, which served his job well. It probably served him well in other areas too.

Like in bed.

Sawyer looked into the bowl of avocado/mayo mix. "What's that?"

"*Not* dip," Maddie said quickly.

"It's hair conditioner," Tara told him. "For the frizzies."

Everyone looked at Sawyer's wind tousled, fawn-colored hair. It fell thick and silky to his collar. No frizzies, the bastard.

"I think I'm good," he said. He was leaning back against the counter, clearly right at home, feet casually crossed, long legs at rest, the muscles of his thighs pressing against the material of his uniform.

Yeah, he was good... "Your skin's dry." Chloe nodded to the bottle next to the conditioner, which held a special blend of vitamin E and tea tree oil in a petroleum jelly base. "That'd cure your problem." Though she had nothing to cure the big, bad, broody thing he had going on. "That is, if you're not still afraid I'm going to poison you..."

He looked at her steadily, then picked up the bottle, which

looked small and feminine in his big hand. Very gingerly, as if maybe he was holding a bomb, he lifted the lid and took a sniff. "Smells like flowers."

"Does that threaten your manhood?" Chloe asked.

Tara opened her mouth to object, but Sawyer laughed, the sound low and slightly rusty, as if he didn't have a lot of reason to laugh lately.

"Use it twice a day," Chloe said. "And you'll be glowing in no time. Just like Maddie here."

He looked like he wanted to say something about Maddie's "glow" but he squelched it. Smart man.

"I heard about what's been going on," Tara said to him. "You okay?"

"Yeah," Sawyer said. "It's another angioplasty. He'll be fine."

Tara paused. "I meant at work. Who's having an angioplasty?"

Sawyer sighed. "My father. It's just routine. He's too ornery to let a heart problem slow him down." His face was calm and blank. The cop face again, which meant he didn't want to talk about it.

"Tell us about the robber," Maddie said.

"What robber?" Chloe asked.

Maddie looked at Sawyer, who just sipped his coffee.

"He single-handedly caught the convenience store robber," Tara told Chloe. "You didn't see it? It was all over the papers. I e-mailed you the link."

Hmm. Maybe she should've checked her e-mail last night instead of hanging out with Lance. "The convenience store got held up?"

"And Sawyer was outside the store when the thief made a run for it," Tara said. "Money falling out of his pockets as he went."

Sawyer shook his head, like he still couldn't believe the stupidity of the guy.

"Sawyer chased him in his car," Tara went on. "And then on foot, with innocent people getting barreled over by the suspect. The librarian broke her ankle."

Chloe gasped. "Ms. Bunyan?"

Tara nodded. "Finally Sawyer pulled his gun and got a few shots off before tackling the guy to the ground. By the time the rest of the cavalry came, Sawyer had the guy subdued and cuffed."

Chloe stared at Sawyer, who was looking mildly annoyed. "Really?" she asked him.

"No. Ms. Bunyan broke her ankle when she came running out of her house looking at her cell phone instead of where she was going, trying to record a video for YouTube. She was nowhere close to the action."

"But there *was* action, right?" Maddie asked. "Gunshots?"

"*No* gunshots," he said.

"Well, damn," Maddie said, disappointed. "I like Tara's version better."

Chloe didn't. Not at all. She was glad there'd been no shots fired, but that still left the chase, the tackle, the wrestling...It wasn't the first time she'd been forcibly reminded of how dangerous Sawyer's job could be, but she marveled just the same at the ease in which he faced it all, day in and day out. "Are you okay?"

Sawyer met her gaze. Right. He was always okay. And if he wasn't, no one would ever know otherwise because he'd keep it to himself. The thought made her wonder if maybe they didn't have more in common with each other than she'd imagined possible.

"The paper said that the perp was in the middle of a divorce, and he just snapped," Tara said. "His ex is taking him to the cleaner's, and he's going around stealing money to pay his lawyers. Takes all kinds of crazy."

Sawyer nodded, and Chloe had to laugh at the resigned look on his face. Clearly he had seen the "all kinds of crazy."

"You were definitely the talk of the town yesterday," Maddie said. "Our hero." She grinned as he grimaced and pushed away from the counter.

"But that's not all that happened to you yesterday," Tara said.

Sawyer slanted her a look. "Yes, it is."

"Nope. You also got called to Mrs. Abbott's house."

"Which turned out to be nothing," Sawyer said.

"Not exactly nothing," Maddie broke in.

"Maddie." Sawyer's voice was meant to scold, but he actually sounded patient and maybe slightly amused. Definitely gentle.

Chloe was fascinated by this glimpse of a gentle Sawyer. But then again, Maddie inspired that in a man.

Chloe sure as hell didn't. "What happened? Is Mrs. Abbott okay?"

"Mrs. Abbott's fine," Sawyer said.

"Only because you rode in on your white horse to save the day." Maddie turned to Chloe. "Her smoke alarm went off, and Sawyer got there first."

"Oh no," Chloe said, genuinely dismayed. Mrs. Abbott was a favorite of hers. Chloe made her a special moisturizer weekly, the only thing that helped ease the older woman's psoriasis symptoms. They had tea, and Mrs. Abbott would regale Chloe with tales of her wild youth. "Was there a fire?"

"No." Clearly trying to get out before Maddie finished her story, Sawyer moved to the door.

Chloe tore her gaze off his very fine ass and glanced at her sister.

"No fire," Maddie assured her. "And not twenty minutes later, the smoke alarm went off again. And then again, with Sawyer responding each time."

Sawyer stopped with a sigh. "Only once more, not twice."

"I have *got* to start reading Facebook," Chloe said. "What was wrong?"

Maddie grinned. "Her smoke alarm needed a new battery."

"Aw," Chloe said. "Those things are a bitch."

"No, the 'aw' is that Sawyer went to the store for her and bought a battery," Maddie said. "Then he came back and put it in for her. So sweet."

Sawyer looked pained. "Not sweet, a necessity. I was tired of driving out there."

"*Sweet*," Maddie repeated.

Chloe snorted, and Sawyer's eyes cut to hers. "Like *you'd* want to be called sweet," he said.

"Not me," she said. "But then again, I'm not even halfway close to sweet."

And truthfully, neither was he, she thought. He was big and bad and alpha and gorgeous and smart and brave and loyal...

But not sweet. *Hell*, no.

"It's okay," Tara told him, patting his shoulder. "Your secret's safe with us."

"Bullshit if it is," he grumbled. "You'll tell Ford and Jax. And Jax's such a girl that he'll tell...everyone."

"And what'll happen then?" Chloe asked. "Will they revoke your man card?"

In tune to Maddie's and Tara's laughter, Sawyer muttered something beneath his breath about the entire female gender and was gone.

Chapter 7

*"Always remember, you're unique.
Just like everyone else."*
—*Chloe Traeger*

The next day Sawyer was sitting in the hospital, waiting to hear how his father's surgery had gone. The TV was tuned to some soap opera, and there was no remote in sight. After two hours, he was feeling a little trigger happy and might have shot the thing, but Chloe showed up. She plopped down next to him.

"All My Children?" she asked. "Didn't peg you as the type."

"I'm not watching it."

She made the exaggerated motion of checking out the room. He was the only one in it.

He pinched the bridge of his nose. "What are you doing here?"

She handed him a bag. "Bringing you pick-me-up muffins from Tara. Banana–chocolate chip. She says they can fix any-thing."

Well, that explained her presence. Tara had sent her on a

Good Samaritan errand. There were four muffins in the sack. He handed one to her and started in on the other three, finishing them before she'd finished hers.

"Hey. How's that a fair division?" she asked.

"Weight ratio."

She slid her eyes over his body, and if he wasn't mistaken, she also sucked in a breath, but all she said was "Hmm."

She finished her muffin before she said, "Oh! Almost forgot!" and pulled out a thermos from her huge purse. "Milk."

He offered her the first sip, and when she shook her head, he downed it.

"Better?" she asked.

He nodded, and she laughed softly. "Don't hog all the words, Sheriff." Not appearing overly insulted, she settled in next to him, leaning back in the uncomfortable chair, her legs stretched in front of her, crossed at the ankles.

"I figure we can do this one of two ways," she said. "Awkward silence, or I could keep talking and you can pretend to listen."

"Or you could leave."

"Yeah, but it's much more fun to stay and make you squirm."

"You don't make me squirm."

Her fathomless green eyes met his. "I make you something."

Yeah. She sure as hell did. "Annoyed?" he offered. "Irritated? Frustrated? Infuriated?"

"Horny."

He shook his head, but hell if she wasn't right. "Option two."

"Irritated?" she asked.

"No. You talk."

She laughed, then talked about her last trip to Belize, where she'd gotten the small tattoo on the inside of her wrist, which apparently meant "Be Yourself." "Hurt like a bitch," she said. "And Tara's certain that I'll never land a corporate job because of the location—it's hard to cover it up. She'd probably freak if she saw my other tat, but she won't because it's...discreetly placed," she said, flashing a grin.

Sawyer thought about that for a very pleasant beat, enjoying the distraction of picturing where and what that might be. "Do you anticipate wanting a job in the corporate world?" he asked, unable to envision her in an office setting, all tamed and subdued.

She laughed. "Sitting behind a desk making nice? No, I'm not sure I have that in me."

"What *do* you have in you?"

Chloe looked surprised at the question. "Well, I'd like to get this natural skincare line I'm creating off the ground."

"That sounds...surprisingly corporate."

"Bite your tongue," she said.

He found himself smiling.

"Wow," she said. "You should do that a *lot* more."

He ignored that. "You like what you do."

"Well, yeah. Isn't that the point?"

He opened his mouth, then closed it again, conceding with a nod. "Did you always know what you wanted to do?"

"Yeah. When I was little, I camped with my mom all the time. Did you know that?"

He shook his head. He didn't know much about her past at all. He'd known Phoebe though, and she hadn't exactly been the mothering type.

"Maddie and Tara grew up with their dads, but I was with Phoebe. Camping," Chloe said. "Mostly we traveled from one Grateful Dead concert to the next; sometimes we'd go off for another adventure. But I always had everything I owned in a little *Saved by the Bell* backpack."

He felt something tighten in his chest, and it took him a moment to speak. "That must have been hard for a little girl." His childhood had been a world away. He'd had a house, a *miserable* house, but a roof over his head regardless.

"Oh, I liked it," Chloe said. "I mean, we were poor as dirt, of course, but I didn't know that. We made the things we needed when we could. Soap, shampoo, stuff like that. I loved figuring out which scents went best with which ingredients."

Of course, she would have made the best of the cards she'd been dealt. But the nomad life had to have been rough. He had no idea how things would have been different for him without Ford and Jax, who'd given him a taste of stability. And then, after getting arrested, he'd found a different, even more stabilizing force in his arresting officer, of all people. Sheriff Allen Coburn had been the first adult to take the time to show interest. To care. He'd straightened Sawyer's ass out by checking on him weekly, and had until his death a few years back.

It didn't sound like Chloe had had any such stabilizing forces, at least not until this past year. "Moving around like that," he said. "How did you go to school and make friends?"

"Phoebe homeschooled me for the most part, until high school. We settled in San Francisco for a while because she had a boyfriend who was a theater stagehand. I went to school there."

"You and your mom lived with the boyfriend?"

"No, he lived in his car in the theater lot. We camped then, too, a lot." She shrugged, like no big deal; it was what it was. "I made friends wherever we were; that wasn't really a problem. It's easier now, of course, having a home."

So the B&B with her sisters was the first real home she'd ever had, which tightened the knot in his chest.

"What about you?" she asked.

"What about me?"

"You grew up here."

"Yes."

She gave him a long look, waiting impatiently for him to open up. "Come on," she said. "Give me something. Do you have any tattoos?" she asked. "Childhood stories? Something you want to share with the class? Anything?"

"I thought the deal was that you talk and I sit."

She shook her head. "I looked you up, you know." She nudged her shoulder to his. "And for a town that loves gossip more than Walmart, there's not a lot about you out there. Actually it's kind of nice that the people here are so protective of their big, bad sheriff."

Protective? He shook his head, but he should have known she wasn't going to let it drop. "Is that no, you're just boring as sin?" she asked. "Or no, you're being obtuse simply because you can and it's what you do best?"

He laughed just as the surgeon came out. Suddenly somber again, Sawyer got to his feet and braced himself for the worst, but the doctor assured him that his father's procedure had gone well. In sheer relief, he sank back to the chair. Why he gave a damn was a complete mystery. Nolan Thompson thought his son wasn't worth his time. That wasn't going to change because of an angioplasty. A heart replacement, maybe...

Chloe sat, too, and slipped her arm around him, resting her head on his shoulder. She didn't speak, just gave him a moment. Which was another surprise. She was always in such perpetual motion, always working so hard at driving him up a wall. Or hell, maybe it wasn't hard work at all, maybe it came easy to her.

But now, right this very minute, she was here. For him. Soft and warm and caring. What the hell was she doing here anyway? And why did it feel so damn right? Unable to resist, he gathered her in close. Just for a minute he told himself, pressing his face into her sweet-smelling hair, absorbing the quiet comfort she was offering.

Finally they rose from their chairs, and in another surprise, she stared up into his face. With a satisfied nod that he was apparently looking okay in her book, she went up on tiptoe and kissed his jaw. And then she walked out of the room just as mysteriously as she'd arrived, leaving in her wake an odd void that he couldn't name.

* * *

Three nights later, after a helluva day, Sawyer dragged his sorry, aching ass into the Love Shack, the bar co-owned by Jax and Ford. That morning, it had snowed for about five seconds, just enough to screw up the roads. Which meant that every call Sawyer had gone on after that had been a life-or-death situation just getting out of his damn SUV. Twice he'd been out on the highway handling traffic control, and twice he'd been nearly hit by some idiot going too fast for the conditions.

But it had been his last call that had gotten to him—a fatal accident just outside Lucky Harbor. A twenty-year-old kid drinking and driving had wrapped himself around a tree.

Once upon a time, Sawyer had nearly been that kid. On that long-ago night, Sawyer hadn't been driving but he'd been just as drunk as the driver when they'd hit a pole.

Sawyer had managed to live through that accident, and while he'd like to think that it had straightened his ass out, it had actually been several more years before that happened.

Now, icy cold to the bone, he headed toward the bar's front door just as another man came out.

Todd, whose eyes narrowed at the sight of Sawyer. Sawyer returned the look evenly. Saying something unintelligible beneath his breath, Todd shoulder-checked Sawyer hard and headed out into the night.

Sawyer was in the mood for a fight and nearly followed Todd to get one. But common sense prevailed, and he let Todd go. He headed into the bar, hoping to warm up.

The Love Shack was done up like an old Western saloon. The walls were a sinful bordello red and lined with old mining tools. Exposed wooden beams high above supported lanterns, which hung over the scarred bench-style tables, now filled with the rowdy weekend crowd.

Sawyer walked straight through the bar to Ford's office in the back. He'd changed out of his dirty uniform at the station and was in plainclothes now, but still armed. He locked his utility belt and the majority of his weapons into an empty locker that the guys kept for him and moved back out to the bar.

"Well, if it isn't the local hero," Ford noted when Sawyer sat at the bar. "Change any smoke alarm batteries lately?"

"Shut up." Sawyer watched him pour his usual soda. "Make that a beer."

Ford raised a brow as he hit the tap. "Fucked-up day?"

"Fucked-up day." Sawyer took a long pull from the beer, still seeing the kid's sightless eyes as he lay forever still on the asphalt forty-five feet from where he'd been flung from his car.

Not five minutes later, Maddie waltzed out from the storage room looking a little tousled, which meant Jax was undoubtedly close by. She smiled at Sawyer and helped herself to an ice water while Ford called out to one of his servers, "An order of fish and chips for the sheriff," he said. "Double the chips." He looked at Sawyer. "Anything else?"

It was a well-known fact that Sawyer ate like a truck driver. He shrugged. "I'm not real hungry."

Ford's brow rose again. "Should I hold the fries?"

"Just the double part."

Maddie and Ford exchanged a worried look, and then Maddie slipped onto the stool next to Sawyer. "You okay?"

It used to be that no one ever asked him that. People just assumed that he was, or at least that he would be. Then the three sisters had come to town. Two of them had snagged his best friends, and now one or another sister was forever asking him if he was okay. "Just not that hungry is all."

Jax came out of the storage room. He pulled Maddie off her stool, sat in her place, then tugged her into his lap, nuzzling at her hair, one hand sliding to her ass. "Hey, babe. Feeling a little better now?"

Jesus, Sawyer thought. They even had Jax asking about feelings.

But Maddie melted against her man. "Much. Sawyer's had a bad day, though. He says he's not hungry."

Jax looked at Sawyer, brows up.

Sawyer ignored him, and when his food came, hunkered in to eat to prove he was fine. Jax leaned close to help himself to a fry. "Since you're not hungry— *Hey*," he grumbled when Sawyer stabbed him with his fork. "Well, there's nothing wrong with your reflexes anyway." Giving Maddie a smacking kiss, Jax went back to work.

Maddie watched him go with a dreamy sigh. "I'm going to marry him."

"God knows why." Sawyer reached for the ketchup, and Maddie laughed.

"He makes me happy," she said. "He makes me...everything. You know?"

Sawyer looked into her warm eyes and nodded, not wanting to disappoint her. She smiled and hugged him, then kissed his cheek. "You're sweet to humor me."

He nearly choked on a fry. There was the *sweet* again. He should have killed someone this week; that would have taken care of that.

A few minutes later, Chloe came in. Sawyer took a deep breath that he hadn't realized he'd been holding. Forget killing someone. He wanted...her.

He'd been thinking about that ever since she'd surprised him at the hospital. Dreaming about it, too. Dreams hot enough to singe his sheets.

She pulled off a black leather jacket, revealing an eye-popping red sweater, a tiny denim skirt, tights, and knee-high boots. And Christ, the boots gave him ideas. Not that he needed more. Her glossy, dark red hair was wind tousled and cascading over her shoulders, making him think of those dreams he'd had. In detail.

Or maybe that was just her. *She* made him think of sex. Hot, wild, no-holds-barred sex...

Chloe came up to the bar and met his gaze for a long, time-less beat. She didn't ask him if he was okay. She didn't weigh him down with her worry. She didn't even give him her usual I-don't-give-a-shit sardonic smile. No, she just looked at him with those deep green eyes, and he found himself wanting to fall in and drown.

He also wanted another drink, and possibly a vacation. Definitely he should get laid. Maybe a tall, stacked blonde who didn't give a damn about his feelings, who's only words would be "Harder, Sawyer, fuck me harder."

Except he didn't want a tall, stacked blonde.

He wanted a petite, curvy, wild, redhead. He wanted *this* petite, curvy, wild redhead.

"After a tough day," Chloe said softly, "I always need some-thing a little...crazy. Something a little off center to nudge me back into place."

He was much farther gone than he'd thought if that made perfect sense to him.

"But maybe that's just me," she said to his silence. "Probably an Eagle Scout doesn't feel the need for crazy."

"Eagle Scout?"

She smiled. "Did I say Eagle Scout? I meant an officer of the law, sorry."

Bullshit she was sorry. She thought he was a straight arrow. He knew that. He'd let her think it because it suited his purposes. They needed distance between them.

Lots of distance.

But tonight he wasn't feeling so straight arrow, and he sure as hell wasn't feeling distant. "Sometimes crazy works."

"Don't tease me," Chloe said. "We have very different ideas of crazy. I mean like zip-lining over snapping alligators." She nudged the drink in front of him. "You mean having a single beer."

"You have no idea what I mean."

She lowered her head slightly in acknowledgment and might have spoken but some guy shoved his way between them and slammed his hands down on the bar. Obviously already two sheets to the wind—hell, make that four sheets gone—he waved a drunken hand in Jax's direction. "Hey, dude, hurry the fuck up. We need another pitcher at our table, pronto!"

"That's the last thing you need," Sawyer said.

The guy whirled on him, eyes flashing with ready-made temper. Sawyer lifted his shirt to reveal the badge hooked on his belt, then pointed for the guy to go back to his table.

"Impressive," Chloe said when the guy did just that. She waited a beat. "You've had a long day."

Sawyer lifted a shoulder.

"Heard about the fatality."

He didn't reply. Nothing to say. But she just kept looking at him, with something far too close to sympathy in her gaze. He didn't want sympathy. He wanted her, wrapped around him, chanting his name as he pounded himself into her over and over again.

She didn't break eye contact, and as tended to happen when he got sucked into her vortex, everything else seemed to fade away. The general din of the bar, the music, the faces of the two men who were more brothers than friends, everything...it was just him and her.

She touched him, just a light stroke of her fingers over his shoulder, and though his body tightened, he felt himself breathe a little easier.

Her mouth slowly curved. Her eyes were warm, with a hint of challenge and quite possibly concern.

He didn't want the concern.

But the challenge...yeah. He'd take that.

"You're tense," Chloe said. Standing up, she moved behind him, putting her hands on his shoulders. She dug her fingers into his tight muscles, working them with a surprising strength, until he melted into a puddle at her feet.

"Better?" she murmured against his ear, making him nearly groan when she pressed her breasts against him.

Was she kidding? The only way for this to be better would be for them to be alone and naked. But someone called her name, and she moved away to talk to friends, leaving him staring after her while pretending not to be. Yeah, they were playing at something new these days, some sort of cat-and-mouse game, and he was pretty sure that he didn't have a complete set of the rules.

She was laughing at something someone said, her red hair gleaming like fire beneath the lights. Her gaze drifted to his. Yeah, definitely something had changed between them. Again. At first he'd thought it was his imagination. After all, she had always baited him, and he'd done the same to her. But he'd always been able to shrug it off, knowing they were just messing with each other.

Nothing more.

Never anything more.

But now they were one spark away from a fire that could burn them both to cinders, and that couldn't happen. He'd worked too damn hard to make this life of his. Every day, every single day, he had to walk the straight road. Discipline was the only thing that he could count on. Not even his friends could help him if he went off the rails as an adult. Coburn was dead, his father didn't count, and Ford and Jax were busy starting new lives. They deserved to be happy and not have to worry about him. That was logic and reason.

But whether it was exhaustion, or the memories stirred from tonight's fatal accident, logic and reason didn't make a dent in his insatiable, drumming, unrelenting need to have Chloe Traeger.

Chapter 8

*"A closed mouth gathers no foot, though that's
hard to remember in the moment."*
—*Chloe Traeger*

Normally Chloe loved being at the Love Shack when it was full like this. She loved the warmth and connection of the people that lived here in Lucky Harbor. She enjoyed the easy camaraderie, especially after being gone for the past few days working. Usually sitting on a barstool listening to stories filled her with a sense of calm. Like she could belong in this place.

Not tonight. She'd been in San Francisco for a few days, and it'd gone well. She had new orders for her skincare line, and she'd even managed to work in some fun, visiting friends she hadn't seen in a while. They'd wanted her to stay a few more days, and she could have easily stretched the work to justify it. But for the first time, she'd been anxious to come back to Lucky Harbor.

Home.

On the drive, she'd started to think of ways to stick closer to home next time and alleviate some of the travel time.

The idea wasn't new. It'd first come to her a few months ago, and it wouldn't leave her alone. She wanted to be more to the inn than just the token dishwasher or night watch for their guests. She wanted more than just filling in. She wanted to be a part of the place in the way Maddie and Tara were. She'd even thought of a perfect way to do that—open her own day spa at the B&B. Several times in the past she'd treated the occasional guest to a complimentary facial in the sunroom, but this would be different. Every day. Officially.

No doubt her sisters would remind her how much time she spent away, but why couldn't she come up with a compromise? Why couldn't she have it all? There was nothing to say she couldn't slowly ease into it, proving she could pull it off. Hell, she could still travel on the days she didn't have anything booked. That would be the best of both worlds, keeping one foot here in this place but being able to get out and spread her wings when she needed.

She'd like that.

Sawyer's name pulled her attention back to the bar. Jax was serving Lucille, telling her a story about his own wild, misguided youth, one that happened to include Sawyer. Apparently the good sheriff had also been a wild, misguided youth, which shocked Chloe. But at the tender age of fourteen, Sawyer had been running a little fake ID business. He'd made both himself and Jax a pair of fake IDs, which they'd attempted to use to buy alcohol.

It hadn't ended well.

Lucille, wearing her customary eye-blinding, neon-pink sweats and white headband, cackled in her been-smoking-for-seventy-years voice. "Oh, honey," she said to Jax. "Do I remember that.

Sawyer's daddy was furious. He gave the both of you boys a stern what for."

"Yeah, more than a what for," Jax said with a remembered wince.

Sawyer appeared to be paying no attention to the story. He was finishing up his French fries with singular concentration, chasing them down with the last of his beer.

Chloe had never seen him drink alcohol before.

And she'd sure as hell never thought that the guy behind the badge would have once upon a time had a fake ID business going, stupid kid or no. It was hard to reconcile the two very different images she had of him.

Sawyer pushed his empty plate away, nodding at the waitress who took it for him. Clearly distracted, he rose to his feet and moved behind the bar, vanishing into the back room.

Chloe watched him go, then saw Ford exchange a look with Jax. Obviously, they knew something was up, which was good because she didn't feel that tangling with Sawyer tonight would be the wisest move. And dammit, she was trying to make wise decisions.

And yet...hell. Neither Ford nor Jax were going after him. She waited another minute, remembered the careful blank look on Sawyer's face and knew that it meant he needed the mask tonight. Heart squeezing, she drew a deep breath and went herself.

He stood alone in the far corner of the back office, in front of an open locker. She remembered Maddie telling her once that the guys kept a locker for him so that he could come from work and unload his weapons in a safe place and be off duty.

Which he'd clearly done earlier in the evening, as he was now in the middle of entering a combination. He opened the locker without turning in her direction, though she knew damn well that he'd heard her come into the room. He was a cat when it came to that stuff, seeing behind his back, sensing things.

She watched as he pulled his utility belt from the locker and slid it around his waist, clicking it securely in place. Next he bent over and clicked the leg strap around his muscular thigh. Selecting his gun next, he carefully held it up and eyeballed something on it. Satisfied, he placed it into the holster on his hip, snapping the small band in place to secure it.

Chloe stood rooted to the spot, shocked to find that watching him arm himself to the teeth was turning her on.

Still not acknowledging her in any way, Sawyer pulled out a knife, sheathed it on his leg, and then slipped another gun into the small of his back.

Whew. Suddenly it felt a little hot in here. "Isn't that a bit of overkill for the kind of calls you get here in Mayberry, USA?" she asked, her voice annoyingly husky. "I mean, sure the traffic jams are irritating, and the occasional drunk stumbling along the pier probably takes up time, but are they really *that* dangerous?"

Sawyer didn't start at the sound of her voice in the quiet room. He merely slid a jacket over his entire ensemble that had DEA in bold white letters on the back. He shut the locker, spun the lock, then slowly turned to face her. "I've been doing extra projects as part of a special task force."

Dangerous projects, from the looks of things, and she felt a prickle of fear for him. "Oh. So you ..."

"Like to be prepared."

She nodded, keeping her concern to herself because he wouldn't want it. She liked to be prepared as well, or at least the semblance of it. And at the moment, she wasn't even close to prepared for what just looking at him was doing to her, so she backed up, right into the door. Wincing, she grabbed the handle. "Well," she said, far too brightly, "sweet dreams." She left the room without another word. She walked straight through the bar, got onto her Vespa, and rode to the B&B in the dark, dark night.

Sweet dreams? Had she really told the man to have sweet dreams? What was going on with her? And dammit, she hadn't even asked about his father. She'd been too busy being distracted by his job, and how good he looked doing it.

Only when she was on the porch of the little owner's cottage behind the inn did she take a deep breath. She was all alone. Alone was good. She really liked alone...

An SUV pulled around the back of the B&B and parked next to her Vespa.

Sawyer, of course. He exited his vehicle and strode up the steps to the porch, looking especially big and bad in the dark. Her knees did an odd little wobble, and she locked them in place, leaning back against the porch railing. "What are you doing here?"

"Wanted to make sure you got home okay."

"Do you follow every woman home from the bar, Sheriff?"

"No. Just the ones who are most likely to go sneaking around late at night near Black Ridge." He braced an arm on the railing at her side and leaned in. "Since I'm too tired to go after you tonight, I thought I'd head you off at the pass."

"You saw us," she murmured, refusing to be intimidated by the size of him looming over her. However, her body didn't fail to get a little thrill from the close proximity. "Lance and I, the night before I left for San Francisco." They'd gone up there because the old Whitney house was scheduled for demolition next Monday. It was out there on thirty acres of thick, remote woods and hadn't been lived in for decades.

Except for the homeless. There was always a small number of them seeking shelter in the place, especially in late fall like this, when the nights got cold. Chloe and Lance, and several others from town, including Lucille and her blue-haired posse, had driven them to various neighboring shelters, to make sure everyone had a place to go before the house came down.

"Got there just as you were leaving." His gaze was hooded. "You help everyone find a place to go?"

Something inside her got a little mushy, which she ruthlessly squelched. "Yes." She drew in a sharp breath as he stepped even closer. For someone who'd been working all day long, he still smelled delicious, like whatever masculine soap he'd used, and man. All man. "So we're back to that Eagle Scout thing," she said. "Stalwart and charitable, worrying about the homeless and women getting home safe and sound."

He gave her a single head shake. "There's nothing stalwart or charitable about how I feel for you, Chloe."

"Well, that's a relief." Her every nerve was on high alert screaming: *Run don't walk*! But there was also something else. The man willingly put his life on the line every day in a thousand different ways, for people like her. It was an odd and uncomfortable realization. But he *was* dangerous, if to nothing other than her heart. She should go inside and lock the door, not because she was afraid of what he might do, but because she was afraid of what *she* might do.

Instead, she found herself taking that last step, closing the gap between them, so that they were toe to toe, only a breath away from each other.

He looked down into her eyes. "What are you up to?"

"No good."

He shook his head and ran a finger along her temple and down her jaw. A little startled by the power of his touch, she covered his hand with hers and held it in place against her. Something flashed in his eyes, an aching hunger that held her captive.

Because it matched hers. She was shocked at the strength of it, at how difficult it suddenly was to breathe. But she wasn't shocked when he nudged her backward until she bumped up against the door. His mouth skimmed her jaw, then her throat, his teeth grazing her skin as he pressed a thigh between hers.

Heat skittered through her belly, then directly south. "Sawyer."

In answer, he brought his head up and kissed her. Deep, hungry, tasting her in a purposely slow, thorough manner before pulling back to once again look into her eyes.

Oh, God. "Sawyer, what are we doing?" she whispered.

He shook his head. "No fucking clue."

She let out a low laugh. "Maybe we should do it some more."

He obliged, pulling her in for another kiss, which grew rougher and more demanding, until she was *vibrating* with need, making little whimpers in her throat for more.

When he stepped back, eyes black as the night, she staggered for balance. "What?" she managed. "Why did you stop?"

"Your phone's going off."

Right. *That* was what was vibrating. Touching her still tingling lips, she pulled her cell phone from her pocket and read the incoming text.

Can you come relieve me at the B&B?

Tara. "I gotta go," she said, blood still rushing through her veins.

Their gazes met. Disaster averted, at least for now. And sleeping with him *would* be a disaster. Well, it'd be an *amazing* disaster. And possibly an out-of-body-experience disaster to boot. And now that she was thinking about it, she'd really like that . . .

"Behave tonight," he said.

That made her laugh, and even he smiled. "Yeah," he said. "I figured that might be a stretch."

"I do occasionally behave, you know."

"Is that right?"

His voice was low, husky. Playful. It was almost as much a turn-on as big, bad Sawyer had been. With the silent night all around them, she tapped her iPhone screen and accessed her Magic Eight app. "You heard the man," she said to it. "Will I behave tonight?"

* * *

The iPhone screen went foggy for a moment, then cleared, and two words floated to view.

Absolutely not.

With a low, mirthless laugh, Sawyer shook his head. Of course, Chloe wasn't going to behave. She didn't know the meaning of the word.

Chloe smiled a little apologetically, like the odds were completely stacked against her, and some of the tension created by that mind-blowing kiss dissipated into the night. But relaxing around her was just as dangerous as whatever had been crackling between them. Sawyer took another look at the screen of her phone to see if it'd changed its mind. A strand of Chloe's long hair stuck to his stubbled jaw. Her scent filled his nostrils, and he shifted closer so that her shoulder bumped into his chest.

He liked being close to her. Way too much.

"Ask it a question," she said.

"Like what?"

"I don't know. Anything. You could ask if you'll catch another idiot convenience store robber, or have to replace any more batteries for Mrs. Abbott anytime soon. Hell, ask it if you'll be getting lucky—I always ask it that. It's good at giving love advice." She turned to the phone and said, "Magic Eight Ball, will Sheriff Sawyer Thompson get laid anytime soon?"

"Jesus, Chloe."

She grinned at him over her shoulder and peered at the screen, which clouded and then cleared, and two more words appeared:

Not likely.

Chloe laughed out loud with what Sawyer thought was a rather nasty glee. "Same question," she told it. "For me this time. Will *I* be getting laid anytime soon?"

Sawyer didn't know what he wanted the answer to be, but before he could decide, the screen came into focus, and two crisp words floated:

Outlook good.

Chloe burst out laughing again, bending at the waist with amusement, which thrust her ass directly into his groin.

As that part of his anatomy was still cocked and loaded from their kiss, it was also now aimed. His hands went to her hips to step back, but somehow his brain mixed up the signal, and he held her still instead.

In the heavy silence, all he could hear was her suddenly accelerated breathing. "Well," she said straightening. "The Magic Eight app has never paid off quite so fast before."

Sawyer was dizzy. He was certain it had to do with the fact that he no longer had any blood in his brain.

"Sex stirs up my asthma."

Sawyer blinked. "What?"

"Yeah. I probably should have told you that sooner."

He shook his head, trying to catch up. He couldn't.

Turning to face him, Chloe grimaced. "Every time. And then I end up overusing my inhaler. But they're expensive, and I have this really crappy catastrophic insurance, and the inhaler isn't covered at all." She drew in a breath. "So I have this thing I do before sex. A test. An 'Is He Inhaler Worthy?' test."

He just stared at her. "There's a test. Before sex."

"Yes. And I should tell you, not many pass."

Somehow they'd ended up tangled in each other again, and she rocked against him, her actions at odds with her words. "There's a test," he said inanely.

"A guy has to pass it before I'll—"

"Have sex with him."

She nodded, her gaze locked on his mouth. He could tell she wanted it on hers, and for once, they were perfectly in sync. Having no idea what he was doing, he kissed her again, another no-holds-barred, tongues tangling, rock-his-fucking-world kiss that left him staggered and her apparently unable to speak as they tore apart for air and waited for the world to right itself.

Didn't happen.

She was breathing hard but not wheezing. Good sign, he thought. He stared at *her* mouth now, still wet from his, and just barely managed not to take a bite out of that full lower lip. It took a hell of a lot more control than he thought possible. Her hands were gripping his shirt, and also a little bit of his skin and some chest hair to boot, but he didn't say anything. Mostly because he wasn't sure if she meant to push him away or pull him closer, and if it was the former, he didn't want to remind her. "Chloe?"

"Yeah?"

"I'd be worth the inhaler," he said, then forced himself to walk away into the night.

* * *

Chloe busied herself with work, which wasn't hard to do. It was early, and she sat in the inn's kitchen with her sisters preparing for their day.

The B&B was thriving. More and more, their weekends were booking up, and people were beginning to schedule during the week as well. Maddie continued to run the inn with supreme efficiency, handling the books, the staffing, the supplies, and the equipment. Tara, as always, handled the kitchen.

And Chloe did her best to pick up the slack. But the restlessness within her was still building, and cleaning and filing and answering phones weren't doing it for her. She had a talent, dammit, and it was time to bring it up. "I've been thinking about a way to get the B&B some publicity."

"Oh, good Lord," Tara said. "Don't tell me you're in the paper again. I mean, your motives with the homeless thing was sweet, but they always refer to you as some sort of troubled rebel. And who the hell is going to want to stay here with a troubled rebel, Chloe?"

"It's okay, I didn't get in the papers again."

Tara let out a sigh of relief and turned back to Maddie. The two of them had spent the past ten minutes arguing over towels. Towels. "Blue," Tara drawled to Maddie. "Blue's soothing as right rain."

Maddie shook her head. "Pale green. Soothing *and* on sale." She turned her laptop to reveal the site that she was looking at. If Maddie gave the place its heart, then Tara added the practical logic. Tara's practical soul was big...and cheap. The word *sale* was one of her favorite words, and she nodded her agreement.

Soothing on-sale green it would be.

"Hey," Chloe said. "About my idea..."

"If you suggest red towels," Tara said, her south showing, "I'm going to hurt you."

"It's not about the towels." Chloe stood up. "And it's more a plan than an idea."

Tara frowned. "The last time you said that, you were calling me collect from Tijuana, needing me to wire you money."

"Okay, first of all," Chloe said, "that was a *long* time ago. And second, this is an actual *good* idea." She drew in some air and held it. "A day spa. Here."

"You already do day spa stuff here," Tara said.

"Yes, I *prepare* here. And sometimes I do freebies for the guests," Chloe agreed. "But I'm talking about making it official and charging for the services."

Tara had turned away from the computer to her island. She was whipping eggs in a bowl now, her whisk moving at the speed of light. "As in a schedule where you set up appointments for our guests?"

"Yes," Chloe said, nodding, feeling the excitement flow just talking about it. "Facials, skin treatments, all the stuff I do for other spas all over the place. But here. Right here."

"What if you're gone on a trip when people want an appointment?" Maddie asked.

"I'd keep a schedule. Like we do for the inn. People would book in advance."

"But you take off on a whim all the time," Tara said. "I wouldn't want to have appointments booked and you off for parts unknown."

"I never take off on a whim anymore," Chloe said, trying not to get defensive. "I go when I get bookings. And I wouldn't leave if there was a booking here."

Neither sister spoke. In fact, there was no sound except the eggs sizzling on the stove, and the heavy weight of Tara and Maddie's misgivings. "Wow," Chloe said, failing at not getting defensive after all, as a ball of hurt clogged her throat. "All I hear are the crickets and doubt."

Tara flipped the eggs with the precision of a brain surgeon. Maddie was head down, forensically examining her fingernails as if they held the secret to the universe.

Chloe stared at them, then let out a mirthless laugh. "You know, all the faith you guys have in me is staggering." She strode to the door with absolutely no idea where she was going.

"Chloe," Maddie said softly, regretful, and Chloe stopped.

"There's a track record to consider," Tara said firmly, not caving to sentiment.

"You think I'd flake on you?" Chloe asked. "When have I ever flaked on you?"

"Well, let's see." Tara turned off her eggs. "Easter. July 4th. My birthday. Maddie's birthday, Mom's service—"

"Hey," Chloe said defensively. "I came to the service." A day late, but she'd had a good reason. She hadn't been ready, not to say good-bye to her mom, nor to face the fact that with Phoebe gone, Chloe had been truly alone. If she'd gone to the funeral, she'd have completely lost it. And she didn't "lose it" well. Truthfully, she didn't do deep emotion well. And birthdays, holidays, and funerals were all about deep emotion. "I've never made an appointment and not shown up."

Maddie, ever the peacemaker, got up and took Chloe's hand. "Why don't we all just think about it? Okay?"

No. No, it wasn't okay. They didn't believe in her. Angry words settled on her tongue, but her chest was too tight to voice them. "I can handle a schedule," Chloe repeated. "I can make us some good money, too. I'd be contributing."

"Honey, you're contributing now," Maddie assured her. "You're a huge help. We couldn't do this without you."

"Yeah, all that taking out the garbage is invaluable," Chloe said, heavy on the sarcasm. "Look, I can do this," she said again, hating that she sounded vulnerable.

Hating that she *felt* vulnerable.

And because she knew that they wouldn't give her what she wanted, the acceptance and the belief she needed, she grabbed her keys and cell phone. Her ever-present inhaler was already in her pocket.

"Chloe," Tara said. "Where are you going?"

"Out. On a whim."

Chapter 9

*"Sisters. Love 'em or fight 'em, but no matter
how hard you try, you can't ignore 'em."*
—*Chloe Traeger*

Frustrated and mad at herself, Chloe rode the Vespa hard. Okay, so there was no riding any Vespa hard, and not for the first time, she wished she could afford a Duc. Or a Harley. Something fast and bad.

She was feeling the extreme need for both.

In substitution, food would work. She'd stop for breakfast, but she didn't have any money on her. Note to self—next time you leave in a diva fit, bring money. Thankfully, it was warmer than it'd been in weeks, which was good, since along with her wallet, she'd also forgotten a jacket.

Okay, so buying food was out. Sex. Sex would be lovely. She didn't need money or a jacket to jump someone's bones. *Sawyer's* very fine bones...

But he'd laid low for days. He'd given her that smoking-hot

kiss—*kisses*—that had melted all resolve and reason, and then nothing. Maybe he'd simply had better sense than she. After all, he was a stable fixture around town. People had respect for him. Getting mixed up with her would undoubtedly put a check mark in his demerit column.

Whatever. She was better off on her own.

Always had been.

She sucked in a calming breath, annoyed with the jitter in her belly. Residual anger. No one could disappoint her quite like the sisters that she hadn't meant to let into her heart. If she'd been thinking straight, she'd have told them about the offer that she'd had two weeks ago in San Diego. The owner of the spa at a luxurious boutique hotel there had asked Chloe to take a permanent space in her salon, where Chloe could work and sell her products on consignment. What would Tara and Maddie think of that? A business acquaintance had more faith in her than they had.

But she hadn't told them, hadn't told anyone, because a little part of her wanted to have a reason to stay here in Lucky Harbor. To be *needed* here . . .

Dammit. She drew as deep a breath as she could and rode. She rode between mountains smothered in forests so thick it was like being swallowed up by a green comforting throw. Above her, the sky was a rare brilliant blue, streaked with a few white, puffy clouds. About fifteen miles out of Lucky Harbor, on a narrow two-lane road that she wasn't exactly sure of the name of, she caught sight of a sign for Yellow Ridge, and then another for some mud springs. She'd heard about the mud springs from Lucille, who knew everything about every square inch of the entire county. Years ago, beavers had created a meadow when they'd chewed their way through the surrounding forest and inadvertently flooded it. Early settlers had then discovered it and come to bathe nude in the mud for its healing effects.

Intrigued, Chloe turned off the highway, riding through a

canyon lush with giant moss-draped trees. A mile or so up the road, she parked in the small clearing, in front of the trailhead to the mud springs. She pulled out her phone to text her sisters that she was alive, but she couldn't send it because she had no cell service.

This didn't stop her. It was a fairly easy climb, which was a good thing. Not anxious to have an asthma attack out here all alone, she didn't push herself. The trail was wet, meaning there was no pesky dust rising as she walked, which helped. The trail branched off several times with no rhyme or reason, or further sign. Staying to the right so that she wouldn't get lost going back, Chloe took it all in. The way was lined with wildflowers and offered up spectacular views of the peaks towering over her. Awe-inspiring, and very effective at clearing her head.

Twenty minutes in, the forest suddenly opened up, and she stood in the small meadow Lucille had told her about, filled with pockets of the promised mud springs.

She sure could use some healing effects right about now, she thought, slipping out of her shoes and socks. And hey, this was research. If the mud was good stuff, well, then she owed it to her clients to check it out before incorporating it into a product. Stepping to the edge, she dipped a toe into the mud.

It was warm.

And she wanted in. Taking a careful look around, she realized just how alone she was. "Crazy," she said out loud. "This is crazy." But she had to admit, she'd done far crazier. Her knit top was long, well past her butt so she stripped out of her jeans and told herself she was still decent if anyone happened upon her. Then she stepped into the mud up to her shins, and it oozed between her toes, toasty and oddly comforting. Wading in a little farther, she sighed in pleasure. The temperature of the mud gliding up her legs was so incredibly soothing that she went out even more, up to her thighs now.

All around her, the woods pulsed with life. Birds, insects, leaves dancing on the light breeze, and she felt…alive. If only she could bottle this feeling, with the sun on her face, the forbidden sense of being outside in her shirt and panties, with the mud soothing her skin in a way she hadn't expected, she'd be a millionaire.

She bet her sisters would take notice then…

She wished she was better prepared, because she would've liked to strip down even more and treat herself to a good soak. But she didn't have a towel or water to wash off with afterward, so she turned back to shore and…

Her foot slipped.

Chloe did a perfect imitation of a cat scrambling for purchase on linoleum, but it was no good. A second later, she was on her butt. She gasped but didn't bother to scramble up. It was too late now; she was in up to her belly button. Never one to waste an opportunity, she took another look around, then carefully pulled off her half-muddy shirt and tossed it to the shore to join her jeans. Relaxing, she soaked in her bra and panties beneath the wide-open sky.

As the mud worked its magic, she finally admitted to herself that what she'd felt earlier was more hurt than anger. She'd honestly tried to fit in, to pick up the slack around the B&B. And just because her mother's death and going into business with her sisters had forced her life into a one-eighty, it didn't mean she could ignore her other responsibilities. Dammit, she'd been serious about the skincare line she'd been working on, and her client list hadn't been developed overnight. Didn't that alone prove she'd grown up some?

But with some distance—and warm mud—she could admit to herself that she understood her sisters' concern. Renovating the sunroom would cost time and money. And yes, they were right, Chloe's track record *was* spotty. But there had to be a compromise. She could promise to commit to a certain number of days a week where she'd stay in town, for instance. And they could promise to believe her. With a resigned sigh, she rose and walked out of the mud.

She looked around, then with a philosophical shrug, she stripped out of her bra and panties, rubbed the excess mud off the best she could, and put her clothes on.

Commando.

Then, with the mud drying on her skin, she moved gingerly back down the trail, telling herself she was merely amplifying the healing affects by keeping the mud on so long. Hell, she'd probably look like a movie star after this. By the time she got to her Vespa, she'd talked herself into believing it. Hard to do when she felt like she'd been wrapped in concrete, but she managed.

That's when she discovered problem number two. Her Vespa wouldn't start. Okay, this was more than a minor setback. With no cell service, she had little choice. She walked down the road to the highway. Unfortunately, by the time she got there, her lungs had had enough. The two long walks had tightened her chest uncomfortably. Her inhaler helped with that, but she still didn't have cell service. She was going to have to flag someone down off the highway while looking like a swamp thing.

So much for being a grown-up.

In less than five minutes, a shiny black truck pulled off to the side of the road. Todd's baby.

"Hey, cutie," Todd said with his good-old-boy smile as he leaned over and opened the passenger door. He wore a Mariner's cap on backward, a ratty T-shirt, equally ratty jeans, and steel-toed boots, none of which took away from his easy good looks and tough build. A roofer by trade when he chose to work, he was clearly on his way to or from a job. "Problem?" he asked.

He didn't blink at the mud. This was probably because he wasn't looking at her limbs. Nope, that honor went to her braless breasts, now outlined with extra-special clarity thanks to the mud acting like an adhesive. "My Vespa's battery is dead," Chloe said. "And I don't have cell service."

"No one does right here." He didn't say a word about the fact that her Vespa was nowhere in sight. "You know what this means, right?" he asked. "You're at my mercy." He grinned, and she sighed. One hundred thousand sperm and *he'd* been the fastest.

"Come on," he said. "That was funny."

"Why are you out here?"

He shrugged. "On my way home from work."

"Isn't this way out of the way?"

Another shrug, and he stared out his windshield. "Sometimes I like to be alone, to hear myself think."

More like he'd gone somewhere remote to get high. But he didn't look buzzed.

"You getting in?" he asked. "Us outcasts need to stick together."

"Outcasts?" She shook her head. "You're not an outcast."

"Misfits, then." Something came and went in his eyes when he said this, but she couldn't read him. "You know what I mean."

"Yeah," she said, softening. Because she did know. Exactly.

He had a duffle bag on the passenger seat, which he took and stuffed behind them instead. Then he patted the passenger seat.

He was Jamie's brother. And Jamie was Tucker's friend, and Tucker was Lance's brother—but six degrees from trouble was still trouble, and she'd been trying so damn hard to stay *out* of trouble. But she was cold now, and getting even colder. Sawyer would hate this, but she couldn't help the extenuating circumstances.

"Come on, sweet thing. I've got somewhere I've gotta be."

Guilt didn't begin to cover how she felt about getting into his truck, but she did it anyway. She glanced over her shoulder and saw his open duffle bag.

She thought she caught sight of ziplock baggies stuffed with—

Todd reached back and shoved the duffle bag farther down so she couldn't see into it. "You're going to owe me," he said, shoving the truck into gear and speeding back onto the highway, flashing her a grin. "Big."

She straightened and looked at him. Was he carrying drugs? She hadn't gotten a close enough look, and she sure as hell wasn't going to ask him while they were out in the middle of nowhere. Besides, she could admit that she hadn't gotten a good enough look to accuse him of anything. "I'll pay for gas."

"Not the kind of payment I was banking on."

"Shut up and drive, Todd."

He grinned again. Ignoring him, she huddled into herself for warmth, staring out the window. Clouds sifted through the trees like wood smoke, distracting her for a while. Out here, the growth was extravagantly thick with spruce and hemlock. Moist air rode in from off the coast, something her lungs liked but made her even more cold.

Twenty minutes later, she sat up straight. "Pull over."

"Yeah, baby," Todd said, and braked.

"Not for that! Lucille has a flat."

"Hell no," Todd said. "I'm not helping that old bat. She's always calling the damn cops on me."

"We can't just leave her there."

"Hell, yeah, we can."

"Todd, goddammit, pull over!"

Todd shook his head and slammed on the brakes as he pulled onto the shoulder. Dirt rose. "I'm not changing her tire. She told Kelly Armstrong I was a menace to society, and her husband, Manny, fired me. Cost me three weeks of work."

"We can't just leave her out here. It's chilly, and she looks cold. I'll help her myself." Chloe swung out of the truck.

"I'm not waiting," Todd warned, revving his truck. "I'm late."

"Then don't wait." She slammed the door, not surprised when he peeled out and was gone, leaving her literally in his dust. "Idiot."

Just as she walked toward Lucille, another truck pulled up.

Sawyer Thompson ambled out of his truck, then stood there in low-slung Levi's and a soft-looking, thin black sweater over a black T-shirt, eyes hidden behind dark, reflective sunglasses.

Off duty, Chloe thought as a violent shiver racked her.

"My white knight," Lucille said, dusting off her hands. "I called him a few minutes ago."

* * *

When Sawyer walked up to Lucille's little Prius, the older woman was giving the flat a kick. He glanced at Chloe, who was very busy studying the highway. "Hey," he said, taking in the mud all over her. "You okay?"

"Perfect."

Okaaaaay. He watched her shiver and handed her his keys. "Go wait in my truck; crank the heat." He headed toward Lucille, not all that surprised when he heard Chloe follow him. "Nice job on listening," he said.

"Maybe I'd listen if you ever asked."

"I ask."

She snorted.

Lucille had stopped kicking her tire and had picked up a lug wrench.

"You didn't mention you had a passenger when you called me," Sawyer said.

"I didn't." Lucille glanced at Chloe. "She just got dropped off."

Sawyer turned to Chloe, who was back to studying the high-way like her life depended on it. "What does she mean, you just got dropped off?"

"I believe I have the right to remain silent," Chloe said.

Shaking his head, Sawyer crouched at Lucille's side by the back rear tire and took the lug wrench.

Lucille backed up and smiled knowingly at Chloe's condition. "Mud springs, right?"

Chloe nodded.

Sawyer narrowed his gaze on Chloe. "You were at the mud springs?"

"Yes."

"How did you get here?"

Before she could answer, Lucille cut in with, "I used to take my stud muffin up there, back in the day. That mud has healing effects, you know. And also, it's an aphrodisiac. Not that you need an aphrodisiac with this one," she said to Chloe, gesturing to Sawyer with a sly smile.

Sawyer grimaced, but Chloe cocked her head and studied him. "You don't think so?" she asked Lucille doubtfully.

"Honey, just look at him."

Both women studied him now, and Sawyer, afraid of nothing except possibly these two, found himself squirming.

"Where's your uniform?" Lucille asked. "I like looking at you in it."

"I'm off duty," he said.

"Aw, and you still came out to help me instead of calling someone else to do it." She patted him on his arm. "Such a sweet boy."

Chloe made an indistinguishable sound, but when Sawyer looked at her, she was all green-eyed innocence.

"I talked to Suzie today," Lucille told Sawyer. "She told me what you did for her boy this week, how you stepped in for him."

Suzie Tierman worked with Sawyer in dispatch. She was a single mom, and she had an eight-year-old terror named Sammy who'd gotten caught last week cutting off a girl's ponytail in class. Her parents had wanted to press assault charges even though their little "princess" had been mercilessly tormenting Sammy for months about being a "stupid loser."

At Suzie's request, Sawyer had stepped in and mediated. Sammy would be doing hard time pulling weeds, and the girl had written an apology for calling Sammy names. Sawyer would have liked to see her do some hard weed pulling as well, but the letter would have to do. "I didn't do much."

"According to Suzie, you're being a father figure to the boy. You call him and take him to your baseball games, and last week you went to his class for career day. She says she couldn't do the single-mom thing without your help."

Uneasy with the praise, Sawyer shrugged. "Being a single mom's hard."

"And you don't want her to give up," Lucille said softly.

"Sammy's a good kid," he said and fixed his attention to the flat.

Lucille and Chloe talked amongst themselves. He wanted to talk to Chloe about the mud springs, but she was doing a damn good job of avoiding the subject. He had no intention of letting it go, but somehow she and Lucille had gotten on the subject of Sawyer at the age of eight. Lucille was telling Chloe about the time when he and Jax had urinated their names in the snow in front of the pier and gotten caught by none other than Lucille herself. And then how several years later, the two of them had moved on to delivering flaming bags of dog poop to the residents on Mulberry Street—until one of the bags had tipped over and caught Mrs. Ramos's dead rosebush on fire. The flames had leaped up to her awning and nearly burned her house down.

Sawyer finished with the tire just as Chloe asked about his

teenage years. Christ, that was the last thing he wanted her to hear about, and he tensed.

But Lucille gave him a reassuring smile, a glint of understanding in her kind eyes as she shook her head at Chloe. "He figured things out," she said. "He had a big heart, even then."

Bless her for lying through her teeth.

"He's one of the good guys," Lucille said, and patted him again.

"Lucille," he started.

"What? It's true. Yesterday alone you saved the peace in town at least twice."

"What happened yesterday?" Chloe asked.

"Honey," Lucille said with exasperation. "Facebook! I have all the good stuff up there, including today's blog on Cute Guy. Someone got a picture of him jogging shirtless on the beach this morning. I'm telling you, if I were thirty years younger—"

"Okay, we're all done here," Sawyer said, gently but firmly ushering Lucille to the driver's side of her car.

"Lucille," Chloe said. "Could you give me a ride?"

"Of course, dear. I can't believe Todd just left you on the side of the road like that. I—"

"I've got her, Lucille," Sawyer said, giving the older woman the bum's rush, shutting Lucille's door on whatever it was that she was going to say. He turned to Chloe, every line of his body saying pissed-off cop.

Well, crap. "You just chased off my ride," she said casually as Lucille drove off.

"Yeah. You're coming with me. Are you hurt?" he asked.

"No."

He pulled off his sunglasses and looked her over for himself, taking in the way that every inch of her skin was covered in mud except for her clothes, which were relatively clean. She knew the exact second when he came to the realization that she'd been skinny-dipping because the carefully blank look vanished. "You and Todd were in the mud springs together."

A logical assumption, she supposed, but she'd had a rough enough day that it pissed her off. "No. I—"

"He's dangerous, Chloe. *Stupid* dangerous."

No shit. She thought about mentioning what she might or might not have seen in Todd's truck, but Sawyer cut her off.

"I realize you like the dangerous part," he said. "But I never pegged you for stupid."

Oh no, he didn't. She reached for the Zen calm she'd found at the mud springs. It was a total stretch. "I don't know exactly how *stupid* I look, but even I know Todd's nothing but a player."

He didn't bend an inch. "Lucille said you were in his truck."

"He gave me a ride."

"So you *were* with him."

"Oh my God!" So much for Zen calm. He was like kryptonite to her Zen. Whirling from him, she stomped along the highway with no concern for how she must look, only knowing that she could feel the steam coming out of her ears. Maybe it'd melt the mud from her body. "Moronic man," she muttered, prepared to walk all the way back to town to avoid talking to Sawyer. "Moronic *men*, all of them, the entire gender is a complete waste of good penises—"

A big, warm hand grabbed her arm, and she spun willingly around, stabbing Sawyer in the chest with a muddy finger. "And you—"

"Moronic," he said mildly. "I know." With a firm grip, he pulled her back to his truck and stopped at his passenger door. "Stay," he said.

"Oh, hell no. I don't *do* 'stay.' I—"

But she was talking to air because he'd moved to the back and pulled a blanket from his emergency kit. Which he wrapped around her shoulders. It was thick wool, and she snuggled into it even as she shook her head. "I'll get it all dirty."

"Done deal," he said. "Get in the truck."

"What about my Vespa?"

"Did you crash it?"

"No. I think the battery is dead. Which is how I ended up in Todd's truck, you...you Neanderthal."

He ignored that. "Your Vespa can wait. You need to get dry and warm. Get in."

She was really quite over the ordering around. "I'm walking." Even to her own ears, she sounded ridiculous, but the words were out. She realized that she was completely contradicting her commitment to being more mature and grown up, but she decided that a few mistakes along the way never hurt anyone.

Sawyer considered her for a brief moment. She'd seen him handle a variety of situations without ever appearing so much as rattled, without even the slight indication that his patience was stretched, yet it seemed ready to snap now. It was in the grimness of his mouth, the narrowing of his eyes. Oh, and his jaw seemed to be bunching and unbunching at random.

"You're not walking," he said.

She took a page from his own book and said nothing.

"Jesus." He pinched the bridge of his nose, then drew in a deep breath. "Just get in the damn truck."

"I'll get it dirty, too."

"It's seen worse." He pulled open the passenger door, bodily picked her up, and plopped her onto the seat. Leaning in, he yanked the seat belt across her and stabbed it into the buckle at her hip. He didn't slam the door. Exactly.

Chloe could have gotten out, but it was warm. And it smelled good. Like Sawyer good. It'd be counterproductive to leave, she decided, and leaned her head back and closed her eyes, ignoring Sawyer when he slid behind the wheel. She went into radio silence as he started the truck, maintaining that quiet as he cranked the heat and aimed the vents at her, and then finally began to drive.

He gave her a full five minutes before he spoke. "You going to tell me what's going on?"

"Thought you had it all figured out," she said.

"Christ. You drive me insane, you know that?"

Yeah. She knew that. She drove everyone insane. It was a special talent of hers.

Chapter 10

*"Just when you think you've hit rock bottom,
someone'll throw you a shovel."*
—Chloe Traeger

Extremely aware of the pissy woman in his passenger seat, Sawyer drove back to Lucky Harbor, occasionally glancing at her. She was no longer shaking, he noted with what he told himself was clinical and professional interest only.

But it wasn't clinical or professional interest that also took in the fact that she looked better covered in mud from head to toe than any woman had the right to look. Her shirt had once been white but was now streaked with mud and sheer as a second skin. Through it, he could see every dip and soft curve, every nuance of her, including two perfect, mouthwateringly tight nipples threatening to burst through the cotton. "Chloe."

Nothing.

"Fine. Let me know when you're done pouting."

Turning her head, she leveled him with yet another icy stare. "Pouting? You think I'm pouting? I'm...*furious*."

"At the Vespa?"

She stared at him like he'd grown a third eye. "At you!"

"Me? What the hell for?"

"You..." She choked, as if she could hardly speak. "You actually think that I'd fuck Todd? In the mud springs? Or anywhere outside of hell freezing over, for that matter?"

Sawyer clenched his jaw. "I found you caked in mud but your clothes are mostly clean. Which means you stripped down to skin. Plus, you're not wearing any underwear. What the hell else am I supposed to think?"

"How can you tell that I'm not wearing any underwear?" she demanded.

"God-given talent."

She closed her eyes and counted to ten. "I was alone in the damn mud springs. I slipped in, then had to ditch my bra and panties. They were...uncomfortable. I didn't see Todd until I got back to the highway to hitch a ride when the Vespa wouldn't start. Halfway back we saw Lucille and I made him pull over to help. He didn't stick around. Not that I should have to explain myself to you."

He was quiet a moment. "I had to ask."

"Why?"

"Why? Christ, Chloe."

"No, I mean it, Sawyer. In the past week, you've made it abundantly clear that we're...well, I don't really know exactly what we are—were—but whatever it was, it clearly wasn't worth your time. So I have to know. What if I *had* been with Todd? What would it matter to you?"

Sawyer reminded himself that she didn't, couldn't, know his history with Todd, or the level of resentment and escalating violence that Todd directed toward him.

Or how the thought of Todd's hands on her twisted him in knots. "It'd matter," he said grimly.

"Why?"

"You don't want to know."

"I *do*."

No way was he going to tell her that once upon a time he and Todd had been fellow thugs. That he and a group of other equally stupid thugs had terrorized the entire county together and had, in fact, outdone themselves on several occasions. The most memorable time being when the four of them had gotten drunk—God so fucking drunk—then stolen a car for a joyride. That had been the night that they'd reduced their gang by two when they'd hit a telephone pole.

Sawyer had earned a trip to juvie.

Todd, the driver, hadn't been as lucky. He'd turned eighteen the week before, had been tried as an adult, and had been convicted for involuntary manslaughter. "There's an old grudge between us," Sawyer finally said.

To say the least.

"What kind of grudge?"

Todd had done some hard time, and when he'd gotten out, he wasn't the same easygoing troublemaker he'd once been.

And even though they'd each made their own decisions, Sawyer had never been able to shake the guilt. This was because he knew without a doubt that if he'd been smarter that night, the accident wouldn't have happened.

Two guys wouldn't be dead.

Todd wouldn't be on a one-way street to Loserville.

And Sawyer wouldn't still be trying to straighten Todd's ass out. "Let's just say that Todd blames me for the way his life has turned out," he said quietly.

"Well, that's ridiculous," Chloe said. "And not your fault. We all make our own path."

"Yes, and his is to fuck with me. I want you to stay away from him, Chloe."

She looked pissed off again. "Look, I understand you're trying to offer me advice, but—"

"Not advice," he said. "I'm flat out telling you. Stay away from him. He's trouble."

She kept her voice low and even, but her eyes were flashing pure fire. "He's a friend of my closest friend's brother. So staying away from him won't always be possible. I get that you have some sort of pissing match going with him, but he's not *that* bad a guy."

"Are you sure about that?"

She had no answer for him, but huddled farther into the seat with a shiver.

Sawyer blew out a breath and checked the heater output, but it was already on full blast.

Chloe sighed. "I need to tell you that Todd maybe had drugs in the back of his car."

He slowed down and looked at her. "Maybe?"

"I can't be sure. He had a duffle bag, and it was filled with small ziplock bags. I couldn't quite see what was in them." She shook her head. "Forget it. I shouldn't have said anything."

"No, I'm glad you did." He fought with what to tell her. "He's under investigation and being watched. If he's got drugs, we'll catch him."

She nodded.

"And no one in Lucky Harbor knows that information."

"Understood."

He glanced at her again, and told her the other thing bugging the hell out of him. "And for what it's worth, I stayed away from you all week because some distance seemed in order. Chloe..." He let out a breath. "We both know damn well we could give each other something we need, but it's a real bad idea."

Her gaze darted away from his, but not before he caught the flicker of unmistakable hurt. "Yes, all the kissing proved that," she said to the window. "It was awful."

He opened his mouth, shut it again, and waited for the traffic to get moving.

* * *

Chloe tried unsuccessfully to ignore the mud that had tightened uncomfortably on her skin. As she squirmed, Sawyer slid her an unreadable gaze. She ignored him, too, and he put the truck into gear, pulling back onto the highway.

She wasn't mad at him anymore. She'd tried to hold on to it, but it was just too hard to stay mad at a guy who stopped to change a woman's tire, not to mention rescued another woman from turning into a mud popsicle. "Tell me the truth," she finally said. "You can't drive and talk at the same time, right?"

He didn't say anything, but his mouth quirked slightly, and she sighed. The ability he had to keep everything to himself drove her nuts. But only because she wanted to be able to do the same. It was another big reason to stay away from him. He wasn't the yin to her yang; he was the Batman to her Joker.

And Batman was fully in his zone right now, complete with the dark reflective sunglasses and the blank face. "So...Lucille says you're sweet."

"She wears rose-colored glasses for everyone."

This made her take a second look at him. "You don't think you're sweet?"

He grimaced and didn't answer.

"It's a compliment," she said, amused. "Sweet is a positive quality."

"Yeah," he said. "In puppies."

Chloe laughed, a little disconcerted by how easily and

effectively he disarmed her, every single time. "Don't worry, Sheriff. I won't tell anyone."

His concentration was on the road. Apparently he'd exhausted his word usage for the day. "So does this happen to you a lot?" she asked, perversely determined to make him talk. "The rescue thing?"

He shrugged. "It's my job."

Maybe. But he wasn't on the job at the moment. "Tell me about the calls yesterday, the ones Lucille brought up."

"They were nothing."

"Fine. I'll just go read Facebook. Probably it's not too overly embellished."

He glanced over at her. "Do you ever use your powers for good?"

"Not if I can help it. Tell me."

He blew out a breath. "I got called out to Mrs. Perez's house because she was shining a light in her neighbor's windows. Apparently the neighbor—Mrs. Cooper—had cheated at bunco earlier in the week and pissed Mrs. Perez off, so Mrs. Perez was retaliating by scaring Mrs. Cooper."

"What did you do?"

"I took the batteries out of Mrs. Perez's high-powered flashlight."

"Fast thinking," Chloe said, impressed. "What else happened?"

"I got called to the Sorenson house."

"Bill and Joanne, with the eight daughters?" she asked.

"Yes. Bill had plowed a pile of mulch in front of his neighbor's driveway."

"Why, had the guy been cheating at bunco too?"

"No," Sawyer said. "The neighbor's son got caught…in a compromising position."

"Compromising position?"

"Pants at his ankles, in the company of one of Bill's daughters."

"Uh-oh. In that case, you're lucky there weren't gunshots."

"No luck involved," he said. "I took Bill's rifle from him two weeks back when I heard the two teens were dating."

She laughed. "You took his rifle? Are you allowed to do that?"

"*Borrowed.* And then accidentally disposed of it."

"How do you accidentally dispose of a rifle?"

Sawyer turned and flashed her a heart-stopping grin, full-wattage. "You go sailing with Ford and dump it three miles out at twelve knots."

Ford had been a world-class sailor, with an Olympic medal and many other awards for his efforts. He didn't go out on the racing circuit so much anymore, but he did sail with Jax and Sawyer on their mutual days off. Chloe had seen them on the docks at the marina. Hell, she had a permanent kink in her neck from all the times she'd stared out the marina building window at the three of them wearing board shorts and nothing else.

The truck's heater was decadently warm on her chilled skin, but the dried mud was still a huge irritant and she squirmed some more.

"What's the matter?"

"You ever go naked on the beach and get sand in places that no sand should go?" she asked.

"Ah. I take it the same applies for mud."

"Little bit." Plus, she'd never worn jeans without underwear before, and it wasn't nearly as fun as she'd thought it might be. The center seam kept riding up, and the zipper was cutting into her. She looked out the side window to distract herself, but all she could see was Sawyer's reflection next to her. *He* wasn't fidgeting. Of course, that was because he didn't have mud in his cracks and crevices. But even if he had, she doubted that he'd fidget. He never wasted a single ounce of energy. He was driving, relaxed—maybe a little too amused at her dilemma—all his carefully controlled energy at rest.

Though he hadn't been so relaxed when Lucille had been recounting the story about how he'd helped Suzie because she was a single mom. Chloe turned to look at him in profile. His hair was windblown, his face tanned. He hadn't shaved that morning, and his square jaw was scruffy. She liked it. But there were lines of tension along the outside corners of his eyes.

He wasn't as relaxed as he appeared to be.

He worked hard. He always did. From what she knew of him, he'd gotten that from his father, a hard worker himself, and a single dad. And it hit her. "How old were you?"

"When?"

"When your mom gave up being a mom."

For a brief beat, he took his gaze off the road and looked at her before turning back. "Eight."

Her heart squeezed. "You were eight when your parents divorced?"

"They were never married. Or together, for that matter. I went back and forth between them until I was around eight." His hesitation was brief. "That's when she left town." He lifted a shoulder, like life happens, no big deal.

But it was a big deal. Chloe knew all too well what it was like to have only one parent, a parent who wasn't always so keen on being one in the first place. It had left its mark on her, and the older she got, the more she was beginning to understand how deep the wounds went. Or maybe being here in Lucky Harbor with her sisters was what had stirred the pot, but all her relationships seemed to be affected by her childhood. Not only that but also her search for stability, for a home, and the ironic fear of those very same things.

Which left her to wonder what the loss of his mother had done to Sawyer. "You ever hear from her?"

"No."

He said it easily enough, but something made her throat

tighten a little. Maybe it was the thought of him at eight years old being utterly abandoned by the one woman in his life who he should have been able to count on. She knew what it felt like to be without a parent, too. It was possible, she supposed, that her own father hadn't known about her at all, but she thought it far more likely that he'd known and simply hadn't wanted her. "Are you close to your dad?"

He let out a low laugh.

"I'll take that as a no."

"There's bad history. I haven't exactly been a model son."

"You were a motherless little boy," she said in his defense.

"I was a complete shit," he corrected. "A holy fucking terror. My father did what he could." He gave a slight shrug. "At least you and Phoebe were of like minds. She was the original wild child." A small but fond smile crossed his lips, taking any of the possible sting out of his words.

"You liked her," she said in surprise.

He glanced at her. "Is that so odd?"

"Well, yeah. You're not always so fond of me, so..."

"Says who?"

She opened her mouth, then closed it again.

"Wow. I just made you speechless. That's new. I like it." He paused. "And yeah, I liked Phoebe, too. She did as she pleased, lived the life she wanted to live."

"Sometimes," she said, staring at him, "you surprise me."

He shot her a rare smile. "So what about your dad?" he asked after a minute. "I've never heard anything about him."

"No? Me either."

"You don't know him?"

"I don't even know who he is."

Again he glanced at her, and she once again turned to the window, annoyed at herself. She never told people that. First of all, it was embarrassing, and second...

Second, it brought out something she hated.

Pity.

She didn't want pity. Most of the time, she didn't give a damn about her father. He was a nonentity. It was only since coming here and being around Tara and Maddie that she'd realized his absence had had such an impact on her. She shifted yet again and sucked in a breath of discomfort.

Beside her, Sawyer made a sound of his own, but when she looked at him, he was watching the road, calm as can be. "Still cold?" he asked.

Fair question. Her nipples were two tight pebbles, so visible that she might as well have been naked. "Yes." She shifted around some more.

"Jesus, Chloe. Stop doing that." He shoved his sunglasses to the top of his head and sent her a look so heated that she nearly went up in smoke. "Get the blanket back on you," he said, reaching behind him, where she'd tossed it to get out of the truck earlier. He threw it over her, including her face.

"Oh for God's sake, they're just nipples," she said, tugging the blanket down so she could breathe. She leaned as close to the vents as her seat belt allowed. "Just let me off in town at Lance's."

"What's with your place?"

"My sisters are going to give me shit about this. We had a fight this morning." A stab of remembered hurt hit her low and deep, but she ignored it. "Among other things, I told them I was all grown up. Which obviously," she said with a mirthless laugh and a gesture at her ensemble, "was a complete lie. Seeing me like this isn't going to help my cause. If you drop me at Lance's, I can check on him and also borrow his shower. And maybe get Tucker to help me fix the Vespa."

"Lance's mother was with him when I talked to him. In your condition, you'll give her heart failure. Hell, *I'm* nearly in heart failure." He pulled off the highway just before her exit.

"So where are we going, then?" she asked.

He drove up a steep street, then turned a couple of times, and pulled into a driveway. The house was the last on the block, a midsized ranch on a bluff overlooking the ocean. Chloe had never been up here, but she knew Sawyer had bought the place earlier in the year.

He turned off the engine and faced her, laying his arm along the back of her seat. "It wasn't a lie, what you told your sisters," he said. "About growing up. You've changed a lot since you moved here."

"Yeah? Then why am I still making stupid moves? Look at me, Sawyer."

He did just that, appearing to like what he saw in spite of the mud. "Just because you're unconventional doesn't mean you're not a grown woman."

It was possibly the nicest thing anyone had ever said to her. "So...is 'unconventional' the new 'sweet'?"

He laughed, and she liked the sound, very much. "Why do we always fight?" she whispered.

"You know why."

Yeah, she did. "It's science."

"Combustible chemistry," he agreed. "Dangerous." His voice was pitched so low as to be nearly inaudible and sent tingles down her spine. Clearly mistaking that for a chill instead of desire, he got out of the truck and came around for her. He held out his hand, but she just stared at it while the fresh fall air slid into her taxed lungs.

"Scared?" he asked.

"Of course not." And she wasn't. Scared. Nope, she was something else entirely, and it was making her breathless, and her chest was tight. She slid out of the truck, and since Sawyer didn't move out of her way, she bumped directly into him, her body pressing close to his.

Given that she could feel him hard against her, she was guessing he wasn't scared of a little combustible chemistry either. "What are we doing?"

"Come on. I'll show you." He pulled her toward the house.

"But I'll get your house as dirty as your truck."

"No, you won't," he said, and that's when she realized that they weren't moving toward his front door but around to the side of the house. Then they were in his backyard, which was nothing more than an open patch of wild grass. Stairs cut into the cliff that led down to the beach about a hundred feet below.

"I run along the beach sometimes," he said. "Or climb the rocks. Clears my head."

She walked to the edge and looked over. The cliff was rocky, jutting out in spots, creating little pockets where trees stuck out like porcupine quills. An entire elemental world of rock, trees, and water that made her itch to explore. "Does it work?" she asked. "The clearing of your head part?"

"Yeah."

She could imagine him climbing to one of the alcoves there on the cliff, staring out at the churning ocean, inhaling the salty air, the wind in his face as the waves crashed on the rocks. "It's a good place," she said.

"It is. And after a run, I come up here." He walked her to the very far corner of his house. "Maybe I'm not muddy, but definitely sandy and sweaty." He gestured to the wall. There was an outdoor shower there, like the ones at the public beaches. But this one wasn't grimy and gross. Instead, it was clean and tiled, and, as she discovered when he leaned in and flicked the handle, equipped with hot water.

She watched the muscles play across his back and shoulders as he straightened, and when she saw what he had in his hands, she paused. "A removable showerhead?"

"For those hard-to-reach spots."

Chapter 11

*"I've always wanted to be somebody.
I should have been more specific."*
—Chloe Traeger

Chloe stared at the pulsing showerhead in Sawyer's hand. Half an hour ago, they'd been furious at each other. Apparently they were going in an entirely different direction now. "Lance would've let me inside his house, you know. Of course, I'd probably have had to strip naked to get past the front door."

"Feel free to strip naked now."

She narrowed her eyes at him. Yeah, okay, they were definitely over their mad. New direction coming at her. Was she ready? And good Lord, that smile should be registered as a lethal weapon, because surely it was as dangerous as anything else he was carrying. She stuck her right jean-covered leg beneath the spray, then moaned against her will as the water soaked past the mud-stiffened denim and warmed her skin. "Ahhh. So warm."

"I might be a—what was it you said? A waste of a penis? But I'm not a complete ass."

"Hmm," she said noncommittally. She kicked off her tennies, then bent over to use her hands to rub her feet beneath the water. The caked-on mud washed away easily, which was nice. She could see this stuff in a really great body mask—

The water suddenly hit high on her thighs and made her jerk upright and squeak in surprise. "Hey!"

"Looked like you could use some help," Sawyer said mildly.

"I've got it, thanks." Because if he stepped in and "helped" by running his hands over her body, getting clean would be the farthest thing from her mind. Her breath hitched just thinking about it, and she thought of her inhaler, which she'd left on the seat of his truck. She considered going back for it, but she felt oddly compelled to stay right where she was even as she grabbed the showerhead from him.

"Don't trust me?" he asked.

"Hell no."

His soft laugh danced along her nerve endings and gave her goose bumps. Or maybe that was the chill that the water left in its wake. In any case, she had a sudden urge to wipe the smirk off his face. She'd been working hard on curbing her impulses, but she decided that not all impulses should be curbed.

So she aimed the water at his chest. "Whoops."

He didn't react other than to narrow his eyes and step directly into the spray. In less than two seconds, he'd wrestled the showerhead from her, twisted her around so that her back was to his chest, and held the showerhead inches from her as he pressed his mouth to her ear. "Are we playing?"

"No!" Laughing and gasping for breath, she squirmed and fought with all her might, but he had her easily restrained against himself. Not a bad place to be—if her chest hadn't felt like it was contracting, the first and most annoying sign of an impending asthma attack. She went still for a beat to mentally assess herself.

"Oh, no you don't." Clearly thinking she was trying to figure a way out of his grasp, Sawyer tightened his grip and lowered the nozzle, letting the water hit her.

She gasped, but couldn't deny the excitement driving through her. There was something to be said for being held captive against a hard, warm chest, completely at his mercy.

With a flick of his wrist, the nozzle shifted higher, near her face.

"Don't you dare," she said.

"I always dare." He nipped her earlobe with his teeth. "But maybe if you beg me real nice…"

Beg, her ass. Besides, she hadn't exhausted all her options yet. She still had some dirty fight left in her, and without qualm, she let her backside grind into his crotch.

He sucked in a breath and instantly went still, his grasp on her slackening slightly. It was enough to whip around, grab the shower handle back, and get him.

Right in the face.

He simply opened his eyes and gazed at her steadily. Calm. His entire body relaxed. *Ready*.

Uh-oh. "Okay," she said, backing up a step. "I got it out of my system."

"My turn, then."

Oh shit. Dropping the showerhead, she whirled to run, but he reacted so fast that all she got out was another squeak as he propelled her forward with his big body, until she was planted cheek against the wall of the outdoor shower. Holding her there with his considerable brawn, he reached up and replaced the showerhead in its bracket. Then, with the hot water now raining down over them, he turned her to face him.

She was breathing hard. "Look at you," she managed. "Now you're as wet and dirty as I am."

His big hands came up to cup her face. "I've told you—I like wet and dirty."

Good thing, since they were plastered together by drenched clothes and warmed-up mud.

"You're still shivering," he said.

"Not from cold." She could feel him, hard beneath his wet denim. No longer playing, she rubbed up against him.

"Chloe." The warning in his voice only turned up the flame on the slow burn in her belly, spreading both north and south now, beyond her soaked clothes all the way to her core.

She moved against him again. "You started it."

His eyes met hers, dark and hungry. With the mist from the hot water swirling around them, he dipped his head and let his lips slide down her throat, igniting flames along each nerve ending. "Stop me now if you're going to," he murmured against the hollow at the base of her throat where her pulse pounded frantically. His voice was thrillingly gruff, and his hands encircled her wrists on either side of her head, slowly sliding them up the wall, holding her pinned as he nibbled at her.

Stop him? Was he kidding? Instead she arched against him, eliciting a rough groan from deep in his chest that reverberated through hers. "Too many clothes," she complained.

In response, he stripped off his sweatshirt and shirt together, and then her top, tossing everything aside. She looked at him and lost even more air. He was sheer perfection, all perfectly toned muscles, with that hint of danger still vibrating from him even now. It was enough to make anyone think twice about making a move on him, but she was fearless, or at least knew how to pretend to be.

His mouth covered hers again, which worked for her because he kissed like heaven on earth. His hands were cold, sending a quick thrill through her when he cupped her breasts, his fingertips teasing her nipples before his fingers slid down her torso on their way to the next barrier. She felt the button on her jeans give, the zipper go down, and then he was pushing the jeans off her legs.

"Kick them off," he said, cupping her ass, pulling her tight to him as she obeyed the quiet demand.

"Yours, too," she panted, annoyingly short of breath. Still ignoring the warning signals dancing in her head, she lent a hand to the cause, helping until they stood facing each other.

Naked.

Wet.

Sawyer was always cool, calm, and utterly in control, but that control was being tested now. She could see it in the line of tension between his eyes, in his tight jaw, and most of all, she could see it in what was quickly becoming her favorite body part of his—the one bouncing happily at the sight of her.

She licked her lips, a nervous little gesture. Sawyer said her name again, voice definitely strained. No more cop face, that was for sure, though his body was hard, strong, and rippling with power. It made her feel her own power, and incredibly sexy. He could probably make any woman with a pulse feel sexy, but she also felt safe, like she could say anything. Do anything.

Temporary, a little voice said. This is just a *Twilight Zone* intermission, and when they were done and once again dressed, they'd return to their separate universes.

But that was a worry for later.

For now, the steam continued to swirl around them, like fog on a humid night. Sawyer's flesh gleamed before her in the weak sunlight, his big body sleek and drenched, taut like a warrior's. Such a beautiful body, she thought, and used her mouth to learn him, tracing her tongue over a pec, flicking at a nipple.

Drawing in a sharp breath, he threaded his hands into her hair and tipped her head up to kiss her. It was long and wet and deep as his hands roamed down her sides, over her hips to her backside again, pulling her in tight, leaving no room between them for so much as a single drop of water.

She tried to suck in more air but couldn't. Dammit. *Not yet.* "Hurry." They had to, because her chest was way too tight. Hell, her airway was already closing. Knowing she was on borrowed time, she dropped to her knees. Sawyer was a big man, *everywhere*, and humming her pleasure, she lightly scraped her nails up the backs of his thighs as she ran her tongue along the length of him.

From above, he hissed in a sharp breath, his fingers tangling in the wild mess of her hair. Not surprisingly, he took over, pulling her away from him, tugging her up to her feet again, pressing her to the tile wall.

Then he dropped to *his* knees. She let out a startled "Wait. What—"

"Ladies first."

Oh, God. She could probably come from his voice alone. "I can't," she whispered, but the words backed up in her throat when he pressed his mouth to the spot just beneath one hip bone, right over the top of her tiny hummingbird tattoo.

"Free as a bird?" he whispered with a smile.

She nodded, her heart pounding in her ears, her breath caught in her throat. And she knew damn well that it wasn't the good kind of can't-catch-your-breath, that she wasn't just near the danger zone but *in* it. She didn't care. He was there, *right* there, looking at her, and it'd been so long. So frigging long . . . "*Sawyer*—"

If he responded, she couldn't hear over the roar of blood in her ears and the water hitting the tiles around them. Then it didn't matter because his hands were on her hips, holding her steady, his thumbs gliding down her quivering belly, then over her trimmed mound. "Pretty," he murmured.

It took her a moment to get enough breath to speak. "Are you going to just look?"

He laughed softly against her, his warm breath caressing her, making her moan. Her hands went to his hair, trying to draw him in close.

"Spread your legs," he said, then took care of it himself with a big, hot hand wedged in between her thighs. Her hips rocked helplessly, and her toes curled. Her heart was going to burst out of her chest, she was certain of it. And, oh God, she really needed air. Little spots were dancing around the very edges of her peripheral vision, but hell if she was going to pass out before she got to the good stuff. No way. "Now. Oh, please now."

Probably thinking she was just impatient, he slowly trailed a finger over her, letting out a raw sound of sheer male appreciation at how wet she was. And then barely, just *barely*, slid it into her, all the while her body racing with equal speed toward the edge of an orgasm *and* an asthma attack.

And still he wasn't hurrying. Pushing him so that he sat back on his heels, she dropped to straddle him right there on the shower floor.

"Chloe—"

She rocked her hips until she had what she wanted, his erection poised at her entrance. "I'm on the pill," she panted.

He ran his hands up to her breasts, then to her ass, yanking her in, angling her so that they were better aligned, the whole time kissing her to the point of madness.

And breathlessness.

But breathing was completely overrated, she assured herself, and then he slid home with one sure, shocking push of his hips, filling her to the hilt, and she didn't need to breathe at all.

They gasped in tandem pleasure. God, the pleasure. He rasped his thumb over her, just above where they were joined, and then again. She cried out, arching against him as the orgasm hit her hard and fast and utterly unexpectedly. Shuddering, she writhed against him in exquisite torture, her body completely under his control.

Heaven.

For one beat, there was such incredible heaven, but in the next, the tightness in her chest spread and completely shut off her air supply, and the dots that had been dancing at the edge of her vision closed in. She heard Sawyer's sudden and urgent "Chloe!" but it was far too late. She'd already faded to black.

Chapter 12

"A guilty conscience needs no accuser."
—Chloe Traeger

Sawyer spent the next half hour in a state of unaccustomed panic. After Chloe had passed out, he'd run with her to his truck, where he'd found her inhaler on the seat. She'd come to enough to use it several times, and now sat in the passenger seat insisting she was fine.

Ignoring her, Sawyer drove toward town, intending to take her straight to the ER.

"Don't," she said. She was wearing sweats—his. He'd grabbed dry clothes from his house. "I'm okay."

"Chloe—"

"Look, I'm still paying off my last two ER visits." Her voice was rough and ragged, and she didn't look nearly steady enough, but she put a hand on his arm. "Please, Sawyer. Just take me home. I have a portable nebulizer there and can give myself a breathing treatment."

He opened his mouth to demand why the hell she hadn't had her inhaler *on* her, but he decided to save that fight for when she didn't look like a slight breeze could knock her on her ass. Against his own instincts, he drove her home and settled her in on the cottage couch, watching as she gave herself a breathing treatment.

At least she had some color back to her lips. That helped, but Christ, he'd never forget the way they'd turned blue, or how she'd gasped, hands at her throat, fighting to draw air into her lungs.

His fault.

"Mr. Magic Eight was right on once again," she rasped over the rumble of her nebulizer.

"What?"

She let out a low, wheezy laugh. "The Magic Eight app. The love advisor, remember? It said you wouldn't get laid, and that I would. Of course, I didn't get *laid* laid, but close enough. I mean, I finished and you didn't get to..."

"Christ, Chloe."

"And now you can confirm I don't sound like a mule in a tar pit, right?"

"You *stopped* breathing."

"Only for a minute."

Head spinning, he dropped it into his hands. "Only for a minute," he repeated dully.

"Yeah." She paused. "Too soon?"

He'd been mentally flogging himself, and she was joking around. He shoved his fingers through his hair and resisted pulling out the strands by the roots.

"Yeah," she murmured. "Too soon. Sorry. Sawyer, look at me. I'm fine."

He gently pushed the nebulizer mouthpiece back in place. She'd passed out from lack of oxygen, and *she* was comforting *him*. "Why wasn't your inhaler on you?"

"Because nothing was on me. We got naked, remember?"

"Fuck, Chloe."

She had the good grace to look sheepish. "Okay, so I didn't exactly realize what was going to happen, or that I'd need it. I told you, I'd been on a sex moratorium."

"No, you absolutely didn't tell me that."

"Oh." She grimaced. "Well, I started to. I told you I couldn't."

Okay, she *had* told him that. And he'd mistakenly—and cockily—believed she'd meant that she couldn't orgasm with a man.

Which mean that he was an ass. A complete ass.

"And technically, it's not that I *can't* orgasm," she said, waving the mouthpiece. "*Obviously*. It's just that the experts recommend measuring your peak oxygen flow and having a portable nebulizer handy."

"Okay. So why didn't we do that?"

"Well, for one thing," she said, "that doesn't exactly scream spontaneity and excitement, and second, I didn't plan on having sex in your shower, it just happened. Which proves point number one."

"Never again, Chloe," he said flatly. "I don't want you to ever again be without that inhaler. Do you hear me?"

She gave him a smart aleck salute that made him narrow his eyes and open his mouth, but before he could say a word, the front door opened and Tara and Maddie came rushing in. Maddie was in the lead, wearing jeans and a USC sweatshirt that Sawyer recognized as Jax's. She sat at Chloe's side and hugged her. "You avoided the ER this time."

Barely, Sawyer thought grimly.

Tara, cool and calm as ever, squeezed in past Sawyer to get closer to Chloe, patting him on the arm as she did, probably assuming that he'd rescued Chloe. If she'd known the truth, he knew he'd have been on the receiving end of a blistering verbal and well-deserved attack. No one did pissed-off-Southern-belle slash protective-mama-bear better than Tara.

But for now, Tara leaned over Chloe and kissed her cheek. "I should have sat on you earlier when you left all half-cocked, making yourself as scarce as hen's teeth. You were wheezing even then."

Chloe left the nebulizer mouthpiece in but rolled her eyes as her two sisters continued to mother and baby her, while Sawyer wondered if they had any idea just how strong she really was.

"Can you tell us what happened?" Tara asked Chloe. "What were you doing, and why in God's name are you streaked with...*mud*?"

A faint blush tinged Chloe's cheeks, and her eyes locked on Sawyer. Slowly she pulled the nebulizer mouthpiece out to speak, but before she could, Tara pushed it back into place.

"No, don't." She fussed at the blanket over Chloe's legs. "It can wait, especially if you're going to tell me you were rock climbing or—"

"She was with me," Sawyer said.

Three sets of eyes landed on him. Maddie's and Tara's were both curious and completely nonjudgmental.

They trusted him, and right now, the weight of that trust sat like an elephant on his chest. He worked so damn hard to earn the respect and trust of the people of his town, and this was a perfect example of why it was all a sham. He knew full well that he'd had no business touching Chloe, and he'd done it anyway.

Coburn had warned him, all the way back when he was eighteen and scared spitless, that all it took was one step out of line. One extra drink before he got behind the wheel. One reckless word, and his whole world could implode. He knew that, and yet when it came to this, he lost it.

Chloe's eyes were narrowed, clearly trying to tell him to keep his trap shut, but he refused to let this be her fault. "I was giving her a ride home from the mud springs."

"The mud springs," Tara said with a frown. "Those are *way* out there. How did she get to your house? When you called me, you said you were bringing her here from your house." She turned to Chloe. "Oh, sugar. What did you do this time?"

Chloe yanked the mouthpiece out. "Nothing!" It wasn't quite a yell, but only because she was clearly still hampered by her inability to breathe freely.

Tara shoved the mouthpiece back in Chloe's mouth. "And yet here you lie, struggling to breathe."

Chloe slapped a hand on the nebulizer power button, and the room went quiet. "You're right," she said. "I did do something. I rode to the mud springs, then hiked all the way back to the highway when I couldn't get the Vespa to start. I tried to hitch a ride, but Sawyer came along and played hero."

"All that hiking," Maddie murmured. "That could have brought on the asthma attack."

Clearly wanting answers, Tara whirled on Sawyer. "Tell me what happened."

"Hey," Chloe said before Sawyer could open his mouth. "Talk to *me*."

Tara reached back and hit the power button of the nebulizer again. "I was asking *him*," she said, eyes on Sawyer. "You picked Chloe up from the highway and then brought her back to your place, and..."

"And I forgot my inhaler," Chloe said. "I left it on the seat of his truck."

"Chloe." Tara's voice was full of censure and dismay.

Maddie looked equally upset with her.

Sawyer met Chloe's intense gaze. Obviously she'd rather them think she was completely irresponsible than blame him.

But she wasn't. Reckless, maybe, yeah. Impulsive, too.

But not irresponsible. So...was she trying to protect him? The notion was unexpected, as was the way it made him feel, but he didn't need her protection. "She's okay," he said to a suspicious Tara, knowing that a good amount of her anger came from a gut-wrenching fear for her sister, the fear that someday they wouldn't get to her in time, and she'd suffocate during an asthma attack.

It also came from the fact that Tara considered Chloe hers. And no one messed with anything that belonged to Tara, even if that possession was a full-grown woman with her own needs and passions.

"He's right, Tara," Chloe said. "I'm okay, like always."

Thankfully, not five minutes later, Sawyer was paged into work by DEA Unit Chief Reed Morris. An ongoing drug investigation that he was working on had some movement, and his presence was required at a task force meeting. From there, he had to go by the hospital to talk to one of the ER docs on staff. The guy had treated a suspect they needed to interview, but he couldn't tell Sawyer anything new about the case. He was just leaving the ER, intending to go check on Chloe, when a nurse came running by, stopping short when she saw him.

Mallory Quinn. Sawyer had dated her in high school. Well, not dated exactly. She'd written his English papers, and in turn, he'd done her science and math. He'd also had a big crush on her, but she'd never returned it, preferring the boys who didn't get arrested when they got bored.

They were friends now and occasionally ran into each other professionally. Seeing him, Mallory skidded to a stop, the relief evident in her eyes. "We need help restraining a patient in bay three."

He didn't waste time asking questions but ran ahead of her. In bay three, two orderlies were struggling with a man on the bed.

"Paranoid schizophrenic," Mallory said. "And off his meds."

He wasn't big, maybe five foot seven, and one hundred forty pounds, but given the odd light in his eyes, he was deep into an episode. When the guy swung out with a fist toward Mallory's face, Sawyer grabbed him, restraining him while Mallory produced a syringe.

It was over in ten seconds, the patient out cold.

"Well, that was fun." Mallory shoved back her hair. She was sweating. They were all sweating. "Thanks. That was about to get ugly."

Sawyer ran a finger over her wrist, where already the bruise in the shape of the man's hand was starting to show. "Get some ice on that."

She laughed shakily. "Will do." She squeezed his hand and smiled at him. "Anything you need in return?" She smiled. "Maybe I can help you out in study hall or something?"

"I've got a Vespa that needs a rescue and a once-over. Possibly a new battery. Your brother still working at the auto shop?"

"Yes." Mallory glanced down the hallway. "I'll call Joe on my break. Would this be Chloe Traeger's Vespa?"

There were no secrets in Lucky Harbor, so he didn't bother to sigh. "Yes."

Her smile went a little teasing. "I suppose she gives better...English than me?"

Sawyer grimaced, and she laughed. "No worries, Sheriff. I won't tell Lucille if you won't."

He walked outside the hospital toward his truck, pulling out his cell to check on Chloe. She didn't answer, so he headed toward the inn, stopping by the Love Shack first because Ford and Jax had texted him ten times. Each.

They were both little girls that way.

Ford was behind the bar. Jax was there as well, not serving but sitting on the counter in the corner, thumbs flying over his phone. They both looked at Sawyer expectantly.

"What?" Sawyer said.

"You know exactly *what*," Jax said. "Start with Chloe being taken home by you in *your* clothes. No, wait. Start just before that."

From beside him, Ford's mouth twitched as he served Sawyer a tall soda. "Way to ease into it, man."

Sawyer tossed back the soda and gestured for another.

Ford refilled him. "Let me save you some time. Tara and Maddie ratted you out. Here's what we know—Todd gave Chloe a ride and dumped her on the side of the road with Lucille. We know this because he came here and knocked a few back, muttering about the idiocy of women. Then somehow you showed up and saved the day with the flat. You gave Chloe a ride and then you two went at it. She had an asthma attack. Oh, and you should watch your back. The sisters are pissed off at you for sleeping with the wild child."

"She's not a child," Sawyer said. "And there was no sleeping involved."

"Nice," Ford said. "But you probably shouldn't mention that in front of my girlfriend—"

"I meant," Sawyer said through his teeth, "that I didn't— *Fuck*. Never mind."

Jax laughed softly. "You didn't...fuck?"

"That's *not* what I said."

Jax looked at Ford. "He's all pissy, too. He didn't get his."

"Hey," Sawyer said. "I was a little busy making sure she didn't die."

"Ah," Ford said with a sage nod to Jax. "You're right. He didn't get his. Which explains the bad attitude."

When they both laughed, Sawyer headed to the door. "You guys are assholes."

"Aw," Ford called after him. "Don't go and get your panties in a wad. That's not good for a guy in your condition. If things get too tight down there, you might do some real damage."

Without looking back, Sawyer flipped them both off and went out into the night. He drove to the B&B and parked in front of the small owner's cottage between Tara's car and Chloe's Vespa, which Joe had indeed rescued and fixed at Sawyer's request.

Tara opened the door, and it was a good thing that looks couldn't kill or he'd be dead on the spot. "She okay?" he asked without preamble.

"Yes."

A tension that he hadn't realized was gripping him released slightly. "I want to see her."

"She's sleeping."

A silent battle of wills commenced, and Tara was good. She had thirty-five years of staring people down and winning, but Sawyer was better, and he held his ground.

She caved with a small sigh and a shake of her head and moved aside to let him in.

He'd have gone in search of Chloe but Tara's hand on his arm stopped him.

"She thinks she's a real tough cookie," she said.

"She is."

"Not when it comes to you."

He met her gaze. "What does that mean?"

"You're going to have to figure that out yourself. I like you, Sawyer. I like you a lot, but hurt her and I'll hurt you."

He stood in front of her armed to the teeth, trained in hand-to-hand combat, outweighing her by seventy-five pounds minimum, and raised a brow.

"Okay," she said. "So I know how ridiculous that sounds, but I mean it."

"We're on the same side," he said.

"No. I'm here for her, always. You're here because there's something going on between you two, something physical and clearly out of control. But when that's done..."

He understood what she was saying. He was temporary in Chloe's life, and Tara was not. "I just want to see her," he said. "I want to see for myself that she's okay."

Tara stared at him for a long beat, clearly fighting the urge to tell him to go to hell. "Fine. I'm going to the inn to check on things. But I'll be back in fifteen minutes, you hear?"

He stopped in Chloe's doorway, propping up the doorjamb with his shoulder. The room was pitch-black, but if he strained, he could hear her breathing and just that sound soothed him. As a few minutes passed, he slowly felt some more of the tension drain out of his body.

Earlier, in his shower, her breathing had started out quiet like this, but then she'd gone up in flames for him. He'd loved it, loved the way she'd panted for more, clutching at him as if she was afraid he'd stop. It had gone straight to his head, more potent than any alcohol or drug.

And then in the very next beat, when she'd started to suffocate, all he'd wanted to do was breathe for her. God, he could still taste the bitter helplessness, and he hated, *hated*, that she'd suffered. That she'd almost died.

There was a chair by her bed, and feeling oddly wobbly, he straddled it. Reaching out, he messed with the shades so that they let in slats of pale light from the moon's glow, enough to see her by.

Chloe lay on her side, a hand tucked beneath her cheek. Her lips weren't blue. He wasn't sure if he'd ever get that image out of his head.

The stuff of nightmares.

The covers had slipped to her waist. She wore a thin camisole top, and one of the straps had slipped off her shoulder, nearly exposing a breast. The thin material was caught on her nipple, and his mouth actually watered.

The hem of the cami was bunched high on her waist, and with

the blanket at her hip, several inches of smooth skin was bared. He watched her stomach rise and fall with each easy breath. No wheezing.

She'd showered. He could smell the scent of her shampoo and soap, and he leaned in for a better whiff. Yeah, he'd completely lost it.

Careful not to wake her, Sawyer ran a finger up her arm, intending to nudge the strap of her cami back into place. But murmuring something in her sleep, Chloe rolled, flopping to her back, covering her eyes with a flung-up arm.

Her breast escaped its confines, and in the cool night air, the nipple puckered into a tight peak.

He bit back a groan and closed his eyes. Not looking didn't help, so he stood and pulled the covers to her chin, hiding her from his gaze. Then he sank back down to the chair, not moving from the spot until he heard Tara return, and then he left like the hounds of hell were on his heels.

Chapter 13

"Smile. It's the second best thing you
can do with your lips."
—Chloe Traeger

Chloe awoke with a start and sat straight up, startled by her cell phone vibrating at her bedside table. "Sawyer?" she whispered. The sun was shining in through the shades, the ones she'd shut the night before.

But she was alone in the room. No Sawyer. Which was odd only because she...*felt* him. Blowing out a breath, she lay back and grabbed her phone. "Hello?"

She'd missed the call. Squinting, she accessed her messages and listened to someone just breathing. She hit delete. The next message was the same, more of her heavy breather.

Delete.

The third message, she finally got a voice. "Hey, sweet thing." Todd. "We need to talk."

No, they didn't. Delete. She sat up and looked around for

Sawyer. But of course he wasn't here. Why would he be here? Just because yesterday they'd—and she'd—and he hadn't—

Don't think about it.

Happy to be the Queen of Denial Town, Chloe flopped onto her belly and closed her eyes, but instead of going back to sleep, she relived yesterday with aching acuity. Sawyer giving her a ride, stopping to change Lucille's tire, his hands moving economically and capably, his shirt stretching taut over the bunch and play of the muscles in his back and shoulders.

Mmm, those muscles. But it had been the fact that he'd helped Lucille that had grabbed her by the heart. He wanted her to think he was so badass, but the truth was, he *was* that good guy Lucille had accused him of. Way too good for the likes of Chloe. Sawyer's world was black and white, and if any gray popped up, well then, he arrested it.

A lot of her life had been spent in the gray. Nothing illegal. At least not *too* illegal. She may not have been raised the way most kids were, but Phoebe had taught her about doing the right thing for the right reasons. That's who she was. At least, that's who she tried to be.

And she wanted to be loved for being that person.

She could play with Sawyer all she wanted but the fact was they were too different, and eventually it would go bad between them. Even if he could put up with her asthma issues—and those were pretty huge considering she couldn't have sex without a tactical plan—he wouldn't be able to put aside his code of conduct, not for the long haul.

He was bound by duty. He hadn't caught her and Lance freeing the dogs, or trespassing, or any of the "gray" area things she did, but what if he had? What would it do to him if someday he had to make a choice between the law and her?

Realizing sleep was nothing but a distant memory, Chloe tossed back the covers and forced herself to get up. After a long, hot shower that only brought more memories, she dressed and went outside.

And came face-to-face with her Vespa.

Confused, she pulled out her cell phone and called Lance. "Hey. You okay?"

"That's my question for you, babe," he said, sounding just as wheezy as she'd been yesterday. Her heart kicked hard. He'd had a long hospital stay last month, complicated and awful, and he'd never quite recovered.

She was deathly afraid this was as good as it got for him. His doctors were starting to discuss lung transplants. "I'm serious, Lance."

"Me too," he said, breath rattling. "I'm good. I'm better."

She wanted desperately to believe that. "Did you fix and bring home my Vespa?"

"No. Sawyer said he'd take care of it."

So he *had* been here...

"Chloe? You still there?"

"Yeah." She shook off the image of Sawyer caring enough to remember her stranded Vespa and getting someone to retrieve it. "Want lunch later? I'll bring you something yum from Tara and also make you some more of that decongestant balm."

"Sure. Hey, did you really go au natural at the mud springs?"

"Not quite but close enough."

"Would have liked to see that," he said wistfully. "How 'bout I make us a mud patch in my backyard?"

Chloe was laughing when she hung up, and her gaze snagged on the Vespa. Sawyer had come through for her. Again. She rubbed at the ache in her chest that had nothing to do with asthma and headed inside the B&B. She found Tara cooking and simultaneously muttering to herself as she wrote something on a recipe card. Maddie was at the table with a stack of paperwork, probably organizing inventory and scheduling for both the inn and her wedding, as evidenced by the handful of bridal magazines spread across the table.

"Hey," Maddie said to Chloe with a smile. "You're up."

Tara turned off the stove, pushed Chloe into a chair, and served her a plate of food. "Feeling better?"

Chloe stuffed her mouth with a bite of something cheesy and moaned in delight. "If I say yes, are you going to yell at me for yesterday?"

"No one's going to yell," Maddie said with a stern glance at Tara.

Chloe tried to tell if Sawyer had come by for coffee yet. She was staring at the pot when her sisters exchanged another glance.

"Let me save you a neck crimp," Maddie said. "The sheriff hasn't been here yet."

"Nope," Tara said. "Not yet." Her grip was tight on her spatula, like maybe she was hoping to hit him upside the back of his head when he did show up.

Maddie shoved an open magazine at Chloe. "What do you think of this dress?"

It was a long-sleeved chiffon in an absolutely hideous Easter-colored floral print that looked like something a great-grandmother would wear. "Um..." Chloe searched for tact. "Thought you wanted a more traditional bridal dress."

"It's for you," Maddie said, beaming with pride. "As my bridesmaid."

Chloe blinked, then slid a cautious look to Tara for help.

"You don't like it?" Tara asked innocently. "Because we've already ordered it for you. You should see the hat that goes with it."

Chloe was chewing on her lower lip, trying to find something tactful to say about the dress from hell when Maddie let out a snort, her face mottled red with the effort of holding in her laughter. "Okay," Chloe said. "That's just mean."

"Sorry," Maddie said, looking anything but. "I was hoping to scare you half as bad as you scared us yesterday."

Chloe ran a finger over the god-awful dress and shuddered in relief. "Yeah, well, consider it done."

Maddie flipped the page over. "*This* is more what I have in mind for you."

This dress was a beautiful spaghetti-strapped sundress the color of a perfect summer sky.

"I can just see you walking along the dock in it," Maddie said, beaming.

The wedding was going to take place here at the marina, right on the water, with the reception inside the inn. Lucille, who'd become an ordained minister online, was going to do the honors.

Chloe, Maddie, and Tara *ooh*ed and *aah*ed over the dresses for a few minutes before Tara went back to the stove and Maddie to her notes. Chloe ate and watched them both. Her sisters were happy, content to be here in Lucky Harbor doing something with their lives. And she . . . she needed to find *her* happy. If she couldn't do that here with them, she wanted to know. "I meant what I said yesterday," she said. "I want to do more around here than just fill in. I think I have more to offer than that."

"Well, of course you do," Maddie said.

"Then give me a chance. Look, I understand that over the years I haven't exactly been the model of responsibility or reliability, but you have to admit I've gotten better. And we could start slow, a few days a week. See how it works out." She took Maddie's hand and pulled her up. Then turned off the stove and grabbed Tara's hand as well.

She tugged them into the sunroom and pointed to the windows lining the wall. "There's where I'd put the spa bed, so the client could look out while getting a facial, or whatever they've chosen. The sea is one of the most Zen things you can look at, and we have a helluva view. And I'd put a chair there," Chloe said, pointing to a corner. "For mani/pedis. A pretty table too, where a guest could be served a delicious lunch prepared by our very own chef—" She smiled at Tara. "It's endless. We can do bridal parties, women's retreats, girls' weekends, all with the promise of being far away from the hustle and bustle of real life. Can't you see it?"

"I can," Maddie said and looked at Tara.

"If I ask you a question," Tara said slowly, "will you get all mad and run off and get naked and muddy with the sheriff again?"

"Jeez, *one* time!" Chloe sighed. "Ask."

"What you're suggesting is a major change in our marketing strategy and planning. It also changes your daily grind, *hugely*." She lifted her hand when Chloe opened her mouth. "I'm not saying it doesn't have potential," she said. "Because it does, but I have to know. If we do this, if we invest and get on board, do you really see yourself happy here, locked in one spot? Because you would be, Chloe. Even if we start with just a few days a week, that's *every* week. You'd be locked in. This is one of those things called a root, sugar—which you've avoided like the plague your whole life. And it's a biggie. We'll be depending on you."

"I know," Chloe said. "And yes. I really see myself doing this." Trying not to get defensive, she stood her ground. "And it's not like it's a cement block attached to my feet for crissake. It's a schedule, and I can work it out to suit me."

"Not if we put a ton of money into it," Tara said. "If we do that, you're going to have to put the clients first, ahead of your need to... whatever."

Chloe swallowed, willing herself to stay calm. "I'll pay for the necessary renovations and marketing," she said, and bit back her retort when Tara didn't look overly impressed at that. Because the truth was that Chloe hadn't been able to put in as much capital for the B&B's renovations as her sisters had. But she was finally starting to make money and was trying to make up for lost time.

"Why don't we draw up plans and get an estimate on what it'd cost to get this room ready?" Maddie suggested with her ever-present mediatory skills. "And like everything else, we'll decide together. Majority rules."

Tara nodded. "Sounds good to me. Chloe?"

Not seeing much of a choice, Chloe nodded. Her sisters went back into the kitchen, and she stayed in the sunroom and let herself envision the spa room. When it was as clear as the ocean outside the window, she sat in the corner and drew her plans. Then she pulled out her cell phone and called the only contractor she knew. "Jax," she said. "Question."

"Me first. You breathing today?"

She had to laugh. "Yes."

"Good. Keep doing it."

"Believe me, I intend to," she said. "I have a new client for you."

"I love new clients. Who is it?"

"Me."

He was quiet a moment. "Why do I have the feeling I'm about to get myself in trouble?"

"No trouble. You know I want to turn the sunroom into a day spa. What I need is an estimate to install a really plush client bed, an industrial sink, hidden speakers, a wall fountain, and a pretty oak wall cubby for storage. Oh! And a soaking tub and a shower for body wraps and things like that. I'll need to know how fast you could get to it, and how much."

Jax promised to get back to her as soon as possible, and satisfied that she was at least on her way, Chloe headed out the back door.

* * *

Their property was about an acre, and though they were off the beaten path, they backed up to the ocean. It was remarkable, really, and Chloe could still feel the shock that had hit her last year when her mother had died and a will had surfaced.

Growing up with Phoebe as Chloe had, she would have sworn on her own life that Phoebe didn't have a spare dollar to her name. After all, they'd lived in tents, or on friends' couches, or even in their car for most of Chloe's childhood. Always at the mercy of Phoebe's need to be free.

Looking back on it brought mostly fond memories, and she'd never suffered for their distinct lack of luxury, but there'd definitely been lean times. Lean enough that a tiny germ of resentment had found its way into Chloe's heart. She'd never admitted it out loud. To do so felt . . . disloyal. But the feelings of resentment sometimes surfaced regardless.

Why hadn't her mother raised her here in Lucky Harbor?

There'd been two short visits, but Chloe had been very young, too young to understand that her mother's parents owned this place. All Chloe remembered was her excitement over having a real bed with a soft mattress and more food than she could eat. When she'd lost her first tooth, it'd been here. The tooth fairy had found her sleeping in a spare bedroom and slipped a crisp new dollar bill under her pillow. After that, there'd been no more dollars, and her young mind had concluded that the tooth fairy must have lost track of her.

Chloe sighed at the jumble of emotions swirling inside of her. She glanced around the property and hoped like anything that she was doing the right thing, and not being influenced by long-ago childhood yearning. Just because she'd felt safe here as a kid once or twice didn't mean this was right for her. She'd always found her own security, her own way.

Still, it felt right, living with the sisters she'd never really known.

With her name on the deed.

Granted, just last year that hadn't meant much. When they'd arrived, the inn had been mortgaged to its eyeballs and in massive disrepair, practically falling down on its axis.

They'd fixed it up, and it was now the three sisters mortgaged to their eyeballs, but it was home.

Home.

Chloe marveled at that and shook her head. On the far side of the property was the marina, which consisted of eight boat slips and a small marina building—basically a one-room warehouse. It held kayaks, canoes, and various other equipment for the marina, and a small office area where Maddie usually worked the books for the B&B, when she wasn't in the kitchen looking at wedding magazines.

As she walked across the yard to the marina building door, she suddenly stopped. The building was always kept locked, with a code lock. But the lock was broken, the door half open.

She took a step back and peered around the corner of the building to the docks. Normally she'd see the fishing boat and houseboat that had come with the inn, and the two boats that Ford kept at the dock as well.

But there was nothing, no boats. Heart stuttering, Chloe whipped out her cell phone.

* * *

The police came, including Sawyer. All four watercrafts were found floating within ten miles, with insignificant damage.

Someone had set the boats loose.

There was no real property damage beyond the broken lock on the marina door, for which Chloe was hugely relieved but still completely unnerved.

"Kids," one of the cops decided.

Tara shook her head. "We've never had problems before."

"And this seems personal," Maddie murmured.

If Sawyer agreed with that, Chloe couldn't tell by his expression, but he stayed back when the other uniforms left.

"We'll make extra drive-bys," he told her quietly. "But you need to think about getting some security. An alarm. A dog."

"I don't want to scare the guests with a big old guard dog," Tara protested.

"Safety is far more important than worrying about what anyone else thinks," Sawyer told her.

"You're right, of course." Tara looked at her sisters. "We'll think about both an alarm and a dog."

"We can borrow Izzy from Jax," Maddie said.

"Sure," Tara said. "And she can lick the next bad guy to death."

When she and Maddie left Sawyer and Chloe alone, Chloe met his gaze. "What are you thinking?"

"That I like the sight of you breathing. How are you feeling?"

"Fine. And don't deflect. Do you think this is just a random vandalism by a kid?"

Before he could answer, his cell phone vibrated. Simultaneously inside his open SUV, he was paged over the radio. He swore and looked at her.

"You have to go," she said.

"Chloe." He put his hand on her jaw and tilted her face up to his, his gaze searching hers.

"I'm fine," she said again. "They need you. Go."

She waited until he'd driven away and then headed inside the marina building. She looked around, hating the fact that someone had invaded their space. She settled at Maddie's desk and booted up the computer. Sometimes being able to compartmentalize was a benefit, and now was no exception. She put the vandalism out of her mind, occupying it instead with thoughts of her day spa.

They needed brochures, a social networking plan, and a

schedule. She worked for several hours, even updating their website, posting a survey to see how many people would be interested in coming into the inn for a day spa.

She took a lunch break to whip up some chest balm for Lance, bringing with it some of Tara's Not Your Granny's Homemade Chicken Noodle Soup and a Don't Call It Just a Grilled Cheese Sandwich. She bullied him into using the balm and into eating, not liking how thin he was. "Lance—"

"I'm *fine*," he said, leaning back on his couch. He lived in a rental duplex with his brother, Tucker, and the decor was late-nineties frat boy. Todd and Jamie lived on the other side of the duplex, though they were at work with Tucker at the moment, which Chloe was glad for. Todd had left a couple of messages reminding her that she still owed him, and that he wouldn't be averse to collecting.

The doorbell rang, and Lance opened the door to a pretty petite blonde holding a plate of brownies. She beamed at him, leaning in to kiss his cheek. "Hey, baby."

Baby? Chloe looked at Lance, who blushed and shrugged. "Renee, this is Chloe."

"Your best friend!" Renee smiled sweetly at Chloe. "I've heard so much about you!"

Huh. Chloe slid another look Lance's way because *she'd* heard nothing about Renee.

"Renee's a nurse and works at my doctor's office," Lance said.

Ah, now it made sense. The crush. Thrilled and amused at Lance's rare shyness, Chloe took a brownie, then left them alone. Hopefully when Lance got lucky—and given the way Renee was looking at him like he was lunch, he was going to get *very* lucky—he wouldn't end up passing out like she had.

She headed back to the marina office and found a happy surprise—there were already hits on the inn's website survey, all of them positive and requesting further info about her spa services. She was working her way through them when the office door opened.

"Whatcha up to?" Maddie asked innocently.

Too innocently. Chloe looked at her, but Maddie had quite the inscrutable face when she chose. "Selling swampland in Florida."

"Or . . . ?" Maddie asked.

"Or organizing Santa's naughty-and-nice list."

Maddie laughed. "Or . . . ?"

"Okay, let's play a different game." Chloe leaned back in her chair. "The one where you tell me what you really want to hear."

"Okay, how about this—when were you going to come clean about hiring Jax to renovate the sunroom?"

Chloe sighed. "He tattled."

"He *mentioned* it."

"That man is *so* whipped."

"Honey, you asked the man I sleep with every night to help you," Maddie said. "Of course he's going to tell me. I thought we were going to do this as a team."

"We are. And I didn't hire him. I only wanted to get an idea of the damage before we worked on the overall business plan. I put a short survey up on our website, just so we could get some feelers about who might be interested." She had to work hard at sounding cool, calm, and collected, when she wanted to grin triumphantly. "Several people have already inquired about booking for day treatments. Two of them are interested in overnight stays at our full rate."

"I like the full rate part," Maddie said.

"I bet Tara likes it even more."

"Let's go get some food and find out."

"Is Tara cooking?" Chloe asked hopefully.

"Not tonight. We have no guests, and we were thinking Eat Me."

Eat Me Café was the diner where Tara had worked up until they'd gotten the B&B running. It was still a quick go-to when they were starving, though lately they'd been too busy to eat together. Well, technically Tara and Maddie had been too busy with their full lives. Chloe not so much. "What's the occasion?"

"Nothing. Just a together meal. And maybe..." She pulled Chloe to her feet. "A certain sister feels like she could have been more supportive, but she's too Southern and mule-headed to admit it so she's buying dinner instead."

"Mmm," Chloe said, grabbing her purse. "I love it when Tara feels the guilt."

* * *

Chloe, Maddie, and Tara had just ordered their dinner when a group of guys entered the diner, laughing and talking so obnoxiously loud that the entire diner went quiet. It was Todd, Jamie, and two others that Chloe had seen around, Dan and Mitch. Filthy from head to toe, they'd clearly just gotten off a job, but that wasn't what made Chloe's gut clench.

It was the look in Jamie's eyes, the one that said he'd been drinking. Mitch too. She was glad Lance and Tucker weren't with them.

The diner was still quiet, the uncomfortable kind of quiet as Jamie gave them all a mocking bow. Next to him, Mitch started laughing into the silence.

"Sit down," Todd said to them uneasily, locking gazes with Chloe.

Arms still wide, Jamie straightened from his bow and knocked the glasses off the table closest to him. "Oops."

Seated at that table was Lucille and her blue-haired posse. Lucille put her hands on the table and rose, her tight bun all aquiver. "Jamie Robinson," she said sternly. Even with her tower of hair piled on top of her head, she was barely five feet tall, but she got right up in Jamie's face, waggling a bony finger. "You can't afford any more trouble, do you hear me? You boys get out of here, and don't come back until you're sober, all of you." She spared a scathing look at Todd. "And you. You should be ashamed of yourself. People are rooting for you to get your life together."

The four guys stared at her like she was an alien, and then Mitch burst out laughing again as they took an empty table.

Amy was the waitress on shift, and she was new to Lucky Harbor. Mid-twenties, she was tall and leggy and tomboy pretty in low-riding cargos, a tank top, and some ass-kicking boots. She was standing behind the bakery counter, gazing at Mitch, clearly unhappy to see him. When she'd first come to town, he'd gotten a little aggressive in his attempt to date her, until she'd actually Maced him one night.

Still laughing, Mitch looked her over and winked lecherously.

Lucille pulled out her cell phone. Probably calling the police, Chloe thought. She wondered if Sawyer was on duty, and how he'd feel about having to face down these drunken idiots.

"Jan should have refused them service," Tara murmured. Jan was the diner's owner and had a zero monkey business tolerance. "They're obviously intoxicated, and they're making Maddie as nervous as a long-tailed cat in a room full of rocking chairs."

"I'm fine," Maddie said. A lie. She was vibrating with nerves. Confrontations did that to her, for good reason. She'd once told Chloe that her ex-boyfriend had been a bully, much like Jamie and Mitch. Smooth and charming on the outside, mean as a snake on the inside.

From the kitchen, the cook dinged his bell. Someone's food was ready, and Amy loaded up a tray. As she walked past the guys' table, Mitch reached out and patted her ass. "Hey, baby. Miss me?"

Amy gave him an eat-shit-and-die look. "Get your hand off my ass."

He laughed like a hyena. "Or what?"

Amy dumped the tray over his head. Soup rained down his hands and face, noodles clinging to his wet skin. "Jesus, that's hot!" he yelled, pulling his shirt away from his body.

Amy glowered at the others as she bent to pick up the fallen dishes. Chloe got up to help her, as did a man from a table behind them.

"Hey, asshole!" Mitch bellowed at the man crouched next to Amy. "Back away from my girlfriend."

Amy stood up. "Are you kidding me? Get out of here, Mitch."

Eyes completely soulless, Mitch merely smiled. "Make me."

Chapter 14

*"They say money talks, but all mine
ever says is 'good-bye, sucker.'"*
—Chloe Traeger

Earlier that morning, Sawyer had given some serious consideration to staying in bed. He was tired, and already knew his desk was nothing but a mountain of paperwork waiting for him. He hated paperwork with the same passion that he hated errands, cooking for himself, and mowing his dad's lawn—which reminded him, he needed to go by there, as he'd been doing every few days.

For all the good it did him.

Hell, Sawyer wasn't even sure the man was eating the food he brought. Nolan Thompson was probably tossing it out soon as Sawyer left, then ordering himself pizza.

Sawyer would've liked a pizza. He thought about it all day, and five minutes from going off duty and getting himself that loaded thick crust, the call came in—overly rowdy customers at the diner. He drove over there wondering what the odds were that he'd get pizza tonight after all.

Not good, he realized in the first two seconds of walking through the diner's front door.

"Who the fuck called the pigs!" Mitch bellowed at the sight of Sawyer. Swinging out, Mitch punched his fist through the bakery display.

Glass shattered to the floor in a slow, musical wave.

He pulled back his arm for another swing, blood blooming brightly from shoulder to wrist as he snagged a surprised Amy around the neck and pressed her against him. "Who did it? Who called? You?" he demanded of Amy, giving her a shake. "You?"

"No," Chloe said, rising from where she'd been crouched on the floor picking up fallen dishes. "I did it. I called the police. Don't hurt her."

"Chloe." Without taking his eyes off Mitch, Sawyer gestured for her to sit back down. "Mitch, let her go."

Mitch shook his head and tightened his grip on Amy.

"Amy didn't do anything to you," Chloe said to Mitch, *not* sitting down.

"Chloe, goddammit," Sawyer said softly. "Sit."

Mitch was glaring at Chloe, clearly wishing he had enough arms to grab her, too.

Lucille stood up next to Chloe. "Mitchell Tyson, if you hurt that girl, I'll tell your mother. Do you hear me?"

Jesus Christ. Sawyer's fingers itched for his gun, but he couldn't pull it. The place was too crowded, each person being an unpredictable variable in this shitty situation.

And Chloe knew that, dammit. Anyone with any common sense would have just let him handle this. But he'd been in enough bad spots to know that common sense wouldn't come into play, not during a time of panic.

And people were panicked, he could practically smell it. The most panicked of all was Mitch. Sawyer watched the blood run down Mitch's arm and wrist to drip on the floor. With any luck, he'd pass out from blood loss. "Let her go, Mitch," he said again.

"No way, man. I watch those cop shows. I know what happens to a guy like me."

Sawyer would have liked to evacuate the diner quickly and quietly, but no one in Lucky Harbor did anything quickly or quietly. "Nothing's going to happen to you if you let her go." He took a few steps forward, stopping only when Mitch tightened his grip on Amy, cutting off her air supply.

Amy clawed desperately at Mitch's bloody arm.

"Stop it," Chloe yelled. "You're strangling her. Stop it!"

Mitch eyed the front door, but Sawyer was blocking it. "Let her go," Sawyer told him. "And I'll let you walk free and clear." He spoke the lie smoothly, without blinking an eye.

"Fine." Mitch shoved Amy hard at Sawyer, but before he could make his escape, Chloe whirled and executed a badass roundhouse kick to Mitch's family jewels.

Mitch let out an unholy scream but didn't go down. He reached for Chloe, but Sawyer was already lunging forward. He vaulted the table between them, hitting Mitch in the middle of the back. They crashed into the center of Chloe's table. The Formica table cracked and broke beneath them, sending them to the floor hard.

Sawyer pulled Mitch's hands behind his back and cuffed him just as the front door opened.

Everyone craned their necks to see what now.

Matt Bowers walked in. Though he was wearing his forest ranger uniform and obviously armed, he was looking loose and relaxed, sipping on a Starbucks coffee. He took in the room with his sharp eyes, not missing a thing. "Aw," he said to Sawyer, taking a slow sip of his coffee. "You get all the fun."

* * *

Chloe, Maddie, and Tara helped Amy and Jan clean up the diner. Chloe did so with an ear half bent toward the action outside, where Sawyer had hauled Mitch.

The parking lot was cop central. Chloe could see Sawyer in profile, looking particularly badass in his uniform and various weaponry, his face the usual impassive blank as he directed Mitch toward the back of an ambulance. Odd how one man could evoke so many emotions within her. Lust? Oh yeah, much of the time. The urge to smack him upside the back of his head? Yep, that was often there, too. Affection? She'd have said no. He didn't need her affection, everyone admired and loved Sawyer, who was just about the most composed, self-assured, capable man she'd ever met.

But there was something suspiciously close to affection filling her now, which had her shaking her head at herself.

Todd, Jamie, and their other pal were out there, seated on the curb being questioned. Inside the diner, things were nearly back to normal, but Chloe didn't think she'd forget anytime soon the way Sawyer had looked facing Mitch. Her stoic sheriff had been steady and calm, his body at ease but ready for anything.

Willing to put his life on the line.

It'd been that willingness that had really brought home the realities of his job. He wasn't playing at getting a thrill, the way she did when she went rock climbing or hang gliding.

His job was real. And potentially lethal.

There'd been that one horrible moment when Mitch's arm had tightened over Amy's throat and Amy had made that little involuntary squeak as she'd used up the last of her air. Terror. More than anyone, Chloe knew what that terror was like, and she'd never felt so helpless in her life, so she'd interfered. She'd just been so afraid that Sawyer's help would come too late.

She'd made it worse, but Sawyer had handled it. He'd had an

entire diner full of scared customers, and yet he'd resolved the situation with minimal damage.

Amy came up next to her at the window.

"You should go home," Chloe said gently.

Clearly made of sterner stuff, Amy shook her head. "I'd rather be here and keep busy. Besides, the police said I'll need to answer some questions for their report in a few minutes. I wanted to thank you for helping. We've got customers pouring in now. Lucille must have put it up on Facebook already."

The cook's bell dinged from the kitchen, and with a tight smile at Chloe, Amy moved off.

Chloe stayed at the window. Without looking, she knew when her sisters closed in and flanked her. A year and a half ago, they'd been complete strangers to each other. Now she could sense their presence without a single glance, just as she also knew that Tara was frowning in concern and Maddie was waiting for the right moment to hug her tight. That was Maddie's thing, hugging. Kissing. Throwing the love around.

Chloe could appreciate that the three of them were very different, that they each had their own way of expressing their feelings, but she herself was of the show-don't-tell school. She showed her feelings through actions, which she thought she'd done over and over again for her sisters by laying down roots here. It certainly hadn't been for herself. At least not at first. "Close call," she murmured.

"You've had a few of those in as many days now," Tara said.

"I'm fine."

"You always say that."

"It's true."

Tara nodded. "You're resilient," Tara agreed. "But we still worry."

"Not necessary."

Together through the window they watched Sawyer, though

Chloe was probably the only one whose good parts twitched at the way his uniform fit his big body.

"Let's go home," Maddie said after a few minutes, slipping an arm around each sister.

Tara nodded.

"I'll meet you there," Chloe said.

"'Kay." Maddie squeezed them both, then kissed Chloe's cheek. "Love you."

"You too," Chloe said, and though she didn't take her eyes off Sawyer, she still felt it when Maddie rolled her eyes at Tara.

Tara didn't hug Chloe, waiting instead until Chloe looked at her. "And you love me, too, right?"

"Sure," Chloe said. Hello, wasn't that implied?

"One of these days," Tara grumbled, "you're going to say it to me, and I'm going to be too old to hear you."

"You're too old now."

Tara sighed. "See you at the inn."

"Mm-hmm." Chloe could see inside the ambulance. Mitch's arm was being wrapped, with Sawyer watching closely. When Mitch shifted as if to run, Sawyer put a hand on his shoulder.

He had big hands. Capable of subduing suspects. Equally capable of taking her straight to ecstasy. He was also of the show-don't-tell persuasion, which she appreciated.

"Hey," Amy called out to Chloe as she strode by, her thin but toned arms straining under the weight of a heavily loaded tray. "No drooling on the glass!"

* * *

Sawyer drove himself to the ER. He'd sliced one palm and also had a cut above his left eye. Regulations required him to go for a hepatitis shot and to get checked out whenever blood was shed.

It took less than an hour. No stitches, just another boatload of paperwork. He was just walking out of the ER when a Vespa pulled up. He watched as Chloe parked illegally and walked to the entrance, stopping when she caught sight of him standing there beneath the overhang.

"Hey," he said. "What are you—" He was deeply startled and stunned when she wrapped her arms around him and squeezed him tight.

When she'd interfered at the café, fear and fury had fought for equal space in his brain. With the fear for her safety gone, it left more room for the temper.

"I just heard you were hurt," she said.

"I'm fine. Chloe—"

She reached up and touched the bandage over his brow.

He grabbed her wrist. "We need to talk."

"Okay, so I butted in and I shouldn't have."

"Damn right you shouldn't have."

She glanced up at him, eyes fierce. "He was hurting her. And I was closer." Her eyes settled on the bandage over his brow. "I'm sorry you got hurt."

"It's nothing. You're the one who could have gotten hurt."

"You had a gun."

He gaped at her. "The diner was full. I couldn't pull my gun. There are rules, protocols—"

"*He was hurting Amy!*" She looked at his cut and frowned.

"I'm *fine*." If this whole thing wasn't an example of their basic differences, he didn't know what was. He'd never actually had to choose between his job and a woman before, and he never wanted to. He closed his eyes and found that his temper couldn't hold up against the feeling of her warm and safe in his arms.

"I was scared," she murmured.

"You're safe now."

"Not for myself! For you!" She took a breath. "But it's your job. I get that, because your job is a part of you. No one gets that more than me."

He'd lost his last girlfriend because of his job. And the one before that, too, now that he thought about it. He'd figured no woman could get it, but he'd forgotten.

Chloe wasn't just any woman.

"I imagine it takes some time to learn to deal with the worry," she said.

He felt an ironic smile twist his lips. "Want a lesson on how to deal with someone in your life who makes you worry?"

She stared at him. Then smiled. "Do you worry about me a lot?"

"Twenty-four seven."

Her smile warmed. "We could start a club." She found the bandage on his palm, and taking his hand in hers, turned it over to inspect it.

"Just a scratch," he said.

Chloe nodded, then kissed the skin just above the bandage. He'd known that she enjoyed baiting him. That she'd also enjoyed driving him nuts. That she was sexually attracted to him.

All those things were mutual.

But this…this felt like more. It felt like a level of caring he hadn't realized existed.

For either of them.

* * *

After the brief ER visit, Sawyer went back to the station to finish up the paperwork before finally dragging his sorry ass toward home.

He probably shouldn't go so far as to call the house he'd purchased earlier in the year *home*. He actually wasn't sure why he'd bought it in the first place, other than Jax had been on his ass to buy instead of rent for years now.

Sawyer had liked renting, liked not being responsible. But now that he'd gone and put his name on the dotted line of a mortgage, he was getting used to it. Plus he had to admit, owning a house gave him an air of unexpected stability, even respectability. It took him one more step away from that reckless guy he'd nearly turned out to be. Like Mitch. Like Todd. Like the thug his father had been so damn sure he'd end up being, rotting in jail somewhere.

But Sawyer hadn't. He'd turned himself around. And he'd bought a fucking house to prove it.

The place needed work. A lot of work, actually. The house was older, built in the 1970s. The color scheme was early Partridge family. A month ago, he'd bought paint for the living room, dining room, and kitchen, and it'd been sitting in his garage ever since. His *garage*. Christ. At least he didn't have a white picket fence and two-point-four kids.

When he'd first told his dad that he'd bought the house, the old man had frowned. "You gonna keep it up?"

No, he'd just spent $250,000 to let the thing rot away. Grimacing, Sawyer ignored his still pea green walls and went straight to the kitchen. The refrigerator held beer, a questionable gallon of milk, something that had maybe once upon a time been cheese, and a leftover...something.

Stomach growling, he took a beer, pulled out his cell phone, and called the diner, surprised when he heard "Eat Me" in Amy's usual brisk cheer.

"Amy, it's Sawyer," he said. "You should have gone home after this evening."

"Are you kidding? Retelling my near-miss is making me some serious bank in tips today. You need a late dinner, Sheriff?"

"Yeah. You have anyone making deliveries tonight?"

"For you, yes. Let me guess—a bacon blue burger, extra blue, side of fries, and a dinner salad with no tomatoes, because tomatoes are a vegetable and despite the fact that you're six feet three of pure man, you eat like a little boy."

"Hey," he said. "Salad's a vegetable."

"Iceberg lettuce is a single step up from water. Doesn't count."

"Good, then forget the salad," Sawyer said. "And make it *two* burgers and double the fries."

While he waited for his dinner, he went into the garage and eyeballed the buckets of paint. "Fuckers," he said to them, but picked one up and carried it into the dining room. "You ready?" he asked his walls.

They didn't have an opinion.

He'd taken a second beer and rolled two very nice plain "ecru" stripes when the doorbell rang. He answered while reaching into his pocket for money to pay the delivery kid.

But it wasn't a delivery kid at all.

It was Chloe, wearing a short denim skirt, emphasis on short, and a black angora sweater that was slipping off one shoulder, revealing a little black strap of something silky. And holy smoking hell, was she a sight for sore eyes.

"Hey," she said.

Ever since their little playtime in his shower, their encounters together had vacillated between awkwardness and their usual lust-filled animosity. Right now it was a little of both. He cleared his throat. "Hey."

"I forgot to say thanks at the hospital earlier, for getting my Vespa back to me."

"Thanks for not dying on me in my shower."

She snorted. "You're just glad you didn't have to explain *that* to Tara."

He felt his brows knit together and his stomach clench.

"I'm kidding." She flashed a smile. "Gonna have to lighten

up, Sheriff, otherwise life sucks golf balls." Looking like sin on a stick, she held up two large bags from the diner. "I went back to the diner to get dinner to go for Maddie and Tara and found Amy bagging your order. She got someone else to deliver to the inn and sent me here with enough food for two normal guys. Or for one starving sheriff." She tried to come in, but he stopped her forward progress.

"Inhaler?" he asked.

"In my pocket, Sheriff. Sir." She added a salute. "Can I come in now?"

This was a very bad idea, of course, but she simply pushed past him, her sweet little ass moving seductively in that skirt as she walked through his nearly empty living room and into the dining room.

She looked at the few swipes he'd taken with the roller. "Coming right along, are we?"

"Been busy."

She'd been busy, too, he knew. Everyone and their mother in Lucky Harbor had felt free to keep him up-to-date on her every move. She'd been taking care of Lance, working at various hotel spas in the state, giving geriatric yoga classes at Matt's studio to Lucille and her cronies, and planning a sunroom renovation at the inn for a day spa.

And if she'd trespassed, done any B&E, or anything else illegal, he hadn't caught wind of it. Or maybe she'd laid low. No doubt she still had that rowdy untethered spirit that he was so inexplicably attracted to. But she'd changed over the last few months. Not settled down—not in any way, shape, or form, but she'd done something else, something better.

She'd found a place to belong.

He wondered if she even knew it yet. Best not to ask. Best not to keep her here one second longer than necessary, as they clearly didn't have themselves under control around each other.

Or maybe that was just him. *He* didn't have himself under control, not when his hands were shoved deep in his pockets to keep them off her. It was getting hard to remember why they were a bad idea.

Because she's the opposite of your type. She was crazy unpredictable, spontaneous...

Okay, that was a load of bullshit. She spoke to the part of him that he kept locked down tight. And that. *That* was why this was a bad idea. He wasn't ever going to be the man she wanted or needed, one who'd fly off a mountain on a hang glider simply for the thrill. One who'd open a vein and bleed out his emotions at the drop of a hat. Or crawl under a fence into private property to rescue a couple of dogs.

He wasn't that guy. He'd committed himself to the obligations of duty and discipline. His job swallowed him whole, and that was just how it was. So he stood in the doorway of the dining room waiting for her to set down the food and leave.

Instead, she turned to him with a little smile that was disarmingly contagious. "You may not know this about me," she said. "But I'm excellent with a paint brush."

Oh, Christ. He was a goner.

Chapter 15

*"Never drive faster than your guardian angel
can fly."*
—Chloe Traeger

Sawyer shook his head at Chloe. "I'm not going to ask you to
help me paint."

"Don't ask. I'm offering." She took a second, longer look
around at his nearly empty living room, the completely empty
dining room, the equally sparse kitchen.

He knew what she saw. She saw what he'd just been thinking
himself...it was a house. Not a home. "You need to go before
the paint fumes aggravate your asthma."

She merely moved to open the windows and turn on his two
ceiling fans.

"Is that enough?" he asked.

"For now. There's good cross ventilation." She picked the
food back up and moved to the middle of the dining room floor
and dropped to her knees.

"What are you doing?" he asked, voice a telltale hoarse,

causing her to glance at him, but he couldn't help it, he'd just flashed to her making that same move in his shower.

"Making you a picnic." She leaned over to pull food from the bags. "Come on."

He didn't budge, riveted by the way her skirt was riding up the backs of her thighs.

"If you don't sit," she said, not looking at him. "I'm going to eat all of this by myself. And trust me, I totally could. I'm starving."

Sawyer sat. She handed him a plate loaded with two burgers and double fries, and then pulled a large bottle of wine from the depths of her huge purse.

"The big guns," he said.

"No, that would have been vodka. But I wanted to relax you, not put you out of commission. Though you're so freaking stoic all the time, it's hard to tell if you need relaxing. Nothing seems to faze you."

He let out a mirthless laugh. "You think nothing fazes me?"

She smiled a secret little smile. "Well, except when I'm naked. You were pretty fazed then."

He shook his head.

"No?" she asked.

"Yes." *Fuck*, yes. "But that's not *all* that gets to me."

"What else, then?"

"Seeing you suffocating," he said. "That fazed the hell out of me."

Her smile faded. "I know. I've been told that's damn hard to watch. I'm sorry."

"Don't be." He shook his head. "God. Don't apologize for that." He paused. "You and your sisters make up?"

"Oh. Yes." Chloe shrugged. "Pretty much anyway. It was my fault. I spent all those years being wild, and then I hate when no one wants to depend on me." She shook her head. "I'm working on that, but the problem is, people tend to assign you the role of the person you are at your worst, you know?"

Yeah. He knew. Exactly.

"Not much I can do about that," she said with a philosophical shrug. "Except hopefully continue to prove them wrong." She set the bottle between her thighs to steady it and went to work the corkscrew, also from the mysterious depths of her purse. When she bent over the bottle, her skirt rose up even more, giving him another quick flash of—yep—something that was definitely black silk beneath. The corkscrew slipped, and with a low breath of annoyance, Chloe ran her fingers up the neck of the bottle to reset its position.

"Keep doing that," he said, mesmerized. "And the top will pop off on its own."

She laughed and handed everything over to Sawyer. He removed the cork, and she took the bottle back, pouring him a glass.

He wasn't much of a drinker, not anymore, and he'd already had the two beers, but she was looking at him with a soft smile. And then there was that sweater, still slipping off her creamy shoulder. Plus she smelled amazing, was wearing black silk under her clothes, and he was suddenly more than a little short on brain power.

They ate and drank in a comfortable silence. After a while, Chloe looked down at his empty plate with a smile. "Better?" she asked.

He'd inhaled everything. Finally full and *definitely* better, he nodded. "Thanks."

"Oh, it's not me." She poured the last of the wine into his glass. "It's the food. And the alcohol."

He was pretty sure it was her, but he kept silent, shaking his head when she pulled a second bottle from her purse. "What else does that suitcase hold?" he asked in marvel.

"Everything."

"Anything worthwhile? Like, say, a house painter?"

"*I'm* your new house painter." She reached for the corkscrew to open up bottle number two.

He stopped her. "Are you trying to get me drunk?"

She tilted her head and studied him. "Is it possible?" she asked, sounding intrigued.

"No." But when she leaned forward, her sweater gaped and he discovered that the black slinky strap belonged to a black, slinky bra. Mouth suddenly dry, he downed the last of his wine, not surprised that he was feeling a nice little buzz.

"I really can paint, you know," Chloe said. "If we keep the windows open, and I wear a mask."

"No way."

"No way?" she repeated in disbelief. "You don't get to tell me what I can and can't do, Sawyer."

He sighed and swiped a hand over his face. This was his own fault for demanding instead of asking. He located one of the paper masks that the paint store had given him with his purchase.

It covered her mouth and nose, and when she got it into position, she looked at him. "I know you're just concerned and not trying to be a domineering asshole," she said benignly through the paper.

"Do you?" he asked, amused in spite of himself. She looked adorable.

And sexy.

"Yes. But I'm a big girl."

And wasn't that just the problem.

Her eyes crinkled so he knew she was smiling as they began painting.

"How's your dad?" she asked.

He watched as she stretched up high as she could with her roller. "Ornery as hell," he said, eyes locked on her bare legs.

"I hear they get that way with age."

He had to laugh. "Then he's always been old."

"You have your moments, too, you know."

That gave him pause. "Are you saying I'm like him?"

"I'm saying that sometimes genetics are annoying."

She was still painting, paying him no special attention, allowing him to look his fill. He wondered if she was referring to Phoebe and the wanderlust lifestyle that had been forced on her, or if she blamed the father she'd never known for not sticking around.

She dipped her roller into the paint tray very carefully. "Sometimes I wonder what I got from *my* dad. If he was...difficult. You know, like me."

Sawyer had liked Phoebe, he really had, but sometimes he wanted her to come back to life just so he could strangle her. How could she never have told Chloe a thing about her father, given her nothing of half of her own heritage—no knowledge, no memories, nothing?

Sawyer had never asked his father much about his own mother. It had hurt that she'd left him, and for a hell of a long time, he'd been positive that he'd been the reason she'd gone. But that was different. Chloe's dad hadn't been there from the get-go. "You're not difficult," he said, meaning it, but when she snorted with laughter, he had to smile. "Okay, maybe you're a little difficult, but I like it."

"You do not. *No one* likes difficult. Which is why I'm so hard to put up with."

It took him a moment to answer because suddenly his throat burned like fire. "If I don't get to tell you what to do, you don't get to tell me how I feel," he said, and watched her eyes crinkle at the corners as she smiled at her own words being tossed back in her face.

Then she scratched the bridge of her nose and left a

smudge of paint there, and another just beneath her left eye. Uncharacteristically silent, she turned back to her wall.

They painted in silence for five full minutes.

"You think he'd like the way I turned out?" she asked her wall casually. Too casually. "You know, my father."

God, she was killing him. "I think he'd be proud of you, of your giving nature and spirit, how you live your life. Everything."

She glanced at him. "Including the way I jump in without thinking things through?"

"Proud," he repeated firmly.

She stared at him, then nodded. "Thanks." She nudged him with her hip when they both bent for the paint tray at the same time. "And I bet your dad's proud of you too."

It was Sawyer's turn to snort.

"Deep down," Chloe said, sounding sure.

Maybe deep, deep, *deep* down, but Sawyer kind of doubted it.

"At least he's around," Chloe said softly. "And he visits with you." She shrugged. "So he's a grumpy old fart. Life's short, Sawyer. Sometimes you have to take what you can get and make it okay."

With this deeply profound statement, Chloe bent over to load more paint onto her roller, pulled back her mask, and flashed him those black panties again, distracting him.

At some point, she put down her roller and went for that second bottle of wine. He doubted the alcohol was good for her asthma, but he'd be damned if he'd point that out. He'd drink the whole bottle himself first before pointing it out. "Before you open that, there's beer in the fridge. I'm going to have one of those instead."

She eyed him, a small mischievous smile tugging at her mouth. Had she seen through him? No telling with her. But she put down the bottle, leaving it unopened. "I'm a little bit of a lightweight anyway. Maybe I'll share a beer with you."

"Sure." He got one out of the fridge and offered her the first sip. She passed it back, and he took a big gulp, watching her as she checked out his empty kitchen.

She hadn't been kidding about being a light drinker. She suddenly wasn't seeming all that steady on her feet after two and a half glasses of wine. But then again, he wasn't all that steady himself after the two beers he'd had before she got here, then the lion's share of the wine.

They moved back to the dining room to eye their handiwork.

"Huh," she said, and rubbed at the streak of paint on her jaw.

"What?" He watched her shake her head as if having a private conversation with herself. She laughed.

So did he. Because two walls looked neat, smooth, and orderly. His.

The other two walls, Chloe's, had been painted in haphazard, uneven strokes utterly without pattern. "Your wall looks...off," he said diplomatically.

"It's your house. Your house's crooked," she said, gesturing to it as she blew a strand of hair from her face. She was paint-spattered and sweaty, and sexy as hell.

He smiled at her. "*You're* crooked," he said, and she burst out laughing, sliding to the floor in a puddle of mirth.

"Probably we shouldn't be painting in your condition," she finally managed, swiping her eyes.

"Your condition is worse than mine."

"Says who?"

"I'm a cop. I know these things. And I know something else, too. We're stopping painting now."

"Yeah?" He heard her breath catch, and when she ran her gaze down his body, she wasn't the only one.

"You have something else in mind, Sheriff?"

"Yeah."

She stared up at him for a long moment, then reached for his beer. He pulled it out of reach, brought it to his lips, and tilted his head back to finish it off in two long swallows.

"Are you drunk?" she whispered.

"More tipsy than I'd like," he whispered back. "You?"

"I don't know." Very carefully, she spread her arms. "Give me a sobriety test, Officer Hottie."

He grinned. "Hottie?"

"Yes, but shh, don't tell yourself that I think so. It'll go to your head. What do I have to do to pass?"

"Walk a straight line."

Affecting a model-on-the-catwalk strut, Chloe headed straight toward him and tripped over her own feet. "Whoops," she said when he caught her up against him. Her eyes were glassy, and her lips were parted. Damp with exertion and warm to the touch, she was both heaven and hell.

Her hands went immediately to his ass, and damn if she didn't cop a feel. "Sorry," she murmured and gave him a squeeze. "I think I failed the test. You should handcuff me now."

Sawyer would like that. He'd like to handcuff her to his bed and bury himself deep. "Chloe—"

"Uh-oh. Did I scare you off, Sheriff Hottie? Because I can stop talking now. Actually, I—"

He set a finger on her lips, and she smiled. "I talk a lot when I'm wasted," she admitted, her lips brushing against the pad of his finger as she spoke.

"Only when you're wasted?"

"Hey, I'm just trying to figure you out, is all."

"What's to figure?" he asked.

"Well, sometimes you're like...the big bad wolf."

"The big bad wolf."

"Yeah. But then you go to Home Depot to save an old lady from her smoke alarm, and rescue a silly fair maiden from the mud springs, and catch a convenience store robber single-handedly."

"I also paint houses."

"See? You're multitalented." It took her three times to say the word.

He laughed and set her back on her own feet. "Okay, it's time to get you some coffee. I have a coffeemaker somewhere..."

It'd been a housewarming present from Tara, actually. He'd never used it, preferring to stop by the inn for his coffee instead. He'd never really examined the reasoning for that too closely and didn't stop to do so now either.

"No, not yet," Chloe said, resisting. "I like being just a little buzzed. I don't have bad dreams that way." Turning away, she gathered the empty wine and beer bottles.

"What do you have bad dreams about?"

"Hmm?"

Sawyer stopped her, taking the bottles from her arms, carrying them to the recycling bin. Then he took her hands in his. "The dreams."

"Oh," Chloe said, peering at the walls they'd painted. "They're silly, really. Not nightmares or terrifying or anything like that. They're mostly annoying." She pulled free and squatted before a bucket of paint and stared into the remains.

He crouched at her side. "Tell me."

"Well, they start out differently." She shrugged, and her sweater slipped off her shoulder again. "Sometimes I'm running and getting really tired. Or I'm in a car and almost out of gas. Or I'm on a plane that can't take off...stuff like that. And I know I need to be somewhere, but something always gets in the way. The stupid thing is, in the dreams, I never really know where exactly I need to be, just that I'm late or I'm missing something or..." She shook her head. "I can't explain it, but I wake up frustrated and angry. And feeling helpless." She fell quiet and ran a finger through the paint. "Silly," she whispered again.

"Doesn't seem silly to me." He pulled her back up to her feet, surprised when they both wobbled. She leaned against him with a dreamy little sigh, and he wasn't sure if that was because he'd managed to catch them both or if she liked the grip she once again had on his ass. "Coffee," he repeated, and they let go of each other.

Then he realized that he didn't actually have any coffee to go in his coffeemaker. "I'll call for another delivery."

She bit her lower lip. "That's not a good idea."

"Why?"

"You can't be seen by anyone." She winced. "I sort of maybe just put paint on your ass. On purpose."

"Yeah, I know. Don't worry, you're going to pay for it."

"Uh-oh." She looked both worried and intrigued. "What's the punishment?"

Pretending to consider that, he stepped toward her and she stepped back, reaching the kitchen wall. Her hands slid behind her, covering her own ass. "I'm not into kinky stuff," she said, then hesitated. "At least I don't think I am. What did you have in mind?"

He smiled at her, and she let out a shaky breath.

"Get your inhaler, Chloe."

She took a hit. Then she settled back against the wall again, looking up at him hopefully. "Ready."

God, she was sweet. So sweet and so hot.

"What do you want me to do?" she asked breathlessly.

"Keep breathing. That's your only job, got it?"

She nodded solemnly. "Got it."

"Good." He cupped her breasts in his hands, and she gasped. When his thumbs rubbed over her nipples, she let out a shaky moan, and her head thunked back against the wall. Slowly her legs gave out, and she slithered down to the floor. Somehow, they both ended up on their knees facing each other.

"You okay?" he asked.

"Yeah." She smiled sheepishly. "I guess I just really liked that."

He smiled. "You won't in the morning."

She broke the eye contact and looked down at herself, finding the two large painted handprints, one on each boob. "Hey, I borrowed this shirt from Tara! And when I say borrowed, I mean stole." Reaching past him, she once again dipped her hand in the paint.

"Don't even think about it," he warned.

"Take your medicine like a man, Sheriff."

"Depends on where you're going to put that hand."

She palmed his erection and squeezed, and he let out a soft groan as her fingers did the walking. "Defacing personal property," he managed.

They both looked down at the handprint she'd left on him.

"What's the punishment for that?" she whispered.

"What's with you and getting punished?"

She grinned. "I don't know. I think it's your handcuffs. I can't stop thinking about them. Can I deface you some more?"

"Only if I get to return the favor."

Again she grinned. "We are so drunk."

"This is a true statement," Sawyer said carefully, and she snorted, falling to her back right there on his floor. Staring up at the ceiling fan slowly swirling above them, she said, "We should keep painting."

"That's a really bad idea."

"Why?" she asked. "Haven't you ever pulled a drunken all-nighter?"

"Sure, when I was a teenager."

"Was this before or after the flaming bags of poop?"

"After."

She grinned. "Hard to believe. You seem so . . ."

"If you say *sweet*," he warned, "I *will* get out the cuffs."

She snorted again, and he pulled her into his lap.

He gripped her ass, feeling the drying paint on the soft material of her skirt. "Hope you didn't steal this, too."

She wriggled a little, and the hem slipped up her thighs to her hips, giving a nice view of her black panties. He slid a finger over the silk, stopping short when he heard her wheeze. "Chloe."

"I'm okay."

Suddenly very sober, he slid out from beneath her. "No, you're not."

"Dammit! One little asthma attack and now you're scared of me." She pushed up to her feet and staggered to the refrigerator. She came back with two more beers and offered him one.

He looked into her eyes and beyond the fresh bravado saw unease. Whatever she said, however she acted, she was no more ready than him to push their luck.

"I thought we were sharing." He took both bottles from her and put one back. She snatched the other one and opened it, even though he hadn't intended on doing so. She took a sip, and he reclaimed the bottle, downing half the beer in one gulp so she wouldn't.

Things got hazy after that.

At some point, Chloe reasoned that since there were no overnight guests at the inn tonight, she was free and clear. She texted her sisters that she'd gone camping and wouldn't be back until morning. And though she and Sawyer kept painting, nothing seemed to get accomplished.

This was probably because Chloe kept stopping to touch him.

Or maybe that was him touching her.

Yeah, probably it was him touching her. He couldn't seem to control it. He, of the famed self-control, couldn't stop and he didn't want to.

Chapter 16

*"Multitasking means screwing up
several things at once."*
—Chloe Traeger

All Chloe knew was that one minute she was blinking sleepily at their handiwork on Sawyer's walls, and in the next, they were on his sole piece of living room furniture—his huge, comfy couch. He was lying lengthwise, and she appeared to be playing the role of his blanket, sprawled over the top of him like she belonged there.

She had no idea how much time had gone by, but it was still dark outside. She lifted her head and met his gaze, and there came the sort of timeless moment that you read about but never really experience. It'd have probably been more classically romantic if Sawyer hadn't had a possessive hand palming each of her butt cheeks, his fingers meeting in the middle, running up and down the Great Divide, but she'd never been all that into the classics.

Their faces were so close that the tips of their noses brushed, and she hoped like hell that he was extremely far-sighted because she was pretty sure she was a complete wreck.

"You're beautiful," he said, reading her mind.

Chloe ducked her head and dropped it to his chest, but he fisted his hand in her hair at the nape of her neck and tugged until she looked at him again. "You are," he said in his brook-no-argument cop voice.

Actually, *he* was the beautiful one. Not in a pretty boy way, he was far too rugged and weathered for pretty. But there was an absolute beauty to his tough, edgy exterior, and she soaked him up. He always moved with such innate grace and ease that she tended to forget what a big guy he really was.

But his poise was gone tonight, which made her smile dopily. She'd relaxed him, which was quite a feat. "We should have a paint party every night until your house is done."

He took his gaze off her and stared at the walls around them, seeming a little befuddled. It was such a shock to see his expression anything other than his usual imperturbable calm that she looked around, too, and winced. "Do the walls seem to be missing a few spots to you?"

He looked at her, then down at himself. "I think we're wearing the missing paint."

His expression cracked her up. "I've never seen you all discombobulated before," she said.

"I'm not discombobulated."

But he was. His hair was standing on end, cemented into place by some paint that might or might not have come from her fingers. His strong, lean jaw was dark with a full day's growth. And his eyes, those mesmerizing warm chocolate eyes, were glossy. But most telling of all was the adorably sexy, bad-boy smile on his face. She grabbed his face and gave him a smacking kiss. "You're so cute."

"Cute." He repeated this slowly, like what she said didn't compute.

At some point, he'd stripped out of his shirt and gun. Both were on the floor next to the couch, both covered in paint. She had no memory of how any of that had occurred but suspected she was at fault. She really wished she remembered the stripping off of his shirt, but between the wine and beer and her silly low tolerance for booze, she wasn't exactly clearheaded. "You *are* cute," she said with conviction.

"Take it back."

Sawyer looked very serious with his paint highlights, and she struggled not to laugh. "No can do, Officer... *Cute*."

His grip tightened on her, and he nipped her bottom lip. She heard a ragged moan and realized it was her own. And that her hands had slid into his hair to hold his face to hers.

"Can't do this," he said against her mouth.

"Why?"

"We're drunk."

"Not that drunk."

"So you're completely aware of the fact that you're grinding against me?"

Yikes. She went still with great effort. Then sat up and carefully got off him. It took her a moment to find her sea legs, and she put her hands out for balance.

"Hey," Sawyer said. "Come back." His voice was deep and steady. A command. She hated commands, but this one suited her. But first, she took a good, long look at him lying there, chest bare, abs hard and flat, jeans slung low. He was so big and bad...

Bad for her, she remembered. She just couldn't quite remember why. "You just said we weren't going to have a drunk make-out."

"We're not having drunk *sex*." He tugged her back over him.

Hard arms encased her, and two hands slid beneath her skirt to grope her ass. "Drunk making out is absolutely allowed," he said against her mouth. "In fact, it's required."

She was smiling when he kissed her. He tasted like the beer they'd shared, smelled like wet paint, and felt like warm promise. It was the best kiss she'd ever had. They stopped to breathe for a minute, and she set her head down on his chest. It was the last thing she remembered until some odd and obnoxious pounding sounded between her ears. When it stopped, she sighed and snuggled into the deliciously heated blanket beneath her...

Then came the sound of a door opening, and a low, shocked "Jesus Christ" woke her all the way up. She opened her eyes to Ford and Jax standing in the doorway.

And behind them was...daylight.

This caused her a moment of confusion. She wasn't at home in her cottage. She was still at Sawyer's, and in fact, was still on the couch, wrapped up in him.

And covered in paint.

So was Sawyer. He didn't open his eyes, but he did tighten his grip on her ass. The man definitely had a thing about her hind quarters.

"What the hell are you guys doing here?" Sawyer said to Jax and Ford without looking. "Besides breaking and entering."

"No breaking. Just entering," Ford said with a laugh in his voice.

"We were supposed to meet at eight to go sailing," Jax said. "Then when you didn't answer your phone..."

Sawyer sighed, then managed to crack one eye and looked at Chloe. "You okay?"

Nodding, she pushed upright and staggered to her feet. When she got her first full-body view of Sawyer, she gasped.

He tilted his head and looked down at himself. He had

fingerprints on each pec. A trail of paint across his perfect, washboard abs.

And a full handprint on his crotch.

To his credit, he didn't so much as blink. But Chloe clapped a hand to her mouth to hold in her horrified laugh. She had a few handprints on herself as well. Big handprints, most notably on her breasts.

Ford was wearing a shit-eating grin. Jax looked as if he was trying not to laugh, but he busted up and had to fake a cough.

Sawyer sat up.

Jax, not being a stupid man, backed away.

Not Ford. He pulled out his cell phone, accessed the camera, and aimed it at Sawyer's crotch. "Hold still, man."

Sawyer got to his feet and shoved Jax out the front door, then turned to Ford, who risked life and limb to take the pic before stepping back over the threshold. "Guess you won't be coming with—"

Sawyer shut the door, locked it, and turned to Chloe. "Sorry about the idiots."

"Yes, well, they're not the only idiots." She put her hands to her head, testing. Still on. That was good. Carefully, she took stock of herself. Everything seemed to be in working order. She looked at Sawyer. "I'm going to assume that since your pants are still on, I didn't get much farther than feeling you up. Right?"

Sawyer went still, his eyes serious. "You don't remember last night?"

"Well, I didn't get lucky. Or I'd have had another asthma attack." She smiled.

He didn't. "I took advantage of you." He sounded extremely unhappy about this.

"Look, if anyone took advantage of anyone, it was me, Sawyer. I mean, look at you."

They both looked at his body decor, specifically at the hand on his crotch. Some good humor crossed his face at that. "You are pretty damn hard to say no to," he said.

She bent for her purse and inhaler. "And yet people manage all the time." Crap, she really hated when her mouth disconnected from her brain. She slipped into her shoes and turned to the door, still kicking herself for that revealing statement.

"Chloe."

She didn't look at him. Couldn't. There was something far too serious in his voice, and it tightened her chest. "Yikes, would you look at the time? Gotta run before my sisters call you to send out a search party for me, which would be awkward considering I'm here." She reached for the door. "Plus, I'm giving facials today at the Garden Society lunch and have to mix up my special antiaging blend." She was babbling. She pressed her lips together and told herself to shut up and get out, but when she tried to open the door, Sawyer's hand appeared above her head, holding it closed.

Dropping her head to the wood, Chloe tried not to absorb the warmth and strength of him standing so close at her back, but then it got worse because he turned her to face him.

She felt more exposed than when she'd been naked with him in his shower. "I really do have to go," she whispered.

"In a minute." Sawyer ran a finger over her jaw. "You helped me paint and made my shitty evening a whole lot less shitty. Thank you for that."

She let out a low laugh. "You could be thanking me for something much more fun except for your damn moral high ground."

His eyes met hers, dark and warm. "Yes, but you wouldn't have remembered it." He reached for her, and she realized he was going to kiss her. Horrified, she slapped a hand over her mouth, blocking him. "Morning breath!"

Sawyer stared at her, clearly torn between amusement and

frustration. "Stay right there," he commanded and vanished into the kitchen, only to come back a few seconds later with a pack of gum. He popped a piece into his mouth and chewed. When he leaned in again, she slapped a hand to his chest. "Not you, me!"

This didn't deter him. He pushed a piece of gum between her lips. "Chew."

Obeying, Chloe narrowed her eyes. "You sure give a lot of orders."

"Yes. And here's one more. We're both minty fresh now, so kiss me."

Laughing, she pulled the gum out of her mouth, and he did the same. Going up on tiptoe, she set a hand on his chest and gave him a peck on his warm, firm mouth. Just when she would have ended it, he planted one hand on either side of her head, caging her in. "Again," he said against her mouth. Yet another command—not that she minded this one.

The brush of his lips was soft this time, though not tentative. Not at all. Nope, she could *feel* the barely leashed power, the carefully restrained passion, but for now, with nothing more than their mouths touching, he held it all in careful check, until her fingers curled into his hard biceps and she heard herself moan for more.

He gave it, settling in against her, deepening their connection to a hot, intense tangle of tongues that would have had her sliding to the floor if his arms hadn't been banded tightly around her. When they finally broke apart, she stared at him, happy that he wasn't breathing any steadier than she. "Okay, then," she said, nodding like a bobblehead, and whirled to leave.

And walked right into the door.

Without laughing at her, though she was quite certain he was doing his damnedest to hold it in, he handed her back her gum, which had stuck to his shirt when she'd grabbed on to him with both fists. Then he popped his back into his mouth with a smirk and reached around her to open the door.

"Thanks," she muttered and flew out of there. Two minutes later, she was on the road, smacking her forehead through her helmet, trying to get the brain cells back in working order. "Don't you fall for him," she ordered herself, peeking into the side mirror to make sure she got the message.

Her image didn't answer, but there was something different about her. Dammit. She had the Maddie glow!

Oh, God, this was bad. Falling for Sawyer would be a colossally stupid move. Sure, he wanted her. But she also drove him crazy. She wasn't right for him, and no matter what he'd said about appreciating her as is, there was no doubt in her mind— in order to become the woman Sawyer needed, she'd have to change. Already facing that very problem with her sisters, it felt too overwhelming for her to even go there.

But it was like a damn song in her head all the same. *Change, and you can have acceptance. Change, and you can catch a man. Change, and...*

God, she was damn tired of that song.

In any case, it wasn't as if Sawyer was going to fall for her. He was smarter than that. The man thought things through, never made a misstep, had himself rigidly controlled.

Well, except for last night. She'd gotten him drunk. She hoped he didn't blame her for that—though why not? It had been her doing. It was *always* her doing.

He'd have to repaint, of course. Or maybe not. He hadn't done much with the place in the way of making it a home. Not that *she'd* had a lot of experience with making anything a home, but she did have Tara and Maddie, both of whom were great at it. The cottage was a little messy but it was full of her things. That's what made staying there feel good, seeing the tangible evidence that she belonged. Even something as small as her favorite glass jars for her creams lined up on her dresser instead of shoved into her backpack made her smile.

But Sawyer had nothing of himself in his house, other than some pretty badly painted walls...A start, she had to admit. He was trying. He didn't have two sisters to show him how. Hell, he probably didn't want sisters. Or a real home for that matter. She actually had no idea. He was quite the puzzle.

All she knew for sure was that he wanted her body.

And that, at least, was very mutual.

* * *

For several days, Chloe kept herself busy. It wasn't hard. She taught yoga, worked on a recipe for a mud skin mask, and baby-sat the inn when Maddie was off doing wedding stuff and Tara attended a culinary conference.

One of the days she brought Sawyer a picnic lunch of Thai food to his station. She found him hunched over his desk scowling at his computer, and he looked so surprised that someone had thought to feed him that she felt an uncomfortable surge of tenderness.

It was incredibly foolish, and she spent two days lying low after that, making sure not to run into him. Because even one more time, her heart told her, and she wouldn't be able to continue to keep things so light and breezy.

It was during those days that she accepted the first four bookings for the following month at their new day spa—the one that didn't quite exist yet. She'd warned the potential clients that they weren't up to full service at this time and hoped that was enough to keep her out of hot water with her sisters. And then she'd called Jax. "We've got a month," she told him.

He hesitated. "Maddie and Tara know this?"

"They will."

"Shit, Chloe."

"I'm not asking for a miracle. Just some basic cosmetic stuff to make the room look warm and inviting. I'll tell Maddie and Tara, I swear, but I need to know what you can pull off and how fast you can do it."

"I'll get back to you," Jax said.

"Thanks." Chloe hung up and buried herself in work once more. She was too busy to think about Sawyer, or so she told herself. But it wasn't true. She thought about him a lot and differently than she used to. Once she'd thought of him as untouchable, but apparently once you finger-painted a man's crotch, things changed in that regard. Plus she'd seen another side to him now, discovered layers and complexity, and learned some more of his past.

He no longer felt untouchable. In fact, he'd become infinitely touchable.

The next night, a windstorm moved in and knocked out power. This wouldn't have bothered Chloe any except that it was a weekend, and they had three of their rooms booked, and she wanted to make sure the guests enjoyed their stay.

With no electricity.

Maddie lit candles throughout the inn, giving it a soft, warm glow for their guests. She used vegetable-based candles so they didn't aggravate Chloe's asthma. Tara barbequed on the covered deck over their brand-spanking-new gas, smokeless grill. "It's older than the mountains and got twice as much dust," Tara had said of their old grill, but they all knew she'd spent a fortune on the new one for Chloe's sake.

Maddie dug a sand pit on the beach and coaxed everyone outside for s'mores. Chloe reminded her that they needed a permit to light a fire on the beach, and Maddie assured her that had been taken care of—and then laughed at Chloe because she'd never been one to worry about breaking any city ordinances before. Maddie's amusement was met with some irritability on Chloe's part, because it was true. Since when did she worry about a city ordinance? "I can't sit at a campfire without getting wheezy."

Maddie handed her a paper surgical mask like the one Chloe had worn at Sawyer's house. "I got a stack from Mallory at the hospital," her sister said proudly. "See if it works."

To Chloe's surprise, it did. Their guests were three middle-aged couples, all friends, traveling together up the coast to Canada. They had a great time making s'mores, and when they'd headed off to bed, Tara stoked the fire while Maddie called the Love Shack. Within ten minutes, the sisters had company.

Ford and Jax, of course.

And Sawyer.

Chloe looked at him from across the fire, and he looked right back. Out of uniform tonight, he was in battered jeans and a CHP hoodie sweatshirt. His eyes were inscrutable, his jaw stubbled, and his thoughts hidden.

Ford had brought beer, which he passed out to everyone except Sawyer and Chloe. "You two kids didn't seem to know your limits the other night," he said.

Sawyer gave him a level look. "This from the guy who once drunk-dialed Tara until I saved his ass by stealing his phone."

Ford winced and offered Sawyer a beer, which he didn't take. Whether he was on call later or had DEA business, Chloe didn't know. What she did know was that Tara and Maddie were staring at her. She knew this was because they'd thought she'd been camping that night she spent at Sawyer's.

"You said you were with Lance," Tara said.

Sawyer arched an amused brow at Chloe.

Suddenly the annoying mask was her best friend, as it allowed her to hide her expression with ease. "I never said I was with Lance."

"You said you were with a *friend*," Maddie said. "We assumed."

"Lance's been busy lately," Chloe said. "With his new girl-friend. Renee the nurse. She's really great for him. She's given him this new lease on life and—"

"Hold it," Tara said, clearly not interested in Lance's love life. Just Chloe's. "So you and Sawyer are..." She waggled a finger back and forth between them.

"No," both Sawyer and Chloe answered in unison.

Chloe sent Sawyer a long look. It was one thing for *her* to say "no," but she sure as hell didn't like that he felt as strongly about it as she did.

"Okay, but since when are you two friends?" Tara asked. "Friends who have *sleepovers*."

"I like those kinds of friends," Ford said.

"We're not *that* kind of friends." Chloe pulled down the mask to make sure she gave the full-effect glare to a silent Sawyer. "Feel free to step in anytime here and defend my honor."

"Chloe's right," Sawyer said, never taking his eyes off of her. "We're not friends." He was looking at her from dark, brooding, heated eyes, which of course helped not at all.

Tara was clearly unhappy. "What the hell is going on with you two?"

"Nothing!" Chloe said.

"They were fully dressed when Ford and I found them the other morning," Jax offered helpfully. "Well, actually, Chloe was dressed. Big guy here was shirtless. Oh, and he had his hands up her skirt, but—"

Sawyer cut his eyes to Jax, who shrugged.

Maddie was staring at her husband-to-be. "And you didn't tell me?"

Ford *tsk*ed in mocking disapproval. "Rookie mistake," he whispered to Tara.

"For God's sake." Surging to her feet, Chloe stabbed at the fire with a big stick, thinking about using it to whack Sawyer across the back of his big, fat head. But since she didn't want to be arrested tonight, she shoved the stick into the fire and pulled out her iPhone. She accessed her Magic Eight application. "For my sisters' sake," she said to it, "please state for the record whether or not I'm capable of running my own life."

The answer was short and sweet.

Without a Doubt.

"Ha!" Righteously triumphant, Chloe sank back to her beach chair. "One hundred percent accurate, as always."

"Actually, statistically speaking," Jax said, ever the lawyer even though he hadn't practiced law in six years, "it has to be wrong fifty percent of the time."

Ford took the iPhone from Chloe. "Magic Eight, will Jax ever learn that he doesn't know everything?"

The screen went cloudy and then cleared.

Don't Count on It.

Everyone laughed except Jax, who was trying—unsuccessfully—to pull a resisting Maddie down to his lap. He snatched the phone from Ford. "Hey," he said to it. "I'm still getting married next month, right?"

Outlook Good.

Jax let out a loud breath of relief. Maddie gave a low laugh, finally allowing him to pull her down to his lap. "Was that really in question?"

"Just making sure."

"See?" Chloe said smugly. "Always accurate."

"That's because you ask it only the easy stuff," Tara said. "Ask it if you're ever going to settle down."

"I already know the answer to that," Chloe told her. "When I'm old. *Reaaaaally* old," she added, catching Sawyer's knowing eyes. "Like when I'm...thirty-five."

The thirty-five-year-old Sawyer smiled at her but didn't take the bait.

However, thirty-five-year old Tara raised a threatening brow. "Ask it if you'll ever be able to say what you're really thinking."

Everyone smiled at this, because they all knew Chloe *always* said whatever she was thinking.

"Hey, she doesn't always," Maddie corrected. "She never says 'I love you.'"

"Maybe because I don't." Chloe said it teasingly enough, but the silly game suddenly felt too serious. It was so simple for her sisters, she thought, surrounded by the security of the men who loved them.

But for someone like her, who'd never experienced that kind of security and love, it wasn't so simple at all.

"So maybe *that's* the real question," Tara said and took the phone. "Magic Eight Ball, will my sister ever say *I Love You*?"

Ridiculously, Chloe found herself holding her breath as she waited for the screen to clear, which pissed her off. She didn't need a stinking app to give her an answer, but it came regardless:

Absolutely Yes.

Chapter 17

*"Sure, good things come to those who wait—but
they're the leftovers from those who got there first."*
—Chloe Traeger

Sawyer watched the reaction cross Chloe's face as she read her phone's screen. Relief, quickly hidden behind a scowl and a derisive snort.

"I like the Absolutely Yes," Tara said.

"Well, don't get excited," Chloe told her. "Because we've finally done it. We've just proven Mr. Magic Eight Ball completely wrong."

"How can you possibly know that?" Maddie asked.

"Because I don't plan on changing a damn thing about myself. Which makes it a little unlikely that I'll get someone to fall in love with me as is, wouldn't you say?"

Sawyer's heart squeezed.

"Actually," Maddie said slowly, sounding as if Chloe's words had made her hurt as much as Sawyer was suddenly hurting.

"I meant you telling Tara and me that you loved us. But I think you're wrong." She said this very gently, eyes bright, her voice soft but utter steel. "There is someone out there for you. I know it."

"I think so, too," Tara said, and it didn't escape Sawyer's notice that *no one* looked at him. Clearly he was not *the some-one* that the sisters had in mind for her. Which, yeah, he already knew, but it still irritated the shit out of him. He was a county sheriff, not some asshole off the street.

Chloe shrugged as if it mattered not one little bit, and it occurred to Sawyer that she had no idea how much she was loved by the people in her life. None.

And *he'd* had no idea that all along she'd been afraid of that love. She hid it well behind that tough, unflappable, hard-edged courage. Not being all that fond of expressing emotions himself, the sympathy coursed through him. With both Tara and Maddie deep in the throes of love themselves, the levels of emotions had to feel like a Hallmark movie at the B&B. He knew because that's how it felt at the bar these days. Kind of nauseating.

Ford snatched the phone again. "Hey, Magic Eight," he said. "Since you're so accurate and all, tell me this—will Tara ever try that one position in the *Kama Sutra*—"

Tara pushed him as everyone cracked up, and just like that, Ford accomplished what he did best and lightened the mood.

"Your turn," Ford said to Sawyer and tossed him the phone.

"Oh no," he said to everyone's expectant face. "Hell no. All I ever get is *Try Again Later*."

"Liar. The odds don't support that any more than Chloe always being right." Jax leaned close and spoke to the phone. "Magic Eight Ball, what about our good sheriff here? Will he ever get a woman and manage to keep her?"

Maddie gave Jax a dark look and a little nudge. Sawyer gave him a nudge, too, one that was actually more of a shove, right off the log he was sitting on, but not before the stupid Magic Eight app answered:

Try Again Later.

Everyone laughed but Jax. "What did the love advisor say?" he wanted to know, from flat on his back in the sand. Sawyer considered dumping his beer on him when, from deep in the woods, a flare went off. At least it looked like a flare.

"What was that?" Tara asked with a startled gasp, getting to her feet.

"I'll go look." Sawyer was already on his. A movement at his side had him turning his head and meeting Chloe's gaze.

"Don't," she warned him. "Don't even try to tell me to—"

"*Stay*," he said firmly.

"Goddammit, Sawyer. A 'please' wouldn't kill you."

Sawyer moved to his SUV and grabbed a high-powered flashlight. Their fire was right near the water's edge and no-where close to the woods. But that flare...They were at an all-time low for precipitation. It would take next to nothing to ignite a catastrophic forest fire. He moved into the woods, Jax and Ford at his side. A few minutes later, they came to a small clearing that Sawyer knew well. He'd come to this very spot as a stupid teenager to get trashed. There was a hastily put out campfire, several empty beer cans, and two cigarette butts.

The three men made sure the fire was out, then headed back to the beach. Chloe stood there, her back to their little circle, lit by the glow of the flames as she squinted to see into the woods. She was waiting, the concern etched on her face.

For him.

That was different. He'd always been the one to look after people and wasn't used to it going the other way. And yet he could see it plain as day. Tough as she was, she let her emotions show, every single one of them.

He wasn't good at that and didn't want to be. He hadn't managed to stay alive on the job by being an open book. Anything he felt, he kept to himself. And actually, sometimes he wasn't sure he even had any emotions to hide.

But all he had to do was look at Chloe and know that he did. He had way too many feelings. It'd been a damn long time since he'd let anything penetrate, but she'd gotten through. In fact, what he felt for her had invaded his life.

Love was a weakness.

Love made a guy soft.

And soft meant mistakes were made. And yet there was Chloe, looking for him. At him. And something turned over in his chest. It was his heart, exposing its soft, vulnerable underbelly. He had no idea what to do with that.

Or her.

* * *

Several days later, Chloe was manning the inn. She was sweeping the living room wood floors and watching an old *Friends* repeat.

Lance called. "Working hard?" he asked.

She glanced at the TV wryly. "Very."

"Is that *Friends*?"

Chloe aimed the remote and turned down the volume. "If you can recognize it by sound alone, you know it too well."

"What season?" he asked.

"Well, Chandler's secretly doing Monica, so season five."

Lance laughed. "If you can name the season, *you* know it too well."

She snorted. "Better than being married to my PS3. Haven't seen you in days."

"Been busy, but not with my PS3."

The smugness in his voice alerted her. "Ah. So how's your nurse?"

"Good. *Very* good."

"Are we ever going to all hang out?" Chloe asked.

"Hell, no."

"Afraid I'll tell her all your secrets and scare her off?" she teased.

"Hell, yes. Listen, we have people coming in this weekend, and they want two rooms. You up for it?"

"Depends." Chloe turned to the front desk and brought up the B&B's schedule on the computer. "Are they normal?"

"Define normal."

"Viable credit card and not any of Tucker's idiot friends."

"You're in luck. They're actually my godparents and their teenage kids, and they're nice. *And* they pay their bills."

"Okay, then. I'll book them."

"Thanks. So what's this I read on Facebook about you and the sheriff sending out save-the-date magnets?"

"*What*?" Chloe nearly fell off the chair. Righting herself, she clicked over to the Facebook page on the computer. Nothing except a Cute Guy sighting had been made in the grocery store. He'd been caught buying an expensive cut of steak, and people were wondering which woman in town he was cooking for. "You made that up!"

"Yeah," Lance said on a rough laugh. "When did you get so easy?"

"When did you get so mean?"

"Aw, you know I love you." Then some of the amusement faded from his voice. "And you should also know, Todd has a new crush."

"Jesus. Amy is *not* interested in *any* of them. Tell them just because she's new and beautiful that she—"

"You," Lance said. "He's crushing on *you*."

"Too bad for him."

"Yeah, well, be careful."

"I'm handling Todd." Mostly by ignoring him, but there wasn't much more she could do.

"He was drunk the other night, Chloe," Lance said. "Talking about snatching you from beneath Sawyer's nose."

Terrific. "I—"

A woman walked in the front door of the inn. "Gotta go," Chloe whispered and hung up. "Hi," she said with a welcoming smile, promptly putting the annoying Todd out of her head. "Can I help you?"

"Um, yeah. I hope so. I don't have a reservation. Do you have any rooms available?" She was a mid-twenties blonde, pretty. And she was nervous as hell. When she clasped her hands together at her chest, her fingers were shaking.

"We do have rooms," Chloe said. "Just you?"

"Y-yes." She squeezed her lips together. "Just me."

Chloe opened a registration page on the computer. "Okay... your name?"

"Um." The woman's gaze shifted toward the television, still turned to *Friends*. "Monica."

Chloe paused. "Last name?"

"Do you really need that?"

"Well, I'll need a driver's license and credit card, so..."

"Oh, but I'm going to pay cash," the woman said, eyes darting around as if someone might object. "So you don't need an ID, right?"

"Actually, we still ask for ID." Chloe looked at "Monica's" luggage—a garment bag from a haute couture store in Seattle and two wrinkled plastic bags from Target. Quite the contradiction. Another was that "Monica's" makeup was theater flawless, with her hair up in an intricate French twist that had been clearly done by a professional and yet she wore cheap, baggy sweats. On her right breast was a tiny round clear sticker with a small black *S*, the size hadn't yet been removed.

And then there was the big tell—the woman's panic was a tangible, living, breathing thing in the room, and Chloe knew right then she was going to cave. But before she could say so, Tara poked her head in from the kitchen. "I've got groceries to unload—Oops, sorry."

"Excuse me for just a minute," Chloe said to Monica and jogged after Tara into the kitchen. Maddie was just coming in the back door as well.

"Problem," Chloe told them quietly. "We have a guest who doesn't want to show ID."

"We have to have a credit card on file," Tara said.

"She's running away from someone." Chloe cracked the kitchen door to peek at their guest, who was pacing the living room. "I want to let her stay here."

"You asking or telling?" Tara asked.

Chloe locked gazes with her.

"We've got to at least get ID," Tara protested.

"Or we could...forget," Maddie said softly. "Because if the poor thing is hiding, it's for a reason, and we should help her."

Chloe nodded her agreement on that score. "She's scared. I'm going back out there." Back in the living room, she smiled reassuringly at their guest. "Just one night?"

"Yes. I need to be on the road at the crack of dawn."

"Sure." Chloe once again bent to the computer. "So where are you headed?"

She bit her lip. "LA?"

Chloe looked up from the screen. "Okay, but tomorrow night, when you're standing at another front desk in some other inn, don't say it with a question mark. Own it."

The woman winced. "Oh, God. You're right." She seemed

to collapse in on herself. "And I don't want to be standing at another inn tomorrow. I've only come from Seattle, and I'm already tired of driving. Can I just book a room here for a week and have you pretend I don't exist?"

"A week might be harder to swing without a credit card."

"Monica" backed to the couch and sat down hard. She was wearing white pumps with her sweats.

Pristine white pumps.

"I know what it looks like," she said. "Like I'm an escapee from the mental hospital, but I'm not."

"Because you're a runaway bride?" Chloe asked softly.

She straightened and stared at Chloe in horror. "I don't—I mean . . ." She bit her lower lip. "I just like white pumps, a lot. So of course, I'm not a runaway bride. Running away from my own wedding would make me a horrible person." She covered her face. "Oh, God, I'm a horrible person! How did you know?"

"The Target sweats with the wedding pumps were a dead giveaway," Chloe said gently, coming around the desk to sit at her side. "So was stealing Monica Geller's identity." She paused. "Are you okay?"

"Sure. I've only broken hearts of all my family and friends and groom-to-be, who I've known since I was ten. But other than that, I'm terrific." And then she burst into tears.

Chloe put a sympathetic hand on her shoulder, and she slumped against her like they were best friends and sobbed.

Chloe awkwardly patted her back while staring helplessly at the door to the kitchen. Where the hell was Maddie the Hugger when she needed her? "Um . . . can I call your family for you? I could tell them that you're safe. They don't have to know where you are, but I'm sure they're worried sick about you."

Maddie came out with some tea, and Tara followed with cupcakes, thank God. The three of them sat on the couch while the woman sniffled and blew her nose. "My name's Allie."

"Cupcake, Allie?" Maddie asked kindly.

Allie nodded and took two, one in each hand.

"Tara calls these Sugar and Spice and Anything but Nice Cupcakes," Chloe said. "She was annoyed at her boyfriend when she baked them."

"Yeah?" Allie shoveled in a cupcake, still occasionally hiccupping and wiping her nose. "What did he do?"

"Oh, she won't tell us," Chloe said. "Whatever it is happened this morning, I think, but she's mum on the subject. He probably left his underwear on the floor. Tara's OCD about that kind of stuff. But then again, I'm still on the fence that Ford actually *wears* underwear." Chloe grinned into Tara's narrowed eyes. Hey, maybe she'd promised to grow up, but she'd never promised to stop poking at her sisters.

"Maddie thinks maybe he's the one who sneaked a piece of Tara's Very Berry Pie without asking, but it wasn't him." She pointed at herself and mouthed "me."

Allie eyed Tara speculatively. "You look so . . . with it. He had to have done something bigger than leave out his underwear, right?"

Tara gave Chloe a meaningful glare but said nothing. The Steel Magnolia wasn't talking.

"Did you ask him how you look and he said fine without taking his eyes off the TV?" Allie asked. "Or did he ogle a woman in the frozen foods aisle at the grocery store because her nipples were hard from standing in front of the ice cream display? Did he tell you that your mother is a pain in his ass?"

"No," Tara said and paused. "He asked me to elope with him to the Greek Islands on his boat."

"Bastard," Allie said, sniffing, while both Maddie and Chloe gaped in shock at Tara.

"*What*?" Maddie whispered, a hand on her heart, a slow smile curving her mouth. "Did he really?"

"Yes." Still looking calm, Tara took a cupcake, cool as she pleased. "The other night, after the bonfire."

Allie was double-fisting cupcake number three and four, mascara smeared on her cheeks. "It's a lot of pressure, isn't it?" she said, mouth full, inhaling sugar like she hadn't eaten in a week.

"What are you going to do?" Chloe asked.

"Well, I could jump off a bridge," Allie said dramatically. "Or maybe I ought to try being a lesbian for a while."

"No bridge jumping," Chloe said firmly. "And the lesbian thing? Two menstrual cycles and double the PMS. That's a big commitment. But actually, I was asking my sister." She looked at Tara. "Are you going to elope with the sexiest man on the planet, or what?"

"Hey," Maddie said. "My man's sexy, too."

Tara patted Maddie's hand, then followed Allie's lead and grabbed yet another cupcake. "I think I have to."

"No," Allie said, eyes glossy from the sugar high. "You don't have to do anything. You can run away to...here." She laughed softly. "I'll share my room. We can do the lesbian thing together."

Tara shook her head. "Got that out of my system in college, sorry."

Maddie choked on her cupcake, but Chloe just grinned. "And they call *me* the wild one."

The phone rang, and Chloe jumped up to take the call. It was a woman wanting to make reservations for her and her sisters for a long weekend.

"How many rooms would you like?" Chloe asked her.

"All of them."

Chloe blinked. "What?"

"We'd like the whole inn for ourselves. It's a reunion, you see. Two of us have been overseas in the military, and another has just gotten her doctorate, and the baby's getting married. We haven't all been together, the eight of us, in five years."

"The whole inn," Chloe repeated, stunned.

"Yes, for at least four days. I hope that's not a problem. We want to utilize the day spa, too. Oh, and do you have yoga classes?"

"Yes." Or they would...Chloe cleared her throat. "How soon are you looking at?"

"What's the soonest you have?"

"Hold on a sec?" Dizzy with excitement, Chloe covered the phone and turned to Tara and Maddie.

"Problem?" Tara asked, rising to her feet at what surely was a look of shock on Chloe's face.

"No. Yes. I don't know." Chloe laughed. "I have a request for a four-day exclusive stay for a family of sisters who wants the entire B&B and day spa at their disposal. *ASAP*."

Tara and Maddie stared at her. "Honey," Maddie said gently, "there is no day spa yet."

"Not yet," Chloe said. "But it's coming." She went back to the phone, catching the warning look in Tara's eyes, the one that said don't you dare be impulsive. Chloe grinned at her while calmly telling the woman on the phone that the spa would be open for limited service in two weeks, or they could wait for the full range of services to be offered in a month. She made the booking, not unhappy that the woman had settled for limited service. "No worries," she said to her sisters when she'd hung up. "Jax promised he could handle it."

Allie sighed. "They all think they can handle it. So there's a day spa?"

* * *

Thirty minutes later, Chloe had shown Allie to her room, then headed into the sunroom, where she was joined by Tara and Maddie. "I think Allie's going to be okay."

"You were good with her," Tara said. "I might have just given her the room key and stayed out of it."

"No, you wouldn't," Maddie said. "You were the first one on board when I was running away from my life and needed to stay here, remember?" She hugged Tara, then reached for Chloe's hand, pulling her in close, too. "I called Jax. Told him we had reservations coming in, that we need this room done yesterday. He said he'd do it at material cost only, and that I could pay the labor later."

"*I'll* pay," Chloe said, trying to figure out how long was long enough to stay in the group hug without being rude. "Whatever it is."

"I've got it," Maddie said. "No worries."

"No, I—"

"Chloe," Tara said dryly. "I'm pretty sure the debt can't be paid in money."

Maddie blushed to the tips of her toes.

"Oh. Gotcha." Chloe laughed. "Well, then, thanks for paying up, sis."

Maddie rolled her eyes and hugged her again. Jesus. Tara was still right there, too, so that now Chloe was sandwiched between them. "Okay . . . Well. I have things to do."

"You always do when we're having a mushy moment," Tara said, not letting go.

Dammit. "Seriously?" Chloe asked. "Because we *just* mushed all over each other a few months back when Maddie got engaged, and I'm still recovering from that."

"That was a year ago," Maddie said. "And now Tara's engaged. It's definitely mush time."

Tara shook her head. "No, first we mush on this." She looked at Chloe. "We owe you an apology."

"Whoa. Can you repeat?"

Tara sighed. "You might be the youngest, but you're not a baby. You've really changed, Chloe. Grown up."

"Okay, thanks. Can you let go of me now?"

"No," Maddie said, tightening her grip, laughing when Chloe swore.

"We're trying to tell you that we're sorry it took us so long to realize," Tara said. "And that though you march to a different drummer, you have it together just fine."

"Sometimes even more than us," Maddie added.

Chloe narrowed her eyes. "Okay, what do you guys want? You're both going away with your lovers this weekend, right? Leaving me with the inn? Is that it?"

Maddie laughed. "No. We love you, Chloe. That's it."

"Oh, good God." She dropped her head to bang it repeatedly on Maddie's shoulder.

Her sisters both laughed, but Chloe didn't feel quite in on the joke. Her mother had been a free spirit and had flung the L-word around to anyone and everyone, so much so that it had lost its meaning. And then there'd been TV and in movies, and everyone knew *that* love wasn't real either, just an easy antidote to bad stuff suffered in the story. Family betrayed you? I love you. All better. Man ripped your heart to shreds? I love you. Perfect Band-Aid. World destruction imminent and you're going to fly into the asteroid leaving your daughter an orphan? I love you. Buck up.

No, to Chloe it seemed like people used "I love you" when they meant "I'm sorry" or "Could we please forget about what a moron I've been?" They weren't words to be used like a Band-Aid, or to be said to make someone feel better in the moment, like the time Phoebe had left a seven-year-old Chloe at a stranger's house for four days or when she'd spent the entire Christmas money on gifts for her boyfriend.

Chloe might not be the smartest kid on the block, but she'd learned early on that those three words had power. No way she would ever let that power be wasted. That would be a sacrilege.

Her sisters could joke all they wanted, but Chloe knew deep in her bones that when it was time to say the words, she'd know. There'd be some cosmic sign. Problem was, she was starting to wonder if her cosmic receiver was faulty.

Wonder if Jax knew a contractor for that?

In any case, she was grateful for what she did have with Tara and Maddie. More than they could possibly know. They were all she had as far as stabilizing forces. They were her only blood ties.

And if she let herself think that way for too long, it made her sad. Lonely.

Afraid.

So she didn't think on it.

Ever.

She just enjoyed having them in her life. And as she'd come to realize in the past year, the more of herself that she gave to the inn, the longer that might be.

"She'll say it when she's ready," Maddie said to Tara. "And we shouldn't be teasing her. Chloe, honey, you're pale. Are you okay? Are you having trouble breathing?"

"It's blood loss from my brain exploding." Chloe jammed her hands into her pockets, suddenly extremely and uncomfortably aware that they were both staring at her with concern. "Not everyone wants to sit around and discuss feelings. Not everyone is in a relationship."

Silence, and she grimaced. When would she learn to stop talking?

"Sugar." Tara's eyes were unusually soft and, dammit, full of sympathy. "Is this about us both getting married?"

"No," Chloe said. "Of course not. I'm thrilled for both of you."

"Is it about you wanting a relationship?" Maddie asked gently.

"If I wanted a relationship, I'd have one."

"Is it about Sawyer?" Tara asked. "Are you're falling for him?"

Yes.

No.

Christ, she had no idea. She shook her head, hoping that covered all the options. "That would be stupid."

Tara let out a breath and nodded. And this, of course, put Chloe in defense mode. "Why are you nodding?"

Tara looked at Maddie, then back to Chloe. "Because," Tara said carefully, "you said it yourself."

"Yes, and *I* know why I said it, but why did *you* say it?"

"Well, there's the whole he-wears-a-badge thing and your whole hate-authority thing. And—"

Maddie put her hand on Chloe's arm. "Honey, what she means is that you've never been all that interested in toeing the line, and Sawyer's life *is* that line, you know?"

Yes, Chloe knew. She knew exactly. And wasn't that just the problem.

Chapter 18

*"Sex is like air; it's not important unless
you aren't getting any."*
—Chloe Traeger

Sawyer's week was an exhausted blur. His counterpart, Tony Sanchez, had been taking a lot of time off because of the new twins, leaving Sawyer overworked and facing too many double shifts. So he wasn't in the best of moods when he should have been getting off duty but instead was heading into an all-nighter and found a car parked oddly on the side of the highway beneath a grove of trees. Sawyer exited his vehicle to check it out, but it roared to life, speeding off, tires squealing, narrowly missing two cars passing by.

Bonehead move. Sawyer jumped back into his vehicle, flipped on his lights, and pulled the car over.

There were two guys in the front seat. Sawyer didn't see anything suspicious inside the car, so he wrote a ticket for reckless driving. The driver bitched about it, then proceeded to pull away, once again squealing his tires and laying down tread, barely missing yet another car.

Sawyer was just pissed off enough to pull him over again, calmly issuing the Idiot of the Day his second ticket.

"Are you fucking kidding me?" the driver yelled. "Another ticket?" He thrust his car into gear.

"Careful," Sawyer warned him. "I have all night."

The guy muttered "asshole" beneath his breath but pulled onto the highway more carefully this time.

From there, Sawyer was called to traffic duty. Construction crews were working on the main street in town and had closed the road. There'd been a flashing sign all week long warning people, and the crew had carefully barricaded the road in several places, posting up "road closed" signs as well as detour signs. And yet several people *still* managed to drive around the barricades and then get angry with Sawyer because they couldn't get through.

"This is ridiculous!" one woman screamed at him. "I can't get out of this mess to save my life. You're all assholes!"

She'd had to drive on the wrong side of the road to get past the barricades—and *he* was the asshole. "See that barricade you ignored and drove around?" he asked her. "You want to drive back the way you came. Go by each of the *road closed* signs that you passed—I believe there were three—and follow the detour directions."

Flipping him off, she turned around.

The next guy to come through the barricades was—oh perfect—Todd. Todd had been questioned after the diner incident as a matter of course and hadn't reacted well. He'd been running his mouth in town, telling anyone who would listen that Sawyer was abusing his power, and that Todd was going to bring him down. The guy wanted a fight, but Sawyer wasn't going to give him one. No way was he going to allow Todd to jeopardize his job or be a menace to innocent people. It'd been *years*; it was time for Todd to get over himself and get his life on track. Unfortunately, Sawyer knew better than anyone that you couldn't make a person do what they didn't want to do. He couldn't save Todd any more than he could gain his own father's approval. There was just some shit that had to be let go.

"What the hell's going on?" Todd said now, not bothering with his usual charm, not for Sawyer. "The road's closed. Why can't you douche bags do this at a more convenient time?"

Sawyer didn't respond to the fact that *he* wasn't actually working on the roads. He was simply attempting to direct the idiots driving on them. Not to mention that it was midnight, how much more convenient of a time could they get?

"How the fuck do I get out of here?" Todd asked.

Sawyer flicked his flashlight into the cab of Todd's truck, knowing he wasn't going to get lucky enough to find a bag of dope in plain sight. "Well, here's the thing, Todd. If you can't follow the detour directions you've been passing, I don't know how you're going to be able to follow the directions I give you to get out of here."

"Fuck you, Thompson. Or maybe I'll just go fuck Chloe."

Sawyer had to work at not reacting at that one.

"Yeah," Todd said, knowing Sawyer enough to see right through him. "She's a sweet piece of ass, and you know what? She's hot for me."

"Stay away from her."

"Or?"

Or I'll kill you wasn't exactly the way to keep his job. And he'd never even had this problem before, the urge to say fuck the job and dive through Todd's window and strangle him.

"Yeah, that's what I thought," Todd said on a grin. "Behind the badge, you're all pussy." He shoved his truck in reverse. "Think of us tonight, cozy in my bed while you're out here playing hall monitor on the roads."

Sawyer gritted his teeth and worked the rest of the night, doing his best to remind himself that Todd was just an angry asshole.

An asshole who knew which buttons to press.

Just past dawn, Sawyer drove to the B&B. It was seven in the morning, and he'd been up for just over twenty-four hours, but he told himself he needed some of Tara's coffee.

"You look like shit, man." This helpful statement was from Jax, who was out of his Jeep and putting on his tool belt.

"Damn," Sawyer said. "And I was planning on going straight to a photo shoot from here, too."

Jax grinned and whistled softly. Izzy, his three-year-old brown Lab snoozing in the passenger seat, scrambled to her feet and barked. When she saw that nothing exciting was happening, she collapsed like a wet noodle, closing her eyes again.

"Come on, lazy girl," Jax said.

Izzy cracked open one eye and stared at him balefully.

"Tara'll have breakfast," Jax coaxed. The dog leaped out of the Jeep and trotted to the B&B's front door.

Sawyer shook his head. "You working on the day spa?" He looked around for Maddie's car. "Or you and Maddie just going to play Contractor and the Missus again?"

"Hey, you're not supposed to know about that. Maddie hates it when people know about our sex life."

"You're the ones who got caught in the attic by Lucille and her damn camera phone."

"Fucking Facebook. And I'd lost a bet with Maddie and the deal was I had to strip. It's not like I do it all the time, but hell, when a pretty woman tells you to drop 'em, you drop 'em, you know?"

"Just be thankful Lucille stuck her head into the attic *before* you stripped down to just that tool belt," Sawyer said.

Jax sighed. "She didn't even get Maddie in the shot. Just me doing the strip dance waving my shirt around. Someone should lower her estrogen dose or something."

"Or you could keep your strip tease to your own bedroom."

"What fun would that be?" Jax shut his Jeep door and took a longer look at Sawyer. "Rough night?"

"*Long* night."

"You stopping by to catch a glimpse of Chloe under the guise of getting coffee?"

Sawyer narrowed his eyes.

His friend gave him the same bland stare that Izzy had given Jax a moment before.

Sawyer blew out a breath but admitted nothing. He hadn't been here in two days. He'd told himself that he was cutting back on caffeine, that he was late, that he didn't need to waste the extra gas. He told himself whatever he'd needed to in order to make it work in his head.

But it didn't. Work.

Jax walked into the inn's kitchen with him. Jax got a *very* friendly kiss from Maddie. Sawyer got coffee. While Jax headed to the sunroom, Sawyer looked around the kitchen for signs of Chloe and found none.

"Looking for anything special?" Tara asked from her perch at the stove.

Sawyer glanced out the window. No Vespa.

"She's not here," Tara said dryly. "She's been sneaking away for a few hours here and there, needing to regroup." She paused. "It's because she lets things build up inside of her. She tries to hide it, pretend nothing gets to her. But things get to her. *People* get to her."

"Tara," Maddie said quietly from the kitchen table.

"*He* gets to her," Tara said to her sister, pointing at Sawyer with a wooden spatula.

"What's wrong?" Sawyer asked. "What's happened?"

Tara shook her head. "Nothing. At least nothing specific."

"Any idea where she might be?"

Tara shook her head. "She said she goes somewhere that gives her peace and quiet, a place where she can think."

At that, some of the tension left Sawyer's shoulders. He had a decent idea where she might be.

"Sawyer?"

"Yeah?" Impatient to be gone, he looked back at Tara.

Her eyes were fierce and protective. "Don't make me sorry I told you." There was an unmistakable threat in her voice.

Normally that would irritate the hell out of him, but he kept his gaze level with hers and shook his head. "I won't."

As he walked out, he heard Maddie say to Tara, "Look at you, meddling like a mother hen."

"She won't thank me," Tara said.

"Depends on what happens next," Maddie said, which was the last thing Sawyer heard as he left the inn.

* * *

Sawyer drove through town, hoping he was right about Chloe's location. *Somewhere that gives her peace and quiet.* Hell, if he thought about it too much, that could be anywhere. The mud springs. Lance's house. Hang gliding...

He shuddered. Christ, he hoped she wasn't doing anything like that, but when it came to Chloe, one never knew. Her idea of peace and quiet was decidedly left of center.

But her partner in crime, Lance, had been seen all over town with his new girlfriend, which hopefully meant they'd all been too busy to get into trouble.

So Sawyer headed home. In the middle of the night, with no traffic and no red lights, it took fifteen minutes to get through town and up the hill to his house. This morning, as the sun rose above the tall mountains cradling Lucky Harbor, bathing the town in a golden glow, he made it in seven.

He idled in his driveway, staring at the Vespa parked there. Not wanting to examine the odd feeling in his chest, the one that felt suspiciously like relief and also something more, he got out. He didn't go inside, but walked around the side of the house. He flicked a glance at the outdoor shower, and as it had every other time since he'd been in there with Chloe, his dick twitched at the memory of her pale skin gleaming, water running in rivers down her curves…

He moved to the cliff and took the stairs to the beach. The sun had risen a little more, casting the overhang in black shadow, the rocks indistinguishable from one another.

At the bottom of the stairs, he kicked off his boots and socks and turned to face the cliffs. The sun was in his eyes, blinding him to anything but the outline of the granite. The beach was utterly empty and completely isolated, especially at this time of year. There was a salty breeze but the waves were subdued, soft and quiet. A lullaby, gently rolling against the rocky sand. A bird squawked. Its mate squawked back.

But there was no sight of a petite, redheaded, wild beauty named Chloe.

When he saw the single-track of small, feminine footprints, he sucked in a breath of pure relief. "Gotcha," he murmured, and followed the prints up the beach and around a large outcropping of rock, heading for the cliff.

Where they vanished at the face of the rock.

If it hadn't been for the footsteps, he'd have missed her entirely. Because even tilting his head back as far as he could, she was invisible to him. But he knew she was up there.

He could feel her.

Shaking his head at himself—he could *feel* her?—he began to climb, telling himself that this would be a hands-off talk.

Halfway up, he levered himself over a large, flat rock that jutted out and found her.

Silent, gaze hooded, arms clasped around her knees, her lovely face was in profile but still projecting a loneliness and darkness that called to him.

Because it matched his own.

He crouched in front of her. "Hey."

Chloe turned her head and studied him, from his bare, sandy feet, to his wrinkled uniform, and finally his face. Whatever she saw there had a small smile curving her mouth. "Long night, Sheriff?"

"Jax asked me the same thing."

"It's because you look like shit."

"Yeah, he said that, too."

She nodded and scooted over, a wordless invitation to join her. He crawled in next to her and mirrored her pose.

They watched the waves for a few minutes in easy, companionable silence. He'd gotten the feeling from Tara that Chloe had been upset, but he wasn't getting that vibe from her at all.

No, just that same sense of needing that vague something that he felt deep in his own gut. "Are you all right?"

"Always." She smiled, but it didn't quite meet her eyes. "Same question back atcha, Sawyer."

She didn't often use his given name. He liked the sound of it coming from her lips way more than he should. "Your sisters are worried."

She blew out a sigh and sank farther back against the rock. "They shouldn't be."

"Want me to take you home?"

"Are you asking, or planning on cuffing me and dragging me back?"

"If I cuff you," he said, "the inn is the last place you'll be headed."

She laughed softly. "You're such a tease. You climb up here in uniform often?"

"Almost never."

She looked at him, that damn concern in her eyes again. "You really do look beat."

"I am." He unbuckled his utility belt and set it on a rock.

"Don't stop there," she said.

"Right, and end up on Facebook."

Chloe laughed. "Lucille wouldn't do that to you."

"Only because she knows I'd arrest her."

"Sure you would." Her smile faded, replaced by a thoughtful frown. "Why is that, I wonder?"

"Why what?"

"Lucille loves to shout to the world what you do as Sheriff Thompson, but the private life of Sawyer seems to be off-limits. She never outs you about anything."

"Nothing to tell. I'm always on the job."

"No, seriously. Remember that day you changed her tire? She was telling me all about your younger years, then totally clammed up when she got to your teens."

No, he wasn't tabloid material anymore, thank God. And he owed a big thanks to Lucille for that. "I'm too tired to have that conversation with you right now." Or ever.

"So...you're off duty."

"Finally, yes."

"Good." She rose to her knees at his side and tugged at his shirt, indicating she wanted him to lose it.

He shouldn't, but he must have been even farther gone than he'd thought, because he peeled out of his Kevlar vest, his uniform shirt, then the T-shirt he wore beneath, setting everything on top of his growing pile.

She ran her gaze over his chest with frank appreciation. Then he shivered, realizing he hadn't really considered the weather. It was forty-five degrees max, but Chloe was giving him a go-on gesture with her hand.

"All I have left is my pants," he said.

"Yes, please."

"It's cold, Chloe."

She tilted her head. "Are you worried about shrinkage?"

Well, he was now.

"I've already seen the goods, remember? Trust me, Sheriff, you have nothing to worry about."

Sawyer laughed in spite of himself, then went still when she straddled him. Before he could so much as blink, she'd bent and kissed his collarbone. Then a pec. She touched her tongue to his skin, and he shivered again. *Not* from the cold. "Chloe." That was all he managed to get out. His hands were on her hips, gripping her tight as she shifted over an inch and licked his nipple. He sucked in a breath.

"It looked cold," she whispered and blew a warm breath over his damp skin.

He shuddered, the cold air the last thing on his mind now, as she rocked slowly over the obvious bulge behind his zipper.

"I thought I wanted to be alone," she said, grinding on him until his eyes rolled to the back of his head.

"I know," he managed, tipping her face up to meet his gaze. "But I didn't want you to be."

She smiled. "I like that about you. You listen to everyone, but then come to your own conclusions and do whatever the hell you want."

"If you knew what I wanted to do right now, you'd probably be shoving me off this bluff."

"Don't count on it." She rose a little and covered his mouth with hers.

The kiss rocked his socks off. Or it would have, if he'd been wearing any. He pulled back and looked into her eyes. She was definitely no longer feeling lonely or sad, or anything negative at all. Her eyes were soft and...dreamy.

Dreamy was troubling, because it was more than just lust. Dreamy meant things he couldn't deliver, such as his own emotions. It wasn't that he couldn't feel things for her. He could, and did.

God, he did.

He just had no idea what to do with them. "Chloe—"

"I was thinking about your shower," she said, nuzzling her face against his jaw. "I was sort of hoping to find you there."

"We never did finish what we started that day."

Chloe smiled against him. "Maybe 'we' didn't finish, but I sure did."

He laughed. So did she. And then somehow they were kissing again. "Hold on," he said, regretfully pulling back. "We can't."

"Sorry. That word doesn't compute."

He let out another low laugh and tightened his grip on her when she nipped at his throat. "I'm not risking you having another post-orgasm asthma attack while we're way up here on the rocks," he murmured, groaning when she rocked the hottest part of her over the hardest part of him.

"I have a better idea," she whispered.

Oh, good. One of them could still think. "What?"

She pulled her inhaler from her back pocket and waved it at him. Leaning over him, she lightly kissed first one corner of his mouth, then the other. "And I want you," she whispered, her mouth brushing his with each word. "So much. Please? Please, Sawyer..."

This was her idea? To beg? Because first, that really worked for him. And second...hell. He couldn't remember.

Chapter 19

"The severity of the itch is inversely
proportional to the ability to reach it."
—Chloe Traeger

Chloe lost herself in Sawyer's embrace. It wasn't a surprise, the man could kiss like nobody's business. She was floating on waves of pleasure and desire when he pulled back. "Not here," he said again, putting his gear back on to climb down. "Not on a sandy rock in fifty-degree weather."

The weather had actually improved. Everything was wet and dewy from the rain, and the sky hung low like a covering tarp, but the sun had begun to peek through. She inhaled the salty air coming off the water and the scents of spruce and pine from the woods. Glorious. So was the man trying to give her the bum's rush down the hill. "We could just free the essentials," she said breathlessly.

"Yes, but it's my essentials I'm worried about." He was following her down, climbing with the agility of someone much lighter and smaller than his size. "I don't want anything freezing off."

She laughed. "It's not cold enough."

"Says the woman who doesn't have a part to freeze off."

"And here I thought you were so tough."

"An illusion." He hopped to the sand and then, because apparently she wasn't moving fast enough for him, snatched her off the rock himself for one more bone-melting kiss. Then he had her by the hand and was pushing her toward the stairs.

Apparently, they were in a hurry. She was on board with that and picked up the pace. But that combined with her undeniable excitement worked against her because after a few steps, she felt her chest tighten. Goddammit. "Sawyer—"

He took one look at her, swore, then lifted her into his arms and took the stairs as if she weighed nothing at all.

Laughing breathlessly, she said, "Don't wear yourself out. I have plans for you."

"You just concentrate on breathing," he said, expression dialed into fiercely intent male. "Inhaler?"

"Got it." She pulled it from her pocket and used it as he carried her through his backyard and past the shower.

"Oh," she said, looking longingly at the showerhead. "But—"

"*Bed*," he said firmly.

She wriggled her gritty toes. "I'm sandy."

"You're going to be hot and bothered in a minute," he promised and shouldered open his back door.

She was already hot and bothered, and a shiver of anticipation racked her as Sawyer carried her through the house so fast that she could barely see. "Hey," she said. "You painted some more—"

This was all she got out before she went sailing through the air.

She landed on a huge bed. Before she'd even bounced once, he was on her. He'd removed his Kevlar vest and shirts again, dropping them to the floor with his other gear. Taking both her wrists in one hand, he raised them above her head and pinned them there as he settled over her. She wriggled and lightly tugged to see if he'd free her hands.

"Not yet," he said.

"No?"

"No." He nipped at her chin. "We need to talk first, and if you touch me, I'll forget what I want to say."

This surprised her. "The big, bad sheriff has a weakness?"

"When it comes to you, more than one," he admitted readily and lightly squeezed her wrists, silently telling her to hold still and stop squirming.

Chloe couldn't help it. He was so nice to squirm against, warm and hard in all the interesting spots, his strength barely held in check. "You don't *really* want to talk right now, do you?" she murmured. "*Really*?"

Sawyer let out a breath and dropped his forehead to hers. "Hell, no. But I have to ask. You said before you couldn't have orgasms."

"Which you proved wrong," she reminded him.

"Yes, at your cost." He paused. "So you don't usually..."

"Not in mixed company, no. I can give myself one, if I concentrate on staying real calm and still."

His eyes dilated black. "That's a hell of a contrast. Trying to come while staying calm and still."

She shrugged. "I manage." Fascinated by the way he was looking at her, as if he wanted to gobble her up whole, she heard herself say, "I could...show you. If you wanted."

"Yes," he said very seriously. "I want you to show me." He backed off of her and sat at her hip.

Suddenly a little shy about this venture that had been her idea, she hesitated.

"Here, let me help." In five seconds flat, he had her out of her shoes, socks, and jeans. He stared down at her sunshine-yellow, boy-cut panties and then ran a finger over the smiley face on her mound. "Show me, Chloe."

Closing her eyes, she slid her hand into her panties. A very rough, male sound of appreciation rumbled above her, and then Sawyer encircled her wrist with his warm fingers. Her eyes flew open.

"Slow," he commanded. "Real slow and easy."

"I didn't say slow," she said. "It doesn't have to be slow. Just calm."

"Lots of calm." His thumb scraped over the pulse at the inside of her wrist. "But let's try slow and easy, too."

She knew that he didn't want an ER run. Problem was, she wasn't a slow-and-easy sort of girl. She was more of a hurry-up-before-she-had-an-asthma-attack sort of girl. "Fast is better. That way I have a shot at it."

"Slow and easy," he repeated firmly and then slid his fingers beneath hers so that he was the one touching her. Gently, so gently that she wanted to weep, he glided his fingers over her core. Back and forth, then again. And again. Teasing.

Arousing.

Her moan echoed around them, and then it was her turn to grip *his* wrist. What he was doing was magic, but she needed... "More."

"Shh," he said and kept up that light touch, opening her a little more with each pass of those diabolical fingers, spreading her wetness until she was writhing beneath him.

Then he just stopped.

Gasping, she sat up.

"You okay?" Sawyer asked, eyes on her face.

When she nodded, he put a hand over her chest and nudged her flat on her back again. "Good," he said. "Keep it slow and—"

"If you say easy, I'm going to hurt you."

"I researched asthma online," he said so quietly that it took a moment for his words to sink in. Or maybe it was because his fingers were driving her to the point of madness, affecting her ability to process. But he'd actually taken enough interest to research her problem? It meant something, it had to, but she wasn't sure what. That he liked her? Okay, she could deal with that. She liked him, too. And maybe it'd also been fear based. Her almost dying had scared him. Yes, of course. That made perfect sense.

"I learned that the key," he said, "is relaxation and having a partner that pays close attention to your breathing patterns. I'm paying close attention, Chloe." His smile was both sexy and reassuring and made her chest tighten until she thought she might burst.

"Hey," he said, his gaze narrow with concern. "Are you—"

"*Fine*. It's not the asthma. It's" —she moistened her lips— "you. I don't want to stop."

His gaze immediately went back to her poised hand. "Then don't," he said a little thickly.

She closed her eyes and took a deep breath. Or as deep as she was able. She wasn't feeling asthmatic—yet—but she did feel a little…exposed. "Maybe you could tell me a dirty story," she whispered and heard his soft chuckle.

"Okay," he murmured. "There's this beautiful, gutsy redhead…" He leaned over her on the bed. "She has curves that drive me insane."

"Curves? Is she chunky, then?"

"She's perfect." Sawyer unbuttoned her top and spread it open. She felt his lips on her collarbone, then the swell of a breast. "And she has this way of moving, so confident and sure of herself. It's sexy as hell."

"Sometimes," Chloe whispered, "she fakes the confidence."

"My story," he said and kissed her nipple through the silk of her bra. His mouth was hot, and she arched up into it, moving her hand faster. Her breath hitched, but his fingers settled over hers, stilling her movements, reminding her about the slow-and-easy decree. Before she could object, he tugged down the cup of her bra with his teeth and ran his tongue over her bared nipple. "You were pierced," he whispered against her skin, kissing the pebbled peak.

"Y—yes."

"Why?"

There was no recrimination in his voice, no judgment. Only curiosity. "I don't know." But she did.

Sawyer lifted his head and met her gaze. Not pressing. Just waiting in that way he had that made her want to spill all her secrets.

"Sometimes, I can't...feel," she said softly.

"Here?" His fingers closed over her nipple, plucking the peak like an instrument, and she quivered.

"No." She shifted his hand to her heart. "Here. I couldn't feel anything, and I needed to."

His gaze dipped to her hand, then rose back to her eyes, his own filled with what might have been understanding.

But she wasn't used to that. And anyway, how could he *really* understand? He didn't give a shit about what anyone thought. He could do whatever he wanted, when he wanted. Run. Climb. Have wild animal sex...

"Did it help?" he asked quietly. "The pain?"

She waited to feel the anxiety build in her chest, festering and clawing at her until she shut down in self-preservation. But she was looking right into his eyes, and there was still no judgment, nothing but a simple acceptance, and she didn't get anxious at all. "Yes, it helped," she whispered. "At the time."

"And now?"

"I don't need the pain anymore."

"Good." He flicked his tongue between her breasts and worked his way south. Her hand was still in her panties, her fingers where she needed them, moving in what felt like tandem with his mouth, making her arch up into him.

"Still pierced here," he murmured against her trembling belly.

"I l-like how it looks with my bathing suit. God, Sawyer."

He settled a hand over hers again and slowed her down. "Easy," he murmured.

"If you say that one more time, I'm going to easy your—"

He hooked his fingers into her panties and pulled them down her legs. Then he wedged his broad shoulders between her thighs, getting up close to all her secrets. A groan wrenched from his throat. "Ah, Chloe. You're so wet. No, don't stop."

She'd always assumed that she could make herself come because there wasn't a lot of aerobic action to a self-serve, at least not the way she did it. No stress or performance anxiety involved, just a slightly boring but gratifying release.

But she was definitely feeling a little breathless now, with him holding her legs open, watching her with such avid fascination. Her chest tightened even more, and she realized this wasn't going to work. "Sawyer—"

"Yeah, I know. You're not very good at following directions." He took her hands in his, pulled them to her sides and held them there. "Don't move."

"I—"

He licked the moisture between her legs, and she gasped.

"Keep breathing," he murmured against her skin. "You're holding your breath. In and out, Chloe. Slow."

Was he kidding her? "I *can't*."

"Thought that word wasn't in your vocabulary."

She huffed out a faint laugh. But his hot mouth was still working her, making her tremble, and his name tumbled from her lips as she slid her hands from his and fisted them in his hair.

He stayed the course, hummed her name against her, making her toes curl. She tightened her grip, but he couldn't be rushed. Whenever she tried, he merely captured her wrists again, pinning her legs with his heavy body to hold her still. "Shhh," he told her and then continued.

Slow.

Easy.

Driving her right out of her mind. "Please. Sawyer, *please*."

But her entreaty fell on deaf ears. He did his own thing at his own pace, gently massaging and teasing and coaxing her right into a blissful explosion that shocked and rocked her to the very core.

While she trembled and shuddered back to Planet Earth, he gave her one last soft kiss and moved back up her body to study her face closely. "Okay?" he asked.

"If I was any more okay, you'd have to peel me off the ceiling."

He smiled, but his eyes were still hot, lines of tension bracketing his mouth.

"I really am okay," she said, stunned to realize it was true. She was breathing heavily but not feeling wheezy. "Sawyer?"

"Yeah?"

"Your turn." She pushed him down to the bed. Leaning over him, she took his wrists and forced his hands up to the headboard and curled his fingers around the spindles. She lowered the timber of her voice to imitate his. "Slow," she commanded. "Real slow and easy."

He smiled. "But I don't have asthma—"

"You're not very good at following directions either. I suppose I'll have to take over."

He raised a challenging brow. He was sprawled beneath her wearing only his uniform trousers, his body warm and strong, his every muscle taut. God, so many muscles. Even his feet were sexy. Lord, she had it bad. "I could look at you all day," she whispered.

A flicker of surprise came into his eyes and then heat. "Look all you want," he said. "But first let me—" He let go of the headboard to adjust himself with a grimace.

"Yeah, those pants do look pretty uncomfortable." Batting his hand away, she popped open the button herself.

"Careful," he said when she reached for the zipper.

"Easy, Sheriff. This won't hurt a bit." She unzipped him with great care and then tugged the pants down his long legs, watching as he sprang free. Sitting back on her haunches, she smiled. "Happy to see me?" Leaning forward, she kissed him on the tip of his very impressive erection, making his low reply unintelligible.

He rose onto his elbows to watch her, reaching to glide his fingers into her hair, but like he'd done to her, she shoved him back to the bed.

He gripped the headboard again, tight enough to turn his knuckles white. "Christ, Chloe. You're killing me."

Ditto, she thought, transfixed as the sight of him spread out for *her* viewing pleasure now, so perfectly in proportion from head to toe and all the glorious spots in between. Wrapping her fingers around the base of his hot, silky length, she licked him delicately, then not so delicately, until he shuddered and slid his fingers back into her hair to pull her away. "God, Chloe. You're going to make me—"

"That's the idea."

"Not yet." He grabbed her, hauling her up his taut, heated body until she was straddling him. She gave a little wriggle to get him right where she...wanted...him—

"Oh no, you don't." Gripping her hips, he held her still. "I want you to stay with me this time."

"I'm with you," she promised. "All the way with you. My lungs are good, see?" She inhaled as deep as she could and let it out.

"Good. Keep doing that, keep breathing," he ordered softly.

"I'll do the rest." Biceps flexing, he lifted her up and then allowed her to sink onto him, and exquisite pleasure washed through her as he slid home.

"Your pace," he said. He sounded a little rough and strained, but his hands loosened their grip on her.

Her pace. Normally she'd kick into gear, desperate to get to the finish before it was too late and she couldn't. But he'd already proven that she didn't have to rush. So for the first time, she set an achingly slow rhythm, letting herself get lost in his eyes as she moved on him, feeling each emotion as it shimmered through her.

Love or lust?

Hard to tell. For all she'd done in her life, she'd had little experience with either. But it'd be nice to know which had driven them to this, which was fueling the passion between them, suspending her in a timeless beat. Sawyer's chest was rising and falling quickly, as if he'd just finished a run. Watching him fight to control himself was a huge turn-on.

It was her, she realized, *her* making him pant. Her eyes drifted closed as a sweet climax washed over her. She heard herself cry out, and then Sawyer's low, ragged answering groan as he joined her.

When she opened her eyes, she was lying on top of him, clinging to him with a quiet desperation that surprised her.

"You okay?" he asked, his incredibly sexy voice rumbling up from his chest where her face was plastered.

Since words were still beyond her, she nodded.

He lifted her head to look into her eyes. "Sure?"

She licked her lips. "*Yes*," she managed in a croak.

"Okay, good. Maybe you could loosen the grip just a little?"

She realized it wasn't just her arms and legs gripping him, but that her fingers were digging into his back. "Oh! I'm sorry!" She started to sit up, but he tightened his grip on her. "Just the nails," he murmured, his hands soothing her, holding her still. "The rest stays."

She relaxed again. Actually, slumped bonelessly against him was more like it. She had no idea how much time passed, but when she surfaced again, he was cradling her against his side, lightly stroking her back from the nape of her neck down her spine, over her bottom and the backs of her thighs, then up again as their breathing slowed.

Love or lust? she asked herself again. And if she asked him, would he have any more of an idea than she? No. She didn't want to know. Because maybe it was a little bit of both. And besides, it wasn't a question that needed answering now. She'd just take their odd mix of frustration, heat, affection, and desire and... enjoy it.

For as long as it lasted.

She lifted her head again to look at him. His eyes were closed, body relaxed, all the tension gone from his face. Feeling her gaze, he opened his eyes. "It's good to be inhaler worthy," he said.

She grinned. "I didn't even need it, not during, not once."

Reaching up, he tugged on a strand of her hair, mouth quirking into a smile. "I noticed."

The joy of it surged through her, and she sat up, unable to contain herself. "I got an orgasm, *and* it didn't cost me a thing."

"I'm a regular blue-light special," he said, shaking his head in amusement. "And you even got a twofer."

This was true. "And no asthma attack," she murmured, still marveling at that. "No ER visit."

Nothing to stop them...

Clearly realizing this at the same time, he rolled her beneath him, pressing her into the mattress, his expression dialed to Wicked Intent.

He was hard, and she shivered with anticipation. "Again, Sawyer?"

"Oh yeah," he said, dipping his head to kiss her breast. "And then again."

Chapter 20

*"You have the right to remain silent.
Otherwise, anything you say might be
misquoted and used against you."*
—Chloe Traeger

Chloe slipped out of Sawyer's bed and scooped up her clothes. Sawyer came up on his elbow to watch her dress, hair tousled, eyes sleepy, looking for all the world like a lazy, sated wild cat.

"Gotta get back to the B&B," she told him, torn between getting under his sheets again and facing her responsibilities. "Jax is working on the spa room today. And I'm bringing Lance some lunch and a chest rub. If Renee's there, I'm going to spend some time teaching her how to make it for him. Oh, and we have a guest. A runaway bride, actually. She's been with us a few days and I've been giving her spa treatments to cheer her up. I promised her I'd give her a body wrap today before I head to Seattle. I'm giving facials at some bachelorette party thingy at the Four Seasons."

She'd pulled on her panties and was wriggling into her bra when Sawyer rolled out of bed and headed toward her with that singular-minded intent of his.

The wild cat once again stalking his prey.

"Oh no," she said with a laugh, backing up. "I told you I'm busy today." She pointed at him. "Stay."

"*Stay?*"

"Yes." She put a hand to his broad chest, feeling the strength of him beneath her palm. It was ridiculous to think that she could push him around. Except he'd given her all the power she'd wanted in his bed, and at the thought, her nipples got perky.

Sensing capitulation, he reached for her but she evaded. "I don't know what this is exactly," she said on a shaky laugh. "But for two polar opposites, we sure get along in the sack." Turning away, she picked up her shirt.

"We're not all that different, you know," he said.

She turned back to him and saw that he was serious. He'd found a pair of jeans and had them pulled up but not yet buttoned. Buttery soft, they fit him perfectly, lovingly cupping one of her very favorite parts of him. "Okay, so maybe we're both...well, sort of single," she allowed. "Alone."

He looked at her for a long moment. "You like believing that, I think. That you're on your own."

"I *am* on my own."

"And your sisters are what, chopped liver?"

"Noooo," she said slowly, not sure how they'd gotten so off track. "I mean I've been on my own until recently. Sometimes I forget that I have them."

"And not just them," he said. "There's Jax and Ford now as well."

"And Jax and Ford," she agreed, looking around for her shoes, trying not to notice that he hadn't included himself.

"And the people of Lucky Harbor who care about you," he said. "Lance, Tucker. Amy. Lucille."

She nodded again, fighting back...what? A growing resentment, she realized. Which was ridiculous. He didn't owe her anything, certainly no pretty meaningless words that she'd doubt anyway. "Fine. I stand corrected. I'm not alone. But thinking otherwise is a hard habit to break."

"Because you like thinking it."

She shoved her feet into her shoes and turned to him, hands on hips. "Are you suggesting I like being a martyr?"

"No, I'm suggesting that I don't buy the alone thing, and neither do you."

Okay, *definitely* time to go. She turned to the bedroom door again, needing out. She hadn't had an asthma attack when he'd been buried inside her, but she was closing in on one now.

"And me," he said quietly to her back. "Are you going to leave me off your list?"

Chloe dropped her forehead to the wood. "You want on the list?" Her voice was strong. Which was good. Because she felt small. Small and weak, and wasn't sure she could face him. And dammit, when had she become a coward?

She wasn't. She was just a realist.

"I care about you," he said.

Her heart skipped a beat, and she turned to him, letting out the question that she could no longer contain. "What's happening here, Sawyer?"

He drew a deep breath and slowly shook his head. "I don't know."

Well, at least he was honest. "Maybe I need to know."

"Do you?" There was no amusement in his expression, no mockery in his voice. He was asking her to think about how deep she wanted to dig, how much she truly wanted to hear.

She nibbled on her lower lip and fought with herself. A part of her wanted to admit that yes, she needed to know how he felt about her, that she was, in fact, dying to know if he was as flummoxed as she was over what was happening between them. She needed to know that she was more than a good time to him, that he thought about her, ached for her like she was coming to ache so desperately for him.

But the other part of her, the stubborn, cynical part, refused to ask. Because that would be putting herself out there, laying herself bare before him, and she didn't do that. Ever.

"Chloe," he said softly, watching her carefully. "You can't even tell your sisters how you feel about them. If I told you how I felt, you'd—"

"Have an asthma attack?" She put her hand to her very tight chest. "*Dammit.*"

"Take a breath," he instructed firmly, moving closer, stopping when she held up her hand. "You're holding your breath."

God, she was. The air whooshed out of her lungs in one big massive exit, leaving her deflated. She had no idea if that was relief that replaced it, or desolation.

"Now inhale," he directed.

She did. And then again, ignoring him when he closed the distance between them and cupped her face. "This is panic," he said, studying her features. "Not asthma."

"I know!" She grimaced and pushed free. "I'm working on that. And for your information, I do care about my sisters." At his raised brow, she crossed her arms. "Which means I'm your normal, average woman. A normal, average woman who's just messing around with her local sheriff."

"Chloe." His laugh was short. "You're beautiful, smart as hell, and can make me lose my mind. But you are not, nor will you ever be, *average.*"

"Hey," she said, not missing that he didn't correct the "just messing around" comment. "I could be average if I tried."

"That wasn't a put-down." He ducked to make eye contact, his hands on her arms. "I like you just the way you are."

Sweet, but doubtful. "Well, I wouldn't mind a little bit of average, you know?"

"Why?"

"Why? Because..." She trailed off and rubbed her chest, which was still way too tight. Because his eyes were reflecting something far too close to sympathy, she scrubbed her hands over her face so she didn't have to look at him. "Never mind. Just ignore me." She got to the front door before he spoke.

"Chloe."

"What?"

"Average is boring." He came close, pulled her inhaler out of her pocket, and shook it for her before handing it over. "Have you ever thought that maybe your asthma's triggered by emotional responses rather than physical ones?"

"It's beginning to occur to me," she admitted. "Not that it matters in this case. We're just...messing around." She felt the doorknob at her back and reached behind to grip it, desperate to flee. God. She was so full of shit. The man had taken the time to research asthma, for God's sake. If showing meant more than telling, then damn, he'd hit the bull's-eye. She opened her mouth, praying something brilliant would come out, but all she managed was a "bye" before she escaped.

* * *

Even after his morning coffee, Sawyer was still thinking about the look in Chloe's eyes as she'd left his bedroom, the look that said he'd somehow disappointed her.

He was good at that, disappointing people, but admittedly, she'd really gotten to him. She'd seemed confused and vulnerable, which had caught him off guard.

He'd felt the same. Christ, they were a pair. And work wasn't the time to think about it or he'd get himself or someone else dead, so he forcibly cleared his mind.

His first not-so-big surprise of the day was to learn that Mitch had been picked up at the crack of dawn, high as a kite. He'd already plea-bargained by naming his drug source.

Todd.

According to Mitch, Todd was doing some heavy dealing for a big drug lord. Unlike Mitch, Todd was smart enough to stay off the crap. Apparently Todd and Mitch were equal partners until Mitch had started caring more about his own consumption than selling for their head honcho, and Todd, worried about losing his meal ticket, cut Mitch out of a deal. Now Mitch was pissed and scared enough to point the finger.

But Todd was only the middleman to the bigger fish, a fish that the DEA was already trying to corner. They were now going to use Todd to lead them to him.

Sawyer couldn't say that he was all that surprised about any of it, but he was certainly angry. Especially as he went to Todd's place to try to talk some sense into the ass.

"Christ," Todd said when Sawyer got out of his SUV. "What do you want?"

"We need to talk."

Todd laughed. "Seriously, man? I have nothing to say to you."

"I can get you a deal if you help us out."

"You want me to give you a name," Todd said.

"Yes."

"Not going to happen." Todd got into his truck.

Sawyer let out a breath. He wanted to say fuck it, but he couldn't just walk away. He had no idea why. "It's not too late. If that's what you're thinking. It's not."

Todd's smirk faded, but his eyes stayed hard. "Yeah, it is."

Sawyer watched him drive off, torn between the feeling of

fury and failure. He knew Todd, whether Todd wanted to admit it or not. Todd was stupid enough to try to warn his supplier.

Sawyer would hopefully be smart enough to catch him at it. Sawyer shook his head and turned back to his vehicle. It was done, then. Todd had had as many opportunities as Sawyer to turn his life around, and at every single turn, he'd chosen to fuck himself over. Not happy, Sawyer called the DEA and gave the information to his contact, Agent Reed Morris, detailing everything that Mitch had provided and what Sawyer knew about Todd.

All they needed now was for Todd to lead them right to his next big deal.

Sawyer tried not to feel guilty, relieved, or any other useless emotion. No matter what went down, Todd would blame him. And with some effort, Sawyer hoped he wouldn't blame himself.

Not your fault...

Chloe had told him that, not even knowing the full story. She was like a spring storm—wild and unpredictable, and yet somehow also a calm, soothing balm on his soul. He didn't understand it, not one bit. Nor did he know what to do about the fact that they hadn't burned out on each other as he'd supposed they would.

He still wanted more of her. And he had a sinking feeling that he always would.

And he was back to thinking about her. Perfect. He shook it off as he was called by dispatch to a house where some drunk guy was allegedly punching out all of his mother's windows. When Sawyer arrived at the house, the front door was open. The woman who'd made the call was standing on the porch. "It's my son," she said, voice trembling. She leaned in to whisper, "Tommy's got a drinking problem."

"Is he still inside?" Sawyer asked her.

"Yes." She was wringing her hands. "What are you going to do to him?"

"I'm going to have Tommy come outside to talk."

"But not arrest him, right? He didn't threaten me or anything."

"Ma'am, he's committed malicious mischief with the windows, and that's domestic violence. Plus those windows are probably at least three hundred bucks a pop. If you add it all up, it's a felony. I have to arrest him."

"Oh, God. He's going to be really mad." She bit her lower lip. "I think he needs rehab," she whispered. "Can you take him to rehab?"

Sawyer looked inside the house. Tommy was mid-thirties but looked fifty, like someone right out of a *Cops* episode. He was sitting on his couch in the living room, and in front of him on the coffee table were two rows of at least twenty empty beer cans. On top of one of the cans was perched a pair of sunglasses.

"What are you doing?" Sawyer asked him.

Tommy just kept staring at the cans with the intense concentration of the extremely inebriated. "Isn't it obvious?"

"Humor me," Sawyer said.

"I'm testing my sunglasses. They say they're polarized, but I think the manufacturer is full of shit. I'm gonna sue." He bent, peering through the lenses, then unexpectedly slashed out with his hand, sending the cans and glasses flying against the far wall. "Fuckers."

"Okay," Sawyer said. "How about we go outside?"

"How about I punch you in the face?"

Sawyer hauled him up to his feet.

For the first time, Tommy looked up at Sawyer. And up, taking in Sawyer's size and bulk, exaggerated by the Kevlar vest. The suspect lost some of his aggression. "I was just testing my sunglasses," he said with far less attitude.

Thirty minutes later, he was testing out the bench in lockup, sobering up.

And Sawyer was at career day at the junior high school. God, he hated career day. He didn't mind the no-drugs speech so much, or the kids' questions. No, what he hated were the censorious looks from teachers who remembered him from his own junior high school days.

When that was over, Sawyer had a baseball game, and to his great satisfaction, they kicked the firefighters' collective asses. Then he had a late dinner with Jax at the bar where he pretended not to be watching the front door for Chloe, who didn't make an appearance. At some point, Sawyer was reminded by Jax that as upcoming best man, he'd better be planning a righteous bachelor party.

Sawyer called Ford and told him to get on that.

The next day, Sawyer was trying to catch up on his ever-growing paperwork when dispatch sent him out to talk to a woman who was claiming she'd been robbed. But when Sawyer got to the beauty salon on the pier, the woman wanted to tell him about her twelve-dollar manicure.

"Ma'am," Sawyer said. "You said you were robbed."

"I'm getting to that. The place is all new on the inside, you see?"

"So?"

"So there's no way they can possibly be making it work with twelve-dollar manicures; clearly it's a front for criminal activity."

Sawyer nearly arrested her for being annoying. Instead, he told her if she stopped talking, he *might* see his way to being charitable enough to not ticket her for making a nuisance call.

Then, since he was there on the pier anyway, he went into Eat Me for food, where Amy took one look at him and promptly served him a double bacon blue burger and a huge helping of pie. "Oh, and heads-up—Chloe's here." She hitched her head in the direction of the table behind him, where Chloe was sitting with Anderson, the guy who ran the hardware store.

Amy left Sawyer alone to eat, and he forced his gaze away from the couple. It was no business of his who Chloe ate with. But as he sat there with his burger, Sawyer wondered how he'd feel if she *were* seeing other people.

Shit, he knew the answer to that without even putting his mind in gear. Two months ago, he'd have laughed at anyone who suggested he'd be this attracted and confused and crazy over a woman. But he felt like he was in a fucking tailspin. When he got a call from dispatch, he jumped on his radio so fast he nearly spilled his soda. Used to eating on the road, he grabbed the second half of his burger and ordered himself not to look over at Chloe as he exited the diner.

But he totally looked.

She smiled and waved as if she were truly happy to see him, and his dumb-ass heart lightened. It took some effort to stop picturing her face as he drove to Delilah Goldstein's house. Delilah was eighty-nine, and alone, and once in a while she called in odd reports to 9-1-1. Lucille had adopted her into her posse, but Delilah wasn't as mobile as the other blue-haired hellions that Lucille hung out with.

"What's the matter, Mrs. Goldstein?" Sawyer asked when he stood on her porch.

She peered at him through the screen. "Sawyer? Is that you, dear? Have you been playing doorbell ditch again?"

He bit back his sigh. "No, ma'am. Not in about twenty-five years. I'm a sheriff now, remember? You called in that you needed help."

"Yes, I do need help. I keep hearing Frank Sinatra singing through my TV when it's turned off."

Sawyer paused a beat, then glanced through the screen into her living room. Her TV was definitely off. "Huh." He scratched his chin. He'd seen and heard it all, or so he thought. But this was a new one even for him.

He walked into her living room and squatted in front of the TV, which was at least fifteen years old. The surface didn't have a spec of dust on it, which took a definite talent. But he wasn't hearing any Frank Sinatra. "Do you like Frank Sinatra?" he finally asked Mrs. Goldstein.

"Oh yes, of course. My Stan—God bless his soul—*loved* Frank. We used to listen to him every afternoon at this time of day. Sometimes we'd dance in the living room." She sighed, the sound an expression of grief as she pressed her hand to her mouth.

To give her a minute, Sawyer made a pretense of checking out the back of the TV, but Christ, sometimes this job sucked golf balls.

"Why do you think it happens?" she whispered. "Do you think it's Stan's ghost, or Frank's? Because as fond as I am of Frank's music, I don't want him here in my house, watching me. It feels...scary."

Sawyer straightened and looked her right in the eyes. "It's Stan," he said. "Not Frank."

"You're sure?"

"*Positive*. And I think that you should just enjoy the music, Mrs. Goldstein. Don't be afraid."

She smiled at him, her voice tremulous. "You're a good man, Sheriff."

At least she hadn't said sweet.

She made him stay for coffee and a brownie. "Are you ever going to corral in that wild child Chloe Traeger and marry her?" she asked, bagging up a brownie for him to take with him.

He was so thrown by this question that he just stared at her.

"I only ask because Chloe comes over when I get the head-aches. She massages my temples with this fantastic homemade balm she creates. It's wonderful. She's wonderful. She'd make such a great sheriff's wife."

Chloe, a wife? The mere thought should've made him laugh, but it didn't.

He knew better. Chloe had to be free to do as she wanted; it wasn't in her nature to be "corralled." And it wasn't in his to try to do so. "I'm not exactly marriage material myself, Mrs. Goldstein."

"Oh, hogwash. That's the silliest thing I've ever heard. You young people have no sense of romance. Why, in my day, if you wanted a girl, you went after her. You made her yours."

Yeah, and wouldn't that go over well with Chloe. She just *loved* it when someone told her what to do. Sawyer moved to the door. "Have a good day, Mrs. Goldstein."

"Don't you mean 'mind my own business'?"

Sawyer grimaced, and she laughed. "Listen, dear. I'm old, and probably far too sentimental, but I'm not dead. Not yet. Don't close yourself off to what could be. Or when you're as old as I am, what will be coming out of your TV?"

Metallica sounded good to him.

It was late afternoon, and he was on the road when he got the call that the convenience store that had been robbed several weeks back had set off their alarm again. He raced over there, lights and sirens blaring, to find the owner and the clerk standing outside waiting for him. When Sawyer got out of his SUV, the owner looked at his watch. "Wow, seven minutes," he said, sounding impressed. He smiled at Sawyer. "We just had a new alarm system installed, and this was our dry run. Nice job, Sheriff. Thank you so much."

Christ. Sawyer did his best to unclench his jaw before point-ing out that he wasn't the convenience store's personal security consultant, and they couldn't call 9-1-1 unless there was a true emergency. And then, what the hell, he also took the opportunity to buy two candy bars.

By the time Sawyer pulled up to his house that night, a rainless lightning storm had moved in. Not good. With how dry it had been, it was like playing Russian roulette with lightning-bolt-sized matches on dry timber.

His place looked dark and empty. Empty, he knew, of food, of warmth, of anything remotely welcoming, new paint or not. He walked through his front yard and stopped short at the sight of Chloe sitting on his porch.

She was wearing a long coat and tight leather boots up past her knees but was still huddled into herself for warmth, and without letting himself think, Sawyer pulled her upright and wrapped his arms around her because *she* wasn't dark and empty. She was the opposite, and as she leaned in to him, a feeling surged through him that felt startlingly like relief. And need.

So much fucking need. "You're frozen solid," he said. "What are you doing out here?"

She simply shook her head and pressed her icy nose to his throat, making him suck in a breath. He opened his front door and ushered her inside, where he cranked the heat before turning back to her.

She stood there hugging herself and flashed him a very small smile. "So, um, have you ever done something stupid and then had regrets?"

His heart contracted painfully. If this was where she said she'd just slept with Anderson, he was going to have to shoot the guy, which would suck because Sawyer's department tended to frown on excessive lethal force. "I try really hard not to do anything stupid," he said carefully. "But it happens. Ditto on the regrets. What's this about, Chloe?"

She looked away, but Sawyer hooked a finger under her

chin, turning her face back to his. "Me?" he asked. "You regretting us?"

"No. Never."

He nodded like he understood, but he didn't. "You and Anderson?"

Her eyes widened. She looked startled, then insulted. "Anderson gave me his twenty-percent employee discount for materials for the spa, so I bought him lunch."

Sawyer let out the breath he hadn't even realized he'd been holding, pulled her in again, and kissed her, his body reacting so quickly that it caught him by surprise, and he heard himself groan into her mouth.

Chloe lifted her head. "Do you remember when I said sometimes I need to feel? And that sometimes I do stupid things to get there, like pierce a nipple or hang glide or—"

He ran his gaze over her, thwarted by her damn coat. "Are you hurt? Are you—"

"No." She fumbled with the buttons, then dropped her coat. Beneath she was utterly, gorgeously naked. And beautiful. So fucking beautiful that Sawyer lost his words and his mind. "God, look at you," he said hoarsely.

"Welcome to my latest crazy," she whispered, wearing nothing but those knee-high boots and an unsure smile. "Oh, and you should probably know, I'm quite possibly hypothermic."

"Luckily I've been trained to handle this situation."

Chloe smiled, and he realized she was nervous. He was nervous, too, which made no sense to him whatsoever. They'd been here before, right here. He pulled off his shirt and reached for her at the same moment she leaped at him, wrapping her legs around his hips. He had one hand on her ass, the other high on her back and in her long hair as he carried her to his bedroom. Lying her on the bed, he stepped back only to get rid of his gun and phone, then strip out of the rest of his clothes, which he did in less than five seconds. *Mother of God, let nobody have an emergency tonight, he thought.*

He had a moment where he stared down at her on his bed in nothing but those fuck-me boots, not wanting to take them off. But then she shivered, and he reluctantly tugged them from her feet and dropped them to the floor before shoving her beneath his thick covers and following her in. "Step one," he said. "We conserve body heat."

"Good plan." She turned to him, wrapping her frozen limbs around him.

He hissed in a breath when she pressed her frozen toes into his calves, but her own breathing wasn't anywhere close to even, and he paused. "Need your inhaler?"

She shook her head. "I need you."

He opened his mouth, but she put a finger over his lips. "I'm done talking now."

Yeah. So was he. But when her icy fingers walked their way down his chest and stomach, he sucked in another harsh breath and grabbed her hand, rubbing it between his to warm it up.

She laughed at him, but he knew how to shut her up. He kissed her hard and long and deep, running a hand down her quivering body, sliding it between her thighs. Ahhhh. She wasn't cold here. She was already hot and slick and ready. "You want me."

She smiled. "Yes. Whatever this is that we're doing, I want you. I've always wanted you."

Her softly whispered words staggered him. It hadn't been a confession of love. Hell, he knew that she didn't do confessions of love.

So why did it feel like one?

Because he wasn't doing so well at controlling his emotions with her, that's why. "I want you, too," he said, sure as hell not able to remember a time that he hadn't.

Pulling him down, she kissed him, and he let himself sink

into the kiss, into her, willingly drowning in her heat, grateful that he couldn't talk and kiss at the same time because he was dangerously close to spilling his guts.

"Now," she said against his lips.

"No, not yet. I want to—"

"*Sawyer.*"

Like he really stood a chance against the sound of his name on her lips. Cradled by her open thighs, he slid into her.

Home.

Slow, he reminded himself, searching her face for signs of distress. But he found only desire and hunger and closed his eyes as her hands ran over his chest, his arms, everywhere she could reach, swamping him with pleasure. He pulled back and thrust again, deeper now, groaning at the feel of her, but hesitated when her nails dug into his shoulders.

"No, don't stop," she said, soft and throaty, still showing no signs of trouble. "Please don't stop." Accompanying this sexy little plea, she made a restless circular motion with her hips, and he lost the tenuous grip on his control.

This morning he'd run three miles on the beach, and he'd been in good enough shape not to feel the exertion overly much. Now, here in her arms, buried in her body, his breath was coming in ragged pants. He reared up on his hands, back arched to get as deep as he could as he began to move. When she cried out this time, he recognized it was a plea for more, and he gave it.

She cupped his face, slid her fingers into his hair, and beamed up at him. God, he loved her smile. She felt so good. Her eyes were a staggering, fathomless green, and looking at her made him ache so much that he ran out of air.

Completely. Ran. Out. He struggled to breathe and thought this must be how she felt. But then she pressed her mouth to his and gave him her air. He groaned and continued to move in and out of her, harder now, faster, and then she came, her eyes filled with a faint, endearing surprise as her body clenched around him.

God, she felt so good. Just watching her sent him spiraling. It began deep inside, racing through his body so that his arms trembled, and he dropped his head with a rough groan, burying his face in the curve of her neck as he completely lost himself.

Chapter 21

"Anything worth taking seriously
is also worth making fun of."
—*Chloe Traeger*

The next day Chloe gave a yoga class for one. Allie never stopped talking the whole time, about the amazing burgers at Eat Me, her Cute Guy sighting at the liquor store, how there was never a line at the post office here... She loved the people and wasn't sure she missed anyone from home.

"Not anyone?" Chloe asked.

Allie lifted a shoulder.

"It's okay to miss him," Chloe said quietly. "It's okay to miss John."

And for the first time all week, Allie clammed up.

They were still stretching on the beach when Maddie and Jax pulled up to the inn. Maddie started to get out of the Jeep, but Jax drew her back, buried his hands in her hair, and kissed her.

"He's going to inhale her right up," Allie noted, sounding a little wistful.

"They're getting married. I think all almost-marrieds act like that." Chloe winced as soon as she said it, remembering why Allie was here. "I'm sorry, I—"

"No. Don't be sorry." Allie sat Indian style on the mat and stared out at the water. "I can't hide out from it forever."

"I know you've been in contact with your family. Have you called John at all?"

"No." She closed her eyes and inhaled deeply. "I made a mistake, Chloe. A big one. Things got intense before the wedding. There was so much to do, and everyone was trying to be involved..." She shook her head. "I lost sight of what I was doing, and why. John wanted to be a part of the planning, and I told him I could handle it. A bride should be able to handle it. I pushed him away. And then when he finally took a big step back, I fell apart and pushed him farther." She bit her lip. "And then on my wedding day, I felt alone. So alone. It was all of my own making, but I couldn't see that." She turned to Chloe. "So I ran. When the going got tough, I ran like a little girl."

Chloe understood both the pushing people away and the feeling alone. And hell, if she was being honest, she understood the running too. She'd spent years perfecting all three. "It's never too late to face a regret." She handed Allie her cell phone. "You don't have to tell him where you are or—"

Allie snatched the phone so fast that Chloe's head spun. She rolled up her mat and moved toward the inn to give Allie some privacy, but before she'd gotten out of earshot she heard, "Baby? It's me." Allie's breath hitched audibly. "John, I'm so sorry— in some Podunk little place called Lucky Harbor. Really? You will? You'll come? Oh, John..."

* * *

Sawyer knocked on his father's door but wasn't surprised when no one answered. For three days now, it'd been the same story. Worried, Sawyer let himself in and dropped the two bags of groceries he'd brought with him on the kitchen table.

From somewhere in the house, he heard a toilet flush, and then his father shuffled into the kitchen, scowling. "Nice knock," he grumbled at Sawyer.

"I did knock. And I called, too. You're avoiding me."

"I was on the pot."

"I've been calling all week. Wanted to help you fix the gutters."

"My boy did it."

Okay, last Sawyer checked, *he* was Nolan's boy. "I would have—"

"I hate carrots," his father said, nosing through the bags. "And blueberries. Christ, this is fucking sissy food."

"It's good for you." Sawyer eyed his father. White wife-beater dulled by years of washings, dark blue trousers hitched up to just beneath a beer belly. "You need to eat healthier."

"I've eaten how I want for sixty years."

"Yes," Sawyer said. "Hence your health problems."

"Goddammit!" His father waved a hand and knocked the bag to the floor. "*My* business, not yours."

Whether he'd accidentally hit the food or not, it pissed Sawyer off. He could handle drug dealers and gangbangers without losing his cool, but five minutes with his father and his temper was lit. "Listen—"

"No, *you* listen," his father snarled, spitting out his words like venom. "Where in the hell do *you* get off telling me how to run my life?"

"Since your doctor said you were going to die if you didn't change!"

"Well, fuck the doctor!" Nolan bellowed. "He's a twelve-year-old, skinny-ass punk kid."

"Dr. Scott is *my* age," Sawyer said, keeping his voice quiet and controlled with great effort. "Josh and I went to school together." In fact, the two of them had spent many, many Saturdays in detention together, driving the high school teachers insane.

"You mean you were good-for-nothing *thugs* together," Nolan snapped.

"Whatever he was, Josh is a doctor now. And a good one," Sawyer said. "Jesus, Dad! You can't hold his past against him." But then he let out a short, mirthless laugh. "What am I saying? Of course you can hold his past against him. You do mine."

Nolan jabbed a meaty finger to the door. "Get out."

"Gladly." Sawyer strode to the door. "Tell your perfect little gofer boy that the porch light's out."

* * *

Exhausted as she was, Chloe did the happy dance around the sunroom. No, she corrected. Not the sunroom—the Lucky Harbor Day Spa.

Well, it was *almost* a spa anyway. It was at least finished enough to have provided a short menu of services for the family of sisters, who as of two hours ago had checked out after a long weekend stay.

The week before, Jax had thrown together a changing room, hooked up the plumbing, and painted the last of the trim an hour before the two massage chairs for pedicures had been delivered, along with the shipment of towels and robes. Chloe already had a portable massage table, so that hadn't been an issue.

Granted, there was still more to do to make it a full-service spa, but she had made it work for now.

Grinning, she spun in a circle and collapsed onto a cushy chair. The important thing was that the weekend had been a huge success. And fun. It'd been a sister-team effort, with Tara making

No-Guilt-Here foods and Maddie introducing "chick night" events complete with knitting sessions and tissues-required classic movies. Chloe had given facials, mud skin treatments, and massages, along with yoga classes.

Every single one of the guests had not only rebooked for other treatments but had bought gift certificates for friends and family.

Chloe was extremely aware of how much she'd enjoyed the weekend, and exactly what she was giving up to have, hopefully, many more. She knew offers like the one she'd had from the San Diego spa didn't grow on trees, but she felt committed to Lucky Harbor, to being here. To her sisters as well.

Her heart wanted to add Sawyer to that list, but her brain reminded her that Sawyer was fun and heat and magic—but that he'd not exactly shown any signs of wanting more.

Neither have you...

She leaned back in the chair and sighed. It was nine o'clock at night, and for the first time in days, she was all alone. Blissful, she put up her tired feet and closed her eyes.

"Aw, look at her, all plum tuckered out. I guess taking people's money is hard work."

At Tara's soft, teasing Southern drawl, Chloe opened her eyes and found her sisters standing in the doorway. "Hey. I thought you'd both left."

"Not yet, sugar." Tara was carrying a bottle of wine in one hand, three glasses in her other. She set them down on the low-lying counter that Chloe had just cleaned, then plopped onto the spa chair and stretched out her long legs. As always, she was in heels. She kicked them off and wriggled her toes. "Lord Almighty, I should have done that about four hours ago." Thoughtfully, she studied the rack of nail colors.

Maddie sat, too. "Long weekend." She smiled at Chloe. "I had a very lovely time just now adding up all the receipts. You've made our bank account very happy."

Chloe wanted to ask *And how about you two, are you happy?* But she didn't. She was afraid of the answer. "I took a booking for six girlfriends for next weekend. Seems we're going to be known for the girls' weekend out sort of thing."

"There's worse things to be known for," Maddie said, covering Chloe's hand in hers. "Heads-up—mushy alert warning."

"What? No, I—"

But before Chloe had finished sputtering, Maddie reeled her in and hugged her.

"Tell her you love her, Mad," Tara said, still prone on her chair. "It'll make her as wild as a peach orchard hog."

Chloe, laughing now, tried to escape, but Maddie squeezed her tighter. "I *lurve* you," Maddie said with as much sap as she could.

Chloe stuck her finger into her mouth and then stuck the wet digit in Maddie's ear.

Maddie collapsed in laughter while screaming "ewwww" and dropped to the floor.

"A wet willy," Tara said calmly, nodding. "Nice tactic."

Chloe brushed her hands together and smirked down at Maddie. "Round two?"

Maddie rolled to her belly and cushioned her head on her arms. "Hell, no. I'm too tired." She crawled to the spa chair where Tara was still sprawled and pulled herself up, curling to share the space. She eyed the nail colors too, then picked out a baby blue. And then a siren red. She looked at Chloe speculatively, then grabbed a metallic silver, and then also a solid black. "Can you open the windows, Chloe? It's not so cold out, and you'll need fresh air for this."

Chloe dutifully opened the windows.

"Now sit," Maddie said.

Which Chloe did gladly since she was exhausted.

Maddie pulled Chloe's feet into her lap. "Nice toes. You got them from Mom. Mine are short and stumpy from my dad, of course." She painted Chloe's big toe the metallic silver, then painted every other toe before filling in the opposite ones with the black.

"Silver and black?" Tara asked, amused. "Different. Suits her."

"Yeah, I thought so, too. You're getting red, by the way," Maddie said, and proceeded to switch to Tara's feet. "And you have pretty feet too, you bitch. Pour the wine, Tara."

Tara arched a brow in Chloe's direction, like *look at our little mouse now*. But she obeyed and poured three glasses of wine, handing one to Chloe and another to Maddie. Finally she took her own and lifted it. "To a hell of a day and a very pretty bottom line."

Tara and Maddie drank deeply to that. Chloe watched them, an unexpected warmth spreading inside her chest. So much had changed so quickly. Tara and Maddie, Ford and Jax, the spa, and of course, Sawyer, who'd made an indelible mark on her life, more than anyone else ever had. She still didn't know what would become of them, and imagining that someday he'd tire of her hurt like hell, so she let her thoughts spin back to her sisters. They would always be here for her. She knew that now. It wasn't just a concept anymore. It was a fact. They were her anchor in a lifetime spent free-floating.

Chloe set aside her untouched wine. She wanted a clear head for this. But more than that, she also wanted to be able to drive herself to Sawyer's later tonight. Thanks to their very busy schedule, it'd been six nights since she'd last been in his bed, naked in his arms, panting his name, letting him take away everything but what they gave each other. Funny, because she'd gone a whole year without sex, and now six days was too long. Or was it simply Sawyer himself that she missed?

"I can't believe it, really," Maddie said.

Chloe started guiltily. "What?"

Maddie began to paint her own toes with the baby-blue polish. "How far we've come. I can't believe it."

Okay, good. They weren't talking about Chloe's sex life.

Tara nodded. "Do you realize that we've each managed to bring a vital part of ourselves to the inn?"

Chloe stared down at her sparkling toes. "Is that it?" she wondered. "Or is it that this place has given each of us something we needed?" When nobody spoke, she looked up. Both her sisters were staring at her, eyes moist.

"Oh, Christ." Chloe sighed and grabbed some napkins, shoving one at each of them. "I swear, if either of you cries, I'm giving out more wet willies, followed by wedgies. I mean it."

"I have a better idea." Maddie stood up. "Our first night here together we stayed up all night decorating our poor Charlie Brown Christmas tree. Do you remember?"

"Hard to forget," Tara said. "Chloe turned our faces and hair green with her facial and conditioner masks, remember?"

"Hey," Chloe said in her defense. "It improved your skin, didn't it?"

"Excuse me." Maddie tapped a fingernail against the wineglass to get their attention, then cleared her throat dramatically. "I'm trying to recount our adventures here, so pay attention. And I do have a point."

"You going to get to it anytime soon?" Chloe asked.

"Do you or do you not remember when we decided to make this place a B&B?" Maddie asked. "We—"

"*We*?" Tara interrupted, laughing. "If we're remembering, then let's remember how it really happened, shall we? *We* didn't decide anything, Maddie. *You* two corralled me into the B&B thing, specifically the chef part. And you did it by dangling Ford in front of me."

"Oh, and that turned out so awful, right?" Chloe responded dryly. "And let me guess—you *hate* being your own boss. You hate ordering us around in the mornings to do your bidding. Is that what you're saying?"

Tara smiled. "No, I really like that part. A lot."

"Hello," Maddie said sternly. "I'm talking here!" She paused for dramatic effect, but when Chloe and Tara just rolled their eyes, she sighed. "Don't you get it? We need to do something. We need a ceremony for this milestone!"

"It's too early for a Christmas tree," Chloe said.

Maddie tossed up her hands. "Something *new*! Something unique. To celebrate *you*," she said. "To celebrate the spa thing." She scrunched up her face to think, then grinned wide, and then slumped. "I had something. But I forgot."

Chloe laughed. "That cheap date thing must be hereditary."

"Yeah," Maddie admitted with a laugh. "Half a glass and I'm gone. Wait, I think I remember. Maybe."

"Uh-oh," Chloe said to Tara. "I feel something inadvisable coming on."

"Well, sugar, if anyone's going to recognize it, it'd be you."

"Recognize this," Chloe said and flipped Tara off.

"We need to mark this milestone," Maddie insisted.

"We can go to the mud baths," Chloe said, knowing damn well that they'd both shoot her down, tell her she was crazy, and then she could finally go jump Sawyer's bones.

And he had such *fine* bones, too...

"That's *brilliant*!" Maddie stood up and grabbed them each by the hand. "We're going to the mud springs!"

"Wait—what?" Chloe asked.

"It's a great idea," Maddie said, tugging them both along.

Chloe dug in her heels. "Hold up."

"Why?" Maddie asked.

"Because first, you're drunk. Second, I was totally kidding."

"Tell me that it wouldn't be the *perfect* thing to do." Maddie let go of them to clasp her hands together and jump up and down. "Oh, come on! Do this for me and...and I won't make you get me a present for my wedding shower!"

"But it's pitch-black outside," Tara said.

"Actually," Chloe said, "it's a full moon." Too late, she clamped her mouth shut. *Dammit*, she had plans for Sawyer and his naked bod beneath that full moon.

"Yeah," Maddie said to Tara. "It's a full moon, pansy ass."

"You know what?" Chloe shook her head. "I don't think it's a good idea."

"You suggested it, genius," Tara reminded her.

"Yeah, but I was joking." But it was the disappointment shining in Maddie's eyes that killed her. "Okay, don't do that. Not the Bambi eyes."

"I thought you'd appreciate the fact that I'm willing to do something that's so *you*," Maddie said. "After all, the spa was your baby."

"Yes, and I do appreciate it." And only a few weeks ago, Chloe would've been the first one out the door, not sitting here considering the fact that it was late and not altogether safe to be slipping and sliding around the springs. She glanced at Tara, then back to Maddie, and sighed. "Fine. *Jesus*. Why the hell not?"

"Yay!" Maddie polished off her wine, grabbed another bottle, then pulled them through the inn to her car, tossing Chloe, the only sober one, the keys.

Chloe thought for a second, then ran back inside for everything she'd wished she'd had the first time: towels, three spa robes, flashlights, and even though it took another trip, she hauled out three big gallons of fresh water to clean off with. When she returned, still laughing at herself a little for being the only grown-up of the bunch—*how scary was that*?—she found Tara still standing outside the car.

"Did she really call me a pansy ass?" Tara asked in a hushed whisper that the people of China could have heard.

"We have to get her a present for her wedding shower?" Chloe whispered back as she tossed the stuff into the trunk. "Because I thought the wedding shower *was* the present."

They got to the trailhead just after eleven, and Chloe felt like a pagan white witch leading her sisters up the trail by flashlight.

Once at the mud springs, they had no trouble seeing. The moon had cast the meadow in a pale blue glow. Steam rose off the mud into the night, and Chloe shivered. "I don't know—"

"And you call yourself the wild child," Maddie chided and stripped down to her tiger-striped panties and bra. "I think we should switch monikers. *You* be the mouse. I'll take wild child, thank you very much!" So saying, she dipped a toe into the mud, then holding the bottle of wine like she was of the highest royalty, waded in up to her waist and sighed in bliss. "Warm."

"Since when do you have tiger-striped underwear?" Chloe asked.

Maddie blushed, her face lighting up like a glow stick in the night. "They were a present from Jax. Isn't it gorgeous out here, all silvery and mysterious? You can almost see the forest fairies."

"Okay, no more wine for you," Tara said. She eyed the mud and sighed. "I must be insane." But she followed suit after Maddie and stripped. Though, of course, *she* took the time to carefully hang her dress over a branch. Her underwear was not tiger-striped but a pale, silky cream and lace that screamed sophistication and elegance. Or at least as much as one can scream sophistication and elegance while standing in your underwear in the woods at eleven.

Chloe was hands on hips staring at them. "For the record, I have never called myself the wild child."

"Come on in, Mouse," Maddie called.

"Nor did I ever call you the mouse." At least not to her face. Chloe kicked off her shoes. "Though I think we should call you Queen Bee-yotch. Damn, it's cold out here!"

"Only until you get in," Maddie promised, tossing back some more of the wine right out of the bottle before handing it over to Tara.

Chloe wriggled out of her jeans, then hesitated there in her panties and sweater. She wasn't wearing a bra.

Tara made the sound of a chicken.

Chloe rolled her eyes and tore off her sweater. When she was up to her chin in the mud, Tara grinned at her. "You took out your nipple ring."

"Last year," Chloe said, watching as Maddie snatched the bottle of wine back from Tara.

"Really?" Tara asked Chloe. "Why?"

"I don't know. It kept catching on my bra." Which was true, but it'd been more than that. Somehow, at some point, she'd realized she'd outgrown the need to be so wildly different. It'd been right about the time that the three of them had agreed to stick together and renovate the inn. They'd been halfway through the renovation when there'd been a bad fire, forcing them to start over. The fire had been devastating in many ways, but by some miracle, they'd survived. And it'd been that night, lying in the ER, suffering from a smoke-induced asthma attack, with a sister on either side of her, that Chloe had known.

She'd been singed nearly to a crisp, lost everything including the clothing on her back, but it hadn't mattered because she had her sisters and she loved them. "I do," she said softly to herself, nodding. "I really do."

"You believe in fairies?" Maddie asked, confused.

Tara took the wine from her. "Shh, sugar. I think Miss Wild Thang's having an epiphany. Let's leave her to it."

Chloe stared at them. Tara was in the middle of carefully

streaking the mud on her jaw in order to get the maximum benefit from it. Maddie had done her face already and looked like a
zebra. And Chloe felt a smile bloom both in her heart and on her
face. "To us," she said softly.

"To us," Maddie said, and drank to that.

* * *

Sawyer got the call from the forest service about midnight. It
was Matt, reporting flickering lights had been seen on the trails
out at Yellow Ridge. Matt was on Mt. Jude, the far side of the
county, a good hour away, and couldn't respond to the call. "I'm
contacting you," he said, "because the caller gave a description
of a hopped-up shiny black truck going off-road, and it sounded
like Todd's. I know you're watching him. I can call another
ranger, but it might be morning before I can get anyone out there,
and as you know, those trails are supposedly closed at nightfall,
thanks to the fire season."

"I'll go," Sawyer said, already in his truck, knowing this was
it. If he caught up with Todd, he'd catch whoever Todd was
working for. It was the break they were looking for. He was
already on call twenty-four seven for the DEA until they closed
in on their drug case, which most likely involved Todd one way
or the other. Twenty minutes later, he was shining his flashlight
on the car in front of the mud springs trailhead, shaking his head
in disbelief.

Maddie's car. What the hell was she doing up here? He
flickered his flashlight in the window and saw a purse on the
passenger floor. He thought maybe it was Tara's. There was a
phone on the backseat. He was pretty sure it was Chloe's iPhone,
which explained why she hadn't picked up any of his calls.
"What are you three up to?" he murmured.

No doubt the three sisters would have an explanation that

would make him dizzy. Chloe might just be the most impulsive person he'd ever met, but she was also one of the sharpest. She had a reason for most everything she did, although sometimes the reason was to turn the world on its ear. But Tara and Maddie? He'd have figured them more sensible than to follow her up here.

Hell, it was fall. Bears were on the hunt to store up their winter fat. Coyotes were doing the same. Not to mention that in spite of the combined efforts of the forestry service and his own county department, there'd been plenty of illegal camping and hunting going on during this long, late Indian summer.

He needed to let it go. They were three grown women and could handle themselves. His job was Todd. If he was out here, he was up to no good, but the demands and conflicts of his job had never been stronger as he caught sight of the iPhone in the backseat of Maddie's car.

Fuck.

He eyed the trailhead, and the sign there, posted by the forest service.

TRAIL CLOSES AT NIGHTFALL.

Swearing beneath his breath, he headed up the path. There were several forks, and he methodically worked his way along each until twenty-five minutes later he came to a clearing and stood staring in utter disbelief. Three heads appeared to be floating disembodied in a mud spring by the light of the moon.

"Hey," he said to the three sisters, hands on hips, "if it isn't Curly, Larry, and Moe."

The three faces grinned. Sawyer had long ago schooled himself to be braced for surprise, trouble, danger... anything. And he had a really good blank, cop face. He knew this because it was that face that allowed him to whip Jax's and Ford's asses in poker every single time. But it was a struggle to stay blank at the sight before him.

Far above them, the moon's glow gave off an unearthly feel, and with nothing surrounding them but isolated wilderness, the three women might have been ancient Indians in their war paint.

The tallest one narrowed her eyes and spoke with a Southern accent. "We were thinking more along the lines of *Sex and the City* than *The Three Stooges*," she drawled.

The next one squealed with delight at that. "Oh! I want to be Carrie! I've always wanted to be Carrie!"

The petite one just studied Sawyer meditatively. "I think we should make him join us," she said, her expression angelic, her voice pure devil. "He doesn't always wear underwear, you know."

Six eyes swiveled to his crotch.

Christ. He resisted cupping himself.

"Come on in, Sheriff," the little minx called softly. "We don't bite."

"You're drunk." Perfect. He should arrest them all for public intoxication *and* public nudity, not to mention being out here on closed trails, but hell if he could make himself do it. Where was Lucille when Facebook needed her? He pulled out his cell phone.

Tara gasped. "What are you doing?"

"Getting a shot for Lucille. You're going to be even more popular than the elusive Cute Guy."

Maddie and Tara squealed and immediately gave him their backs.

Chloe held her ground, watching him. "You wouldn't."

"I should."

"Come in."

"Not gonna happen." If she'd been alone, he'd have been

tempted. Which was a sorry thing. Before she'd come along, the thought not only wouldn't have entered his mind but would've appalled him.

He pressed the button on his phone to check for calls from Agent Morris before he remembered—no service up here. "Okay, everyone out." He held out his hand to Maddie first because she was finger-painting Chloe's face and looked to be the most gone. She didn't come out. No one did. Tara was gathering the hair off her neck, her skin gleaming pale and smooth beneath the moonlight, looking like some sort of Greek goddess. Maddie finished with Chloe's face and began humming a song to herself while doing some sort of dance. Chloe grabbed her before she could dance her way farther into the shadows. "Whoa there, Pocahontas," she said, snagging her sister by the arm, surging up out of the mud to her waist to do so.

She wasn't wearing a bra, and Sawyer swallowed hard. "Chloe—"

She sent him an innocent smile and pulled both sisters out of the mud, wrapping them each up in towels before reaching for her own towel.

Sawyer turned his back and stared hard up at the stars. He tried a few multiplication tables, but it couldn't hold up against the images of three gorgeous women covered in mud, washing each other off.

By the time Chloe came up to his side, cleaned and grinning, he was sweating. "You can look now," she murmured.

They were all dressed, thank God. He could stop picturing Ford's and Jax's women, nude by the pale moon's glow.

But he didn't have to stop picturing Chloe.

They walked together down the path, making it in twenty minutes back to Maddie's car. He then followed them down the road to the highway in his truck, getting out when Chloe pulled Maddie's car over to the side.

"Just wanted to say thanks for checking on us," she said when he'd walked up to the driver's door and she'd rolled her window down.

His phone beeped as his cell service kicked in, and he realized he had messages. From where he stood, he could also hear dispatch trying to get him on his radio. *Shit*. He listened to the first message on his cell and his blood ran cold.

"Sawyer?" Chloe's smile faded. "You okay?"

He held up a hand, listening. Dispatch had been trying to reach him. Agent Morris had been trying to reach him. Everyone and their mother had been trying to reach him. In the forty minutes he'd been out of range, all hell had broken loose. There'd been a reported drug deal before the DEA could mobilize. They had a witness, a hiker, who claimed that he'd seen the whole thing but by the time the authorities had arrived, everyone had scattered.

It'd been only a few miles from here.

The DEA had gone to Todd's place to discover that not only had they missed whatever had gone down tonight, Todd had cleared out entirely, probably holed up waiting until the heat was off.

No doubt thanks to Sawyer going to Todd, trying to interrogate him about his drug source and offering him a deal. Instead Todd had packed up his shit and vanished.

"Sawyer?"

"I've got to go." He strode back to his truck, vibrating with anger. Jamming his key in the ignition, he tossed his cell on the seat, then peeled out of the parking area, furious at himself. He'd known he was the only one on the DEA task force actually stationed in Lucky Harbor, and he'd also known better than to be out of cell service that long, but as always, being anywhere near Chloe stole his good sense.

Not her fault. Nope, this one was all on him, and it'd been at the expense of the job that meant everything to him.

Chapter 22

*"Women might not like to admit their age,
but men don't like to act theirs."*
—*Chloe Traeger*

Chloe stared after Sawyer's truck, Maddie's headlights cutting through the cloud of dust in his wake.

"What the hell was that?" Maddie asked. She sat in the backseat, a towel wrapped around her hair. She didn't sound drunk now. "He seemed mad."

"He wasn't angry before," Tara said from her shotgun position in the front seat.

Now that the dust had settled, Chloe pulled back onto the road, replaying the evening in her head. "It wasn't about us," she said. "I think it was about his messages. Something must have happened."

"I hope everything's okay," Maddie said. "I'd hate it if he missed helping someone because of us."

Chloe, too. She'd never seen Sawyer react like that before.

It wasn't his style. Usually when things went to hell, he got calm and quiet. Steady as a rock. It had to be something bad. Her thoughts went first to his father, but that didn't hold up. If he'd had a heart attack, Sawyer would have been concerned, not angry.

"He sure was surprised to find us in the mud," Maddie said. "I can't imagine what he was expecting, but I can guarantee it wasn't the three of us in war paint."

Chloe thought of Sawyer's expression when he'd come into view at the edge of the trail and found them. He'd been irritated, then relieved to find them. Then he'd looked right at her and hadn't even tried to hide his affection.

The memory brought an unexpected lump to her throat. Jax and Ford had known Sawyer forever, and yet he hid his emotions from them all the time. His emotions and his weaknesses...

But not from her.

He let her see him, all of him. It was a gift, she realized. The gift of himself.

She'd never had such a thing offered to her before, and she was still thinking about it, marveling at it, when she dropped Tara and a very groggy Maddie at the inn. No one even bothered to suggest cleaning out the car tonight. Jax and Ford were waiting to pick up their women.

Chloe parked and walked around back to the cottage. It was with mixed feelings that she went inside, alone.

She stripped there in the doorway and stepped gingerly to the bathroom, where it took her nearly an entire bottle of her own shea butter body wash to get clean. Afterward, she slid naked between the soft sheets of her bed and listened to the quiet creaks and groans of the place around her. Several months ago, she and Lance had joked about the sounds coming from a ghost, a lonely one.

Chloe knew the feeling...

No. Life was good, she reminded herself firmly. She and her sisters seemed to be in sync. The inn was doing well. Her past was her past, and her present was actually moving along.

It was only her future in question. A future she couldn't quite see or imagine. She flopped over and told herself she'd never given her future much of a thought, so why the sudden worry now?

The answer was terrifyingly simple.

For the first time, she was feeling content. And she wanted the feeling to last, even though she knew from experience that nothing lasted.

Sleep didn't come. Just more concern. She debated calling Sawyer, but... but she had a bad feeling about whatever it was that had happened tonight. She didn't want to interrupt him from something important.

But on the other hand, he could already be home, and not calling her because he thought *she* was asleep.

Which settled it. She'd go to his place, see if his truck was there. If he was mad, he could tell her in person.

When she pulled into his driveway twenty minutes later, she let out a breath at the sight of his truck. Parking the Vespa next to it, she headed up the walk and knocked softly.

Sawyer opened the door in low-slung jeans and nothing else but a decent amount of testosterone-driven attitude. For the first time since they'd been doing this, he didn't seem happy to see her, and dread enveloped her heart. "Is it too late?" she asked much more mildly than she felt.

"Since when has that stopped you?"

She stared at him for a beat, then turned to go. "I shouldn't have come—"

"Chloe." He sighed and pulled her back around. "Come in. You're cold."

No, she was scared. Not of him, never of him, but of what was going to happen between them.

Or not happen.

With butterflies flying around in her gut, she shut the front door and leaned back against it. She tried to get a read on him, but as usual, his face was giving away nothing. "I didn't think you were upset about the mud springs," she said. "Which, by the way, wasn't my idea." She winced. "Okay, so it was, but I'd been just kidding, and then Maddie was all over it, and—"

"It's not about the mud springs."

"Are you sure, because—"

"Not everything revolves around you, Chloe." And at that, he walked away.

"Well, I know that—" But he wasn't listening. He was gone. Her initial thought was to walk out the door, just let everything go. The old Chloe would've done that in a heartbeat. But she didn't want to be that Chloe anymore, that person who skipped town rather than face hard reality.

So she pressed a hand to her nervous stomach, dropped her purse in the entry, and forced herself down the hall after him. That's when she saw the low wooden coffee table, and against the wall, an entertainment unit.

Sawyer had been busy making the place look more like a home.

She found Sawyer in the master bathroom, reaching through the shower to open the window there. To her surprise, one wall was half painted. It'd been a rather outdated shade of green, which he was covering up with the wildly imaginative off-white. "How did you decide on a shade?" she asked.

"It was on sale."

She might have smiled if it hadn't been for the knots in her gut. "It's two a.m."

"Yep." He reached for the roller.

Every part of her wanted to run for the door, say what the hell, it'd been fun while it lasted, because she'd known, God, she'd known, that this couldn't last.

But the hell with being a big, fat chicken. She was braver now. She didn't understand. She needed to understand. "So what was that call about earlier? More crazy women skinny-dipping by moonlight somewhere?"

"No." He rolled a careful stripe of paint, perfectly even. No crooked walls tonight.

"Your dad okay?" she asked.

"He's fine. Blowing me off, but fine."

"Blowing you off?"

He shrugged. "He told me to stay away, that he'd got some kid to do odd jobs around his place. A really great kid who's always on time and doesn't try to screw him and is a fucking pillar of virtue."

"Well, good for him," she said. "Those pillars of fucking virtue are really hard to find."

He tossed the roller down. "There's no damn kid, Chloe. He's making him up."

"Maybe he's trying to save you the time or save face."

"Save face?"

"Yes, you know, stupid male pride?"

"You don't understand," Sawyer said grimly. "And how could you? I've never told you about who I used to be."

"So you were a punk-ass kid," she said. "So what? A lot of us were."

"You don't know."

"I know who you are now," she said. "And that's all that matters. You're loyal, strong, caring—"

He snorted and went back to painting. Clearly they were done discussing this. Shock. She stared at his broad, expansive back, watching with avid interest as the muscles there flexed and bunched while he stroked the walls with the roller. "Do you have another roller?"

"No."

She squeezed in between him and the wall. "Hi. My name's Chloe, and you might not have noticed, but we're friends. Naked friends, sure, but friends nevertheless. And friends share. If it wasn't your father tonight that pissed you off, what was it?"

He met her gaze. "We're more than just messing around naked friends," he said.

She did her best to squelch the burst of emotion those words caused. "Then talk to me."

He made a restless movement with his shoulders, like he was to-the-bone exhausted. "If you're mad at me," she murmured, "I think I deserve to know why."

He stared at the wet paint on the wall above her head. "It's not you I'm mad at."

"Then who?"

"Me." He drew a careful breath. "I'm between a rock and a hard place here with what I can say."

"Okay."

"It's DEA business. We've been waiting on a break. I'm on call now, but thanks to me being out of range tonight, our lead went underground and took any evidence with him."

Chloe closed her eyes, stricken with guilt. This was because he'd been at the mud springs checking on her and her sisters. "Oh, Sawyer. I'm so sorry. Is there anything I can do?"

His gaze swiveled to hers, and he studied her meditatively. "That's your only question?"

"No, I have at least a dozen, but I'm working on not being an impulsive pain in your ass."

With a quiet laugh to himself, he asked, "How is it you're so good for me, and yet so bad at the same time?"

Well, if that didn't reach out and punch her in the gut. "It's a special talent of mine," she managed.

His gaze roamed her face, and she hated this, hated standing here waiting for him to tell her that they were through. Because that's where this was going, she knew it. She *felt* it. Everything about his voice and expression told her so, and she knew that she should have left when she had the chance, left and pretended she'd never found contentment and security in his arms.

"You asked if there was something you could do for me," he said quietly.

She nodded numbly.

"You could come here."

Without hesitation, she moved closer, pressing her cheek against his warm, naked chest, finding comfort in the strong, steady beat of his heart against her ear, as his arms surrounded her hard. "I'm not the man you think I am, Chloe," he said into her hair.

"Wrong," she said and pulled him closer. "You are exactly who I thought you were." She kissed him, hard. He responded by pressing her up against the one dry wall, holding her there with two hundred pounds of solid, hard muscle. And he *was* hard, *everywhere*.

"Feeling better, then?" she whispered.

"I'm feeling something. Where's your inhaler, Chloe?"

"In my purse by your front door. I just used it." She slid her arms up around his neck and again pulled his head down to hers. "As a precaution." The wall behind her was giving her a chill, but Sawyer's mouth was hot and urgent on her throat. The hard curves of his back burned warm against her fingers. "I'm sorry about tonight, Sawyer. So sorry."

"It can't happen again. Not ever again."

The words skittered down her spine, causing a shiver. Because it was going to be over. She'd known that. A part of her had always known that. But it was going to destroy her.

Tomorrow.

Jill Shalvis

For now, right now, she still had this, had tonight. He wanted her, that much she knew, and she wanted him.

More than she'd ever wanted anyone in her entire life.

Not willing to waste another second of it, she slid her hand between them to unsnap his jeans. He lifted his head, his gaze searching hers. His expression softened, and he took over, stripping out of his jeans. He was commando, and she took him in, one taut muscle at a time.

Heart-stopping.

Breath-taking.

He unzipped her sweatshirt and groaned at the strip of skin he exposed from the pulse point of her throat to the hip-hugging waistband of her jeans. Then he tugged the sweatshirt off, letting it fall to the floor on top of his jeans. Her bra went next. "Turn around."

When she didn't move fast enough, he spun her so that she faced the mirror, setting her hands on the countertop like he was going to frisk her. Instead, he pressed up close behind her.

Together they looked at her body in the mirror.

She could feel his warm breath on her neck, coming a little faster than his usual hibernation rate of breathing, and it gave her a little thrill. "What?" he murmured when she shuddered, bending to kiss her neck.

She gasped as his hands skimmed up her torso to cup her bare breasts, his fingers plucking at her nipples. "I make you feel things," she said.

He rocked into her. "Yeah. You sure as hell do." He unfastened her jeans and nudged them down along with her panties, kicking all the fallen clothes away from their feet. His hands settled hers on the counter again, one foot nudging her legs farther apart. When he had her arranged to suit him, he put his hands on her hips and met her gaze in the mirror.

"Are you going to search me now?" she teased.

"Mm." He skimmed one hand up her belly to cup a breast, the other between her thighs. "I could look at you all day," he said.

She soaked up the warmth of both his words and his big body behind hers. "Look later." She wriggled. "Do now."

He didn't hesitate. He plunged into her, and she cried out in sheer, mindless pleasure, gripping the counter with white knuckles as she thrust back against him.

With a groan, he pushed even deeper. "Open your eyes."

She hadn't even realized she'd closed them, but they flew open now and met his in the mirror.

They were hot and demanding, much like the man.

"You want this, Chloe?"

"Yes. God yes."

Cursing beneath his strained breath, he bent her over the counter, one hand on her hip, the other between her thighs, using it to drive her straight to the edge. There were no other words for what he did to her. He controlled their movements, and he knew what he was doing. In no time, she was flying, sobbing his name as she came. Pulling her head back, he kissed her deep as he followed her over.

Her legs were wobbling, and he felt like her only anchor in a spinning world. They sank to their knees there on the bathroom floor, his arms hard around her as if maybe she was his anchor as well.

After a few minutes, he kissed her sweaty temple. "Okay?"

If she didn't let herself think. "If I say no, can we do it again?"

He let out a low chuckle and leaned over her, pushing damp hair from her face. "You're breathing pretty hard."

"Yes, but that's your doing," she said.

"It's okay. It's going to be okay." He rose to his feet in one quick, economical movement, scooping her up in his arms.

"Sawyer—"

"Save your breath." They were on the move down the hallway.

He snatched up her purse in the entryway and kept moving, right into the kitchen. Flipping on the lights, he set her on the countertop.

It was icy cold on her bare ass, and she squealed. He merely held her there with one hand and rifled through her purse with the other. Yanking out her inhaler, he thrust it into her hands. She took a puff and held it in, watching him.

He'd gone from her lover to the cop in a blink, cool and calm and completely in charge. "Impressive," she murmured when she exhaled. "You're good in an emergency. But you do realize that I'm not having an emergency, right? I was just..." She let out a low laugh. "You're pretty potent, Sheriff. You sent me out of the stratosphere. I'm still coming down, that's all."

"I thought—" He shook his head. "I thought you were having an asthma attack because I pushed too hard, rushing you—"

"No." She ran her hands up and down his tense arms. "I'm sorry I scared you, but I'm fine."

He stared at her, then backed into a chair, minus some of his usual grace, given that he was naked, too. "I thought you were in trouble," he said.

Oh, God. How was she going to give him up? *Don't go there, not now. Tomorrow...* She hopped down off the counter, walked over, and straddled him, sliding her fingers into his hair.

His hands went to her ass and squeezed.

With a smile, she bent over him, lightly brushing her lips with his. "I actually forgot I had asthma," she murmured. "You know that's only happened with you."

"Yeah?"

"Yeah. You must be special to make me forget such a thing."

Between them, he stirred, and he tightened his grip on her ass, palming her possessively. Still holding her, he rose and turned to eye the kitchen table speculatively.

"Sawyer," she said on a laugh. There were a few things on

the table—a stack of mail, an empty paper plate, his wallet and keys—but with one swipe of his hand it all hit the floor.

A ridiculous flutter went through her belly.

He laid her down on the surface of the table and towered over her, planting his hands on either side of her head. "Let's see what else I can make you forget."

Chapter 23

*"Just when you think you have
a handle on life, it breaks."*
—*Chloe Traeger*

The next day, Sawyer had just finished reading a kid the riot act for shoplifting his lunch at the convenience store when his phone vibrated. *Chloe*, he thought, his chest squeezing with the painful reminder of how she'd slipped out of his bed at some point in the middle of the night.

But it wasn't Chloe. It was Josh calling to tell him that his father had been admitted into the ER for chest pains.

"It's not a heart attack," Josh said when he'd met Sawyer in the hallway outside Nolan's room.

Sawyer took his first breath in the twenty minutes since he'd gotten the phone call. "So what is it?"

"He said he was trying to mow his lawn early this morning when the chest pains came on. He waited until now to come in because he's Nolan Thompson."

Sawyer gritted his teeth. "He said he'd hired someone to do that for him," he muttered, though why he felt inclined to defend himself he couldn't guess. Nearly everyone in town knew about his rocky relationship with his dad, including Josh.

Josh shrugged. He was looking like it'd been a long day already in wrinkled blue scrubs, a stethoscope hanging around his neck, his dark hair ruffled and dark eyes lined with exhaustion. "It's anxiety. I'm going to prescribe some mild anti-anxiety meds, but he needs to go low stress."

"You tell him that?"

Josh gave a tired smile. "Yeah." He clapped a hand on Sawyer's shoulder. "Try to take it easy on him."

Sawyer walked into the room. His father was prone on his back, hooked up to an IV and oxygen, looking frail, small, and old, and yet he *still* managed to make a sound that perfectly conveyed what he thought at the sight of Sawyer. "Gee, Dad," he said. "I'm happy to see you, too."

Nolan closed his eyes. "You'd be sarcastic to your dying father?"

"You're not dying. You're going to outlive me out of sheer orneriness."

His father's eyes opened and narrowed.

"It's anxiety, not your heart," Sawyer told him, standing at the foot of the hospital bed.

"The fuck it is. I was mowing the lawn. No stress in that."

"And why were you mowing the lawn, Dad?"

"Because I . . ." Nolan clammed up.

Sawyer was trying his damnedest to ignore *The Fresh Prince of Bel-Air* rerun blaring on the TV behind him. He had no idea how to proceed here without further infuriating his father. "Dad, I know there's no kid."

"He got busy."

"There's no kid," Sawyer repeated.

Nolan frowned. "You're standing in front of the TV."

"I'm trying to talk to you."

"Move."

Sawyer felt the helplessness reach up and choke him. It was a new feeling, but it'd become his best friend since Chloe had sneaked out of his bed, and, he suspected, out of his life. What was it she'd once told him—life was too short? She'd been right on. "What do you want from me, Dad?"

"Nothing. Take your fucking bad attitude and get the hell out of here."

He could have no idea how much Sawyer wanted to do just that. But no more putting this kind of shit off. "Look, I know I disappointed you as a kid. I get that. I disappointed *me* as a kid."

For the first time since Sawyer had walked into the room, Nolan met his gaze.

"And I know," Sawyer went on, "that you did the best you could with me."

There was a long, painful silence during which Sawyer kicked a chair closer to the side of the bed and sat.

Getting the message that Sawyer wasn't leaving, Nolan finally cleared his throat. "Maybe I could have done better with you."

"I don't know how," Sawyer admitted. "I was a complete shit. We both know that. In fact, raising me probably put you in here." He reached for his father's hand. It was the first time they'd touched in years. "But I'm trying to make up for it. It'd be great if you let me."

"How?" Nolan asked warily.

"By eating some pride and letting your sorry-ass son help you out once in a while."

"You're busy," Nolan said.

"Not that busy."

His father said nothing to this. His gaze drifted to the TV again.

Sawyer stood up. "But it can't be one-sided. You're going to have to meet me halfway."

Nolan shrugged noncommittally.

"Do you know how many times you've called me, Dad?" Sawyer asked.

Nolan hunched over the remote, squinting at it since he didn't have his glasses. "Fucking remote needs new batteries. Get the nurse for me, will you?"

"Never. You've called me never," Sawyer said. "I don't even know if you have my phone number."

Nolan aimed the remote and gave it another try.

Sawyer sighed. Maybe he deserved this. He'd been so busy preserving his own pride and playing super sheriff to make up for the past that he hadn't recognized his father's pride. The man was getting old, and Sawyer was starting to get how much it sucked when the world you worked so hard to build fell down around you like a house of cards. He took the damn remote and walked out of the room to find some batteries. He was halfway down the hallway when his phone rang. Sawyer looked at the screen with disbelief. It was his father.

"I have your number because when you bought me the phone last year, you put your number in it," Nolan said. "I never called you before because I had nothing to say."

Sawyer walked back into his father's hospital room and stared at his father, the both of them still holding their cell phones to their ears. "You have something to say now?" Sawyer asked.

"Yeah. Except we have to hang up first because I'm not supposed to have this cell phone on in here." His father lowered his arm.

Sawyer reached up and manually turned off the TV because a new episode was starting, and if *The Fresh Prince of Bel-Air* theme song got stuck in his head, he was going to have to kill himself.

Nolan cleared his throat, his eyes going to the now dark screen of the TV. He looked uncomfortable and embarrassed, but he still spoke. "I saw you in the paper. You caught that guy trying to hurt that pretty waitress at the diner."

"Amy," Sawyer said. "She's okay."

"I know." His father cleared his throat. "Because of you."

Sawyer waited, but he said nothing else. Apparently that was as big an *atta boy* as he was ever going to get, but it was so much more than he'd expected that he found himself speechless. "So you're saying?"

His father scowled, the lines etched deep in his jowls. "That you didn't totally fuck it up."

Sawyer had to laugh. "Wow. That's going to go straight to my head, Dad."

"Watch it. I can still kick your ass." But there was a small smile around the corners of Nolan's mouth when he said it. "Now get out so I can get some sleep." In fact, his eyes were already closed.

But Sawyer knew it was going to be okay. Not great, maybe never great, but at least they could do something they'd never quite managed before—peacefully coexist.

* * *

"You look different, Clo."

Chloe glanced at Lance and then quickly averted her gaze, afraid he'd see her misery. She needed sleep. Even more, she needed to understand what had happened at Sawyer's last night.

Or maybe it was best if she didn't.

They were at the cottage. Lance had caught another nasty cold that had kept him in the hospital for the past few days. His doctors had wanted him to stay, but two hours ago he'd had enough and had walked out, calling Chloe for a ride.

She'd brought him here because his duplex was being watched for the still-missing Todd. Plus Tucker was on a job out of town until Friday. Trying to help make Lance comfortable, she had him stretched out on her bed and was giving him a massage while they waited for Renee to get off work and come get him.

"If Renee ends up with overtime again, you're going to stay here with me tonight," Chloe said. Leaning over him, she worked her special oil blend into the knots of tension in his shoulders and back. "You're like a rock quarry. Breathe as deep as you can. Positive visualization. Picture your lungs all clear and at one hundred percent. Puppies and rainbows."

After a pained laugh, Lance shifted a bit, then turned his head just enough to be annoying. "Puppies and rainbows? What's going on with you? You're off today." He tensed and grunted when she hit a particularly sore spot. "Ouch."

"You're not concentrating on visualizing your good health."

He dropped his head down and was obedient for about fifteen seconds. "It's about Sawyer, right? What happened? It got too real, and you bailed?"

"Hey, I don't do that."

Lance was facedown, but she knew he was also brows up, and she sighed. "Jeez, you go and get laid and you turn into a relationship expert."

He snorted. "Yeah, I'd make a fine shrink. I'd tell everyone to fuck the rules and just live." He paused. "And it's more than getting laid, by the way. We're a thing, Renee and me."

Chloe stared down at Lance's painfully thin, pale, disease-ravaged body. She could count his every rib. His breath rattled with each inhale. "Does she understand—I mean, is she—"

"Okay with me dying?" He sighed. "No. Hell no, not even close. But she loves me." He shook his head, sounding marveled. "And if she can love this body and the man inside it, then you sure as hell can find someone to love your sorry—but fine—ass."

Love hadn't been in Chloe's plans when it came to Sawyer. Wild sex, yes. Love, no. So of course that's what she'd done. She'd gone and fallen. Stupid, stupid, stupid. But what was done was done, and she couldn't unfall. She'd tried. Didn't work. She'd only fallen harder, even hoping that he'd caught the bug, too. But she wasn't sure.

God, she was so confused. One lousy minute of contentment, and boom, everything had fallen apart.

"Smell something burning in there," Lance teased. Shoving up to his elbows, he gave her a terrifyingly gentle look. "I've seen him look at you, you know. He accepts you, Chloe. As is."

Maybe. But could he love her?

"Just promise me you won't waste your time doubting or second guessing," he said. "It's not worth it. Just go for it." His eyes were unsettlingly clear and serene. "Look, we both know I'm no shrink, but I know what I'm talking about here. And I want to know you're okay before…"

Before he was gone.

He didn't say it out loud, he didn't have to. It was the big, fat elephant in the room. Why the hell did it seem as if everyone was saying good-bye to her? "We are *not* having this conversation." Her chest was going tight. "People with CF have a median survival age of thirty-seven years now. You have ten years left before I will even *think* of having this conversation with you."

"Chloe, that's the *median* age. People die at two, or ten, or twenty-seven." His voice was low and rough, and he shrugged his too-thin shoulders. "Shit happens."

"Yeah, shit happens. I could get hit by a bus," she said grimly. "Or smack you upside the head for being annoying."

"Goddammit, Chloe, I want to know you have someone."

Suddenly she couldn't breathe. Just couldn't. She struggled for air, couldn't manage it, and staggered backward, tripping over her own legs to fall to her butt.

"Fuck." Lance leaped off the couch and crouched in front of her in nothing but his boxers. He shoved her purse in her lap. "Your inhaler in here?"

She managed a nod, and he opened the thing like it was a ticking bomb.

"Pocket," she wheezed. "Inside pocket."

Looking squeamish, he rooted past a lip gloss, a pack of birth control pills, and the latest *Cosmo* to get to the pocket. "Jesus fucking Christ," he was muttering. "If I find a tampon in here, I'm going to hurt you." He opened the pocket, plunged his hand in, and came out with a... "*Argh!*" He flung the tampon across the room like it was a hand grenade, and she was both laughing and sobbing for breath when he finally located her inhaler.

She took a long puff. Then another. It didn't help fast enough, and she felt the licks of that familiar horrific panic gripping her. Lance stayed with her, holding her face. "In and out, baby, that's all you gotta do. In and then out."

Chloe caught enough breath to croak out a shaky joke. "That's what *she* said," she gasped, making Lance laugh.

After a few minutes, she'd caught her breath a little more and glared at him. "Okay, don't you *ever* fucking say good-bye to me again."

"How the hell is telling you that it's okay to fall for someone saying good-bye?"

"It *felt* like a good-bye. *God.*" She felt the tears well up. *Tears.* She never cried. "Goddammit."

Lance let go of her face and sat back on his heels. "Chloe," he said softly. "You know it's coming."

"No, I don't! And you can't think like that!"

"I *have* to think like that." When her phone vibrated, he rose to his feet a little shakily and reached out a hand for her. "But you don't. You have your whole life ahead of you."

She swallowed a sob, ignored his hand, and scrambled to her

feet on her own. She read the text from Tara requesting some help. "I have to go," she said. "Renee will be here soon. Call me if you need anything." She refused to look at him as she shoved her inhaler in her pocket and ran out the door. She stepped off the cottage porch and wiped the tears from her eyes. It was all she could do to not drop down to the stairs and weep like a child. Clearly she hadn't gotten nearly enough sleep. She and Sawyer had turned to each other over and over again in the night like . . . like they were never going to have each other again.

Don't go there.

Another sniff, another swipe of the back of her hand, and she was almost at the inn. As Chloe moved, she saw a swirl of dust fade at the edge of the woods, which was odd enough to catch her attention. There wasn't a road there, just an old hiking path.

With a quick change of direction, she followed the dust and caught sight of tire tracks in the still-moist mud. She could hear an engine. A truck, probably. Something with four-wheel drive. It wasn't far, but she was wondering who'd be out there in the first place.

At the edge of the woods, she stopped and listened again. Not one truck.

Two.

Chloe took out her cell and called Tara. "Hey, there's a couple of trucks moving around out here in the woods. I'm going to go take a look, and I didn't want to be the stupid chick in the movies who doesn't tell anyone where she's going."

"Hang on, I'll come out."

"It's probably nothing. Maybe the forest service checking on the fire lanes. I'll call you right back." She disconnected, then headed down the trail. She could still hear the engines ahead of her. The trail wasn't meant for a vehicle so it'd be slow, rough going.

And then the engines cut off. There was the faint sound of

male voices. And then a truck door closing. An engine revved, coming back her way. Shit. Chloe dove into the bushes and ducked low.

A blue truck drove past her, going far too fast for the terrain. She recognized the driver and covered her mouth to hide her gasp, even though no one could have heard her.

Nick Raybo.

The forest had come down around her like a theater curtain, surrounding her with mossy pines, spruce, and the scent of Christmas. There was still someone ahead of her, and she made her way a little closer, then went utterly still because there, behind a huge outgrowth of sage, was a truck. New. Black. Shiny.

Todd's.

Todd and Raybo. Oh, God, that couldn't be good.

Chloe shifted behind a large pine and dialed Sawyer this time, watching Todd behind the wheel talking on his cell phone. She took a hit from her inhaler and held her breath as Sawyer answered, sounding distracted. "Thompson."

But Todd was exiting his truck now. Afraid to reply and tip Todd off, Chloe bit her lower lip.

"Chloe," Sawyer said. "You there?"

"Raybo. And Todd," she whispered, hearting pounding, chest tight. Too tight. That half-mile walk had taxed her.

"Todd? He's with you?"

"In the woods. Raybo's leaving." It was all she could say. She took another peek from around the tree. She could see the whole left side of Todd's truck, but not Todd. There was something in the bed of his truck that looked like camouflage netting. She knew marijuana growers used it to hide their crops, which made sense given what Todd was suspected of.

"Chloe," Sawyer said. "I'm on my way. Where are you exactly?"

"I'm half a mile or so in." She pressed a hand to her chest.

She was wheezing badly. "Lance knows the trail. I think Todd's hiding his stash."

"I've called it in, Chloe," Sawyer said. "We're all on our way. You did great. Now get the fuck out of there." He paused, then added, "Please. Please get the fuck out of there. For me."

Despite the fear and asthma attack now fully upon her, Chloe smiled as she left her tree and started to head back. "Like the please," she whispered. "Nice...touch."

"Use your inhaler."

"Did." She was a safe enough distance away now that she slowed, then stopped. "Okay, I'm in trouble," she admitted. "I have...to rest." She dropped to her knees, gasping for breath. She opened her mouth to tell Sawyer that she was going to hang up when a hand clamped down on her mouth, and her scream was swallowed before it started.

Chapter 24

*"If they don't have good adventures
in heaven, I'm not going."*
—*Chloe Traeger*

Every muscle in Sawyer's body tightened as he heard Chloe's attempt at a hoarse scream and then the beep of the call being cut off. A dozen horrible images raced through his mind, but he cut them off, swerving around slower cars as he called Morris.

The DEA agent was still pissed at Sawyer for not being available when he'd been needed last night, and when Sawyer told him he wasn't waiting for backup as he raced toward Chloe's last-known location, the man started to tear Sawyer a new one.

Sawyer didn't give a shit. The job, the bust, the drugs, none of it mattered. The whole world could go fuck itself if something happened to Chloe. He waited for Morris's rant to end, confirmed the location one more time, and clicked off.

Raybo—he'd been the missing link, the big dealer the DEA had been looking to nail. It made perfect sense. Sawyer knew

Morris's team would get Raybo on the road or at his compound. Sawyer was certain of it.

What he wasn't certain of, what he was terrified of, was what was happening to Chloe right this very second. He wasn't far from the B&B, but every second felt like an hour. If that fucker touched one hair on her head, he was going down. Sawyer had no more mercy left. He cut the sirens and the lights as he approached the turnoff. When he pulled up at the inn, Tara was standing on the porch holding her cell phone. "Chloe called," she said. "I think she's in trouble."

"Which trail?"

Lance came around the corner. "I'll show you." They moved to the marina building, Lance doing his best to keep up, but he was breathing hard. "There," he said, pointing the way. "That one."

Sawyer knew the trail all too well. It was the same one that he, Ford, and Jax had taken the night they'd seen the odd flare. It was also the trail to the hidden clearing where he and Todd had partied through their high school years. "Stay here," he said to Lance. "More are coming. Tell them which way I've gone." He drew his gun. No matter what happened, Chloe *was* coming out of this in one piece, but he'd make no guarantees about anyone else.

* * *

Todd had his arm across Chloe's throat. Just tight enough that a regular person would have trouble breathing. She'd passed trouble halfway to his truck.

"This is just great," Todd was muttering, dragging her along with him. "Fucking great. I spent a year trying to get your fucking attention, and you could give a shit. And now that I'm headed out, you want a piece of me."

"I don't—"

He tightened his grip on her, cutting off her words. He smelled of sweat and fear, and his body shook with tension as he walked her forward. There was a gun in his free hand, a semiautomatic, and she hoped the safety was on because he was swinging it around like a laser pointer. "I'm not going back to jail," he said, his jaw pressed to hers. "Not even for your sweet ass. But I can't let you go, either."

"Yes, you can. It's Raybo, right? It's all him. You—"

Again he tightened his grip, and she choked. "Shut up," he said. "Shut up and listen. I'm not taking the fall for Raybo. Hell, no. And I'm not narcing him out, either; the fucker is crazy. He'd kill me for sure."

"No—"

"You should be worried about you, Chloe," he said. "Our fun is over. I could have had you that day at the mud springs. That pisses me off. You were hot for me up until then, but something changed."

"I was never hot for you," she managed.

"Liar. But after that, Sawyer had you. That pissed me off, too. You're not his usual type."

"What's that supposed to mean?"

"I don't know what it is about you, but you jump knee deep in shit all the time and still come out smelling like a rose. I fucked with the boats at the marina," he said. "I told everyone that you were pissed off at your sisters and wanted to get out of this place. I thought everyone would blame you, but no one did, no one even believed the rumors. Nothing sticks to you. Too bad you can't teach me that trick," he said almost wistfully.

"I don't—"

He tugged viciously on her hair. "We're gonna load up now, and then we're getting the hell out of here. Just be a good girl. That's all you gotta do."

Todd marched her past a burnt-out tree, then headed for a wild mass of Manzanita bush canopied by two-hundred-foot pines. There was something about the lush growth. It looked like the rest of the forest, but then it kinda didn't, and she struggled to inhale again. She didn't know what would happen if she passed out. Todd wouldn't lift a finger to help her; she knew that.

"Stay," he said, and the minute he removed his arm from her neck, she dropped to her knees. She was gasping, shaking, sweating, and freaking out in general, but he pointed the gun at her, and she sat back on her haunches.

"Jesus. I'm not gonna hurt you as long as you shut up."

"I . . . can't help it."

"Do you have to gasp like that? I'm not even touching you. Shut the fuck up."

She was trying. Not that she believed him about not hurting her. God, she hoped Tara wasn't following the trail at this moment, trying to find her. Or Sawyer. She was afraid Todd would shoot anyone who came upon them. Hell, she was afraid he'd shoot *her*. She was going to die, either by Todd's hand or by suffocation, and she hadn't told anyone how she felt about them. She hadn't said the words because she was a goddamn chicken, and now she was gonna die, and they'd never know. Not Sawyer, and not her sisters. It wasn't right, and she was so mad at herself *and* Todd that she could shoot him herself.

"Get up," Todd said. He was holding several bundles in his arms. "Chloe, I fucking mean it! Get up or I'll drag you."

If she could, she would. She'd get up, punch his lights out, and run like hell.

Except she couldn't run. Not even on a good day, which this wasn't shaping up to be.

She couldn't do anything but attempt to inhale. She certainly couldn't get any more terrified, which sucked. She'd thought she'd been afraid of three little words. What a joke.

Todd dropped the load in his truck and turned back to her just as she caught some movement out of the corner of her eye. At first she thought it was a deer, but then she realized it was Sawyer. It had to be.

In front of her, she heard the unmistakable sound of a belt being pulled loose from denim. For a second, she got frightened in a whole new way, then realized Todd was going to tie her up using his belt. Still holding his gun, he moved behind her. Vision wavering, she closed her eyes and concentrated on the little air that she was getting, waiting for an opportunity to help Sawyer. Mostly, she wanted to get Todd before Sawyer shot him. She wanted first blood, dammit.

The snap of a twig sounded loud as a gunshot. Todd grabbed her by the throat and spun her around.

"Let her go, Todd," Sawyer said, stepping right into Todd's line of sight, gun aimed, face so fiercely determined that Chloe forgot to breathe.

Until Todd squeezed her throat again. He hadn't gotten her hands tied, and she clawed at his arm around her neck, her vision graying at the edges.

"Drop your gun," Todd grated out. "Or I'll shoot her dead."

Not going to be necessary, Chloe thought hazily . . .

"There's no reason to hurt her," Sawyer said, moving slowly but steadily forward. "The DEA is five minutes away. They've got Raybo. They got him on the highway and he's in custody. It's over, Todd. Don't make things even worse."

"Worse? How could it be *worse*? You've fucked me over for the last time, man. I'm not going back to jail. You know what they did to me in jail? You were still seventeen. Why the hell didn't you tell them that you were driving? All you had to do was say you were driving!"

"I was unconscious, you asshole. We both were. They found us in the car. We never should have been drinking and driving. You know it as well as I do."

"Yeah, well, easy for you to say. You got juvie, and I got hard time for second-degree murder. You think I ever had a chance for anything after that? Eighteen, and my life was fucking over."

"It's only over if you don't walk away from this. Let Chloe go, and I'll do what I can for you. I swear it, Todd. I know you didn't mean for Sammy and Cutter to die. Nobody wanted that. I'm sorry it was you driving. I am."

Chloe's eyes drifted shut. She felt Todd look down at her, and she used the last of her strength to twist and bring her knee up hard between his legs.

He let out a strangled, high-pitched cry, and then she was free.

Free to tell Sawyer that she loved the stupid kid he'd once been, that she loved the man he'd become now, that she always would. But free of Todd wasn't the same thing as home free.

She fell, bracing for the hard ground rushing up to meet her, but she never felt it.

* * *

Sawyer had spent lots of time in the ER. He'd brought in injured suspects, he'd gone to interview witnesses, and he'd been there not three months ago after a power tool incident when Jax had accidentally stapled his thumb to a shelving unit he'd been building.

But until now Sawyer had never sat in a tiny, cramped ER cubicle with panic gripping him by the balls. He stared at the woman in the bed. Pale and clammy. *Him* not her.

Though Chloe was pale, too.

Her hair still had flecks of dirt in it. The silky strands had long ago escaped the hair band to riot around her face. Sawyer might have stroked it back, but the nurse was hovering, moving like a busy bee around them: giving Chloe a breathing treatment, hooking up the monitors, checking the nebulizer, supervising oxygen levels. And all the while, the nurse's mouth was moving, too, though she may have been speaking Chinese for all Sawyer was paying attention. He couldn't do anything but look at Chloe, because if he took his eyes off her she might stop breathing again.

So he pulled a chair as close as he could get next to her bed and watched her struggle. Even with the nebulizer and the corticosteroids and the Beta-2 agonists, she still wasn't out of the woods. But at least her lips weren't blue, and she was starting to get some color in her cheeks.

Christ, it'd been close, too fucking close, and he'd never been so scared in his life.

The nurse finally left and in her wake were the beeping monitors, hissing oxygen, and the steady patter of people moving up and down the hallways on the other side of the curtain. Chloe opened her eyes, and Sawyer took his first real breath in the past hour of hell. He had no idea what to say. He was still struggling to think of something when she pulled the mouthpiece of the nebulizer from her mouth and spoke first.

"Did I miss the Jell-O? I really like it when they give me Jell-O."

His throat constricted. "I'll get you an entire tray."

She reached out and took his hand, running her icy fingers over his knuckles, which were raw and red and a little swollen from where he'd punched the outside wall of the hospital. His form of stress relief.

"Chloe," he said, but her eyes were closed again.

She'd replaced the nebulizer and fallen back to sleep.

Two minutes later, Tara and Maddie arrived. Tara sat in the chair that Sawyer vacated for her. Maddie moved to Chloe's other side, the two of them staring down into her face.

"She's so damn much a part of me that I feel like I can't breathe either," Maddie whispered, hand to her own heart.

"Luckily, she's stubborn enough to breathe for the both of you," Tara said.

Sawyer nearly smiled at the truth of that statement and looked down at his vibrating phone. Morris was here and needed to talk to him. Code for yell at him. Sawyer rose and met him in a hallway, where he spent the next ten minutes explaining exactly why he'd broken protocol and hadn't waited for backup. Morris listened, both pissed off and acknowledging that Sawyer had nailed Todd.

Of course, it hadn't been Sawyer at all, but Chloe and a well-placed knee, leaving Todd in possession of one dislocated nut and relieved of possession of his entire stash.

The DEA had their case and the drugs, and there were a *lot* of drugs. Raybo had been even bigger than they'd thought, and he was already singing. Todd had been making some side deals, storing most of his own shit in his duplex attic, but when Mitch ratted him out, he'd had to change his plans and quick.

Todd had rigged up some duck blinds in the woods, the way they'd done with their booze when they'd been kids, covering it with the military camouflage netting.

Stupid. But Sawyer was done wasting a single second of his time thinking and worrying about Todd.

Life was too short.

* * *

Chloe woke up with a little start. "I got him in the nuts!"

Tara and Maddie, seated at her side, smiled. "You sure did," Tara said. "Proud of you, sugar."

Chloe smiled, relieved it was over.

"So is it that you don't have enough work at the B&B and the spa that you had to add crime fighting to your résumé?" Tara asked.

Chloe choked out a low laugh. She sat up a little, testing her lungs, and was relieved to find herself in relatively good working order. "I, um, thought of something when I was out there."

"Before or after you spoon-fed Todd his left family jewel?"

Chloe smiled. "Before. Actually, way before. I thought of it a while back, but...well, to be honest, I can't explain the why or how of what took me so long." That's how love worked, she thought. It was confusing and messy and wonderful and real. God, so real. And she'd meant it. It *had* been growing in her for a while. But right here, right now, looking at her hodgepodge family crowded around her, she felt it expanding inside of her even more, like her chest was going to explode. In a good way for once. "In the mud springs last night, Tara teased me for having an epiphany. She was right, I *was* having one."

"You 'bout done with it yet?" Tara asked.

"Yeah, I believe I am. But I want you to know, once I tell you, it's not an all-access pass to any group hugs. Those need to be put on the schedule in advance." She drew a deep breath, or as deep as she could anyway. "I love you. I love you both."

"Well, would you listen to that." Tara's tone was dry, in direct contrast to her suspiciously wet eyes. "You just emotionally compromised yourself and lived to tell the tale."

There was a knock on the open door, and they all looked up at Sawyer standing there, eyes locked on Chloe. Yes, she'd just emotionally compromised herself.

And she was about to do it again.

"The nurse says you'll be out of here in less than an hour," Sawyer said. "Need a ride?"

Chloe looked at her sisters. Maddie jumped up, grabbing Tara by the hand. "Oh, that would be great. We're expecting a few scheduled guests, and..."

"Just say good-bye, sugar," Tara said, shaking her head. "And remind me to teach you how to lie better than that."

And then they were both gone.

An hour later, Chloe was dropped down on Sawyer's couch and gruffly told to "hang on." She sat on the couch, shivering. "I'm n-not c-cold. It's just what happens sometimes after a bad asthma attack and all the meds." Her heart raced, too, like it was trying to get outside of her chest, and it pissed her off.

Sawyer wrapped her in a blanket, then carefully lifted her into his arms. She cuddled in, absorbing his body heat as her eyes locked in on the nebulizer on the coffee table. "What's that?"

"A nebulizer."

"I know that. I mean, what's it doing here?"

"I bought one."

Her heart squeezed. "When?"

"What does it matter?"

"When, Sawyer?"

"A few days ago."

She stared into his eyes. "Why did you buy a nebulizer if you were going to dump me?"

"I believe you dumped me," he said lightly.

She stared at him. "Okay, we're going to circle back to that in a minute. Sawyer..." She looked around at the living room. Painted walls. Furniture. "Up until a week ago, you didn't have anything in here, and now you have a nebulizer. Do you know what that means? It means," she went on without waiting for an answer, "that you like me." She smiled, feeling the warmth of the knowledge chase away the chill. "You really, really like me."

"Don't get excited. I like all my house painters." He settled her head against his chest. She knew he was giving her time to settle. And also, she realized as he stroked a big hand up and down her back, he was giving her his heat, strength, and reassurance—the last of which wasn't exactly second nature to him. She knew his job didn't allow for much softness, or a lot of emotion for that matter. Obviously he'd let that spill over into his life, but she knew he was trying his damnedest to offer her what he thought she needed.

Damn. Damn, she was a goner, and she curled into him, tracing little patterns on his stomach with her fingers, enjoying the hard ridges of his abs. Wriggling to get comfortable, she pressed her face into his throat and inhaled him, then rested her head on his chest. Unlike her, he wasn't trembling or shaking at all. "Sorry," she murmured. "I can't stop shaking."

"Adrenaline letdown."

"What about you?" she asked. "You ever get adrenaline letdown? Because I just can't imagine anything getting to you."

Sawyer tugged her hair until she met his gaze, his own clear and unguarded. "You," he said, shockingly gently. "You get to me. You scared the hell out of me today."

"Makes two of us."

His grip tightened on her. "If anything had happened to you . . ." He shook his head and cut the words off.

"I'm okay." She touched his scruffy jaw. "You make a comfy chair, Sheriff. Sure you're a little hard in spots, but—"

"Chloe." He laughed and pressed his forehead to hers. "You get to me," he said again quietly. "I want you to know that. You get to me, just the way you are." He leaned in close. "No changing."

She absorbed the words as she'd absorbed his heat and felt a weight lift from her shoulders. "What if being myself isn't always pretty or polite?" she whispered.

"Well, Christ, I hope not," he said. "Polite is fucking exhausting. Chloe, listen to me. You being you is who I fell for. Now, as for who *you* fell for . . ." He drew in a deep breath. "What Todd said today, about when we were teenagers."

"I don't care. It doesn't change how I feel about you."

"Be sure. Because most of it was true." He ran his thumb over her fingers. She stared down at his large, tanned, callused hand against her much smaller, pale one, which looked almost frail in his. "It's not easy to talk about."

"It's me, Sawyer. You can tell me anything. You know that, right?"

"I do now. But until recently, my life was all about work. Only work. I figured I owed it to everyone here for the second chance the town gave me."

"Sawyer, you do realize that the reason no one talks about your past. And that the reason it's not plastered on that damn Facebook page isn't because they're asking for penance. It's because they're protective of you. They care about you and respect you." She hugged him. "So stop punishing yourself. It's over and done."

He was quiet a moment. "Is everything over and done?"

Her breath caught, and she pulled back to look into his eyes. "I don't want it to be."

"What do you want?"

"To know you," she said without hesitation. "All of you. I want to know what makes you feel good."

"Your laughter," he said without hesitation. "Feeling your hands on me. The way you look at me, whether I've been a complete dumbass, or just made you come—"

With a laugh, she ducked her head, but he dipped his down until she was looking at him again. "You want to know what scares me?" he asked.

"Yes."

He leaned even closer and slid a hand to the nape of her neck. "The thought of never having those things with you again. I'm a little slow but not an idiot, Chloe, and I learn from my mistakes." He cupped her jaw. "I love you, Chloe."

"Dammit!"

He blinked. "That wasn't quite the reaction I'd expected."

"No, it's just that I meant to say it first!"

He stared at her. "You could say it now."

"I love you. God, I love you." She let out a breath. "Whew. That's more exhausting than an asthma attack."

He smiled. A real slow, glorious, sexy-as-hell smile. "Maybe it just requires practice."

She returned his smile, feeling so light and happy she could float to the ceiling, although that might have been all the drugs in her system. "Or confirmation."

"Confirmation?"

She pulled out her phone, and he appeared puzzled. "You say I love you, and it reminds you that you have to make a call?" he asked.

"You knew loving me was going to require patience." She accessed her Magic Eight Ball app. "How about it?" she said to the screen. "Me and Sawyer. Yes?"

"Christ, Chloe." Sawyer straightened with a scowl. "You know what it's going to say, what it always says when it's referring to me."

"It's been right every single time with us." She looked at him. "Are you scared?"

"No. But if it says Try Again Later, it's going out the window."

Absolutely yes

Epilogue

"A closed mind is a good thing to lose."
—*Chloe Traeger*

A month later

On the afternoon of Maddie and Jax's wedding rehearsal, the sisters stood together in the cottage, holding hands at the front door.

"This is it," Maddie whispered. She bit her lower lip, looking pale. Very pale. "I mean this is really it."

"Uh-oh." Chloe turned to Tara. "Lock the back door quick; we've got a flight risk."

"Really, really it..." Maddie whispered, sounding bewildered, like she hadn't been beating them all over the head with her bridal magazines for the past six months.

"No, honey, it's just the rehearsal," Tara said gently, stroking Maddie's hair. "It's not the *it* it."

"Which means you can still make a run for it if you want," Chloe said. "I'll drive."

"Chloe!" Tara scolded.

Maddie just kept biting her lower lip.

"Seriously," Chloe told her. "I'll call Jax right now and tell him we're going out for a bag of chips. He'd totally buy it. We get on the Vespa and just keep going as far as the tank of gas will take us. Which, granted, isn't all that far, but—"

"Stop it," Tara said, covering Maddie's ears.

"We'll leave the Steel Magnolia behind, too," Chloe said, studying Maddie. "Your call, Mad."

Maddie closed her eyes. "I have the pretty dress. It's all ready for tomorrow. I'd sure hate to waste that dress."

"No problem," Chloe said. "We'll Craigslist it. *For Sale: a wedding dress, size eight, almost worn once by accident.* You'll get good bucks for it."

Tara reached around Maddie and pinched Chloe. Chloe pinched her back.

Normally, Maddie would have smacked them both, but she ignored them to peek out the window. Jax was waiting for them at the marina, along with Ford, the two of them standing between the marina building and Ford's docked boat. Sawyer wasn't here yet because he'd gotten held up at work, but Chloe had gotten a text that he was on his way.

Maddie watched Jax tip his head back and laugh at something Ford said, and a soft smile crossed her lips. "I really do want him, you know. As mine."

Chloe smiled triumphantly at Tara. "Good to know."

Tara let out a relieved breath, and they all took each other's hands again. "Ready, Maddie?"

"Ready," Maddie said, not quite so pale now. She squeezed her sisters' fingers. "Let's do this. Let's go get me a husband."

Together they walked to the marina just as Lucille pulled up in her old clunker. "Perfect timing!" the older woman called out. "I've got thirty minutes between happy hour and bingo night."

They all settled on the dock. Tomorrow, the railings would be lined with potted flowers. There'd be a runner for them to walk on. Guests would line the way, lots of them.

But for now, it was just Lucille and the five of them—

Six, Chloe corrected, hearing Sawyer drive up. The sound of his truck made her all warm and mushy on the inside, and she laughed at herself. *Sap.*

Lucille pointed everyone to their places, then looked around for Sawyer.

"Here." He was sauntering toward them with his long-legged stride, eyes on Chloe, a small smile threatening the corners of his mouth at the sight of her.

Jax had taken his place at the end of the dock, the water at his back. Following Lucille's direction, Ford escorted Tara to the end of the walkway.

Watching, knowing she was next, Chloe turned to Sawyer, who offered his arm.

He was still in uniform, still armed to the teeth, still looking a little tense from what had undoubtedly been a long day on the job.

They hadn't seen each other in three days. She'd been in Los Angeles, fulfilling the last of her traveling spa obligations. She looked up at him, trying to keep herself in check when she really wanted to throw herself into his arms. Whether it was the happiness emanating off Maddie, or Chloe's own swelling emotions, she wasn't sure, but she felt far too close to tears.

She had no idea why.

Except she did.

Sawyer escorted her down the makeshift aisle and she moved to stand next to Tara.

Maddie came down the aisle next, beaming, her face radiant. Lucille walked them through the short ceremony, and when it was over, Jax practiced kissing Maddie.

Since that went on for some time, Ford suggested that he should practice kissing Tara.

While they were working on that, Sawyer pulled Chloe in tight. "Hey." He nuzzled at her ear. "You okay?"

Because she didn't know, she cupped his face and pulled it to hers for some practicing of their own. When the kissing was over, everyone was talking and laughing about the wedding, about Ford and Tara's engagement, about honeymoons and futures.

Chloe took it all in, wishing her smile didn't feel congealed on her face. She needed to just suck it up. Truly she was happy for her sisters. So happy. Tomorrow Maddie and Jax would be married.

And then in the next month, Tara and Ford would follow suit.

They'd still be sisters, of course. They'd always be sisters, but it would never again be just the three of them.

Chloe was going to go back to being on her own.

Sawyer took her small hand in his much larger one and squeezed. There was a silent inquiry in the touch, and she looked up into his eyes.

He searched her gaze for a long moment, then brought their joined fingers up to his mouth. "You're not okay," he said, as always, seeing what no one else did. "You're sad."

"Of course not."

"You're sad," he repeated with quiet understanding.

She sighed. "Don't you have to go take Jax out and get him drunk now?"

"What's wrong?"

"Nothing." She closed her eyes. "I'll be alone."

Sawyer waited until she looked at him. "I should be insulted."

"No," she said, shaking her head, her control beginning to slip. "No, I don't mean it like that—"

His eyes never flinching, never leaving her face, he said, "Marry me."

"What?" Her heart stopped. Had she heard him correctly? "Because you feel sorry for me?"

"Feel sorry for you? Not likely." He smiled. "Marry me because we're good together." He waggled a brow. "Especially in the shower."

"Oh my God. Shh!" She glanced around, and his grin broadened, probably because the old Chloe wouldn't have given a rat's ass if anyone had overheard. She still didn't, not really, it was just that clearly he'd lost his frigging mind.

"You could marry me right here, right now," he said.

Oh, God. He was serious. "You like your own space," she told him, trying to give him an out.

He lifted a shoulder, cool as could be, while she was ready to burst something. "I like sharing it with you."

Hope kindled and ignited. "I'll drive you crazy," she whispered.

"Already done," he assured her, "in the best possible way." He ran a finger over her temple, gently pushing back a strand of hair. "I want to come home to you every night, Chloe."

"There will be nights I have to be here, when we have guests."

He shrugged. "Then we'll hire someone to work part-time at night and give you breaks, or I'll come to you. I don't care what bed I go home to, as long as you're in it. Say you'll think about it, that you'll think about giving us a real shot."

She stared at him, knowing she'd never wanted anything so much in her entire life. Which made it simple, really. "For you," she said, "I believe I'd do anything."

His eyes went hot. "*Anything*?"

Her knees were wobbling, but she had enough strength to shove him.

A guy to the very core, he laughed and reeled her back in. Leaning close, he pressed his mouth to her ear and nipped the lobe with his teeth. "Trust me. It'll be good."

"The marrying part, or the—"

"Everything."

Since she did trust him—with her heart, her soul, her life—she wrapped her arms around his broad shoulders, pressed her face to his throat, and kissed him there, loving how his arms tightened around her. "I love you, Sawyer. So much."

"I know." His eyes were serious. "It's my very own miracle, and I count on it every single day."

"It would never be boring..." she said.

"Counting on that, too. Say yes, Chloe."

She lifted her face and smiled. "Yes. To everything."

Lucky in Love

To Laurie, Melinda, and Mary for finding all my mistakes. If there are more, it's all on me.

To Helenkay Dimon, Susan Anderson, Kristan Higgins, and Robyn Carr for the bestest limo ride I've ever had (okay, ONLY limo ride I've ever had) on the day after I'd turned in this book (and winning a Rita that night was the icing on the cake!).

To Jolie and Debbie for the help in putting Ty together.

To Robyn Carr, for just about everything else.

Love you all!!

Prologue

*All you need is love. But a little chocolate
now and then doesn't hurt.*

Lightning sent a jagged bolt across Ty Garrison's closed lids.
Thunder boomed and the earth shuddered, and he jerked straight
up in bed, gasping as if he'd just run a marathon.

A dream, just the same goddamn four-year-old dream.

Sweating and trembling like a leaf, he scrubbed his hands
over his face. Why couldn't he dream about something good,
like sex with triplets?

Shoving free of the covers, he limped naked to the window
and yanked it open. The cool mist of the spring storm brushed
his heated skin, and he fought the urge to close his eyes. If he
did, he'd be back there.

But the memories came anyway.

"Landing in ten," the pilot announced as the plane skimmed
just beneath the storm raging through the night.

In eight, the plane began to vibrate.

In six, lightning cracked.

And then an explosion, one so violent it nearly blew out his eardrums.

Ty dropped his head back, letting the rain slash at his body through the open window. He could hear the Pacific Ocean pounding the surf below the cliffs. Scented with fragrant pines, the air smelled like Christmas in April, and he forced himself to draw a deep, shaky breath.

He was no longer a SEAL medic dragging his sorry ass out of a burning plane, choking on the knowledge that he was the only one still breathing, that he hadn't been able to save a single soul. He was in Washington State, in the small beach town of Lucky Harbor. The ocean was in front of him, the Olympic Mountains at his back.

Safe.

But hell if at the next bolt of lightning, he didn't try to jump out of his own skin. Pissed at the weakness, Ty shut the window. He was never inhaling an entire pepperoni pizza before bed again.

Except he knew it wasn't something as simple as pizza that made him dream badly. It was the edginess that came from being idle. His work was still special ops, but he hadn't gone back to being a first responder trauma paramedic. Instead, he'd signed up as a private contractor to the government, which was a decent enough adrenaline rush. Plus it suited him—or it had until six months ago, when on an assignment he'd had to jump out a second story window to avoid being shot, and had reinjured his leg.

Stretching that leg now, he winced. He wanted to get back to his job. *Needed* to get back. But he also needed clearance from his doctor first. Pulling on a pair of jeans, he snagged a shirt off the back of a chair and left the room as the storm railed around outside. He made his way through the big and nearly empty house he'd rented for the duration, heading to the garage. A fast drive in the middle of the night would have to do, and maybe a quick stop at the all-night diner.

But this first.

Flipping on the lights, Ty sucked in a deep, calming breath of air heavy with the smells of motor oil, well-greased tools, and rubber tires. On the left sat a '72 GMC Jimmy, a rebuild job he'd picked up on the fly. He didn't need the money. As it turned out, special ops talents were well-compensated these days, but the repair work was a welcome diversion from his problems.

The '68 Shelby Mustang on the right wasn't a side job. She was his baby, and she was calling to him. He kicked the mechanic's creeper from against the wall toward the classic muscle car. Lowering himself onto the cart with a grimace of pain, Ty rolled beneath the car, shoving down his problems, denying them, avoiding them.

Seeking his own calm in the storm.

Chapter 1

Put the chocolate in the bag, and no one gets hurt.

The lightning flashed bright, momentarily blinding Mallory Quinn as she ran through the dark rainy night from her car to the front door of the diner.

One Mississippi.

Two Mississippi.

On three Mississippi, thunder boomed and shook the ground. A vicious wind nearly blew her off her feet. She'd forgotten her umbrella that morning, which was just as well or she'd have taken off like Mary Poppins.

A second, brighter bolt of lightning sent jagged light across the sky, and Mallory gasped as everything momentarily lit up like day: the pier behind the diner, the churning ocean, the menacing sky.

All went dark again, and she burst breathlessly into the Eat Me Café feeling like the hounds of hell were on her very tired heels. Except she wasn't wearing heels; she was in fake Uggs.

Lucky Harbor tended to roll up its sidewalks after ten o'clock, and tonight was no exception. The place was deserted except for a lone customer at the counter, and the waitress behind it. The waitress was a friend of Mallory's. Smartass, cynical Amy Michaels, whose tall, leggy body was reminiscent of Xena, the warrior princess. This was convenient, since Amy had a kick-ass 'tude to life in general. Her dark hair was a little tousled as always, her even darker eyes showed amusement at Mallory's wild entrance.

"Hey," Mallory said, fighting the wind to close the door behind her.

"Looking a little spooked," Amy said, wiping down the counter. "You reading Stephen King on the slow shifts again, Nurse Nightingale?"

Mallory drew a deep, shuddery breath and shook off the icy rain the best she could. Her day had started a million years ago at the crack of dawn when she'd left her house in her usual perpetual rush, without a jacket. One incredibly long ER shift and seventeen hours later, she was still in her scrubs with only a thin sweater over the top, everything now sticking to her like a second skin. She did not resemble a warrior princess. Maybe a drowned lady-in-waiting. "No Stephen," she said. "I had to give him up. Last month's reread of *The Shining* wrecked me."

Amy nodded. "Emergency Dispatch tired of taking your 'there's a shadow outside my window' calls?"

"Hey, that was *one* time." Giving up squeezing the water out of her hair, Mallory ignored Amy's knowing snicker. "And for your information, there really was a man outside my window."

"Yeah. Seventy-year-old Mr. Wykowski, who'd gotten turned around on his walk around the block."

This was unfortunately true. And while Mallory knew that Mr. Wykowski was a very nice man, he really did look a lot like

Jack Nicholson had in *The Shining*. "That could have been a *very* bad situation."

Amy shook her head as she filled napkin dispensers. "You live on Senior Drive. Your biggest 'situation' is if Dial-A-Ride doesn't show up in time to pick everyone up to take them to Bingo Night."

Also true. Mallory's tiny ranch house was indeed surrounded by other tiny ranch houses filled with mostly seniors. But it wasn't that bad. They were a sweet bunch and always had a coffee cake to share. Or a story about a various ailment or two. Or two hundred.

Mallory had inherited her house from her grandma, complete with a mortgage that she'd nearly had to give up her firstborn for. If she'd had a first born. But for that she'd like to be married, and to be married, she'd have to have a Mr. Right.

Except she'd been dumped by her last two Mr. Rights.

Wind and something heavy lashed at the windows of the diner. Mallory couldn't believe it. *Snow*. "Wow, the temp must have just dropped. That came on fast."

"It's spring," Amy said in disgust. "Why's it frigging snowing in spring? I changed my winter tires already."

The lone customer at the counter turned and eyed the view. "Crap. I don't have winter tires either." She looked to be in her mid-twenties and spoke with the clipped vowels that said northeast. If Amy was Xena, and Mallory the lady-in-waiting, then she was Blonde Barbie's younger, prettier, far more natural sister. "I'm in a 1972 VW Bug," she said.

As Mallory's own tires were threadbare, she gnawed on her lower lip and looked out the window. Maybe if she left immediately, she'd be okay.

"We should wait it out," Amy suggested. "It can't possibly last."

Mallory knew better, but it was her own fault. She'd been ignoring the forecast ever since last week, when the weather guy had promised ninety-degree temps and the day hadn't gotten above fifty, leaving her to spend a very long day frozen in the ER. Her nipples still hadn't forgiven her. "I don't have time to wait it out." She had a date with eight solid hours of sleep.

The VW driver was in a flimsy summer-weight skirt and two thin camisoles layered over each other. Mallory hadn't been the only one caught by surprise. Though the woman didn't look too concerned as she worked her way through a big, fat brownie that made Mallory's mouth water.

"Sorry," Amy said, reading her mind. "That was the last one."

"Just as well." Mallory wasn't here for herself anyway. Dead on her feet, she'd only stopped as a favor for her mother. "I just need to pick up Joe's cake."

Joe was her baby brother and turning twenty-four tomorrow. The last thing he wanted was a family party, but work was slow for him at the welding shop, and flying to Vegas with his friends hadn't panned out since he had no money.

So their mother had gotten involved and tasked Mallory with bringing a cake. Actually, Mallory had been tasked with *making* a cake, but she had a hard time not burning water so she was cheating. "Please tell me that no one from my crazy family has seen the cake so I can pretend I made it."

Amy *tsk*ed. "The good girl of Lucky Harbor, lying to her mother. Shame on you."

This was the ongoing town joke, "*good girl*" Mallory. Okay, fine, so in all fairness, she played the part. But she had her reasons—good ones—not that she wanted to go there now. Or ever. "Yeah, yeah. Hand it over. I have a date."

"You do not," Amy said. "I'd have heard about it if you did."

"It's a *secret* date."

Amy laughed because yeah, that *had* been a bit of a stretch. Lucky Harbor was a wonderful, small town where people cared about each other. You could leave a pot of gold in your backseat, and it wouldn't get stolen.

But there were no such things as secrets.

"I do have a date. With my own bed," Mallory admitted. "Happy?"

Amy wisely kept whatever smartass remark she had to herself and turned to the kitchen to go get the birthday cake. As she did, lightning flashed, followed immediately by a thundering boom. The wind howled, and the entire building shuddered, caught in the throes. It seemed to go on and on, and the three women scooted as close as they could to each other with Amy still on the other side of the counter.

"Suddenly I can't stop thinking about *The Shining*," the blonde murmured.

"No worries," Amy said. "The whole horror flick thing rarely happens here in Mayberry."

They all let out a weak laugh, which died when an ear-splitting crack sounded, followed immediately by shattering glass as both the front window and door blew in.

In the shocking silence, a fallen tree limb waved obscenely at them through the new opening.

Mallory grabbed the woman next to her and scurried behind the counter to join Amy. "Just in case more windows go," she managed. "We're safest right here, away from flying glass."

Amy swallowed audibly. "I'll never laugh at you about Mr. Wykowski again."

"I'd like that in writing." Mallory rose up on her knees, taking a peek over the counter at the tree now blocking the front door.

"I can't reach my brownie from here," Blondie said shakily. "I really need my brownie."

"What we need," Amy said, "is to blow this popsicle stand."

Mallory shook her head. "It's coming down too hard and fast

now. It's not safe to leave. We should call someone about the downed tree though."

Blondie pulled out her cell phone and eyed her screen. "I forgot I'm in Podunk. No reception in half the town." She grimaced. "Sorry. I just got here today. I'm sure Lucky Harbor is a very nice Podunk."

"It's got its moments." Mallory slapped her pockets for her own cell before remembering. *Crap.* "My phone's in the car."

"Mine's dead," Amy said. "But we have a landline in the kitchen, as long as we still have electricity."

Just then the lights flickered and went out.

Mallory's stomach hit her toes. "You had to say it," she said to Amy.

Blondie rustled around for a moment, and then there came a blue glow. "It's a cigarette lighter app," she said, holding up her phone, and the faux flame flickered over the screen like a real Bic lighter. "Only problem, it drains my battery really fast so I'll keep it off until we have an emergency." She hit the home button and everything went really, really dark.

Another hard gust of wind sent more of the shattered window tinkling to the floor, and the Bic lighter immediately came back on.

"Emergency," Blondie said as the three of them huddled together.

"Stupid cake," Mallory said.

"Stupid storm," Amy said.

"Stupid life," Blondie said. Pale, she looked at them. "Now would be a great time for one of you to tell me that you have a big, strong guy who's going to come looking for you."

"Yeah, not likely," Amy said. "What's your name?"

"Grace Brooks."

"Well, Grace, you're new to Lucky Harbor so let me fill you in. There are lots of big, strong guys in town. But I do my own heavy lifting."

Grace and Mallory both took in Amy's short Army camo cargo skirt and her shit-kicking boots, topped with a snug tee that revealed tanned, toned arms. The entire sexy-tough ensemble was topped by an incongruous Eat Me pink apron. Amy had put her own spin on it by using red duct tape to fashion a circle around the Eat Me logo, complete with a line through it.

"I can believe that about you," Grace said to her.

"My name's Amy." Amy tossed her chin toward Mallory. "And that's Mallory, my polar opposite and the town's very own good girl."

"Stop," Mallory said, tired of hearing "good" and "girl" in the same sentence as it pertained to her.

But of course Amy didn't stop. "If there's an old lady to help across the street or a kid with a skinned knee needing a Band-Aid and a kiss," she said, "or a big, strong man looking for a sweet, warm damsel, it's Mallory to the rescue."

"So where is he then?" Grace asked. "Her big, strong man?"

Amy shrugged. "Ask her."

Mallory grimaced and admitted the truth. "As it turns out, I'm not so good at keeping any Mr. Rights."

"So date a Mr. Wrong," Amy said.

"Shh, you." Not wanting to discuss her love life—or lack thereof—Mallory rose up on her knees to take another peek over the counter and outside in the hopes the snow had lightened up.

It hadn't.

Gusts were blowing the heavy snow sideways, hitting the remaining windows and flying in through the ones that had broken. She craned her neck and looked behind her into the kitchen. If she went out the back door, she'd have to go around the whole building to get to her car and her phone.

In the dark.

But it was the best way. She got to her feet just as the two windows over the kitchen sink shattered with a suddenness that caused Mallory's heart to stop.

Grace's Bic lighter came back on. "Holy shit," she gasped, and holding onto each other, they all stared at the offending tree branch waving at them from the new opening.

"Jan's going to blow a gasket," Amy said.

Jan was the owner of the diner. She was fifty-something, grumpy on the best of days, and hated spending a single dime of her hard-earned money on anything other than her online poker habit.

The temperature in the kitchen dropped as cold wind and snow blew over them. "Did I hear someone say cake?" Grace asked in a wobbly voice.

They did Rock-Paper-Scissors. Amy lost, so she had to crawl to the refrigerator to retrieve the cake. "You okay with this?" she asked Mallory, handing out forks.

Mallory looked at the cake. About a month ago, her scrubs had seemed to be getting tight so she'd given up chocolate. But sometimes there had to be exceptions. "This is a cake emergency. Joe will live."

So instead of trying to get outside, and then on to the bad roads, they all dug into the cake. And there in the pitch black night, unnerved by the storm but bolstered by sugar and chocolate, they talked.

Grace told them that when the economy had taken a nose-dive, her hot career as an investment banker had vanished, along with her condo, her credit cards, and her stock portfolio. There'd been a glimmer of a job possibility in Seattle so she'd traveled across the country for it. But when she'd gotten there, she found out the job involved sleeping with the sleazeball company president. She'd told him to stuff it, and now she was thinking about maybe hitting Los Angeles. Tired, she'd stopped in Lucky Harbor earlier today. She'd found a coupon for the local B&B

and was going to stay for a few days and regroup. "Or until I run out of money and end up on the street," she said, clearly trying to sound chipper about her limited options.

Mallory reached out for her hand and squeezed it. "You'll find something. I know it."

"I hope you're right." Grace let out a long, shaky breath. "Sorry to dump on you. Guess I'd been holding on to that all by myself for too long, it just burst out of me."

"Don't be sorry." Amy licked frosting off her finger. "That's what dark, stormy nights are for. Confessions."

"Well, I'd feel better if you guys had one as well."

Mallory wasn't big on confessions and glanced at Amy.

"Don't look at me," Amy said. "Mine isn't anything special."

Grace leaned in expectantly. "I'd love to hear it anyway."

Amy shrugged, looking as reluctant as Mallory felt. "It's just your average, run-of-the-mill riches-to-rags story."

"What?" Mallory asked, surprised, her fork going still. Amy had been in town for months now, and although she wasn't shy, she was extremely private. She'd never talked about her past.

"Well rags to riches *to rags* would be a better way of putting it," Amy corrected.

"Tell us," Grace said, reaching for another piece of cake.

"Okay, but it's one big bad cliché. Trailer trash girl's mother marries rich guy, trailer trash girl pisses new step-daddy off, gets rudely ousted out of her house at age sixteen, and disinherited from any trust fund. Broke, with no skills whatsoever, she hitches her way across the country, hooking up with the wrong people and then more wrong people, until it comes down to two choices. Straighten up or die. She decides straightening up is the better option and ends up in Lucky Harbor, because her grandma spent one summer here a million years ago and it changed her life."

Heart squeezing, Mallory reached for Amy's hand, too. "Oh, Amy."

"See?" Amy said to Grace. "The town sweetheart. She can't help herself."

"I can so," Mallory said. But that was a lie. She did like to help people—which made Amy right; she really couldn't help herself.

"And don't think we didn't notice that you avoided sharing any of *your* vulnerability with the class," Amy said.

"Maybe later," Mallory said, licking her fork. Or never. She shared just about every part of herself all the time. It was her work, and also her nature. So she held back because she had to have something that was hers alone. "I'm having another piece."

"Denial is her BFF," Amy told Grace as Mallory cut off a second hunk of cake. "I'd guess that it has something to do with her notoriously wild and crazy siblings and being the only sane one in the family. She doesn't think that she deserves to be happy, because that chocolate seems to be the substitute for something."

"Thanks, Dr. Phil." But it was uncomfortably close to the truth. Her family was wild and crazy, and she worked hard at keeping them together. And she did have a hard time with letting herself be totally happy and had ever since her sister Karen's death. She shivered. "Is there a lost-and-found box around somewhere with extra jackets or something?"

"Nope. Jan sells everything on eBay." Amy set her fork down and leaned back. "Look at us, sitting here stuffing ourselves with birthday cake because we have no better options on a Friday night."

"Hey, I have options," Grace said. "There's just a big, fat, mean storm blocking our exit strategies."

Amy gave her a droll look and Grace sagged. "Okay, I don't have shit."

They both looked at Mallory, and she sighed. "Fine. I'm

stalled too. I'm more than stalled, okay? I've got the equivalent of a dead battery, punctured tires, no gas, and no roadside assistance service. How's *that* for a confession?"

Grace and Amy laughed softly, their exhales little clouds of condensation. They were huddled close, trying to share body heat.

"You know," Amy said. "If we live through this, I'm going to—"

"Hey." Mallory straightened up in concern. "Of course we're going to live. Soon as the snow lets up, we'll push some branches out of the way and head out to my car and call for help, and—"

"Jeez," Amy said, annoyed. "Way to ruin my dramatic moment."

"Sorry. Do continue."

"Thank you. If we live," Amy repeated with mock gravity, "I'm going to keep a cake just like this in the freezer just for us. And also..." She shifted and when she spoke this time, her voice was softer. "I'd like to make improvements to my life, like living it instead of letting it live me. Growing roots and making real friends. I suck at that."

Mallory squeezed her hand tight in hers. "I'm a real friend," she whispered. "*Especially* if you mean it about the cake."

Amy's mouth curved in a small smile.

"If we live," Grace said. "I'm going to find more than a job. I want to stop chasing my own tail and go after some happy for a change, instead of waiting for it to find me. I've waited long enough."

Once again, both Amy and Grace looked expectantly at Mallory, who blew out a sigh. She knew what she wanted for herself, but it was complicated. She wanted to let loose, do whatever she wanted, and stop worrying about being the glue at work, in her family, for everyone. Unable to say that, she wracked her brain and came up with something else. "There's this big charity event I'm organizing for the hospital next weekend, a formal dinner and auction. I'm the only nurse on my floor without a date. If we live, a date would be really great."

"Well, if you're wishing, wish big," Amy said. "Wish for a little nookie too."

Grace nodded her approval. "Nookie," she murmured fondly. "Oh how I miss nookie."

"Nookie," Mallory repeated.

"Hot sex," Grace translated.

Amy nodded. "And since you've already said Mr. Right never works out for you, you should get a Mr. Wrong."

"Sure," Mallory said, secure in the knowledge that one, there were no Mr. Wrongs anywhere close by, and two, even if there had been, he wouldn't be interested in her.

Amy pulled her order pad from her apron pocket. "You know what? I'm making you a list of some possible candidates. Since this is the only type of guy I know, it's right up my alley. Off the top of my head, I can think of two. Dr. Josh Scott from the hospital, and Anderson, the guy who runs the hardware store. I'm sure there's plenty of others. Promise me that if a Mr. Wrong crosses your path, you're going for him. As long as he isn't a felon," she added responsibly.

Good to know there were some boundaries. Amy thrust out her pinkie for what Mallory assumed was to be a solemn pinkie swear. With a sigh Mallory wrapped her littlest finger around Amy's. "I promise—" She broke off when a thump sounded on one of the walls out front. Each of them went stock still, staring at each other.

"That wasn't a branch," Mallory whispered. "That sounded like a fist."

"Could have been a rock," Grace, the eternal optimist, said.

They all nodded but not a one of them believed it was a

rock. A bad feeling had come over Mallory. It was the same one she got sometimes in the ER right before they got an incoming. "May I?" she asked Grace, gesturing to the smart phone.

Grace handed it over and Mallory rose to her knees and used the lighter app to look over the edge of the counter.

It wasn't good.

The opened doorway had become blocked by a snow drift. It really was incredible for this late in the year, but big, fat, round snowflakes the size of dinner plates were falling from the sky, piling up quickly.

The thump came again, and through the vicious wind, she thought she also heard a moan. A pained moan. She stood. "Maybe someone's trying to get inside," she said. "Maybe they're hurt."

"Mallory," Amy said. "Don't."

Grace grabbed Mallory's hand. "It's too dangerous out there right now."

"Well, I can't just ignore it." Tugging free, Mallory wrapped her arms around herself and moved toward the opening. Someone was in trouble, and she was a sucker for that. It was the eternal middle child syndrome and the nurse's curse. Glass crunched beneath her feet, and she shivered as snow blasted her in the face. Amazingly, the aluminum frame of the front door had withstood the impact when the glass had shattered. Shoving aside the thick branch, Mallory once again held the phone out in front of her, using it to peer out into the dark.

Nothing but snow.

"Hello?" she called, taking a step outside, onto the concrete stoop. "Is anyone—"

A hand wrapped around her ankle, and Mallory broke off with a startled scream, falling into the night.

Chapter 2

If it's a toss up between men and chocolate,
bring on the chocolate!

Mallory scrambled backward, or tried to anyway, but a big hand on her ankle held firm. The hand appeared to be attached to an even bigger body. Fear and panic bubbled in her throat, and she simply reacted, chucking Grace's phone at her captor's hooded head.

It bounced off his cheek without much of a reaction other than a grunt. The guy was sprawled flat on his back, half covered in snow. Still holding her ankle in a vice-like grip, he shifted slightly and groaned. The sound didn't take her out of panic mode but it did push another emotion to the surface. Concern. Since he hadn't tried to hurt her, she leaned over him, brushing the snow away to get a better look—not easy with the wind pummeling her, bringing more icy snow that slapped at her bare face. "Are you hurt?" she asked.

He was non-responsive. His down parka was open, and he

was wet and shivering. Pushing his dark brown hair from his forehead, she saw the first problem. He had a nasty gash over an eyebrow, which was bleeding profusely in a trickle down his temple and over his swollen eye. Not from where she'd hit him with the phone, thankfully, but from something much bigger and heavier, probably part of the fallen tree.

His eyes suddenly flew open, his gaze landing intense and unwavering on her.

"It's okay," she said, trying to sound like she believed it. "It looks like you were hit by a large branch. You're going to need stitches, but for now I can—"

Before she could finish the thought, she found herself rolled beneath what had to be two hundred pounds of solid muscle, the entire length of her pressed ruthlessly hard into the snow, her hands yanked high over her head and pinned by his. He wasn't crushing her, nor was he hurting her, but his hold was shockingly effective. In less than one second, he'd immobilized her, shrink-wrapping her between the ground and his body.

"Who the hell are you?" he asked, voice low and rough. It would have brought goose bumps to her flesh if she hadn't already been covered in them.

"Mallory Quinn," she said, struggling to free herself. She'd have had better luck trying to move a slab of cement.

Breathing hard, eyes dilated, clearly out of his mind, he leaned over her, the snow blowing around his head like some twisted paragon of a halo.

"You have a head injury," she told him, using the brisk, no-nonsense, I'm-In-Charge tone she saved for both the ER and her crazy siblings. "You're hypothermic." And he was getting a nice red spot on his cheek, which she suspected was courtesy of the phone she'd hurled at him. Best not to bother him with the reminder of that. "I can help you if you let me."

He just stared down at her, not so much as blinking while the storm railed and rallied in strength around them. He wasn't fully conscious, that much was clear.

Still, testosterone and dark edginess poured off him, emphasized by his brutal grip on her. Mallory was cataloguing her options when the next gust hit hard enough to knock his hood back, and with a jolt, she recognized him.

Mysterious Cute Guy.

At least that's how he was known around Lucky Harbor. He'd slipped into town six months ago without making a single effort to blend in.

As a whole, Lucky Harbor wasn't used to that. Residents tended to consider it a God-given right to gossip and nose into people's business, and no one was exempt. All that was known about the man was that he was staying in a big rental house up on the bluffs.

There'd been sightings of him at the Love Shack—the town's bar and grill—and also at the local gym, and filling up some classic muscle car at the gas station. But Mallory had only seen him once in the grocery store parking lot, with a bag in hand. Tall and broad shouldered, he'd been facing his car, the muscles of his back straining his shirt as he reached into his pocket to retrieve his keys. He'd slid his long legs into his car and accelerated out of the lot, as she caught a flash of dark Oakleys, a firm jaw, and grim mouth.

A little frisson of female awareness had skittered up her spine that day, and even wet and cold and uncomfortable beneath him, she got another now. He felt much colder than she, making her realize she had no idea how long he'd been out here. He was probably concussed, but the head injury would be the least of his problems if she didn't get him warmed up and call for help. "Let's get you inside," she said, ceasing to struggle beneath him, hoping that might calm him down.

No response, not even a twitch of a single muscle.

"You have to let me up," she said. "I can help you if you let me up."

At that, he seemed to come around a little bit. Slowly he drew back, pulling off her until he was on his knees, but he didn't let go of her, still manacling both of her wrists in one hand. His eyes were shadowed, and it was dark enough that she couldn't see their color. She couldn't see much of anything but she didn't need a light to catch the tension coming off of him in waves.

His brow furrowed. "Are you hurt?"

"It's you who's hurt."

"No, I'm not."

Such a typical guy response. He was bleeding and nearly unconscious, but he wasn't hurt. Good to know. "You're bleeding, and we need to get you warmed up, so—"

He interrupted this with an unintelligible denial, followed by another groan just before his eyes rolled up. In almost slow-motion, he began to topple over. She barely managed to grab onto his coat, breaking his fall with her own torso so he didn't hit his head again. But he was so heavy that they both fell.

"Oh my God," came Grace's quavering voice. "That's a lot of blood."

Mallory squeezed out from beneath him and looked up to see both Grace and Amy peeking out from between the fallen tree branches and the door frame.

"Holy shit," Amy said. "Is he okay?"

"He will be." Mallory scooped Grace's phone from the snow and tossed it to her. "I need help. I told him I'd get him inside but my car's better, I think. My phone's there, and I have reception. We can call for help. And I can turn on the engine and use the heater to warm him up."

Amy leaned over him, peering into his face. "Wait." She looked at Mallory. "You know who this is, right? It's Mysterious Cute Guy. He comes into the diner."

"You never told me," Mallory said.

Amy shrugged. "He never says a word. Tips good though."

"Who's Mysterious Cute Guy?" Grace wanted to know.

"When you get reception on your phone, pull up Lucky Harbor's Facebook," Amy told her. "There's a list of Mysterious Cute Guy sightings on the wall there, along with the Bingo Night schedule and how many women managed to get pulled over by Sheriff Hotstuff last weekend. Sawyer's engaged now so it's not as much fun to get pulled over by him anymore, but at least we have Mysterious Cute Guy so it doesn't matter as much."

Grace fell silent, probably trying to soak in the fact that she'd landed in Mayberry, U.S.A.

Or the Twilight Zone.

Mallory wrapped her arms around Mysterious Cute Guy from behind, lifting his head and shoulders out of the snow and into her lap. He didn't move. Not good. "Grace, get his feet," she said. "Amy, take his middle. Come on."

"It's karma, you know that, right?" Amy said, huffing and puffing as they barely managed to lift the man. Actually *dragged* was more like it. "Because you promised you'd go for the first Mr. All Wrong who landed at your feet. And here he is. Literally."

"Yes, well, I meant a conscious one."

"He's going on the list," Amy said.

"Careful!" Mallory admonished Grace, who'd dropped his feet. Too late. With the momentum, they all fell to their butts in the snow, Mysterious Cute Guy sprawled out over the top of them.

"Sorry," Grace gasped. "He weighs a ton."

"Solid muscle though," Amy noted, being in a good position to know since she had two handfuls of his hindquarters.

Somehow, squinting through the snow and pressing into the wind, they made it to Mallory's car. She hadn't locked it, had in fact left her keys in the ignition, which Grace shook her head about.

"It's Lucky Harbor," Mallory said in her defense.

"I don't care if it's Never Never Land," Grace told her. "You need to lock up your car."

They got Mysterious Cute Guy in the backseat, which wasn't big enough for him by any stretch. They bent his legs to accommodate his torso, then Mallory climbed in and again put his head in her lap. "Start the car," she told Amy. "And crank the heat. Get my phone from the passenger seat," she said to Grace. "Call 9-1-1. Tell them we've got a male, approximately thirty years of age, unconscious with a head injury and possible hypothermia. Give them our location so they can send an ambulance."

They both did her bidding, with Amy muttering "domineering little thing" beneath her breath. But she started the car and switched the heater to high before turning toward the back again. Her dark hair was dusted with snow, making her look like a pixie. "He still breathing?"

"Yes."

"Are you sure? Because maybe he needs mouth to mouth."

"Amy!"

"Just a suggestion, sheesh."

Grace ended her call to dispatch. "They said fifteen minutes. They said to try to get him warm and dry. Which means one of us needs to strip down with him to keep him warm, right? That's how it's done in the movies."

"Oh my God, you two," Mallory said.

Amy turned to Grace. "We're going to have to give her lessons on how to be a Bad Girl, you know that, right?"

Mallory ignored them and looked down at her patient. His brow was still furrowed tight, his mouth grim. Wherever he was in dreamland, it wasn't a happy place. Then suddenly the muscles in his shoulders and neck tensed, and he went rigid. She cupped both sides of his face to hold him still. "You're okay," she told him.

Shaking his head, he let out a low, rough sound of grief. "They're gone. They're all . . . gone."

The three women stared at each other for a beat, then Mallory bent lower over him. "Hey," she said gently, knowing better than to wake him up abruptly. "We've got you. You're in Lucky Harbor, and—"

He shoved her hand off of him and sat straight up so fast that he nearly hit his head on her chin, and then the roof of the car.

"We've called an ambulance," she said.

Twisting around, he stared at her, his eyes dark and filled with shadows.

"You okay?" she asked.

"Fine."

"Really? Because the last time you said that, you passed out."

He swiped at his temple and stared at the blood that came away on his forearm. "Goddammit."

"Yeah. See, you're not quite fine—"

He made a sound that managed to perfectly convey what he thought of her assessment, which turned into a groan of pain as he clutched his head.

Mallory forced him to lie back down. "Be still."

"Bossy," he muttered. "But hot."

Hot? Did he really just say that? Mallory looked down at herself. Wrinkled nurse's scrubs, fake Uggs, and she had no doubt her hair was a disaster of biblical proportions. She was just about the furthest she could get from *hot*, which meant that he was full of shit.

"Mr. Wrong," Amy whispered to her.

Uh huh, more like Mr. *All* Wrong. But unable to help herself, Mallory took in his very handsome, bloody face, and had to admit it was true. She couldn't have found a more Mr. All Wrong for herself if she'd tried.

Ty drifted half awake when a female voice penetrated his shaken-but-not-stirred brain.

"I'm keeping a list of Mr. Wrongs going for you. This one might not make it to the weekend's auction."

"Stop," said another woman.

"I'm just kidding."

"I still vote we strip him down." This was a third woman.

Wait. Three women? Had he died and gone to orgy heaven? Awake now, Ty took stock. He wasn't dead. And he had no idea who the fuck Mr. Wrong was, but he was very much "going to make it." He was stuffed in the back of a car, a *small* car, his bad leg cramping like a son-of-a-bitch. His head was pillowed on...he shifted to try to figure it out, and pain lanced straight through his eyeballs. He licked his dry lips and tried to focus. "I'm okay."

"Good," one of them repeated with humor. "He's fine, he's okay. He's also bleeding like a stuck pig. Men are ridiculous."

"Just stay still," someone close said to him, the same someone who'd earlier told him that he'd been hit by a branch. It felt more like a Mack Truck. Given where her voice was coming from, directly above him, it must be her very nice rack that he was pillowed against. Risking tossing his cookies, he tilted his head back to see her. This was tricky because one, it was dark, and two, he was seeing in duplicate. Her hair was piled into a ponytail on top of her head. Half of it had tumbled free, giving her—both of her—a mussed-up, just out-of-bed look. Looking a little bit rumpled, she wore what appeared to be standard issue hospital scrubs, hiding what he could feel was a very nice, soft, female form. She was pretty in an understated way, her features delicate but set with purpose.

A doctor, maybe. Except she didn't have the cockiness that most doctors held. A nurse, maybe.

"I know it looks like you've lost a bit of blood," she said, "but head injuries always bleed more, often making them appear more serious than they are."

Yeah. A nurse. He could have told her he'd seen more head injuries than she could possibly imagine. One time he'd even seen a head blown clear off a body, but she wouldn't want to hear that.

Her blessedly warm hand touched the side of his face. He turned into it and tried to think. Earlier when he'd woken up to the nightmare, he'd gone to work on the Shelby before taking it for a drive. He'd needed speed and the open road. Of course that had been before the snow hit, because even he wasn't that reckless. He remembered winding his way along the highway, the cliffs on his right, and far below on his left, the Pacific Ocean. The sea had been pitching and rolling as the storm moved in long, silvery fingers over the water. He remembered making it into town, remembered wanting pie and seeing the lights in the diner, so he'd parked.

That's when it'd started to snow like a mother.

He'd gotten nearly to the door when his memory abruptly ended. Damn. He hated that. He tried to sit up but six hands pushed him back down. Christ. That'd teach him to wish for a dream about triplets.

Someone's phone lit up, giving them some light, and Ty ordered himself to focus through the hammering in his skull. It wasn't easy, but he found that if he squinted he could see past the cobweb vision. Sort of.

Leaning over the back of the driver's seat was the waitress from the diner, though she was looking a little bit like a drowned rat at the moment. The woman riding shotgun next to her was a willowy blonde and unfamiliar to him.

As was the woman whose breasts were his pillow. "Thanks," he said to her. "For saving my ass."

"So... would you say you *owe* her?" the waitress asked.

"Amy," his nurse said in a warning tone. Then she shot Ty a weak smile. "You've had quite a night."

And so had she. She didn't say so—she didn't have to—it was all there in her doe-like brown eyes.

"The ambulance will be here soon," she said.

"Don't need one."

She didn't bother to point out that he was flat on his back and obviously pretty damn helpless. She kept her hands on him, her gaze now made of steel, signaling that in spite of those soft eyes, she was no pushover. "We'll get you patched up," she said. "And some meds for your pain."

"No." Fuck, no.

"Look, it's obvious you're hurting, so—"

"*No narcotics*," he growled, then had to grip his head to keep it on his shoulders, grinding his teeth as he rode out the latest wave of pain. Stars danced around in front of his eyes, shrinking to pinpoints as the darkness took him again.

"They passed us up," Grace said worriedly, twisting to follow the flashing blue and red ambulance lights moving slowly through the lot and back out again.

"Did you tell them that we were inside my car, and to look for us here?" Mallory asked.

"No. Dammit." Grace grabbed Mallory's phone again. "Sorry. I'll call them back right now."

Mallory looked down at her patient. Dark, silky hair. Square scruffy jaw. An old scar along his temple, a new one forming right this very minute on his eyebrow. His eyes were still closed, his face white and clammy, but she could tell he was awake again. "Easy," she said, figuring she'd be lucky if he held off getting sick until they got him out of here.

"What happened?" he said, jaw tight, eyes still closed, his big body a solid weight against her.

It was not uncommon after a head trauma to keep forgetting what had happened, so she gave him the recap. "Tree on the head."

"And then Nurse Nightingale here came to your rescue," Amy told him. "And you said you owed her."

"Amy," Mallory said.

"She needs a date this weekend," Amy told him.

"Ignore her." Over his head, Mallory gave Amy the universal finger-slicing-at-the-throat signal for *Shut It*.

Amy ignored her. "If you go with her to the charity auction on Saturday night at the Vets' Hall, you'd save her from merciless ridicule. She can't get her own date, you see."

Mallory sighed. "Thanks, Amy. Appreciate that. But I can so get my own—"

Unbelievably, her patient interrupted her with what sounded like a murmured ascent.

But Amy grinned and bumped fists with Grace. "Five bucks says Mr. Wrong will rock her world."

Grace looked down at the prone man in Mallory's lap with clear doubt. "You're on," she whispered back.

Mallory gave up trying to control Amy and eyed her patient. Even flat on his back, he was lethally gorgeous. She could only imagine what he'd be like dressed to the nines and on his feet.

"She'll meet you at the event, of course," Amy said to him. "Because even though this is Lucky Harbor, we're not giving you her address. You might be a serial killer. Or worse, just be a completely Mr. Right."

Another sound of ascent from Mysterious Cute Guy. Which, actually, might have been more of a moan of disbelief that he'd agreed to this craziness.

Right there with you, Mr. Wrong. Right there with you.

Chapter 3

By age thirty-five, women have only a few taste
buds left: one for alcohol, one for cheese,
and one for chocolate.

One week later, Mallory was walking around in a cloud of anticipation in spite of herself. The auction was tonight, and although she
knew damn well Mysterious Cute Guy wasn't going to show up,
she could admit a tiny part of her wanted to be proven wrong.

Not that she'd actually *choose* to date a man like him, with the
guarded eyes and edgy 'tude. She didn't even know his name.
Not to mention she'd chucked a phone at his face.

Mr. Wrong, aka Mysterious Cute Guy...

Truthfully, that whole stormy night at the diner was still pretty
much a blur to her. The ambulance had eventually found them
and loaded up her patient. The snow had stopped, and Mallory
had been able to drive home, after a solemn pinky-swear vow
with both Amy and Grace to meet weekly, at least for as long as
Grace stayed in town.

Chocoholics—CA for short—was their name, chocolate cake was their game.

Mallory had then spent the rest of the week alternating between long shifts in the ER and working on the auction. A portion of the evening's take would go to her own pet project, the Health Services Clinic she planned to open in conjunction with the County Hospital Foundation. HSC would be a place for anyone in the county to get community recovery resources, teen services, crisis counseling, and a whole host of other programs she'd been trying to get going for several years. She still needed hospital board approval, and hopefully the money from the auction would ensure that. It's what should have been foremost in her mind.

Instead that honor went to one Mysterious Cute Guy. For the first time that day, Mallory walked by the nurses' station and eyed the computer. Thanks to HIPPA, a very strict privacy act, she couldn't access a patient's records unless she'd actually worked on the patient that day. This meant that if she wanted to know his name, she'd have to ask the nurse who'd seen him in the ER that night. Unfortunately, her own mother had been his nurse, so she decided against that option.

Luckily, she had six patients to keep her occupied. The problem was that her counterpart, Alyssa, was very busy flirting with the new resident, doing none of her duties. This made for a long morning, made even longer by the fact that one of Mallory's patients was Mrs. Louisa Burland. Mrs. Burland was suffering from arrhythmia complicated by vasovagal syncope, a condition that was a common cause of dizziness, light-headedness, and fainting in the elderly. She was also suffering from a condition called Meanness. "I brought you the juice you asked for," Mallory said, entering Mrs. B's room.

"I asked for that three hours ago. What's wrong with you? You're slower than molasses."

Mallory ignored this complaint because it'd been five minutes, not three hours. And because Mrs. B was so bitter that even the volunteer hospital visitors skipped her room. Before retiring, the woman had been a first grade teacher who had at one time or another terrorized most of town with a single bony finger that she liked to waggle in people's faces. She was so difficult that even her daughter, who lived up the road in Seattle, refused to call or visit.

"I remember you, you know," Mrs. Burland said. "You peed yourself in front of your entire class."

Mallory was surprised to find that she could still burn with shame at the memory. "Because you wouldn't let me go to the bathroom."

"Recess was only five minutes away."

"Well, obviously, I couldn't wait."

"And now you make me wait. You're a terrible nurse, letting your treatment of me be clouded by our past interactions."

Mallory ignored this too. She set the juice, complete with straw, on Mrs. Burland's bedside tray.

"I wanted *apple* juice," Mrs. B said.

"You asked for cranberry."

Mrs. Burland's hand lashed out and the juice went flying, spilling across the bedding, the floor, the IV pole, and Mallory as well. Juice dripping off her nose, Mallory sighed. Perfect. It took twenty minutes to clean up the mess. Ten more to get Mrs. Burland back into her now fresh bed, which had Mallory huffing a little with the effort.

Mrs. B *tsk*ed. "Out of shape, or just gaining some weight?"

Mallory sucked in her belly and tried not to feel guilty about the cinnamon roll she'd inhaled on a quick break two hours ago. She reminded herself that she helped save lives, not take them, and walked out of the room, purposely not glancing at herself in the small mirror over the sink as she went.

Paramedics were just bringing in a new patient, a two-year-old with a laceration requiring stitches. Mallory got him all cleaned up and prepped the area for the doctor. She drew the lidocaine, got a suture kit, 4x4s and some suture material, and then assisted in the closing of the wound.

And so it went.

At her first break, she made her way to the nurses' break room and grabbed her soft-sided lunch box out of the fridge. Her older sister Tammy was there and Mallory sidled up to her. Once upon a time, Tammy had been wild. For that matter, so had Mallory's younger brother Joe. And Tammy's twin, Karen. All three of them, as out of control as they came.

Not Mallory. She'd always been the good one, attempting to distract her parents from the stress of raising wild, out-of-control kids.

Then Karen had died.

Tammy and Joe had carried on for Karen in the same vein, but for Mallory, everything had pretty much skidded to a halt. Blaming herself, she'd fallen into a pit of desperate grief. She'd always walked the straight and narrow path, but she'd taken it to a new extreme, terrified to do anything wrong, to screw a single thing up and make things worse for her parents. Once during that terrible time, she'd accidentally forgotten to pay for a lip balm and had turned herself in as a thief. The clerk of the store had refused to press charges, instead calling Mallory's mother to come get her.

Mallory had felt as if she'd needed to be punished in some way for not paying enough attention to Karen, for being a bad sister, for something, *anything*. She'd put all of her energy into healing her family, but had not been even remotely successful. Her parents divorced and her father had left to go surf in Australia. He'd never come back, and Tammy and Joe...well, they'd gone even further off the deep end.

Joe was doing better these days, spending far less time at cop central and more time on the job. Tammy had improved, too. Sure, last year she'd headed to Vegas for a weekend and had come home with a husband. But to everyone's shock, the wedding hadn't been because of an unplanned pregnancy. It hadn't even been alcohol-related.

Well, it might have been a little bit alcohol-related, but unbelievably, Tammy and her hotel security guard-turned-shotgun husband were still married. She'd applied for and landed a housekeeping job at the hospital and—gasp—had actually held onto the job, the same as her marriage. And since their mother was a supervisory nurse, that meant there were *three* Quinns at the hospital working together. Or, more accurately, Tammy and Ella working as opposing magnets, with Mallory doing her best to hold onto them both.

Tammy had been on shift the night of the freak storm, and because she liked to know everything, in all likelihood she knew Mysterious Cute Guy's name.

Mallory knew that asking her would be better than asking her mom—or looking in the computer and losing her job, not to mention completely invading the guy's privacy—but not by much. Her best hope was for his name to come up in a conversation, all casual-like, maybe even "accidentally." The trick was to not let Tammy know what Mallory wanted, or it'd be Game Over.

The break room was crowded, as it usually was at this time of the day. Mostly it was filled with other nurses and aides. Today Lucille was sitting on the couch as well, sipping a cup of coffee in her volunteer's uniform.

No one knew exactly how old Lucille was, but she'd been running the art gallery in town since the dawn of time. She was also the hub of all things gossip in Lucky Harbor, and she gave one-hundred percent in life. This included her volunteering efforts, and since she knew *everyone*, she'd been hugely influential in helping Mallory gain interest in the Health Services Clinic. Fond of her, Mallory waved, then sat next to Tammy at the large round table in the center of the room.

Tammy smiled and put down her phone. "Heard about tonight."

Mallory stopped in the act of pulling out her sandwich. This might be easier than she thought. "What about tonight?"

"Rumor is that you have a hot blind date for the auction."

"No, I—" She went still. "Wait a minute. How did you hear that?"

"I'm psychic," Tammy said and stole Mallory's chips from her lunch bag.

Dammit, she *needed* those chips. Then she remembered what Mrs. Burland had said about gaining weight and sighed. "Just because you paid for an online course to learn to manage your Wiccan powers does not mean you actually *have* powers. How did you hear about the date?"

"Amy told me when I grabbed lunch at the diner yesterday."

Okay, she'd kill Amy later at their Chocoholics meeting. For now, it was just the opening Mallory needed. "First of all, the date thing is just a silly rumor." Even if she was secretly hoping otherwise. "And second...did Amy happen to tell you *who* this silly rumor date might be with?"

"Yep." Tammy was munching her way through the chips and moaning with pleasure, damn her. Mallory hoped she gained five pounds.

"I can't believe you actually landed Mysterious Cute Guy," Tammy said, licking salt off her fingers.

"*Shh*!" Mallory took a quick, sweeping glance around them, extremely aware of Lucille only a few feet away, ears aquiver with the attempt to eavesdrop. "*Keep it down*."

Unimpressed with the need for stealth, Tammy went on. "It's pretty damn impressive, really. Didn't know you had it in you.

I mean, your last boyfriend was that stuffy accountant from Seattle, remember? The only mysterious thing about him was what you saw in him."

"You were here last weekend when he came in," Mallory said.

"The accountant?"

"My *date*."

Tammy smiled. She knew she was stepping on Mallory's last nerve. It was what she did. And this wasn't going well.

"So is it a silly rumor?" Tammy asked. "Or a real date?"

"Never mind!" Mallory paused. "But . . . did you hear anything about him?"

"Like . . . ?"

Lucille was nearly falling off the couch now, trying to catch the conversation. Mallory turned her chair slightly, more fully facing her sister. "Like his name," she whispered.

This got Tammy's attention in a big way. "Wait a minute. You don't know his name?"

Shit.

"Wow, how absolutely naughty, Mal. You haven't done naughty since you were sixteen and turned yourself in for shoplifting. Now you may or may not have a date with a guy whose name you don't know. A fascinating cry for attention." Tammy turned her head. "You catching all of this, Lucille?"

"Oh, you know I am." Lucille pulled out a Smartphone and began tapping keys with her thumbs. Probably writing on the Facebook wall. "This is good; keep talking."

Mallory dropped her head to the table and thunked it but unfortunately she didn't lose consciousness and she still had to finish her shift.

After work, she drove home and watered her next door neighbor's flowers because Mrs. Tyler was wheelchair-bound and couldn't do it for herself. Then she watered her grandma's beloved flowers. She fed the ancient old black cat that had come with the house, the one who answered only to "Sweet Pea" and only when food was involved. And before she showered to get ready for the night's dinner and auction, she clicked through her e-mail.

Then wished she hadn't.

She'd been tagged on Facebook.

Make sure to buy tickets for tonight's elegant formal dinner and auction, folks! Supported by the hospital, organized by the nurses and spearheaded by Mallory Quinn, all proceeds will go into the Hospital Foundation's coffers toward the Health Services Clinic that Mallory's been working on shoving down our throats. (Just kidding, Mallory!)

And speaking of Ms. Quinn, rumor is that she'll 'maybe' have a date for the event after all, with Mysterious Cute Guy!

Go Mallory!

p.s. Anyone at the event with their cell phone, pictures are greatly appreciated!

Chapter 4

Chocolate will never fail you.

Ty's routine hadn't changed much in the six months he'd been in Lucky Harbor. He got up in the mornings and either swam in the ocean or went to the gym, usually with Matt Bowers, a local supervisory forest ranger and the guy who owned the '72 GMC Jimmy that Ty was fixing up.

Matt was ex-Chicago SWAT, but before that he'd been in the Navy. He and Ty had gone through basic together.

When Ty had injured his leg again, Matt had coaxed him out West to rehabilitate. They'd spent time hitting the gun range, but mostly they enjoyed beating the shit out of each other on the mats.

They had a routine. They'd lie panting side by side on their backs in the gym. "Another round?" Matt would ask.

"Absolutely," Ty would say.

Neither of them would move.

"You doing okay?" Matt would then ask.

"Don't want to talk about it," Ty would say.

Matt would let it go.

Ty would hit the beach, swimming until the exhaustion nearly pulled him under. Afterward, he'd force himself along the choppy, rough rocky beach just to prove he could stay upright. He'd started out slow—hell, he'd practically crawled—but he could walk it now. It was quite the feat. Or so his doctor kept telling him. He supposed this was true given that four years ago, he'd nearly lost his left leg in the plane crash thanks to a post-surgical infection.

Which was a hell of a lot less than Brad, Tommy, Kelly, and Trevor had lost.

At the thought of that time and the loss of his team, the familiar clutching seized his gut. He hadn't been able to save a single one of them. He'd been trained as a trauma paramedic, but their injuries, and his own, had proven too much. Later he'd been honorably discharged and he'd walked away from being a medic.

He hadn't given anyone so much as a Band-Aid since.

Working in the private sector had proven to be a good fit for him. In actuality, it wasn't all that different from being enlisted, except the pay was better and he got a say in his assignments. But six months out of work was making him think too much. He wasn't used to this down time. He wasn't used to being in one spot for so long. His entire life had been one base after another, one mission after another. He was ready to get back to that world.

He *needed* to get back to that world, because it was the only way he had of making sure that his team's death meant something.

But Dr. Josh Scott, the man in charge of his medical care until he was cleared, took a weekly look at Ty's scans and shook his head each time.

So here Ty was, holed up and recuperating in the big, empty house that Matt had leased for him, the one that was as far from his world as he could get. Far away from where he'd grown up, from anyone he'd known. Just as well, since they were all gone now anyway. His dad had been killed in Desert Storm. His mom had passed two years ago. With his closest friends resting beneath their marble tombstones in Arlington, there was no one else: no wife, no lover, no kids.

It made for a short contact list on his cell phone.

Instead of thinking about that, he spent his time fixing cars instead of people—Matt's 1972 Jimmy, his own Shelby—because cars didn't die on those they cared about.

On the day of the big hospital auction, after replacing the transmission on Matt's Jimmy, Ty degreased and showered, as always. Unlike always, he passed over his usual jeans for a suit, then stared at himself in the mirror, hardly recognizing the man looking back at him. He still had stitches over one eye and a bruise on his cheek from the storm incident. His hair was on the wrong side of a haircut, and he'd skipped shaving. He'd lost some weight over the past six months, making the angles of his face more stark. His eyes seemed...hollow. They matched how he felt inside. His body might be slowly getting back into lean, mean fighting shape, but he had some work yet to do on his soul. He shoved his hand in his pocket and pulled out the ever-present Vicodin bottle, rolling it between his fingers.

The bottle had been empty for two months now, and he'd still give his left nut for a refill. He had two refills available to him; it said so right on the bottle. But since Ty had started to need to be numb—with a terrifying desperation—he'd quit cold turkey.

This didn't help his leg. Rubbing it absently, he turned

away from the mirror, having no idea why he was going to the auction.

Except he did. He was going because the entire town would be there, and in spite of himself, he was curious.

He wanted to see her again, his bossy, warm, sexy nurse.

Which was ridiculous. It'd been so dark the night of the storm that he honestly wasn't sure he even knew what she looked like. But he knew he'd recognize her voice—that soft, warm voice. It was pretty much all he remembered of the entire evening, the way it'd soothed and calmed him.

Shaking his head, he strode through the bedroom, slipping keys and cash into his pockets, skipping the gun for the night although he'd miss the comforting weight of it. His cell phone was up to fifty-five missed calls now, which was a record. Giving in, he called voice mail and waited for the inevitable.

"Ty," said a sexy female voice. "Call me."

Frances St. Claire was the hottest redhead he'd ever seen and also the most ruthless. The messages went back a month or so.

Delete.

"Ty," she said on one of them. "Seriously. Call me."

Delete.

"Ty, I'm not fucking around. I need to hear from you."

Delete.

"Ty, Goddammit! Call me, you bastard!"

Delete.

As the rest of the calls were all variations on the same theme, with slurs on Ty's heritage and questionable moral compass, he hit *delete, delete, delete…*

There was no need to call her back. He knew exactly what she wanted. Him, back at work.

Which made two of them.

* * *

Mallory paced the lobby of Vets' Hall in her little black dress and designer heels knock-offs, nodding to the occasional late straggler as they came in. From the large front gathering room, she could smell the delicious dinner that was being served and knew she should be in there. Eating. Smiling. Schmoozing. Getting people fired up for the auction and ready to spend their money.

But she was missing one thing. A date.

Her Mr. All Wrong hadn't showed, not a big surprise. She hadn't really expected him to come, but…hell. Amy had gotten her hopes up. And speaking of Amy, Mallory blinked in shock as the tall, poised, *gorgeous* woman stopped in front of her.

"Wow." She'd never seen Amy with makeup, or in a dress for that matter, but tonight she was in both, in a killer slinky dress and some serious kick-ass gladiator style heels, both of which emphasized endless legs.

Amy shrugged. "The hospital thrift store."

"*Wow*," Mallory repeated. "You look like you belong in a super hero movie."

"Yeah, yeah. Listen, I came out here to ask you if we need to review your mission tonight with Mr. Wrong."

"Nope. Mission cancelled."

"What? Where's your date?"

"We both know that I didn't really have a date." Mallory shook her head. "You look so *amazing*. I hardly even recognize you."

"Can't judge a book by its cover," Amy said casually. "Have you seen Grace? She didn't know any guys in town, and there's no one I'm interested in, so she's my date tonight."

In the time since Amy had shown up in Lucky Harbor, Mallory had never known her to go out on a date. Whenever Mallory asked about it, Amy shrugged and said the pickings were too slim. "Maybe I should be making you two a list of Mr. Rights," Mallory said.

Amy snorted. "Been there, done that."

Matt Bowers walked by and stopped to say hi to Mallory. She was used to seeing him in his ranger uniform, armed and in work mode. But tonight he was in an expensive dark suit, appearing just as comfortable in his own skin as always, and looking pretty damn fine while he was at it. He was six feet tall, built rangy and leanly muscled like the boxer he was on his off days. He had sun-kissed brown hair from long days on the mountain, light brown eyes, and an easy smile that he flashed at Mallory. "Hey," he said.

She smiled. "Hey, back."

Matt turned his attention politely to Amy, and then his eyes registered sudden surprise. "*Amy?*"

"Yeah, I know. I clean up okay." Her voice was emotionless, her smile gone as she turned to Mallory. "See you in there."

Matt's gaze tracked Amy as she strode across the lobby and vanished inside. Yeah, he looked very fine tonight—and also just the slightest bit bewildered.

Mallory knew him to be a laid-back, easygoing guy. Sharp, quick-witted, and tough as hell. He had to be, given that he was an ex-cop and now worked as a district forest ranger supervisor. Nothing much ever seemed to get beneath his skin.

But Amy had. Interesting. This was definitely going on the list of topics to be discussed during their next little Chocoholics meeting. "You forget to tip her at the diner or something?" she asked him.

"Or something," Matt said. With a shake of his head, he walked off.

Mallory shrugged and took one more look around. At first, she'd been so busy setting up, and then greeting people, that she'd been far too nervous to think about what would happen if Mr. Wrong didn't show up.

But she was thinking about it now, and it wasn't going to be pleasant. She paced the length of the lobby again, stopping to look once more out the large windows into the parking lot. Argh. She strode back to the dining area and peeked in.

Also filled.

This was both good and bad news. Good, because there was lots of potential money in all those pockets.

Bad, because there was also a lot of potential humiliation in having to go in there alone after it'd been announced that she had a date.

Well, she'd survived worse, she assured herself. Far worse. Still, she managed to waste another five minutes going through the displays of the auction items for the umpteenth time, and as she had every single one of those times, she dawdled in front of one display in particular.

It was a small item, a silver charm bracelet. Each of its charms were unique to Lucky Harbor in some way: a tiny Victorian B&B, a miniature pier, and a gold pan from the gold rush days. So pretty.

Normally, the only jewelry Mallory wore was a small, delicate gold chain with an infinity charm that had been Karen's. It had been all she ever needed, but this bracelet kept drawing her in, urging her to spend money she didn't have.

"Not exactly practical for an ER nurse."

Mallory turned and found Mrs. Burland standing behind her, leaning heavily on a cane, her features twisted into a smile, only named so because her teeth were bared. "Mrs. Burland. You're feeling better?"

"Hell, no. My ankles are swollen, my fingers are numb, and I'm plugged up beyond any roto-rooter help."

Mallory was well used to people telling her things that would never come up in normal conversations. "You need to stay hydrated. You taking your meds?"

"There was a mix-up at the pharmacy."

"You need those meds," Mallory said.

"I tried calling my doctor. He's an idiot. And he's twelve."

Mrs. B's doctor was Dr. Josh Scott. Josh was thirty-two, and one of the best MDs on the West Coast.

"Trades on his cute looks," Mrs. Burland sniffed.

Mallory wouldn't have described Josh as cute. Handsome, yes. Definitely striking as well, and...serious, even when he smiled. So serious that he always looked like he'd been to hell and back. And had learned plenty along the way.

None of which had anything to do with his ability to do his job. Josh worked his ass off. "You're being very unfair to a man who's given you your life back. I'll check into the med issue for you first thing in the morning."

"Yes, well, see that you do. Where's your date?"

Mallory took a deep breath. "Well—"

"You've been stood up? A shame, since you're dressed to put out." Then the woman walked away.

Mallory went back to staring down at the bracelet. Mrs. B was right about one thing: it *was* totally impractical for anyone who had to be as practical as she did on a daily basis. The charms would snag on everything from patients' leads to the bed rails.

"Sweetheart, what are you doing out here?"

Perfect. Her mother. Ella was in her Sunday best, a pale blue dress that set off the tan she'd gotten on the hospital's upper deck during her breaks, where she sat reading romance novels and plotting her single daughter's happily-ever-after. "Pretty," Ella said of the bracelet, "but—"

"Impractical," Mallory said. "I know."

"Actually, I was going to say it's the type of thing a boyfriend would buy you. You need a boyfriend, Mallory."

Yeah, she'd just pick one up at the boyfriend store later.

"Where's your date?"

Oh good, her favorite question.

"Oh, honey. Did you get stood up?"

Mallory made a show of looking very busy straightening out the description plaque with the bracelet display. "Maybe he's just running a little late is all."

"Well, that doesn't bode well for the relationship."

Yeah, and neither did the fact that they didn't *have* a relationship. "You should have a date too, Mom."

"Me?" Ella asked in obvious surprise. "Oh, no. I'm not ready for another man, you know that."

Mallory did know that. Ella had been saying so for the past decade, ever since The Divorce, which Mallory—however twisted—still one-hundred-percent blamed herself for.

"You look a little peaked, sweetheart. Maybe you're catching that nasty flu that's going around."

No, she was catching Stood-Up-Itis. "I'm good, Mom. No worries."

"Okay, then I'm going back inside. Dessert's up next." Ella kissed her on the cheek and left.

Mallory walked around the rest of the auction items. She checked the parking lot again for Mysterious No-Longer-So-Cute Guy. By then, dessert was just about over. When the lights dimmed and the PowerPoint slide show started—the one she'd put together to showcase the auction items—she sneaked in. Tip-toeing to one of the back tables, she grabbed the first empty seat she could find and let out a breath.

So far so good.

She took a surreptitious peek at the people at her table but it was too dark to see across from her. To her right was an empty chair. To her left was a man, sitting still in the shadows, his face turned to the slide show. She was squinting, trying to figure out why he seemed so vaguely familiar when someone came up behind her and put a hand on her shoulder. "Mallory, there you are."

Her boss. *Crap.* She craned her neck and smiled. "Hello, Jane."

"I've been looking everywhere for you. You're late." Jane Miller was the director of nurses, and probably in her previous life she'd been queen of her very own planet. She had a way of moving and speaking that demanded attention and subtly promised a beheading if she was disappointed in the slightest.

"Oh, I'm not just getting here," Mallory assured her. "I've been behind the scenes all night."

"Hmm," Jane said. "And...?"

"And everything's running smoothly," Mallory quickly assured her. "We have a full house. We're doing good."

"Okay, then." Rare approval entered Jane's voice. "That's terrific." She eyed the chair to the right of Mallory. The empty spot. "Your date didn't show up?"

And here's where Mallory made her mistake. She honestly had no idea what came over her: simple exhaustion from a very long week, or it might have been that her heels were already pinching her feet. But most likely it was sheer, stubborn pride—which her grandmother had always told her would be the death of her. "My date is right here," she whispered. As discreetly as she could, she gestured with her chin to the man to her left, praying that his date didn't take that moment to come back from the restroom.

"Lovely." Jane smiled politely at the back of his head. "Aren't you going to introduce us?"

Oh for God's sake. Mallory glanced over at the man, grateful he was paying them no attention whatsoever. "He's very busy watching the slide show."

Jane's smile didn't falter. She also didn't budge. It was her patent alpha dog stance, the one that hospital administrators, politicians, and God himself bent over backward for.

Mallory gritted her teeth and again glanced at her "date," expecting him to still be watching the slide show.

He wasn't.

He was looking right at her, and naturally the slide show ended at that very moment and the lights went up.

He had a bandage above his eye, which she knew covered stitches, and there was a small bruise on his cheek, where she'd nailed him with Grace's cell phone.

Mysterious Cute Guy.

Chapter 5

Do Not Disturb: Chocolate fantasy in progress.

Mallory's first thought at the sight of Mysterious Cute Guy: *Holy smokes.* The night of the storm she hadn't gotten a good look at him, but she was getting one now. Edgy expression, dangerous eyes, long, hard physique clothed in the elegant, sophisticated packaging of a dark suit. He'd managed to pack a wallop while prone and bleeding but that had been nothing compared to what happened to her now when he was upright and conscious. Before she could speak, a spotlight hit the stage, revealing a microphone.

"That's you," Jane said, pulling Mallory out of the chair. "You're introducing the auction, yes?"

Saved by the bell. Or by the end of the slide show. "Yes, that's me."

"Well?" Jane said to Cute Guy. "You're her date, aren't you? Escort her up there."

The expression on his face never changed from that cool,

assessing calm. And even though Mallory had no idea what he did for a living, or even his name, she'd bet the last three dollars in her wallet that few people, if anyone, *ever* barked an order at him. "Oh," she said in a rush to Jane. "It's okay, he doesn't have to—"

But he was already on his feet, setting his hand at the small of her back, gesturing for her to go ahead of him.

Craning her neck, she stared up at him.

He stared back, brow arched, mouth only very slightly curved.

Hot, he'd called her. Sure, he'd also called her "bossy," and he hadn't been in full possession of his faculties at the time, but even now, the memory gave her a tingle in some places that had no business tingling.

"Mallory," Jane said in that Displeased Queen voice again. "Get on with it."

"Yes, *Mallory*," her "date" said, his voice low and grainy, with just a touch of irony. "Let's get on with it."

She nearly let out a short, half-hysterical laugh but she slapped her hand over her mouth. Later. She'd die of embarrassment later. She forced a smile for anyone looking at them, and *everyone* was looking at them. Speaking out of the corner of her mouth for his ears alone, she whispered, "You don't have to do this, pretend to be on the date you didn't want in the first place."

For the briefest flash, something flickered in his eyes before he smoothed it out and went back to his impassive blank face. Confusion? She wasn't sure, and it no longer mattered. Sure, an apology for standing her up would be nice, but beggars couldn't be choosers. For whatever reason, he was willing to play along, and at the moment, with Jane staring holes in her back, Mallory was grateful.

She threaded her way through the tables to the stage, managing a smile at everyone who caught her eye. But she couldn't have come up with a single name to go with those faces. Not when she was so completely aware of that big, warm hand at the small of her back to go along with the big, strong, gorgeous guy escorting her. He was close enough for her to catch his scent.

Which, by the way, was still fantastic, damn him.

As they got to the stage stairs, she caught the fact that he was limping. She glanced down at his leg. What had happened? He hadn't injured his leg in the storm that she knew of. "Are you okay?"

"Later," he said, and nudged her up the stairs to the stage.

With five hundred sets of eyes on her, she let it go and took the mic. "Good evening, Lucky Harbor," she said.

The crowd hooted and hollered.

In spite of herself, she felt a genuine smile escape at their enthusiastic greeting. She'd grown up in this town, had found her life's passion working as a nurse in this town, and knew that even if she somehow ended up on the other side of the world some day for whatever reason, she'd always smile at the thought of Lucky Harbor. "Let's make some money for health care tonight, okay?"

More wild applause. Then someone yelled out, "Who's the hottie with you?"

This was from Tammy, of course, sitting at one of the front tables, her hands curled around her mouth so that her voice would carry to the stage.

Mallory ignored her sister's heckling as best she could and turned to the big screen behind her. "Okay, everyone, get your bidding paddles ready because we have some great stuff for you tonight. Our favorite auctioneer, Charles Tennessee, is going to come up here, and I expect to see lots of action. I want cat fights, people. Hair-pulling if necessary. Whatever it takes to keep the bidding going. So let the fun begin—"

"We want to meet your date!"

Mallory let out a breath and looked down at Lucille, sitting at another front table.

Lucille gave her a finger wave, which Mallory also ignored, but it was hard to ignore the "*Do it, do it, do it*" chanting now coming from Tammy's table. Her brother was there too, looking every bit the part of the mountain biking bum that he was, with the perpetual goggle tan, the streaked, long brown hair. Tall and lanky lean, Joe sat with an arm slung around the blonde he was dating this week. Mallory caught movement at her right and glanced over as her so-called date strode up the stairs to the stage. Oh God, this wasn't going to help anything, and she shook her head vehemently at him to stop, to go back.

Instead he joined her.

She shook her head again, and she'd have sworn he was laughing at her without his mouth so much as twitching. His eyes were sharp with intelligence, wit, and absolutely no hint of remorse or shame at standing her up. She should probably get over that—and quickly—because the entire audience was now fixated on both of them, the anticipation palpable. With no choice but to be as gracious as possible, Mallory shook her head at the crowd. "Bloodthirsty lot, all of you."

Everyone laughed.

"One of these days," she said. "You're all going to get a life."

Everyone laughed again, but she knew no one was going to move on to the auction until she did this, until she introduced Mysterious Cute Guy. "Fine," she said. "But don't try to tell me you don't know the man standing next to me. I've seen his FB stats."

More laughter, and what might have been slight bafflement from the man himself. "Everyone," she said. "Meet..." She trailed off with one thought. *Crap*. Hard to believe that she could possibly have yet another embarrassing moment in her tonight, but she shouldn't have underestimated herself. Drawing a deep breath, she had no choice. She turned to him and she knew damn well that he knew what she needed.

His name.

Again, the very hint of a smile touched the corner of his lips as he looked at her, brow quirked. He was going to make her *ask*, the big, sexy jerk. Well, that's what she got for wanting Mr. All Wrong. Mr. Bad Boy. Mr. Smoking Hot. He was going to burn her, for sure, and she would lay the blame at the Chocoholics' feet. But she'd yell at Amy and Grace later. For now, she had to deal with this. The question was how? She hadn't a clue. *Uncle*, she finally mouthed to him.

Leaning in close so that his broad chest bumped her shoulder, he wrapped his fingers around hers on the mic. They were tanner than hers, and work-roughened. And the touch of them made her shiver.

"Mallory's just being shy," he said to the audience, then slid her a look that she couldn't begin to decipher. The man was most excellent at hiding his thoughts. "I'm Ty Garrison. The . . . date."

Shy her ass. And she knew damn well he hadn't known her name either, not until Jane had said it. And now he was giving her that bad boy smirk, and she wanted to smack him, but at least she finally knew his name.

Ty Garrison.

It suited him. She'd known a Ty once in first grade. He'd pulled her hair, torn up her homework, and told Mrs. Burland that she'd stolen his. It fueled her temper a little bit just thinking about it. "So there you have it," she said, commandeering the microphone. "Now let's get to the auction, and have a good time." She quickly introduced the auctioneer and gratefully stepped down off the stage, happy to be out of the spotlight.

She walked quickly through the crowd, even happier to note that no one was paying her any attention now; they were all glued to the auctioneer.

Except Lucille.

Lucille, in a silver ball gown that looked like a disco ball, snapped a photo of Mallory with her phone and then winked.

Mallory sighed and was bee-lining for her seat when she was waylaid by her mom, who pulled her down for a hug. Mallory had no idea where her supposed date had gone. Apparently he'd vanished when she'd left the stage, which worked for her. She did not want to subject him to her mother.

The auction had begun with her bracelet, and Mallory quickly grabbed an auction paddle from Ella's table, unable to help herself. No one else was bidding, so she told herself it was a sacrifice for the cause, and raised her paddle.

"Mallory," her mother admonished. "You can't afford that bracelet."

This was true. Annoying but true. "I'm thirty, mom. I get to make my own dumb decisions now, remember?"

"Like going out with a man whose name you didn't even know?" She sounded scandalized. "That's as bad as finding a man on..." She lowered her voice to a horrified whisper, as if she was imparting a state secret. "—the *Internet*!"

"I'm not looking for a man on the Internet. And it's just a one-night thing with Ty."

Someone behind them won the bracelet, and the auctioneer went on to the next item.

"Listen to me, honey," Ella said. "Ty Garrison is not the kind of man who's going to marry you and give me grandchildren."

Well, her mom was absolutely right on that one. "I'm not looking for that, either." At least not right this moment.

"What *are* you looking for?"

Good question. "I don't know exactly." She looked around

at the social crowd, who were all far more into the party atmosphere than bidding. "I guess I'm...bored."

Her mother looked as if she'd just admitted to smoking a crack pipe.

"And I'm restless too," Mallory said. "And...sad, if you want to know the whole ugly truth." She hadn't even realized that was true until it popped out of her mouth without permission, but she couldn't take it back now.

"Oh, honey." Ella squeezed her hand, her eyes suspiciously damp. "Out of all you kids, you've always been my easy one." The crowd got louder and so Ella did too. "The good one, and sometimes I forget to check in and make sure you're okay. Especially after Karen—"

"I *am* okay." And if she wasn't, well then she could handle it. But dammit, she was tired. Tired of doing what was expected, tired of feeling like she was missing something.

"Mallory," Ella said softly, concerned. "You've also always been the smart one. I depend on that from you, honey." She paused. "You're not going to do anything stupid tonight that you'll regret later, right?"

Well, that depended on her mother's definition of *stupid*. As for regrets, she tried hard to live without them. "I hope so."

Her mother looked at something over Mallory's shoulder and made a funny little noise in her throat. Mallory froze, closing her eyes for a beat before turning to find—*of course*—Ty.

Looking bigger than life, he stood there holding two glasses of wine. He handed one over to her while she did her best to stay cool. Downing half the glass went a long way toward assuring that. *Please let him not have heard any of that....*

"Ty Garrison," Ella said as if testing out the name. "Is my daughter safe with you?"

"*Mom*," Mallory said quickly. "Jesus."

"Don't swear, honey." But Ella held up a hand in concession.

"And fine. I'll reword." She looked at Ty. "Are you going to hurt my daughter?"

Ty looked at Mallory as he answered. "She's too smart to let that happen."

Okay, so he *had* heard every word. Terrific. God, she was so far out of her league she could no longer even *see* her league. Her mom had asked if she was going to do anything stupid. And Mallory was pretty sure that the answer was a resounding yes.

As if he could read her thoughts, Ty gave her a sardonic little half toast with his glass, then surprised her by moving away.

Which meant *he* was smart too. "Well," Mallory said. "This has been lots of fun."

"I'm going to assume that was sarcasm," her mom said.

"Always knew I got my smarts from somewhere." Mallory leaned in and kissed Ella's cheek, then went back to her own table where she'd left her purse. That's when she realized that her problems were bigger than her own stupidity issues. Although the room was filled with the sounds of happy, well-fed people, they really were doing far more socializing than bidding. When a "Boating at the Marina" package came up and no one lifted their paddle, Jane locked her unhappy gaze on Mallory's.

Mallory smiled reassuringly while quivering inside. *Someone bid, someone please bid*, she thought with desperation, trying to make it happen by sheer will.

Finally, someone did, but it didn't bring in the money she'd expected.

The next item was a big ticket one, an expensive night on the town in Seattle, which included a limo, a fancy dinner, and an orchestra concert. The bidding began at another low, modest rate, and Mallory's heart landed in her throat.

They were going to have to do better than this. Much better. Again her gaze locked in on Jane, and her unease grew. Someone sank into the chair next to her and since her nipples got hard, she knew it was Ty. "Go away," she said, not taking her gaze off the stage.

Ty said nothing, and she glanced over just as he rose his paddle, bidding two hundred dollars higher than she could have even *thought* about offering.

She stared at him. "What are you doing?"

He didn't even look at her, just eyed the crowd with interest and a smile she hadn't seen from him before. It was a killer smile, she admitted to herself, and when someone joined him in the bidding across the room, he flashed it again and raised his paddle to up the bid.

And then the oddest thing happened.

More people joined in. Unbelievably, the bidding for the "Night on the Town" continued for five more minutes, until the money offered was nothing short of dazzling.

Ty won.

Apparently satisfied, he set down his paddle and leaned back, long legs stretched out in front of him, perfectly at ease as he watched the proceedings. Mallory should have been watching too, but couldn't take her eyes off him, while around them the night kicked into full gear with a new excitement. Everyone in the whole place was now bidding on all the items, playfully trying to outdo each other, or in some cases, not so playfully. It was . . . wonderful. But she couldn't get her mind off the fact that Ty had spent hundreds of dollars to get it going. "What are you going to do with that package you just won?"

"Have a night on the town, apparently."

There was no way he was an orchestra kind of guy. "But—"

"Trouble at three o'clock," he said casually.

She turned to look and found Lucille and another biddy from her blue-haired posse bidding fiercely for the next auction item—a date with Anderson Moore, the cute owner of the hardware store in town.

"This Anderson guy," Ty said to Mallory, still watching the old ladies upping the bid with alarming acerbity, "he's ninety, right?"

The auctioneer jokingly suggested the two older women share the date, and the bidding ended peacefully.

Ty winced in clear sympathy for Anderson, who now had to date not one, but two old ladies.

"Don't feel sorry for him," Mallory said. "He's got it coming to him. He goes after anything with breasts."

Ty slid her a look. "You have a little bit of a mean streak."

She laughed. It was true, even if not a single soul in Lucky Harbor would believe it. She had no idea what it said about her that Ty, a perfect stranger, saw more of her than anyone who actually knew her.

At her smile, Ty leaned close, his gaze dropping from her eyes to her mouth. "I like a woman with a mean streak."

She stared into his eyes, nearly falling into him before letting out another low laugh, this time at herself. God, he was good. Really good. "Save the charm. I'm immune." And look at her displaying another shockingly bad girl characteristic—lying through her teeth.

"Explain something to me," he said.

"What?"

"Why does everyone think I was your date tonight?"

She stared at him. "Last weekend, when I pulled you out of that storm, Amy told you about the auction and how I needed a date, remember?"

"No, actually."

She gaped at him. "Seriously?"

"I remember the storm," he said slowly, as if wracking his brain. "I remember getting hit by the tree. I remember you."

She was wondering if that was good or bad when he added, "Sort of."

Sort of? He "sort of" remembered her? What did *that* mean? She reached for her wine, wishing it was something harder.

"I remember there being a list," he said. "A list of... Mr. Wrongs."

She choked on her wine.

"And I definitely remember waking up in the ambulance with a mother of a headache."

She was silent for a shocked beat while she digested this astonishing fact. He had absolutely no memory of the fact that he was supposed to be her date tonight. Well, that certainly explained a lot of things. Like being stood up. Damn, it was going to be hard to hold that against him, though she was willing to give it a try. "So I guess that the next time I make a date with a concussed guy, I should pin a note to his collar so he doesn't forget."

"Good plan." His hand was next to hers on the table. He let his thumb glide over her fingers, a small, almost casual touch that sent a shudder through her. "I'm sorry I forgot our date," he said. He was so close she could see every single hue of green in his eyes, and there were many. She could feel the warmth of his exhale at her temple. In the crowded Vets' Hall, their nearness was no different from any other couple in the room, discussing their next bid, or laughing over a joke. But Mallory wasn't bidding or laughing. Her heart was suddenly pounding in her throat and there were butterflies going crazy low in her belly.

"Am I on that list, Mallory?" he asked, low and husky. "Am I a Mr. Wrong?"

Oh God, she was in trouble now, because she liked the sound of her name on his lips. Too much. "Don't get too cocky. There are others on the list." She lifted her hand to touch the bruise on his cheek.

He caught her hand in his. "Not what I asked."

"Yes," she admitted. "You're on the list. You're at the top of the list."

Chapter 6

What came first, woman—or the chocolate bar?

Ty had no idea what the hell he thought he was doing, flirting with Mallory.

Scratch that.

He knew exactly what he was doing. He was feeling alive for the first time in six months. Possibly in four years.

She was looking at him, her sweet brown eyes lit, cheeks flushed. She was feeling alive too, he was guessing. But she probably wasn't wondering if he still had a condom in his wallet, trying to calculate how old it might be.

But if she had a list, so did he. A short list of one, and she was it. "Why does a woman like you need a list at all?"

"Like me?"

"Pretty. Smart. Funny."

She laughed, then shook her head. "I don't know. I guess I don't have a lot of time to date."

He could understand that. Hell, it'd been a long time since

he'd dated. It'd been a long dry spell without a woman at all, and she was all woman. Her dress was a deceptively modest black number that had little straps criss-crossing across her back and fell to mid-thigh, molding her curves and whetting his appetite for more. Her heels were high and strappy, emphasizing world-class legs that had been hidden beneath her scrubs. She had her hair up in some loose twist with a few tendrils falling across one temple and at the nape of her neck. Her only jewelry was a little gold necklace—no earrings, nothing to stop his mouth from nipping her throat along his way to her ear where, if he was so inclined, he'd stop to whisper promises.

He shouldn't be inclined. Mallory Quinn was sweet, warm, and caring. She was a white picket fence and two-point-four kids. She was a diamond ring.

She was someone's keeper.

Not his. Never his. He didn't do keepers.

And yet in that beat, with her mouth close to his, a smile in her eyes, he...ached. He ached and yearned for something. Someone. He wanted to wrap his arms around a woman, *this* woman, and lose himself in her.

A woman tapped Mallory on the shoulder, the same woman from before; tall, thin, and coldly beautiful, with a tight pinch to her mouth that said she was greatly displeased about something. Or possibly constipated. She wore authority and bitchiness as easily as she wore the strand of diamonds around her neck.

Mallory glanced up and straightened, her expression going carefully blank. "Jane," she said, in a tone that told Ty that the woman was either her boss or her executioner.

"I need a moment," Jane said.

Boss, Ty thought.

"Absolutely." Mallory followed Jane out of the hall and into the foyer.

The auction was moving ahead at full steam now, and people

were into it, jumping up and waving as they bid. Telling himself he had to stretch his aching leg, that he wasn't at all curious about what had come so briefly over Mallory's face, Ty left the hall.

In the entranceway, Mallory had her back to him, facing Cruella Deville. "Absolutely," she was saying. "I'll go upstairs and get it right now. Thank you for your addition, Jane."

And then Jane went one way and Mallory the other, her sweet little ass sashaying as fast as she could move in those sexy heels.

Let it go, man. Let her go, he told himself. He'd heard enough from her mother to know she was a good girl just looking for a walk on the wild side. Probably she'd grown up in Lucky Harbor, which was pretty much the same thing as being in bubble wrap all her life. She was not for him.

Except.

Except here she was, clearly doing her damnedest to meet some pretty tough expectations from family and work and whatever, all while looking to spread her wings. She had guts, and he admired that. She was sexy and adorable, but no matter what she did to spread her wings, she wasn't going to match him in life's experiences.

Not even close.

She was clean and untainted and *not* jaded. She was his opposite. She was too good for him. Far too good, even when she was out there risking it all. She deserved *way* more than he had to offer, and he needed to just walk away. After all, he was out of here, maybe as soon as one more week. Gone, baby, gone.

He told himself all this, repeated it, and then followed her down the hallway anyway.

Mallory walked up the stairs, cursing the heels that were pinching her toes. Jane had sent her up here on a wild goose chase for an antique vase that had been accidentally left off the auction chopping block.

Mallory knew Jane's family had built the Vets' Hall in the early 1940s. Apparently the missing vase had sat in the entry for years, until last spring when the building had been renovated. The vase had never been put back on display and now Jane wanted it gone.

All Mallory had to do was find it.

The second story ran the length of the building. On one side was a series of rooms used by the rec center and other various groups like the local Booster Club. The other side was one big closed-off storage room. Mallory let herself in and flipped on the lights. Far above her was an open-beam ceiling and a loft area where more crap had been haphazardly shoved away. Mallory hoped like hell she wouldn't have to climb up there in her dress and annoying heels to find the vase.

The place was warm, stuffy, and smelled like neglect. She took a good look around and felt a lick of panic at the idea of finding her way out of here, much less locating the missing vase. She moved past a huge shelving unit that was stuffed to the gills with long-lost play props and background sets, and various other miscellaneous items for which there was little use.

Not a single vase.

She walked past more shelves and around two huge, fake, potted Christmas trees before coming to a large stack of boxes leaning against the wall. Assuming the vase wouldn't be stuffed away, she walked farther, gaze searching. Near the center of the room, she came to another long set of shelves. Here were some more valuable items, such as office equipment and furnishings, and miraculously, sitting all by itself on a shelf, a tall vase, looking exactly like the one Jane had described. Mallory couldn't believe it. She picked it up and turned to go, and ran directly into a brick wall.

A brick wall that was a man's chest.

Ty.

He'd appeared out of thin air, scaring her half to death. The vase flew out of her hands and would have smashed to the floor except he caught it.

His sexy suit might have given him an air of sophistication, but it did nothing to hide his bad-boy air. His hair was a little mussed, like he'd run his fingers through it repeatedly. In another man, this would have softened his look but not Ty. She wasn't fooled. There was nothing soft about him. He was sheer trouble, and she knew it. "What are you doing?" she gasped, hand to her pounding heart.

"What are *you* doing?"

She snatched the vase from his hands. "Working."

"Well, I'm helping my date work then."

"You're not my real date. You didn't even know you had a date."

He looked amused. "So you're one of those women who holds a grudge?"

"No! I'm—"

From somewhere far behind them, the storage room door opened. "Hello? Mallory, dear?"

"*Shit,*" Mallory whispered, horrified. "It's Lucille."

"Your mother told you not to swear."

She narrowed her eyes at him.

"Mallory?" Lucille called out.

Mallory slapped her hand over her own mouth.

"Yoo-hoo...I saw your hot date follow you in here. I just want to get a picture of you two for Facebook."

Oh no. No, no, no...Mallory turned in a quick circle in the warm, dusty, overstuffed storage room, desperate for a place to hide.

Ty must have seen her panic because he briefly held a finger to her lips to indicate he needed her silence, then took the vase in one hand and her wrist in his other and tugged her along, farther into the shadows.

She followed, walking on her tiptoes to avoid the clicking of her heels, when suddenly Ty pressed her against the wall. "Shh," he breathed in her ear.

Stealth. She got it. She was depending on it. She also got something else, an unexpected zing from the feel of his mouth on her ear and his body pressing into hers.

"*Mallory*?" Lucille called out.

Ty had gone into 007 mode. His eyes were searching their surroundings, his body ready and alert. He opened a panel she hadn't even noticed, then pulled something from his pocket and used it inside the panel. In the next second, the lights went out.

Startled, she nearly gasped but he slid a hand over her mouth. That, combined with the way he was holding her against the wall, caused a tsunami of inappropriate feelings to rush through her.

"Don't move." He remained still until she nodded, and then he was gone.

Only not completely gone.

She jumped when she felt his hands on her ankles. He was crouched before her, removing first one heel and then the other. Her hands went out for balance and smacked him in the head. She heard his soft laugh, then he had her hand again and they were on the move. She couldn't see a thing, but Ty didn't appear to have that problem. He was navigating them both with apparent ease, leading her through the maze of the vast storage unit as if he could see in the dark. They turned corners and squeezed into spots, his hands sliding to her hips, guiding her exactly where he wanted her to go, taking care that she didn't bump into anything. She had no idea how he could see, or even know where they were going, but she followed him.

Blindly.

It was better than the alternative.

Each time they stopped, she was pulled up against his big, warm body, until she began to anticipate it.

Crave it.

"Mallory?" Now, accompanying Lucille's voice came a small beam of light.

Good Lord. The woman was using the same Bic app that Grace had. "Oh for the love of—"

Warm lips covered hers. "*Shh.*"

Right. Shh. Her knees were still melting. Her one hand was in his, trapped between their bodies, but her other hand slid up his chest, around the back of his neck and into his hair. Because she needed a hand grip, she told herself.

"How bad do you want to keep out of her sight?" Ty wanted to know, each syllable rumbling from his chest and through hers. He'd set the vase down, freeing up both his hands. She felt herself rock into him and tighten her grip on his hair, and it took a long moment to process his words because her brain was no longer firing on all cylinders.

"Mallory."

God, she liked the sound of her name on his lips. And she liked the feeling that had come over her too, the languid yet throbbing beat of anticipation. She certainly wasn't bored or sad now. "Hmm?"

"How bad?"

How bad did she want him? *Bad.*

With a little huff against her jaw that might have been another low laugh, he tightened his grip on her and spun her away from him, setting her hands on something that felt like cold steel.

"Hold on tight," he whispered and nudged his big body up behind hers, his biceps on either side of her arms, his chest against her back.

Her mind went utterly blank, but her body didn't. Her body went damp at the wicked thought of doing it right here, like this. From behind.

"Up," he said, and the fantasy receded. No, he didn't want sex. He had her in front of a ladder and wanted her to climb it.

Good thing it was dark because it hid the heat of the blush she could feel on her face. She pulled herself up, *extremely* aware that her butt was in his face, and then she was directly above him.

He was still apparently able to see in the dark. Which meant that he could see right up her dress. She was wearing a brand new silky black thong, her very best, but still, it couldn't be a very good angle for her.

At the top of the ladder was the loft. Moonlight slanted in from the sole round window, revealing more stored items, a couch and a large table with chairs. The table was stacked with more stuff. There were also rows of framed pictures and empty planters, and a whole horde of other crap. Everywhere.

Mallory moved aside for Ty to join her but the standing space was so small she lost her balance and fell onto the couch.

Ty followed her down.

On the night of the storm, Mallory had been beneath him too, but it felt different this time. Sexy different, and she let out a small, half hysterical laugh.

Ty covered her mouth with his hand, shifting a little to get the bulk of his weight off of her. In the execution, one of his thighs pushed between hers and *oh sweet baby Jesus*. She promptly stopped laughing and moaned instead. A total involuntary, accidental moan that sounded needy and wanton. And horrifyingly loud.

Ty's hands tightened on her and they both stilled, craning their necks, looking down into the dark storage area, following the little beam of light as Lucille weaved through the aisles below.

Ty pulled his hand from Mallory's mouth. "Unless she can climb a ladder, we're good here until she gives up and leaves."

Yes. Yes, they were good here. Or very bad, depending on how one looked at it.

Above her, Ty was still as stone, a solid heated package of testosterone and sinew holding her down on the couch. She wasn't sure what it said about her that she felt just a little bit powerless and helpless, and that she liked it.

A lot.

Another thing she liked? The fact that every time he breathed, his leg shifted up against her core, putting her body on an entirely different page than her brain.

On the *get-more-of-him* page.

"She won't give up," she whispered, more than a little breathless.

"Watch." Ty shifted again—oh God *his thigh*!—and pulled something from his pocket, which he threw.

Mallory heard the ping of the coin as it landed with deadly precision all the way across the huge room near the storage room entrance.

Holy shit he could throw.

"Oh!" they heard Lucille exclaim, whipping around toward the sound. "You're escaping, you smart girl. Darn it all!"

They watched as the little beam of light wobbled back through the room to the entrance, and then in the next moment, vanished completely.

Silence reigned.

Well, except for Mallory's thundering heartbeat. She was in an attic loft, flat beneath her Mr. Wrong. Her common sense was screaming *flee*! But her secret inner bad girl was screaming *oh please, can't we have him? Just once?*

"You okay?" Ty asked.

Loaded question. "You have some impressive skills," she said. "I feel like a Bond girl."

"You weren't so bad yourself," he said. "The way you shimmied up that ladder is going to fuel my fantasies for some time."

So he *could* see in the dark. And now that they were up here with moonlight coming in the window, she could see too. She bit her lower lip because she could feel, too. She could feel him, *all* of him. Her breasts were mashed up against his chest, plumping out of her dress suggestively. She wasn't sure he'd noticed, but then he very purposely dropped his head, his lips just barely brushing her exposed skin. She sucked in a breath and felt him stir against her.

Yeah. He'd noticed. "I have lots of ladder practice," she said inanely.

"Yeah?" he asked, sounding intrigued. "You climb a lot of ladders in the ER?"

"Uh, no." Nerves had her laughing. And babbling. "But I had to clear the gutters on my house last fall before the rains hit. I nearly fell when I found a fist-sized spider waiting for me but managed not to accidentally kill myself."

A low laugh escaped him.

"So why did you do it?" she asked.

"The ladder? Nowhere else to go but up."

"No, I mean why did you help me hide? And thanks, by the way. You pretty much saved my butt." *Again.*

He slid a hand down her arm, squeezing her hip before shocking the hell out of her when he slid that hand further, cupping said butt. "My pleasure."

At the words, at the touch, her body liquefied. Or maybe that was his fingers, tightening on her hindquarters, making her want to squirm and rock into him.

The brand new bad girl in her took over and did exactly that.

Ty went still. She wasn't sure what that meant exactly, but she was feeling things she hadn't in far too long, and she intended to go with those feelings. So she squirmed again.

"Mallory." There was a warning in that low, sexy tone of his, a very serious warning.

She'd wanted a kiss, but hearing him say her name like that was almost as good. And now she wanted more. She wanted things she didn't even have names for. So she wriggled some more, hoping like hell she was getting her message across because she wasn't all that practiced in the bad girl department. Amy had been right; she needed lessons. She made a mental note to address this as well at the next Chocoholics meeting. For now, she'd wing it. "Yeah?"

"Are you coming onto me?"

"Well, technically, you're on top of me," she pointed out. "So I think that means that *you're* coming onto *me*."

With a groan, he pressed his forehead to hers and swore beneath his breath, and not the good kind of swear either. And though she should have seen this coming, she hadn't.

He didn't want her.

It was perfect, really. Perfect for the way the rest of the night had gone. Horrified, humiliated, she pushed at him. "Sorry. I got caught up in the moment. I'm not very good at this, obviously." He didn't budge so she shoved him again. "Excuse me."

He merely tightened his grip. "Not good at what, exactly?" he asked.

"Really? You need me to say it?"

When he just waited, she sighed. "Attracting men. I'm not good at attracting men. Now if you could please *get off*."

He lifted his head and cupped the back of hers in one big hand, his eyes glinting with heat. "You first," he said rough and gravelly, leaving no mistake to his meaning.

She gasped, and he took advantage of that to kiss her, his lips moving against hers until she gasped again, in sheer pleasure this time.

Things went a little crazy then. Ty's mouth was firm and

hungry, his tongue sliding against hers, and God, she'd almost forgotten what it was like to be kissed like this, like there was nothing on earth more important than her. That long-forgotten thrill of feeling soft and feminine rushed over her.

Then Ty lifted his head, and she realized she was touching his face, the stubble on his jaw scraping against the pads of her fingers.

"To be clear," he said, "I'm *very* attracted to you." And she believed him because the proof of that statement was hard against her hip.

"I think it's your eyes," he said.

She was a little startled by the unexpected romance of that. And then she was drowning in *his* eyes, which were smoldering. But then they were kissing again, and she couldn't think because he happened to be the world's most amazing kisser. Ever. She lost herself in it for long moments, loving the fact that he didn't seem to be in a hurry at all, or using the kiss as a means to an end. Kissing her was an act all unto itself, and she was panting for air when he finally broke from it. He shifted to pull away and she reflexively clutched at him. "Wait—We're stopping?"

Dropping his head, he rubbed his jaw to hers. "Yeah."

"But...why?"

He let out a low, innately male groan. "Because you're not the fuck-a-stranger-in-a-storage-room-with-her-boss-waiting type of woman."

Well, when he put it like that...Damn. Her inner bad girl retreated a little. More than a little.

You don't think you deserve to be happy.

Amy's words floated in her head. No, she'd never been the type to let a stranger into her heart, much less her body.

But this wasn't about her heart.

And Ty was no longer a complete stranger. He was the man

who'd good-naturedly stepped in tonight when she'd needed him. Multiple times. He was the man who'd just given her the most amazing kiss of her life.

She wanted him to also be the man to vanquish her restlessness and loneliness. "I am for tonight," she said, and wrapped herself around him.

"Mallory." He stared down at her, the moonlight casting his features in bold relief. "I'm not a long-term bet. Hell, I'm not even a short-term bet."

"I just want this," she said. "Here. Now. With you."

This won her another long look, interrupted by a very rough, very male groan when she undulated against him, trying to sway the game in her favor.

"Christ, your eyes," he said on a long breath. "Come here then." Before she could, he pressed her down farther into the couch, his mouth trailblazing a path over her throat and collar bone.

Apparently, he wasn't one to over-think or second-guess a decision. Good to know. And when he came up against the material of her dress, he wasn't deterred by that either. A quick tug of his fingers and her straps slid down her shoulders to her elbows, trapping her hands at her sides and baring her breasts all in one economical movement.

Apparently, Ty didn't waste energy unnecessarily. Also good to know.

"Mmm," he said, a growl of approval low in his throat. He made his way to her breasts, paying such careful homage to her nipples that she was writhing beneath him by the time he moved down her stomach.

"So soft," he murmured against her, his breath gently caressing her skin. But there was nothing gentle about him as his work-roughened fingers pushed the hem of the dress up to her waist. He looked down at her black thong, gave another low growl of approval, then slid the tiny swatch of black silk to one side. This bared all her secrets both to the night air and his hot gaze. Lowering his head, he put his mouth on her, using his lips and his tongue, making her arch up into him. She was crying out within minutes, her hands fisted in his hair as stars exploded behind her eyes.

Before she'd even stopped shuddering, he'd shoved off his jacket, then unbuckled, unzipped, and was rolling on a condom. The sight made her moan, and then he was pushing inside of her and she lost her breath. He gave her a moment to adjust to his size, then his mouth found hers again and she could taste herself on his tongue. It was wildly sensuous, and so far out of her realm of experience she could only dig her fingernails into his back and hold on.

He swallowed her cries as he thrust into her, running a hand beneath her knee, lifting her leg up to wrap around him so he could get even deeper.

Deeper worked. Oh, how it worked. He took her right out of herself, and she thrilled to it. He was powerful and primal, and if he hadn't taken such care to make sure she was right there with him, she might have doubted herself. Instead, she rose to meet him halfway, unable to do anything but feel as he pushed her over the edge again, his hard length pounding into her, his tongue mimicking his body's movement as he claimed her. And it was a claiming, a thorough one. She was deep in the throes when he joined her, shuddering in her arms, his hands digging hard into her hips as he lost himself in his pleasure.

In her.

The knowledge nearly sent her over again, as did the low, hoarse, very male sound he made when he came. Tearing his mouth from hers, he dropped his head into the crook of her neck, his broad shoulders rising and falling beneath her hands as he caught his breath.

He was still buried deep inside of her when he lifted his head to see her face.

"What?" she whispered.

"Wanted to make sure you're okay. You're smiling."

"Am not." But she was. God, she so was. It would probably take days to get rid of it. But apparently she'd taken the Chocoholics modus operandi to heart. She'd just had her Mr. Wrong.

In a storage room.

Which just proved exactly how wrong Mr. All Wrong was for her, because she'd never had sex without a commitment in her entire life. She braced herself for the guilt.

None came.

In fact, Mallory felt unexpectedly fantastic. "No regrets," she whispered.

He gave her a curious look, then that almost-smile. "I like the way you think."

She ran a finger over the Band-Aid on his forehead, and then along the bruise on his cheek. "I'm sorry about this," she said. "About throwing the phone at your head when I thought you were a bad guy."

He shook his head, but his almost-smile became a full smile. "I don't remember that part."

"Oops. Then never mind." She heard a thunderous applause from below them and remembered. The auction! "Oh my God, we've got to go. You first. Hurry." She gave him a nudge but he didn't move.

"I'm not going to just leave you up here," he said.

"Yes, you are! We can't be seen leaving here together." Just the thought brought more panic, and she pushed him again. "Go. Hurry!"

Not hurrying at all, he looked at her for another long moment. Leaning forward, he pressed his lips to her damp temple and finally pulled away. He helped her straighten out her clothing before taking care of himself.

She was still lying there with no bones in her body when he disappeared over the edge of the loft, vanishing into the night, giving her exactly what she'd asked for. Just this, here, now.

And now was over.

Chapter 7

There is no kiss sweeter than a chocolate kiss.

Ty slept hard that night, and apparently lulled by post-orgasmic glow, he didn't dream. Sex was the cure for nightmares. Good to know. His morning went pretty much status quo. Matt met him on the beach, and they'd gone several miles when Matt got a cramp and went down.

Ty was too far away, and his heart nearly stopped before he got to Matt and dragged his ass out of the water.

Matt rolled around in agony on the sand while Ty dug his fingers into Matt's calf and rubbed the cramp out. When he had, he collapsed to the sand next to Matt. "No more."

Matt was gasping for breath. "You're right. You're a fucking animal in the water. No one should be able to swim that long and hard."

"No, I mean because you nearly drowned yourself."

"Well," Matt managed, sitting up with a smile. "Only half drowned, thanks to you."

"Fuck it, Matt, I'm not kidding. You're not swimming with me anymore."

Matt's smile faded as he studied Ty for a long moment. "You do realize that not everyone's going to die on you, right?"

"Shut up."

"What crawled up your ass today?" Matt asked. "You had a good time last night. I saw you actually crack a smile at Mallory."

Mallory. God, Mallory. Ty pushed upright and despite his trembling limbs, he started walking.

"Good talk," Matt called out after him.

Ty kept going, heading back to the house. He wanted to run but his leg didn't have the same want. Brooding about that, he pushed hard, forcing himself to stay at the tide line where the sand was the softest and choppiest because that made the going extra teeth-grindingly difficult.

Difficult worked. He wanted to feel the pain, to remind himself why the hell he was here. Which was *not* to dally with the sweet, warm, giving, sexy-as-hell Mallory Quinn.

Though God, she'd been all those things and more, and she'd revved his engine but good. Every time he thought about how hot she'd looked lying all spread out for him on that couch, he got hard.

Stupid. What he'd done last night had been *beyond* stupid and he knew it. It was also selfish, and he had no excuse other than she'd blindsided him with her open, honest sweetness. He should have ignored the attraction, had fully intended to, but that hadn't worked out so well for him.

And now he could add being an asshole to his list of infractions. Because taking advantage of Mallory last night had been a real dick move. But she was...well, everything he wasn't.

Still, she didn't deserve the likes of him, or what he'd done. Probably she already hated him for it. He told himself this was for the best and took a long, hot shower. He pulled on clothes while eyeballing the empty Vicodin bottle on the dresser. This was a ritual, the stare down. In the end, he shoved the bottle into his pocket as he always did, wanting the reminder close at hand. The reminder to keep his head on straight, keep his mind on the goal—getting back in the game.

With that in his head, he left for his doctor's appointment.

"Looking better," Josh said an hour later, eyeing the latest screen of Ty's leg.

"I feel all better," Ty said, lying through his teeth. After this morning's exercise, he hurt like hell.

Not fooled, Josh gave him a long look.

"I'm good for light duty."

"Uh huh." Josh leaned back in his chair and studied him. "Lighter duty than what, rappelling out of helicopters, rescuing dignitaries, etcetera?"

This was the problem with having your boss put you on leave until you were medically cleared. Thanks to Frances, Josh knew far too much about him. Ty blew out a breath. It wasn't Josh's fault. He was a good guy, and under different circumstances, would even be considered a friend.

If Ty had friends. He didn't. He'd let his friends die on a mountaintop four years ago.

So what was Matt, a pesky little voice asked. *Or Mallory?* Accidents, he decided.

"Look," Josh said, leaning forward, "you want out of here. I get that. You're getting closer. But let's give it another week, okay?"

Another fucking week. But reacting badly wasn't going to help him. He'd use the week to finish Matt's Jimmy. And the Shelby. He couldn't leave without the Shelby. "Fine. But *you* tell her."

"Frances?" Josh smiled grimly. "Gladly."

When Ty got back to the house, his phone was blinking missed calls. He deleted them without a glance, then went to work on Matt's Jimmy. Later he switched to his real love, the Shelby, stopping to look up some parts on the Internet. There he got distracted by an e-mail from Matt with a link.

He'd been tagged on Facebook. In fact, on the Lucky Harbor page there was an entire note on him, listing sightings and news. They called him *Mysterious Cute Guy*.

It was enough to give a guy nightmares.

Except he was already having nightmares...

He waited until hunger stopped him and drove into town. Lucky Harbor was nestled in a rocky cove, its architecture a quirky, eclectic mix of the old and new. The main drag was lined with Victorian buildings painted in bright colors, housing the requisite grocery store, post office, gas station, and hardware store. Then there was a turnoff to the beach itself, where a long pier jutted out into the water, lined with more shops, the arcade and Ferris wheel, and the diner.

Eat Me was like something from an out-of-time Mayberry, except in Mayberry he'd probably not have gotten laid at Vets' Hall, in a storage attic above the entire town.

Noticing the brand new front door, he entered the diner and took a seat at the counter. Amy silently poured him a mug of coffee. This was routine; they'd been doing the same dance for months, rarely speaking. He really appreciated that in a waitress, and he liked her infinitely more than the eternally grumpy diner owner. Jan scared him, just a little bit.

Then Amy dropped the local paper in front of him and cocked a hip tableside.

Ty slowly pushed his sunglasses to the top of his head and gave her a level look. Her return look had bad attitude all over it. She wore a black tee with some Chinese symbol on the front and the requisite frilly pink apron that looked incongruous with her short denim skirt, boots, and general kick-ass attitude. She gestured with a short jerk of her chin to the paper, and he took a look.

The headline read: COUNTY HOSPITAL'S AUCTION—A HUGE SUCCESS.

So far so good, he thought, then read the first paragraph, which credited the success of the auction to the nurses, specifically Mallory Quinn, who along with her new boyfriend had gotten the entire Vets' Hall on its feet by starting off the bidding with a bang.

Ty reread the article. New boyfriend? *Mysterious Cute Guy*? He graced Amy with his no-nonsense, don't-fuck-with-me look. It had cowed many.

But Amy didn't appear impressed or even particularly intimidated.

He set down the paper and pushed it away.

She pushed it back with a single finger.

"Do you have a point?" he asked.

"Several, actually. First, Mallory's my friend. And I recently encouraged her to make a change in her life. You were that change. Don't make me sorry."

Ty wasn't much used to threats, however sweetly uttered. Never had been. He'd been raised by two military parents who'd taken turns parenting him when one or the other had been on tour overseas. He'd been loved, but weaknesses had not been tolerated. Even his current job added up to a life lived by rules, discipline, sheer wits, and honor.

The honor part was troubling him now.

Somehow in spite of himself and his reclusiveness, he'd managed to find celebrity status in this crazy-ass, one-horse town, and even worse, there was Mallory, wanting him to take her for a walk on the wild side.

Bad idea.

The *baddest*.

He'd done it anyway, fallen captive to those melted chocolate eyes, even knowing he planned on being out of Lucky Harbor any minute now. "She's a big girl," he finally said.

Amy stared at him for a long moment, then shook her head and walked away, muttering something beneath her breath about the entire male race being genetically flawed.

Ty was inclined to agree with her. He paid for his coffee and received another long, careful look from Amy.

Message received.

As to whether he was going to heed the warning, the jury was still out. He went straight back to his big, empty house. Cranking the music to ear-splitting levels, he worked on the Shelby. He'd seen the car in the newspaper on his first day in Lucky Harbor had hadn't been able to resist her.

He'd never been able to resist a sweetheart of a car.

Or, apparently, a sweetheart of a woman...

Mallory sat in a hospital board meeting surrounded by a bunch of administrators that included her boss and her mother, in what should have been the meeting of her life. Instead, her mind was a million miles away. Or more accurately, in a certain storage room.

Memories of that storage room, and what Ty had done to her in it, were making her warm. *Very* warm.

She still couldn't believe how fast she'd gotten naked with him.

Well, not quite naked, she reminded herself. She'd been in such a hurry that she hadn't even lost her panties, not completely.

Ty had simply slipped them aside with his fingers.

Just remembering made her damp all over again. God. She'd never gone up in flames so hard and fast in her entire life.

Heaven.

He'd taken her to heaven in seven minutes. A record for her. And she'd do it again, in a heartbeat.

That is, if the man who'd taken her to heaven hadn't vanished from the auction without a word. That should teach her to have completely inappropriate sex with a man whose name she'd learned only twenty minutes earlier.

But all it'd really taught her was that she'd been missing out. Man, had she been missing out. Worse, she knew the magnitude of her attraction for him now, and she was afraid that the next time she saw him, she was going to shove him into the nearest closet for round two.

And round three.

Mallory took a moment to fantasize about that, about what she'd be wearing the next time. Maybe her little black dress again; he'd seemed to really like it. And maybe next time she'd leave the panties at home—

"Mallory?"

She blinked away the vision of Ty and her panties and came face to face with a *not amused* Jane.

"The amount?" Jane asked in a tone that said she'd repeated herself several times already.

"Eighteen thousand." Mallory looked down at the check in her hands, a check she was incredibly proud of—the total of the proceeds from the auction. "You said the board would donate twenty-five percent of it to the Health Services Clinic."

"There isn't an HSC," Jane said. "Not yet."

Mallory bit back her retort, knowing better than to show weakness. "There will be. We've proven need."

"Have we?" Jane asked.

"Yes." Mallory forced herself to look the other board members in the eyes as she spoke, no matter how resistant they were. Dr. Scott was there, rumpled and gorgeous as usual. His eyes warmed when he met her gaze. No one else made eye contact. She took a big gulp of air. "The need is obvious. There's no-where else in the entire county providing drug programs, teen pregnancy counseling, women's services, or an abuse hotline. We all know that. The ER is losing money because we're taking on patients who'd be better served by a Health Clinic."

"You mean people who can't, or won't, pay." This from Bill Lawson, head of the board of directors. He was tall, lean, and fit, looking forty instead of his fifty-five. He had sharp eyes, a sharper mind, and was all about the bottom line. Always. He *was* listening though, and Mallory appreciated that. This was important to her, had been since Karen had died because she'd had no place to go and get the services she'd so desperately needed.

People rarely talked about Karen and what had happened to her. But Mallory hadn't forgotten a thing, and she intended to make sure that no other scared eighteen-year-old girl ever felt the helplessness and terror that Karen had.

"We've run the numbers," she said, talking directly to Bill now. The hospital, just outside of Lucky Harbor, serviced the entire county but was private, run by a board of directors who all tended to bow to Bill's wishes. She needed his support. "A Health Services Clinic is eligible for programs and funding that the ER isn't. I've written the grant requests. If you go with my proposed plan and allow use of the old west wing, then one hundred percent of the HSC revenue will go right back into the hospital's pockets."

"It would also mean that the full financial responsibility for the Health Services Clinic would be the hospital's," Bill pointed out.

He already knew this. He just didn't like it. "Yes," she agreed. "But with the grants and donations, HSC will run in the black, and in the long run, it'll save your ER losses. We've got most of the first year's funds already."

"You're short ten big ones."

"True, but I won't stop until we have the rest," she promised. "This makes sense for our community, Bill, and it's the right thing to do." She paused, then admitted the rest. "I'm going to be a pain in your ass over this."

"Going to be?" Bill shook his head wryly. "Listen, Mallory, I believe in what you're trying to do, and I want to be on your side. But let's face the truth here—your proposed programs will bring a certain...demographic to Lucky Harbor, a demographic we typically try to divert away to other parts of the county. The town isn't really behind this."

"The town can be persuaded. People are in need, and HSC can meet that need."

Bill was quiet a moment, and Mallory did her best not to fidget. She was only moderately successful.

"I'll make you a deal," Bill finally said. "At this week's town meeting, I'll give everyone a formal spiel, then ask for thoughts."

People went to town meetings like they went to the grocery store or got gas. It was simply what everyone did. If Bill asked for opinions, he'd get them, in droves.

"If we get a positive response, I'll consider a one-month trial run for HSC. One month, Mallory," he said when she smiled. "Then we'll reevaluate on the condition of the actual costs and the bottom line at that time. If you've got the budget for the rest of the year after that month, and if there've been no problems, you're on. If not, you drop this." He gave her a long look. "Is that acceptable to you?"

There was only one answer here. "Yes, sir," she said with carefully tempered excitement.

"Oh, and that budget of yours better not include paying you to go to the pharmacy and pick up meds for our patients and then delivering them."

He was referring to how she'd picked up Mrs. Burland's meds for her just that morning and brought them to the woman's home. How he'd found out wasn't too much of a mystery. Lucky

Harbor had one pharmacy. It was located in the grocery store, and everyone in town was in and out of that store often. Anyone from the pharmacist, to the clerk, to any of the customers could have seen her, and she hadn't made a secret of what she was doing.

Nor had Mrs. Burland made a mystery out of how she'd felt about Mallory delivering her meds.

"Do you expect a tip?" she'd asked. *"Because here it is. Put on some makeup and do something with your hair or you'll never catch a man."*

At the memory, Mallory felt an eye twitch coming on but she didn't let it dampen her relief. She was closer to opening the HSC than she'd ever been. "I did that on my own time."

Bill nodded. "And if by some miracle, the town meeting goes well, how long would you need to get up and running?"

She'd had volunteer professionals from all over the county on standby all year. "I would open immediately with limited services, adding more as quickly as I can get supplies and staff scheduled."

"See that 'immediately' is actually immediately," Bill said. "And I'll expect to see numbers weekly."

"Yes, sir."

An hour later, Mallory was on the ER floor, still doing the happy dance. Finally she had something other than sexy Ty to think about, because hoping for town approval and actually getting it were two very different things.

Not that she had time to think about that either, thanks to a crazy shift. She had a stroke victim, a diabetic in the midst of losing his toes, a gangbanger who'd been shot up in Seattle and made it all the way to Lucky Harbor before deciding he was dying, two drunks, a stomach-ache, and a partridge in a pear tree.

In between patients, she worked the phones like mad, preparing for a *very* tentative Health Clinic opening the following week.

The west wing in the hospital had once been the emergency department before the new wing had been built three years ago. It was perfectly set up for the clinic, easily accessible with its own parking lot. It needed to be cleaned and stocked. And she needed staff on standby. The list of what she needed and what she had to do went on and on.

When she yawned for the tenth time, Mallory went in search of coffee. As she stood there mainlining it, waiting for it to kick in— her mind danced off to revisit a certain storage room...*big, warm hands, both rough and gentle at the same time, stroking her—*

"Mallory, my goodness. Where are you at in that pretty little head, Disneyland?"

Mallory blinked and the daydream faded, replaced by the sight of her mother, who stood in front of her smiling with bafflement. "I called your name three times. And the same thing happened in the board meeting. Honey, what in the world are you thinking about today?"

She'd been thinking about the sound Ty had made when he'd come, a low, inherently male sound that gave her a tingle even now. "Dessert," she said faintly. "I'm thinking about dessert."

"Hmmm." Ella looked doubtful but didn't call her on it. "You've seen the paper."

"You mean the local gossip rag masquerading as legit news?" They'd labeled Ty her *boyfriend.* Who'd run the fact check for *that* tidbit? "Yeah, I saw it." Every person she'd come across had made sure of it.

"Honey, I just don't think it's a good idea to risk so much on a man you know nothing about."

"It's not about taking risks, mom." And it wasn't. Mallory had risked nothing, not really. Well, maybe she'd risked getting caught having wild sex in a public place, but she'd felt safe enough or she'd never have done it. No, for her it'd been about being selfish for the first time in recent memory, taking what she wanted. And yeah, maybe that was going to wreak some havoc on her personal life. But since when was worrying about what people thought a life requirement?

Since a long time ago. Since she'd got it in her head that she had to be good to be loved.

"Mallory, honestly," Ella murmured, her tone full of worry. "This is so unlike you, seeing a man you don't even know."

Yes, Mallory, the shock. The horror. The good girl actually wanting something for herself. How dare she? "We're not seeing each other," she said. At least not how Ella meant.

"But the newspaper said—"

"We're not," Mallory repeated. Ty hadn't said so in words, not a single one in fact, but he couldn't have been more clear as he'd vanished.

"So you're telling me that I'm worrying about nothing?" Ella asked.

"Unless you enjoy having to wash that gray out of your hair every three weeks, yes. You're worrying about nothing."

Her mother patted her brunette bob self-consciously. "Four weeks and counting. Do I need a touch-up?"

Just then, Camilla came running through, looking breathless. Camilla was a fellow nurse, twenty-two years old and so fresh out of nursing school she still squeaked when she walked. She was a trainee, and as such, got all the crap jobs. Such as signing in new patients. "He's here," she whispered dramatically, practically quivering with the news. "In the waiting room."

"He?" Mallory asked.

Camilla nodded vigorously. "*He.*"

"Does 'he' have a name?" Ella asked dryly.

"Mysterious Cute Guy!"

Her mother slid Mallory a look. But Mallory was too busy having a coronary to respond. *Why was he here?* "Is he hurt or sick?"

"He asked for Dr. Scott," Camilla said in a rush. "But Dr. Scott's been called away."

Mallory moved around Camilla. "I'll take him."

"Are you sure?" Camilla asked. "Because I'd be happy to—"

"I'm sure." Heart pounding, Mallory headed down the hallway toward the ER waiting room, taking quick mental stock. She had nothing gross or unidentifiable on her scrubs, always a bonus. But she couldn't remember if she was wearing mascara. And she really wished she'd redone her hair at break.

Ty was indeed in the waiting room. There was no noticeable injury. He was seated, head back, eyes closed, one leg stretched out in front of him. He wore faded Levi's and a black T-shirt, and looked like the poster boy for Tall, Dark, and Dangerous. Pretty much anyone looking at him would assume he was relaxed, maybe even asleep, but Mallory sensed he was about as relaxed as a coiled rattler.

He opened his eyes and looked at her.

Inexplicably nervous, she glanced at the TV mounted high in a corner, which was tuned to a soap opera. On the screen was a beautiful, dark-haired woman getting it on with a guy half her age in a hot tub. She was panting and screaming out, "Oh, Brad. Oh, please, Brad!"

Oh, good. Because this wasn't awkward enough. She hastily looked around for the remote but it was MIA. Naturally.

Ty's brows went up but he said nothing; he didn't need to. The last time she'd seen him, he'd been pouring on the charm and getting into her panties with shocking ease.

Okay, maybe not so much on the charm. Nope, he'd drawn her in with something far more devastatingly effective—that piercing, fierce gaze, which had turned her on like she'd never been turned on before.

Apparently nothing much had changed in that regard. She'd just handled three emergencies in a row without an elevation in her heart rate, but her heart was pumping now, thudding in her chest and bouncing off her rib cage at stroke levels.

He'd walked away from her, she reminded herself, clearly not intending to further their relationship—if that's what one called a quickie these days.

The woman on the TV was still screaming like she was auditioning for a porno. "Oh God, oh Brad, *yes!*"

The air conditioning was on, which in no way explained why she was in the throes of a sudden hot flash. Whirling around, she continued to search in desperation for the remote, finally locating it sitting innocuously on a corner chair. It still took her a horrifyingly long time to find the mute button, but when she hit it, the ensuing silence seemed more deafening than the "Oh Brad, please!" had been.

She could feel Ty looking at her, and she bit her lower lip because all she could think about was that he'd made her cry out like that too.

But at least she hadn't begged.

"I'd offer a penny for your thoughts," he said. "But I have the feeling they're worth far more."

"I'm not thinking anything," she said far too quickly, then felt the heat of her blush rise up her face.

"Liar." He rose from the chair and shifted closer, and she stopped breathing. Just stopped breathing. Which wasn't good because she *really* needed some air.

And a grip.

Ty leaned into her a little bit, his lips brushing her ear. "You weren't quite as loud as she was."

She closed her eyes as the blush renewed itself. "A nice guy wouldn't even bring that up."

He shrugged, plainly saying he wasn't a nice guy. And in fact, he'd never claimed to be one.

Of course there was no one else in the waiting room, but just across the hall at the sign-in desk were Camilla and her mother, neither of them bothering to pretend to be doing anything other than staring in open, rapt curiosity.

Mallory turned her back on them. "I wasn't loud," she whispered.

Oh good Lord. That hadn't been what she'd meant to say at all, but it made him smile. A genuine smile that crinkled the corners of his eyes and softened his face, making him even more heart-stoppingly handsome, if that was possible. "Yeah," he said. "You were."

Okay, maybe she had been. But she couldn't have helped it. "It'd been a while," she admitted grudgingly. And he'd *really* known what he was doing.

As Tammy had reminded her, Mallory's last boyfriend had been Allen, the Seattle accountant, who'd decided Mallory wasn't worth the commute. That had been last year. A very long, dry year...

Ty's eyes softened, and she realized that they weren't clear green, not even close. Lurking just beneath the surface were layers of other shades, which in turn softened *her*. He'd held her like no other, whispered sweet, hot nothings in her ear as she'd indeed panted and cried out, and begged him just like the soap opera actress. Damn, but she could still get aroused at just the memory of the strength of his arms as he'd held her through it, that intoxicating mix of absolute security and wild abandon.

"It'd been a long time for me too," he said, surprising her. How did a guy who looked as good as he did and exuded pheromones and testosterone like they were going out of style *not* have sex for a "long time"?

On the screen behind him, the woman was still going at it, and watching her without the sound made it seem even more X-rated. "I did *not* go on like that," she murmured, and though

Ty wisely held his tongue, his expression said it all. "What, you think I *did*?" she asked in disbelief.

His gaze flicked to the screen, then back to her face. "If it helps, you looked way hotter and sounded much better while doing it."

Oh, God. She turned away from him and was at the door before his low, husky voice sounded again. "Where are you going?" he asked.

"Walking away. You should recognize it."

"I'm actually here as a patient."

At the only words in the English language that could have made her turn around, she did just that. "You are? Are you sick?"

He pointed to his head. "Josh told me to come back in ten days to get the stitches out."

Josh? He was on a first-name basis with Dr. Scott? "Dr. Scott got called to Seattle." She let out a long breath. "But if he left the order, I can remove the stitches for you."

Her mother and Camilla were still watching, of course, now joined by additional staff who apparently had nothing better to do than attempt to eavesdrop on Mallory and Mysterious Cute Guy. Mallory would lay odds that *this* Cute Guy sighting would go wide and be public by the end of her shift.

Nothing she could do about that. "Let's get this over with."

"Is it going to hurt?"

She looked at Ty, at his big, tough body, at the way he limped ever so slightly on his left leg, and then into his eyes. Which were amused.

He was teasing her.

Well, fine. She could give as good as she got. "Something tells me you can handle it."

Chapter 8

Eve left the Garden of Eden for chocolate.

Ty followed Mallory through the double doors to the ER and to a bed, where she then pulled a curtain around them for privacy.

In the military, Ty had learned defense tactics and ways to conceal information. He'd excelled at both. As a result, concealing emotion came all too easily to him. Not to mention, there wasn't much room for emotion in the underbelly of the Third World countries he'd worked in. So he'd long ago perfected the blank expression, honed it as a valuable tool. It was second nature now, or had been.

Until Mallory.

Because he was having a hell of a hard time pulling it off with her. Like now, for instance, when he was relieved to see her and yet struggling to hide that very fact. Clearly not so relieved to see him, she said "I'll be right back" and vanished.

Fair enough. As she'd pointed out, he'd vanished on her, and a part of him had figured he'd never see her again.

But another part had hoped he would.

He'd known that she worked here and imagined she was a great nurse. On the night of the storm, she'd been good in an emergency, extremely level-headed and composed.

Unlike at the auction, in his arms. Then she'd been hungry, and the very opposite of level-headed and composed. He'd loved that about her. Now she was back to the calm persona. She looked cute in her pale pink scrubs with the tiny red heart embroidered over the pocket on her left breast. He especially liked the air of authority she wore.

Hell.

He liked everything he knew about her so far, including how she'd tasted. Yeah, he'd really liked how she'd tasted. Which was the only explanation he had for being here, because he sure as hell could remove his own damn stitches.

From nearby, someone was moaning softly in both fear and pain. He stood, instinctively reacting to the sound as he hadn't in four years. Four years of ignoring the call to help or heal.

The moan came again, and Ty closed his eyes. Christ, how he suddenly wished he hadn't come. Unable to help himself, he stuck his head out the curtain of his cubicle. In the next bed over, a guy was hooked up to a monitor, fluids, and oxygen. He was in his early forties, smelled like a brewery, and either hadn't showered this month or he'd rolled in garbage. His hair was gray and standing straight up, missing in clumps. A transient, probably, looking small and weak and terrified.

"You okay?" Ty asked, staying where he was. "You need the nurse?"

The man shook his head but kept moaning, eyes wide, his free hand flailing. His eyes were dilated, and there was a look to him that said he was high on something.

Cursing himself, Ty moved to the side of his bed. He glanced at the IV. They were hydrating him, which was good. Catching the man's hand in his, Ty squeezed lightly. "What's going on?"

"Stomach. It hurts."

The guy's clothes were filthy and torn enough to reveal a Trident Tattoo on his arm, and Ty let out a slow breath. "Military," he said, feeling raw. Too raw.

"Army," the man said, slurring, clearly still heavily intoxicated, at the least.

Ty nodded and might have turned away but the guy was clinging to his hand like it was a lifeline, so Ty continued to hold onto him right back as he slowly sank onto the stool. "I was Navy," he heard himself say. He left out the Special Ops part; he always did. It had nothing to do with not being proud of his service and everything to do with not wanting to answer any questions. And there were *always* questions. "I'm out now."

Technically.

"You never get out," the man said.

Well, that was true enough.

"They should pay us for the long nights of bad dreams." The guy took a moment to gather his thoughts. This seemed to be a big effort. Ty wanted to tell him not to work too hard but before he could, the man spoke again. "They should give us extra combat pay for all the ways our lives are fucked up."

Ty could get behind that. They sat there in silence a moment, the man looking like he was half asleep now and Ty feeling a little bit sick. Sick in the gut. Sick to the depths of his soul. Yeah, definitely the hospital had been a stupid idea. This was absolutely the *last* time he let his dick think for him.

"I still think about them," the man said softly into the silence.

Ah, hell. Ty didn't have to ask who. He knew. All the dead. Ty swallowed hard and nodded.

The man stared at him, glassy-eyed but coherent. "How many for you?"

Ty closed his eyes. "Four." But there'd been others, too. *Way* too many others.

The man let out a shuddery sigh of sympathy. "Here." He lifted a shaky hand and slid it into his shirt, coming out with a flask. "This helps."

Mallory chose that very moment to pull back the curtain. "*There* you are," she said to Ty, then smiled kindly at the man in the bed. "Better yet, Ryan?"

Ryan, caught red-handed with the flask, didn't meet her gaze as he gave a jerky nod.

"Why don't I hold that for you, okay?" Gently, she pried the flask from Ryan's fingers, confiscating it without another word.

Ty didn't know what he'd expected from her. Maybe annoyance, or some sign that she resented the duty of caring for a guy who was in here for reasons that had clearly been self-inflicted. But she ran a hand down Ryan's arm in a comforting gesture, not shying away from touching him.

More than duty, Ty thought. Much more. This was the real deal, *she* was the real deal, and she cared, deeply.

"I've called your daughter," she told Ryan. "She'll be here in ten minutes. We're just going to let the bag do its thing, refilling you up with minerals, potassium, sodium, and other good stuff. You'll feel better soon." She patted his forearm as she checked his leads, making physical contact before she looked at Ty, gesturing with her head for him to follow her.

"Is he going to be okay?" Ty asked quietly on the other side of the curtain.

"Soon as he sobers up."

"He's on something besides alcohol."

"Yes."

"Does he have a place to stay?"

She gave him a long once-over. "Look at you with all the questions."

"Does he?"

She sighed. "I'm sorry, but you know I can't discuss his case with you. I can tell you that he's being taken care of. Does that help?"

Yeah. No. Ty had no idea what the fucking lump the size of a regulation football was doing stuck in his throat or why his heart was pounding. Or why he couldn't let this go. "He's a vet," he said. "He's having nightmares. He—"

"I know," she said softly, and reached out to touch him, soothing him as she had Ryan. "And like I said, he's being taken care of." She paused, studying him for a disturbingly long beat. "Not everyone would have done that, you know. Gone in there and held a vagrant's hand and comforted him."

"I'm not everyone."

"No kidding." The phone at her hip vibrated. She looked at the screen and let out a breath. "Wait for me," she said, pointing to his cubicle. "I'll be right there." And then she moved off in the direction of the front desk.

In front of Ty was yet another bed. This curtain was shut but it was suddenly whipped open by a nurse who was talking to the patient sitting on the bed. "Change into the robe," she was saying. "And I'll go page your doctor."

The patient had clearly walked in under his own steam, but he wasn't looking good. He was a big guy, mid-thirties, dressed in coveralls that had the Public Utilities Department logo on a pec. He was filthy from head to toe, clearly just off the job. As Ty watched, he went from looking bad to worse, and then he gasped, clutching at his chest.

Oh, Christ, Ty thought. Why the hell was he here? He should have left. Instead, he was hurtled back in time, back to the mountain, squinting against the brilliant fireball that had been a plane. He'd sat on the cliff holding Trevor in his arms, Trevor clutching at his crushed chest.

A million miles and four years later, the guy on the hospital bed groaned, dropping the gown he'd been holding. He slithered to the floor, his eyes rolling up in the back of his head.

Ty took a step back and came up against a rolling cart of supplies even as his instincts screamed at him to rush over there and help.

But the cart moved out from behind him, and he staggered on legs that felt like overcooked noodles.

Then suddenly people came out of the woodwork, including Mallory.

"He's coding," someone yelled.

And the dance to save the man's life began. Someone pulled Ty out of the way and back to his cubicle, where he waited for what might have been five minutes, or an hour.

Or a lifetime.

Mallory finally came in. When she found him still standing, she gave him a sharp look. "Sorry about that. You okay?"

"The guy. Is he . . . ?"

"He's going to make it." She gestured to the bed. "Sit. You look like you could use it."

Like hell he did.

"Sit," she said again, soft steel.

Fine. He sat. On the stool, not the bed. The bed was for patients, and he wasn't a patient. He was a fucking idiot, but he wasn't a patient.

"Not a big hospital fan, huh?" she asked wryly.

"No."

She washed her hands thoroughly. "Personal experience?"

He didn't answer, wasn't ready to answer. Apparently okay with that, she pulled on a pair of latex gloves, then opened a couple of drawers. "Are you squeamish?"

He didn't answer that either. Mostly because only yesterday he'd have given her an emphatic *no*. Except what had just happened to him in the hallway said otherwise.

He'd changed.

Once upon a time, nothing had gotten to him, but that was no longer true. Case in point was Mallory herself. She got to him, big time.

She lifted a big, fat needle, and he blinked.

She smiled and put the needle down, and he realized she'd been fucking with him to lighten the mood. He heard the surprised laugh rumble out of him, rusty sounding. Muscles long gone unused stretched as he smiled and shook his head. "Guess you owed me that."

"Guess I did." After she'd loaded up a tray with what she wanted, she came at him. She set the tray on the bed and perched a hip there as well, letting out an exhale that spelled exhaustion. "If you don't want to sit here, I sure as hell do."

He found himself letting out another smile. "Tired?"

"I passed tired about three hours ago." She soaked a gauze in rubbing alcohol.

"So you're an RN."

"Yes," she said. "I bought my license online yesterday." She dabbed at the wound over his eyebrow and then opened a suture kit, which he was intimately familiar with. As a medic in the field, he'd gone through a lot of them patching guys up.

"Don't worry," she said, picking up a set of tweezers. "I've seen a guy do this once."

He wrapped his fingers around her wrist, stopping her movement.

"I'm kidding," she said.

"Oh I know. I just don't want you to be cracking yourself up when you put those things near my eye."

"Actually, I'm not all that amused right now," she said.

"What are you, then?"

She hesitated. "Embarrassed," she finally admitted.

This stopped him cold. That was the *last* thing he wanted her to be. "Don't be embarrassed," he said. "Pick something else, *anything* else."

"Like?"

"Mad. Mad would be better."

"You want me to be mad at you?" she asked, looking confused. "Why? I'm the one who said the 'here' and 'now,' remember?"

Yeah, he remembered. He'd loved it.

"And *I'm* the one who wanted a one-time thing," she said. "No strings attached."

"So why be embarrassed then?"

She sighed.

"Tell me."

"Because I'd never done that before." She lowered her voice to a soft whisper. "Sex without an emotional attachment," she clarified. "And now..." Her eyes slowly met his. "I'm thinking I should have requested a two-time thing."

This left him speechless.

She winced, shook her head, then laughed a little at herself. "Never mind." She leaned in close to look at the stitching. "Nice work. Dr. Scott's the best," she said. "But you'll probably still have a decent scar. Shouldn't be too much of a problem for you, women like that sort of thing. Apparently they'll fall all over themselves to sleep with you."

Still holding her wrist, he ran his thumb over her pulse. "You didn't fall all over yourself," he said quietly.

"Didn't I?"

"If you did, there were two of us doing the falling."

Again, her eyes met his, and he watched her struggle to accept that. "Well," she finally said, pulling her hand free, "as long as there were two of us." Some of the good humor was now restored in her voice. Which meant she was compassionate, funny, *and* resilient. His favorite qualities in a woman.

But he wasn't looking for a woman. He wasn't looking for anything except to get back to his world where he functioned best.

She leaned in close and used the tweezers to pull up a stitch, which she then snipped with scissors. "A little sting now," she warned, and pulled out the suture. "So what was it that you said you do?"

Oh, she was good, he thought. Very good. "I didn't say."

She pulled out another stitch and then gazed steadily at him.

She had the most amazing eyes. Mostly chocolate brown, but there were specks of gold in there as well. And a sharp wit that stirred him even more than her hot, curvy little bod.

A woman poked her head around the curtain, the same one who'd been at the front desk. Young. Eager. "Need help?" she asked Mallory, her eyes on Ty.

"Nope," Mallory said. "I've got this."

Her face fell, but she left without further comment.

Two seconds later another nurse appeared, and this one Ty recognized as Mallory's mother from the night of the auction.

"New arrival," she said to Mallory, eyeing Ty.

"It's your turn," Mallory told her.

Her mom frowned. "*Mal.*"

"*Mother.*"

The curtain yanked shut, and they were alone. "She hates when I call her 'mother.'"

"You work with your mom."

Mallory took a page from his book and went silent. It made him smile. *She* made him smile.

"She looked pissed," he said, fishing. Which was new for him. He never fished. He hated fishing.

"Oh, she is," Mallory said. She pulled another stitch, and he barely felt it. She had good hands, as he had reason to know.

"Because of me?" he asked.

"Now why would you think that?" she asked. "Because I left my own fundraiser to have sex in a storage room with a man whose name I barely knew?"

"Really great sex," he corrected. When she slid him a long look, he added, "Imagine what we could do with a bed."

She let out a short laugh, and he stared at her face, truly fascinated by her in a way that surprised him. She was supposed to be just a woman, a cute nurse in a small town that soon he'd forget the name of.

Except…he wasn't buying it.

"Hey, Mal." Yet another woman peeked into the cubicle, this one mid-thirties and wearing a housekeeping outfit. "Need anything?"

"*No!*"

"Jeez," she said, insulted. "Fine, you don't have to take my head off."

When she vanished, Mallory sighed. "My sister." She dumped the instruments she'd used into the sink, and still facing away from him, spoke. "What about your leg?"

"What about it?"

"Does it need to be looked at, too?" she asked.

"No."

She turned to look at him with an expectant air, saying nothing. It made him smile. "You can't use that silence thing against me. I invented it."

"What silence thing?" she asked innocently.

"You know what silence thing, where you go all quiet and I'm supposed to feel compelled to fill it in with all my secrets."

She smiled. "So you admit to having secrets."

"Many," he said flatly.

Her smile faded. "You're engaged. Or worse, you're married. You have ten kids. Oh my God, tell me you don't have kids."

"No. And I'm not engaged or married. I'm not…anything."

She just looked at him for a long moment. "Some secrets are toxic if you try to keep them inside. You know that, right? Some secrets are meant to be told, before they eat you up."

Maybe, but not his. In no time, he'd be long gone, back to a very fast-paced, dangerous life that would eventually, probably kill him. But not her. She'd find someone to share her life with, grow old with. "You watch too much *Oprah*."

She didn't take umbrage at this. She pulled off her gloves and tossed them into the trash.

"Does your whole family work here?" he asked, running a finger over the healing cut, now sans stitches. She'd done a good job.

"Just my mom, my sister, and me," she said. "And I also work at the Health Services Clinic."

"I didn't know there was one here."

"Well, there's not. Not yet. But if we get approval at the town meeting tomorrow night, it's a go for a tentative opening this weekend."

"Is there a need in a town this small?"

"This hospital services the entire county," she said. "Not just Lucky Harbor. And there's a huge need. We have a high teenage pregnancy rate, and drug abuse is on the rise as well. So is abuse and homelessness. We need counseling services and advocacy and educational programs. And there's going to be a weekly health clinic on Saturday for those who can't afford medical care."

God, she was so fierce she made his heart ache. They could use her at his work, he thought, but was doubly glad that she pretty much embodied Lucky Harbor. Hopefully she'd never live through some of the horrors out there, or lose her genuine compassion to jaded cynicism. "So what makes a woman like you take on such a thing?" he asked.

"What do you mean?"

"Usually this sort of thing is driven by a cause. What's yours?"

She turned away, busying herself with washing her hands again.

"Ah," he said. "So I'm not the only one with secrets."

She turned back to him at that, eyes narrowed. "Tell you what. I'll answer one question for every question you answer for me."

He knew better than to go there. He might have treated her like a one-night stand but he knew damn well she was different. By all appearances, she was pretty and sweet and innocent, but beneath that guileless smile, she held all the power, and he knew it. She'd have him confessing his sins with one warm touch.

She isn't for you...

"Yeah," she said dryly, hands on hips. "I figured that'd be too much for you."

It was. Far too much. He was leaving...and yet he opened his mouth anyway. "What time do you get off?"

This shocked her, he could tell. Fair enough. He'd shocked himself too.

"Seven," she said.

"I'll pick you up."

"No," she said. "You know the pier?"

"Sure."

"I'll meet you there. In front of the Ferris wheel."

She didn't trust him. Smart woman. "Okay," he said. "In front of the Ferris wheel."

"How do I know you're going to remember to show up for *this* date?"

A date. Christ, it was utter insanity. But he looked into her beautiful eyes and nearly drowned. "Because this time I'm in charge of all my faculties," he said.

Except, clearly, he wasn't.

Chapter 9

*Stress wouldn't be so hard to take if it were
chocolate covered.*

As Mallory got into her car after her shift, her phone rang from
an unfamiliar number.

"*He came to the hospital to see you?*" Amy asked.

Mallory didn't bother to ask how Amy knew Ty had been
at the hospital earlier. It was probably put out as an all points
bulletin. "Whose cell phone is this?"

"I just found it at the diner. Don't tell Jan; she likes to keep
all the leftover phones for herself."

"Amy! You can't just use someone's phone."

"And that," Amy said dryly, "is why you need Bad Girl lessons.
Okay, impromptu meeting of the Chocoholics commencing right
here, right now, because you're in crisis."

"I am not."

"Lesson number one," Amy went on without listening. "*Always* use a situation to your benefit."

"*That's* lesson number one?" Mallory said. "What's lesson number two?"

"Lesson number two is *not* to get your exploits recounted on Facebook. Rookie mistake, Mal."

Mallory sighed. "Do you have any wisdom that might actually be helpful?"

"Yeah." There was some muffled talking, and she came back on. "Grace is here. She needed a big, warm brownie after pounding the sidewalk today looking for a job. She says lesson number three is to understand that guys are about the visuals, and she's right. Always wear Bad Girl shoes and Bad Girl panties. They create the mood."

The panties were self-explanatory. "Bad Girl shoes? *You* wear steel-toed boots."

More muffled talking as Grace and Amy conferred on this subject.

"Okay," Amy came back to say. "Grace thinks it's a frame of mind. I'm a shit-kicker, so the boots work. You're...softer. You need high heels. Strappy. Sexy."

The thought of high heels after being on her feet all day made Mallory want to cry. Then she remembered how it had felt when Ty had put his hands on her ankles and removed her heels for her. She'd liked that, a lot. "My only heels hurt my feet."

"Get another pair. Lesson number four," Amy said. "Get a hold of his phone and scan through the contacts."

"I'm not going to run through his contacts!" Mallory paused and considered. "And what would I be looking for, anyway?"

"Anyone listed as *My Drug Dealer*. That's when you'd run not walk."

Mallory blinked. "The guy who left his phone at the diner has a contact that says *My Drug Dealer*?"

"And also *Bitch Ex-Wife*. Oh, and *Mommy*." Amy sighed. "*Not* a keeper."

Grace got on the phone then, her mouth sounding quite full. "You're going to have to make the next meeting in person, Mallory. This brownie is orgasmic."

She could use an orgasmic brownie. "One of you take a turn now."

"Well, Grace here has been turned down for all the jobs she applied for from the Canadian border to San Diego," Amy said. "So I'm considering pouring her a shot of something to go with the brownie. In the meantime, I called Tara at the B&B, and they had no problem giving her the local discount to keep staying there for cheap, since she's a local now. As for me," Amy said, "I'm status quo. Waiting for warmer weather to make my move."

"Your move on what?" Mallory asked.

"Life. In the meantime, we'll concentrate on you," she said. "You're the most screwed up so it makes the most sense. Get some bad girl shoes."

Mallory hung up and drove to the pier. When she got out, she took a moment to inhale the salty ocean air as the sound of the waves hitting the shore soothed her antsy nerves. At the pier's entrance, flyers were posted, one for an upcoming high school play, another for a musical festival the following week. But it was the flyer for the town's monthly Interested Citizens Meeting that caught her interest.

This was where Bill Lawson would pitch her Health Services Clinic and get the town's collective reaction.

In the meantime, she had another meeting, one that, according to her heart rate, was imminent. She'd changed into a summer dress she'd borrowed from Tammy's work locker. Tammy had superior clothes. This was what happened when one was married to a mall cop. By way of her husband, Tammy got a hell of a discount.

Walking to the Ferris wheel, Mallory took quick stock of

her appearance. Not too bad, she thought, although her walking sandals were definitely not up to Bad Girl code.

Next time.

The night was warm and moist, and the waves rocked gently against the pylons far below the pier. The power beneath her feet made the pier shudder faintly with the push and pull of the tide, which matched the push and pull of anticipation drumming through her.

You are not going to sleep with him again, she told herself firmly. *That was just a one-time thing. You're only here now because you're curious about him.*

And also because he'd looked hot today at the hospital. Damn, she had a problem. A big, attracted-to-him-like-a-moth-to-a-flame-type problem. How that was possible, she had no idea. Their good-bye on the night of the auction had been...abrupt. Although *nothing* about what had occurred before that had felt abrupt. Nope, everything had been...*amazing*.

She stopped at the entrance to the line for the Ferris wheel. When her inner drumming turned into a prickle at the base of her neck, she turned in a slow circle.

And found Ty watching her.

He was leaning back against the pier railing, legs casually crossed at the ankles, looking for all the world like a guy who made it a habit to be carefree enough to walk a beach pier.

They both knew that wasn't true.

And good God, just looking at him did something to her. His hair was tousled, like he'd been shoving his fingers through it. Stubble darkened his jaw, and his firm, sensuous mouth was unsmiling. The scar above his brow was new and shiny, and the mirrored sunglasses only added to the whole ruffian look he had going on.

It suited him, in a big way.

He was dressed in cargoes and a dark T-shirt snug across his broad chest and loose over his abs. He looked big, bad, built, and dangerous as hell.

And he was hers for the evening.

Hers.

Not one of her smartest moves. But stretching her wings wasn't about keeping her head. It was about...being. Living.

Feeling.

And the man definitely made her feel, a lot. Already in their short acquaintance, he'd made her feel curious, annoyed, frustrated, and the topper...

Aroused.

She was feeling that right now in fact, in spades. She wanted to shove up his shirt and lick him from Adam's Apple to belly button.

And beyond.

Slowly he pushed the sunglasses to the top of his head and his stark green eyes locked unwaveringly on hers. She knew he couldn't really read her mind, but she jumped and flushed a little guiltily anyway for where her thoughts had gone.

He pushed away from the railing and came toward her, all those muscles moving fluidly and utterly without thought. She had no idea what she'd expected, but it wasn't for him to take her hand in his and pull her around to the side of the Ferris wheel, out of view, between a storage shed and the pier railing.

"W-what are you doing?"

He didn't answer. He merely put his big hands on her, lifted her up to her tiptoes, and covered her mouth with his.

Her purse fell in a thud at her feet. Her fingers slid into his hair. And when his tongue slid over hers, all her bones melted away.

Then before she knew it, the kiss was over and she was weaving unsteadily on her feet, blinking him into focus. "What was *that*?"

He scooped up her purse and handed it to her. "I lost my head. You're distracting."

"And you're not?"

His eyes heated. "We could fix that."

"Oh no," she said. "You said you weren't a long-term bet. You said you weren't even a short one."

"But I'm on your list. Your list of Mr. Wrongs."

"Yeah, about that. I've rearranged the order of the list." This was a bold-faced lie. She'd not rearranged the list. He *was* the list.

He raised a brow. "Did what's-his-name from the hardware store get ahead of me? The one who sleeps with anyone with boobs?"

"Maybe."

"I was at the hardware store today," he said. "Anderson was there, flirting with some cute young thing." Leaning in, his mouth found its way to her ear. "You can take Anderson off your list."

Oh no he didn't. He didn't just tell her what to do. "I—"

He pressed her into the railing and kissed her again. Apparently he didn't want to hear it. That was okay, because she forgot her own name, much less who was on her list. She had her tongue in his mouth, her hands in his silky hair, and her breasts mashed up to his hard, warm chest. She'd have climbed inside him if she could.

You came here to ask him questions.

In an attempt to go back to that, she squeezed her thighs, thinking *keep them together*, but his knee nudged hers, and then he slid a muscled thigh between hers. Good. Lord. He felt so . . . *good*. Drawing on some reserve of strength she didn't know she had, she pushed on his chest. For a beat he didn't budge, then he stepped slowly back, his eyes heavy-lidded and sexy.

"Okay," she said shakily. "Let's try something that's *not* going to lead to round two of sex in a public place." His expression was giving nothing away. Not exactly open, but she was a woman of her word, and she wanted to know he was a man of his. "What do you do for a living? Are you...military?" she asked, letting loose of the one thing she couldn't seem to get out of her head. It was the way he carried himself: calm, steady, looking ready for anything, and that bone-deep stoicism. Not to mention how he'd looked while at Ryan's bedside—like he knew to the depths of his soul what Ryan was feeling.

A low, wry laugh rumbled out of him. "So we're going to ease into this then."

"Yeah." She was glad to see the smile. "You don't know this about me, but I tend to jump in with both feet."

"I noticed." He looked at her, his eyes reminding her that he knew other things about her as well, things that made her blush. "At the moment I'm rebuilding a few cars."

This didn't exactly answer her question, and in fact, only brought on *more* questions. "So you're a mechanic?" she asked.

"While I'm here in lucky Harbor."

"But—"

"My turn. The other night. Why me?"

She squirmed a little at this, although it was a fair enough question. He already knew that what they'd done that night at the auction had been a first for her, but what he didn't know, *couldn't* know, was that she'd only been able to do it at all because she'd felt something for him. Which was crazy; they'd been perfect strangers. "Like I said, it'd been a long time."

"So I was handy?"

"Well, Anderson already had a date, so..."

He growled, and she laughed. "I don't know exactly," she admitted. "Except..." *Just say it.* "I felt a connection to you."

He was looking very serious now, and he slowly shook his head. "You don't want to feel connected to me, Mallory."

"No, I don't want to. But I do. And there's more."

"The whole bored and restless thing?" he asked.

So he'd *also* overheard her entire conversation with her mother. The man had some serious listening skills.

"You used me to chase away your restlessness," he said quietly.

"Yes." She winced. "I'm sorry about that."

"Mallory, you can use me any time."

"But you said one-time only," she reminded him.

"Actually, *you* said that. And plans change. Apparently I left you needing more, which is the same thing as unsatisfied in my book." His gaze went hot and dark. "We'll have to fix that."

She felt her body respond as if he'd already touched her. He hadn't left her unsatisfied at all. In fact, she'd never been more satisfied in her life. "Ice cream," she whispered, her throat suddenly very dry. "I think I need ice cream."

He smiled knowingly but didn't challenge her. They walked to the ice cream stand. The server was small for a guy in his early twenties and painfully thin, but the warm smile he flashed at Mallory distracted from his ill appearance. "Hey, Mal," he said. "Looking good today."

Lance gave her this same line every time that he landed in the ER. He could be flat on his back, at death's door—which with his Cystic Fibrosis happened more than anyone liked—and he'd *still* flash Mallory those baby blues and flirt.

He was one of her very favorite patients. "Where's your pretty girlfriend?" she teased, knowing he'd been dating another nurse, Renee, for months now.

An attractive brunette poked her head out from behind Lance and smiled. "She's right here. Hey, Mallory" Renee's eyes locked onto Ty and turned speculative. "Seems like Lance isn't the only one with a pretty date."

Mallory laughed at the look on Ty's face. He actually didn't react outwardly, but it was all in his eyes as he slid her a glance.

She decided to take mercy on him and wrap things up. "I'll need a double scooped vanilla."

"So the usual," Lance said. "You ever going to branch out? Add a twist of cookie dough, or go for a walk on the wild side and add sprinkles?"

Mallory very carefully didn't look at Ty. "Not this time." She'd already taken her walk on the wild side, and wild walk on the dark side was standing right next to her.

Lance served Mallory, then looked at Ty, who shook his head. No ice cream for him.

Which was probably how he kept his body in such incredible shape, Mallory thought as she reached into her pocket for cash. Ty beat her to it, paying for her ice cream.

"Watching your girlie figure?" Mallory asked him, licking at the ice cream as they walked.

His eyes never left her tongue. "Girlie figure?"

There was nothing girlie about him, not one thing. "Maybe you're dieting," she said. Another lick. "Fighting the bulge."

Ty Garrison didn't have an ounce of fat on him, and they both knew it. But he did have a very dark, hot look as he watched her continue to lick at her cone. Like maybe he was a hungry predator and she was his prey. The thought caused another of those secret tingles.

"You think I'm fighting the bulge?" he asked softly.

She reached out and patted his abs. Her hand practically bounced off the tight muscles there. "I wouldn't worry about it. It happens to all of us," she said lightly, taking another slow lick of her ice cream. "Does your break from work have anything to do with your leg?"

"Yes." His eyes never left her mouth. She was playing with fire, and she knew it.

"You know this whole man of mystery thing isn't as cute as you might think," she said. "Right?"

"I'm not cute."

"No kidding!"

A very small smile curved his mouth as he studied her for a moment, as if coming to a decision. "You asked if I'm military. I was."

Her gaze searched his. "And now?"

"Like I said, I'm working on cars."

"And when you're not working on cars?" she asked with mock patience. "What do you do then?"

Again he just looked at her for a long beat. "It's in the same vein as mechanics. I locate a problem and...rectify it."

"But...not on cars."

"No," he agreed. "Not on cars."

Huh. He was certainly *not* saying more than he was saying. Which wasn't working for her. "And the leg?" she asked.

"I was in a crash."

He hadn't hesitated to say it but she sensed a big inner hesitation to discuss it further. "I'm sorry," she said, not wanting to push. She knew exactly what it felt like to *not* want to discuss something painful, but she was definitely wishing he'd say more. And then he did.

"I'm in Lucky Harbor until I'm cleared," he said. "Matt and I go way back. He set me up in a house to recoup."

"Are you...recouping okay?" she asked softly.

"Working on it."

She nodded and fought the ridiculous urge to hug him. He wouldn't want her sympathy, she knew that much. "The leg is giving you pain. Are you taking anything for it?"

"No," he said, and with a hand on the small of her back, led her into the arcade. Conversation over, apparently. He handed some money over to the guy behind the first booth.

Shooting Duck Gallery.

"What are you doing?" she asked.

"I'm going to shoot some ducks. And so are you."

"I'm not good at shooting ducks," she said, watching him pick up the gun like he knew what he was doing. He sighted and shot.

And hit every duck, destroying the entire row.

"Show off," she said, and picked up her gun. She didn't know what she was doing. And she didn't hit a single duck. She set the gun down and sighed.

"That's pathetic." Ty handed over some more cash and stood behind her. "Pick up the gun again." He corrected her stance by nudging his foot between hers, kicking her legs farther apart. Then he steadied her arms with his.

This meant he was practically wrapped around her, surrounding her. If she turned her head, she could press her mouth to his bicep. His very rock-solid bicep. It was shocking how much she wanted to do just that. She'd bet he'd taste better than her ice cream.

He went still, then let out a low breath, his jaw brushing hers. "You're thinking so loud I'm already hard."

She choked out a laugh, and he pressed himself against her bottom, proving he wasn't kidding. "How do you know what I'm thinking?" she asked, embarrassingly breathless. "Maybe I'm thinking that I want another ice cream."

"That's not what you're thinking. Shoot the ducks, Mallory."

With him guiding her, she actually hit one, and her competitive nature kicked in. "Again," she demanded.

With a rare grin, Ty slapped some more money onto the counter. "Show me what you've got," he said to her, and to her disappointment, this time he remained back a few steps, leaving her to do it alone.

She hit one more out of the entire row, which was *hugely* annoying to her. "How do you make it look so easy?"

"Practice," he said in a voice that assured her he'd had lots. "Your concentration needs some work."

Actually, there was nothing wrong with her concentration. She was concentrating just fine. She was concentrating on how she felt in his arms, with his hard body at her back.

She liked it. Far too much. "Maybe I don't care about being able to shoot a duck."

"No problem." He tossed down another few bucks and obliterated another row of ducks himself.

"Dude," the guy behind the counter said, sounding impressed as he presented Ty with a huge teddy bear as a prize.

Ty handed it to Mallory. "My hero," she murmured with a laugh, and he grimaced, making her laugh again as she hugged the bear close, the silly gesture giving her a warm fuzzy. Which was ironic because nothing about the big, tough Ty Garrison should have given her a warm fuzzy.

She knew he didn't want to be her hero.

He dragged her to the squirt gun booth next, where he proceeded to soundly beat her three times in a row. Apparently he wasn't worried about her ego. He won a stuffed dog at that booth, and then laughed out loud at her as she attempted to carry both huge stuffed animals and navigate the aisles without bumping into anyone.

Ridiculously, the whole thing gave her another warm fuzzy, immediately followed by an inner head smack. Because no way was she going to be the woman who fell for a guy just because he gave her a silly stuffed animal that she didn't need. *You're not supposed to fall for him at all*, she reminded herself. "This is very teenager-y of us," she said.

"If we were teenagers," he said, "we'd be behind the arcade, and you'd be showing me your gratitude for the stuffed animals by letting me cop a feel."

"In your dreams," she quipped, but her nipples went hard.

They competed in a driving game next, the two of them side by side in the booth, fighting for first place. Ty was handling his steering wheel with easy concentration, paying her no mind whatsoever. Mallory couldn't find her easy concentration, she was too busy watching him out of the corner of her eye. When she fell back a few cars as a result, Ty grinned.

Ah, so he *was* paying attention to her. Just to make sure, she nudged up against him.

His grin widened, but he didn't take his eyes off the screen. "That's not going to work, Mallory. You're going down."

Not going to work, her ass. She nudged his body with hers again, lingering this time, letting her breast brush his arm.

"Playing dirty," he warned, voice low, both husky and amused.

But she absolutely had his attention. She did the breast-against-his-arm thing again, her eyes on the screen, so she missed when he turned his head. But she didn't miss when he sank his teeth lightly into her earlobe and tugged. When she hissed in a breath, he soothed the ache with his tongue, and her knees wobbled. Her foot slipped off the gas.

And her car crashed into the wall.

Ty's car sped across the finish line.

"That's cheating!" she complained. "You can't—"

He grabbed her, lifting her up so that her feet dangled, and then kissed her until she couldn't remember what she'd meant to say. When he set her back down, she would have fallen over if he hadn't kept his hands on her. "You started it," he said. He gave her one more smacking kiss and then bought them both hot dogs for dinner. They sat on the pier, she and Ty and the two huge stuffed animals, and ate.

"So what are you doing to recover from the crash?" she asked.

"Swimming. Beating the shit out of Matt." He took the last bite of his hot dog. "Who's Karen?"

If her life had been a DVD, in that moment it would have skipped and come to a sudden halt, complete with the sound effect.

"I heard your mother say her name," he said, watching her face carefully. "And you got an odd expression, just like now."

"Karen's my sister." She paused, because it never got easier to say. "She died when I was younger."

Concern flashed in his eyes, stirring feelings she didn't want to revisit. Thankfully he didn't offer empty platitudes, for which she was grateful. But he did take her hand in his. "How?"

"Overdose."

His hand was big and warm and callused. He had several healing cuts over his knuckles, like he'd had a fight with a car part or tool. "How old were you?" he asked.

"Sixteen."

He squeezed her hand, and she blew out a breath. "You ever lose anyone?" she asked.

He didn't answer right away. She turned her head and looked at him, and found him studying the little flickers of reflection on the water as the sun lowered in the sky. "I lost my four closest friends all at the same time," he finally said and met her gaze. "Four years now, and it still sucks."

Throat tight, she nodded. "In the Army?"

"Navy. We were a crazy bunch, but it shouldn't have happened."

"All three of my siblings are a crazy bunch," she said. "Not military, of course, just . . . crazy."

He smiled. "Not you though."

"I have my moments." She blew out a breath. "Well, moment."

"Us."

She nodded.

"So I really am your walk on the wild side." He paused, then shook his head. "I'm still not clear on why you chose me."

"I'm not clear on a lot of things about myself." She met his gaze. "But in hindsight, I think it's because you're safe."

He stared at her, then laughed and scrubbed a hand over

his face. "Mallory, I'm about as unsafe as you can possibly get."

Yeah. But for some reason, she'd somehow trusted him that night. She still did. "If you're swimming," she said, "you must be healing up pretty good. When do you get cleared to go back to work?"

He looked into her eyes, his own unapologetic. "Soon."

"And it won't be in Lucky Harbor," she said quietly. She knew it wouldn't, but she needed to hear it, to remind herself that this wasn't anything but an...interlude.

"No," he agreed. "It won't be in Lucky Harbor."

The disappointment was undeniable, and shockingly painful. She'd really thought she could do this with him, have it be just about the sex, but it was turning out not to be the case at all. With a sigh, she stood. He did as well, gathering their garbage and taking it to a trash bin before coming back to stand next to where she was looking out at the water.

"I can't do this," she whispered.

He nodded. "I know."

"I want to but I—"

"It's okay." He brushed a kiss over her jaw and then was gone, proving for the second time now that he was, after all, her perfect Mr. All Wrong.

Chapter 10

*Chocolate is cheaper than therapy,
and you don't need an appointment.*

Two days later, Mallory entered the Vets' Hall for the town meeting and felt the déjà vu hit her. Pointedly ignoring the stairs to the second floor storage room, she strode forward to the big central meeting room. It was full, as all the town meetings tended to be.

Heaven forbid anyone in Lucky Harbor miss anything.

With sweaty palms and an accelerated heart rate, she found a seat in the back. Two seconds later, her sister plopped down into the chair next to her.

"Whew," Tammy said. "My dogs are tired." She leaned back and wriggled her toes. "You medical professionals are slobs, you know that? Took me an hour to clean up the staff kitchen, and I was ten minutes late getting off shift. And I was scheduled to have a quickie with Zach on his twenty-minute break too. We had to really amp it up to get done in time."

"That's great. I really needed to know that, thank you." Mallory glanced over at the glowing Tammy. There was no denying that she seemed...well, not settled exactly, and certainly not tamed, but *content*.

"Why are you looking at me like that?" Tammy asked. "Do I look like I just had a screaming orgasm? Cuz I totally did."

Mallory grimaced. "Again, thanks. And I'm looking at you because you look happy. Really happy."

"I should hope so. Because Zach just—"

Mallory slapped her hands over her ears, and Tammy grinned. "Wow, Mal, you almost over-reacted there for a second. One would almost think you hadn't had sex in forever, which isn't true at all."

"How in the world did you know that?"

Tammy grinned. "Well, I didn't know for sure until now. Mysterious Cute Guy, right? When? The night of the auction when you vanished for an hour and then reappeared with that cat-in-cream smile? *I knew it*."

Mallory choked. "I—"

"Don't try to deny it. Oh, and give me your phone for a sec."

Still embarrassed, Mallory handed over her phone, then watched as Tammy programmed something in. "What are you doing?"

"Making sure you can't forget your new boyfriend's name," Tammy said. "Here ya go."

Mallory stared down at the newest entry in her contact list. "Mysterious Cute Guy, aka Ty Garrison." She stared at Tammy. "Where did you get his number?"

"He left a message for Dr. Scott at the nurse's desk, including his cell phone number. I accidentally-on-purpose memorized it."

"You can't do that—"

"Oh relax, Miss Goodie Two-Shoes. No one saw me."

"*Tammy*—"

"Shh, it's starting." Tammy turned to face forward with a mock excited expression as the meeting was called to order.

Mallory bit her fingernails through the discussion of a new measure to put sports and arts back in the schools, getting parking meters along the sidewalks downtown, and whether or not the mayor, Jax Cullen, was going to run for another term.

Finally, the Health Services Clinic came up. Bill Lawson stood up and reiterated the bare bones plan and the facts, and then asked for opinions. Two attendees immediately stood up in the center aisle in front of the microphone set up there. The first was Mrs. Burland.

"I'm against this health clinic and always have been," she said, gripping her cane in one hand and pointing at the audience with a bony finger of her other. "It'll cost us—the hardworking taxpayers—money."

"Actually," Bill interrupted to say. "We've been given a large grant, plus the money raised at auction. There's also future fundraising events planned, including next week's car wash." He smiled. "Mallory Quinn talked everyone on the board into working the car wash, so I'm expecting each and every one of you to come out."

There was a collective gasp of glee. The hospital board was a virtual Who's Who of Lucky Harbor, including some very hot guys such as the mayor, Dr. Scott, and Matt Bowers, amongst others.

"Even you, Bill?" someone called out.

"Even me," Bill answered. "I can wash cars with the best of them."

Everyone *woo-hoo*'d at that, and Mallory relaxed marginally. Bill had just guaranteed them a huge showing at the car wash. People would come out in droves to see the town's best and finest out of their positions of honor and washing cars. They'd pay through the nose for it as they took pictures and laughed and pointed.

Lucky Harbor was sweet that way.

Still in the aisle, Mrs. Burland tapped on the microphone, her face pinched. "Hello! I'm still talking here! HSC will bring *undesirables* to our town. And we already have plenty of them." Her gaze sorted through the crowd with the speed and agility of an eagle after its prey, narrowing in on Mallory way in the back.

"Bitch," Tammy muttered.

Mallory just sank deeper into her seat.

"You all need to think about that," Mrs. Burland said and moved back to her seat.

Sandy, the town clerk and manager, stood up next. "I'm also against it," she said with what appeared to be genuine regret. "I just don't think we need to deplete our resources with a Health Services Clinic. Not when our library has no funds, our schools are short-staffed due to enforced layoffs, and our budget isn't close to being in balance. We could be allocating donations in better ways. I'm sorry, Mal, very sorry."

The audience murmured agreement, and two more people stood up to say they were also against the Health Services Clinic.

Then it was Lucille's turn. She stood up there in her bright pink tracksuit and brighter white tennis shoes, a matching pink headband holding back her steel grey/blue hair. She took a moment to glare at Mrs. Burland in the front row. The rumor was that they'd gone to high school together about two centuries back, and Mrs. Burland had stolen Lucille's beau. Lucille had retaliated by eloping with Mrs. B's brother, who'd died in the Korean War—not on the front lines but in a brothel from a heart attack.

Lucille was so short that the microphone was about a foot

above her head. This didn't stop her. "A Health Services Clinic would be nice," she said, head tipped up toward the microphone, her blue bun all aquiver. "Because then, if I thought I had the clap, I'd have a place to go."

The audience erupted in laughter.

"What?" she said. "You think I'm not getting any?" She turned and winked at Mr. Murdock in the third row.

Mr. Murdock grinned at her, his freshly washed dentures so unnaturally bright white they appeared to be glowing.

Lucille winked back, then returned to the business at hand. "Also, we couldn't have an HSC in better hands than those of our very own Mallory Quinn. She's a wonderful nurse and has her degree in business as well. She's one smart cookie."

Tammy turned to Mallory. "Did you actually graduate with both of those degrees?" she asked, clearly impressed.

Mallory slid her a look. "You were at my graduation."

Tammy searched her brain and then shook her head. "I've got nothing. In my defense, I spent those years pretty toasted."

Lucille was still talking. "I know some of you might say that Mallory's too sweet to handle such a big responsibility as the HSC, and that her programs involving drug rehab and teenage pregnancies will be overrun by dealers and pimps. But we're not giving our girl enough credit. If she can't handle the riffraff that her clinic brings into town, well then her new boyfriend certainly can."

"Oh my God." Mallory covered her eyes. "I can't look."

Tammy snorted. "At least she didn't call him your lover. And that's not even your biggest problem. That honor goes to the fact that your only supporter so far is a crazy old bat."

"You know, *you* could get up there and support me," Mallory said.

"Not me," Tammy said. "I'm shy in front of a crowd."

Yeah, right.

Lucille took her seat. Four more people had their say, not a single one of them in favor of the HSC. Tammy had to practically sit on Mallory to keep her in her chair.

"Beating them up isn't going to help," Tammy said.

Mallory's phone was buzzing with incoming texts, like the one from her mother that said:

He's your boyfriend?

Finally, a tall, broad-shouldered guy in faded jeans and mirrored sunglasses stood at the microphone, which came up to his chest.

Ty Garrison.

By this time, Mallory was so low in her chair that she could hardly see him, but to make sure she couldn't, she once again covered her face with her hands.

"Gee, Mallory, that works like a charm," Tammy whispered. "I can't see you there at all."

Mallory smacked her.

Ty spoke, his voice unrushed and clear. "The Health Clinic will improve the quality of life for people who'd otherwise go without help."

The audience murmured amongst themselves for a beat. Then came from one of the naysayers, "There's other places in other towns for people to get that kind of help."

"Yeah," someone else called out. "People here don't need the HSC."

"You're wrong," Ty said bluntly. "There are people in Lucky Harbor who *do* need the sort of services that HSC will provide. Veterans, for instance."

No one said a word now, though it was unclear whether they were scared of Ty's quiet intensity or simply acknowledging the truth of what he said.

"You can keep sticking your heads in the sand," he went on. "But there are people who need help managing their addictions, people who don't have a way to find a place to go that's safe from violence, teens who can't get STD education or birth control. These problems are real and growing, and a Health Services Clinic would be an invaluable resource for the entire county." He paused. Could have heard a pin drop. "And Lucille's right," he said into the silence. "You couldn't have a better person running such a place than your own Mallory Quinn. Each of you should be trying to help. I'll start by donating enough money for a program for veterans, where they can get assistance in rehabilitation or job opportunities, or simply to re-acclimate to society."

Mallory's mouth fell open.

The entire place went stock still. A real feat when it came to the people of Lucky Harbor. No one even blinked.

"He is so hot," Tammy whispered to Mallory. "You really ought to keep him."

"Can't," Mallory said, staring at Ty in shock through the fingers she still had across her eyes. "We've agreed it was a one-time thing."

"Well, that was stupid. You can put your hands down now. It's safe. No one's going to dare cross him. He's pretty badass."

He *was* pretty badass standing up there, steady as a rock, speaking his mind. *Offering his help...*

"Hey, didn't he also save your ass at the auction too by getting the bidding going?" Tammy asked.

Yeah, he had, and here he was at it again. Saving her ass.

As if sensing her scrutiny, he met her gaze for one long charged beat across the entire audience before walking back up the aisle to leave.

He'd stood up in front of the entire town and defended her. Her, a one-night stand. *What did that mean?* It meant he cared, she decided. The knowledge washed over her, and she sat up a little straighter, craning her neck to watch him go.

"My boyfriend's ever so dreamy," Tammy whispered mockingly.

Mallory smacked her again.

In spite of Ty's rather commanding appearance, the next three people who stood up opposed the clinic. Then Ella Quinn had her turn. Still in her scrubs, she grabbed the microphone. "This is poppycock," she said. "Anyone against this clinic is selfish, ungiving, and should be ashamed of themselves. As for my daughter Mallory, you all know damn well that she can be trusted to handle the HSC and any problems that might arise. After all, she's handled her crazy family all her life without batting so much as an eyelash." She searched the audience, found Joe in the fourth row, and gave him a long look. "And call your mamas. No one's calling their mamas often enough. That is all."

Joe slunk in his seat, his shoulders up around his ears. The little blonde sitting next to him gave him a hit upside the back of his head.

The meeting ended shortly after that, and Mallory was rushed with people wanting their questions answered. Would she really be supplying drug dealers? Doling out abortions? It was an hour before she was free, and even knowing she wouldn't find him, she looked around for Ty.

But he was long gone.

That afternoon, a spring storm broke wild and violent over Lucky Harbor. Ty worked on the Shelby, and when he was done, he drove through the worst of the rain, flying through the steep, vivid green mountain canyons, his mind cleared of anything but the road. For once he wasn't thinking of the past, or work.

He was thinking of a certain warm, sexy nurse.

He'd shelved his emotions years ago at SEALs training camp,

long before he'd ever met one Mallory Quinn. But no amount of training could have prepared him for her.

She was a one-woman wrecking crew when it came to the walls he'd built up inside, laying waste to all his defenses. Only a few weeks ago, there wasn't a person on earth who could have convinced him that she would have the power to bring him to his knees with a single look.

And yet she could. She had.

A few hours later, the storm was raging as he came back through Lucky Harbor. At a stop sign, he came up behind a stalled VW. Through the driving rain, he could see a woman fiddling beneath the opened hood, her clothes plastered to her. Well, hell. He pulled over, and as he walked toward her, she went still, then reached into the purse hanging off her shoulder.

Ty recognized the defensive movement and knew she had her hand on some sort of weapon. He stopped with a healthy distance between them and lifted his hands, hopefully signaling that he was harmless. "Need some help?"

"No." She paused. "Thank you, though. I'm fine."

He nodded and took in her sodden clothes and the wet hair dripping into her eyes. Then he looked into the opened engine compartment of the stalled car. "Wet distributor cap?"

Her eyes revealed surprise. "How did you know?"

"It's a '73 VW. Get the cap wet, and it won't run."

She nodded and relaxed her stance, taking her hand out of her purse. "I was going to dry the cap on my skirt but it's too wet." She shoved her hair back from her face and blinked at him. "Hey, I know you. You're Mysterious Cute Guy."

Christ how he hated that moniker. "Ty Garrison."

"I'm Grace Brooks. One of your three guardian angels in that freak snowstorm last week." She flashed a grin. "I'm the one who called 9-1-1."

"Then the least I can do is this." He came closer and took the distributor cap from her, wiping it on the hem of his shirt, which hadn't yet gotten drenched through. When he had the inside of the cap as dry as it was going to get, he replaced it and got her off and running.

Back in his own car, he ended up at the diner. Amy and Jan were there, Jan's gaze glued to the TV in the far corner. *American Idol* was on, and she was very busy yelling at the screen. "Okay, come on! That *sucked*. God, I miss Simon. He always told it like it was."

Amy rolled her eyes and met Ty at a table with a coffee pot. Guardian Angel Number Two, in a pair of low-slung cargoes and a snug, lacy tee. Normally she was alert as hell and on-guard but tonight her face was pale, her smile weak. "Pie?" she asked.

"Sure."

She came back two minutes later with a huge serving of strawberry pie. "You're in luck," she said. "It's Kick Ass Strawberry Pie from the B&B up the road. That means Tara made it," she explained to his blank look. "Best pie on the planet, trust me."

That was quite the claim but one bite proved it to be true. Ty watched Amy refill his cup, then gestured to the towel she had wrapped around the palm of her left hand. "You okay?"

"Fine."

Bullshit. Her other hand was shaking, and she looked miserable. But hell, if she wanted to pretend she was fine, it was none of his business. Especially since he was the master at being *fine*.

Problem was, there was blood seeping through her towel. "Do you need a doctor?"

"No."

He nodded and ate some more pie. Good. She was fine and didn't need a doctor. And God knew, he sure as hell didn't want to get involved. But when he was done, he cleared his own plate, bringing it to the kitchen himself.

"Hey," Jan yelled at him, not taking her gaze off the TV. "You can't go back there. It's against the rules."

"Your waitress is bleeding. That's against the rules too."

This got Jan's attention. Jan glanced into the back at Amy and frowned before turning back to Ty. "You going to patch her up? She has an hour left on her shift."

He had no idea what the hell he thought he was doing. He hadn't "patched" anyone up in a damn long time. Four years, to be exact. He waited for the sick feeling to settle in his gut, but all he felt was a need to help Amy. "Yeah. I can patch her up."

Amy was standing at the kitchen chopping block, hands flat on the cutting board, head bowed, her face a mask of pain. She jumped when she saw Ty and shook her head. "Guests aren't supposed to clear their own dishes."

"I'm going to ask you again. Do you need a doctor?"

"It was just a silly disagreement with a knife."

Not an answer. He unwrapped her hand himself and looked down at the cut. "That's more than a silly disagreement. You need stitches."

"It's just a cut."

"Uh-huh. And you need the ER."

"No, I don't."

There was something edgy in Amy's voice now, something Ty recognized all too well. For whatever reason, she had a fear or deep-rooted hatred of hospitals. He could sympathize. "You have a first-aid kit?"

"Yeah."

He drew a deep breath, knowing if he didn't help her, she'd go without it. "Get it."

The diner's first-aid box consisted of a few Band-Aids and a pair of tweezers, so Ty went to his car. He always kept a full first-aid kit in there, even though he hadn't ever cracked this one open. He returned to the kitchen and eyed Amy's wound again. He had Steri-strips but the cut was a little deep for that. "Trust me?" he asked her.

"Hell no."

Good girl, he thought. Smart. "Me or the hospital, Amy."

She blew out a breath. "All I need is a damn Band-Aid. And hurry. I have customers."

"They'll wait." She was looking a little greener now. He pushed her onto the lone stool in the kitchen. "Put your head down."

She dropped it to the counter with an audible thunk. He disinfected the wound, then opened a tube.

Head still down, she turned it to the side to eyeball what he was doing. "*Super glue?*" she squeaked.

"*Skin* glue. And hold on tight, it stings like hell." He started, and she sucked in a breath. "You okay?"

She nodded, and he worked in silence, finally covering the wound with a large waterproof bandage.

"Thanks." Amy let out a shuddery sigh. "Men are assholes. Present company excluded, of course."

With a shrug—men *were* assholes, himself included—he gestured to her hand. "How's that feel?"

She opened and closed her fist, testing. "Not bad. Thanks." She watched him put everything back into his kit. "Does Mallory know that you're as good with your hands as she is?"

"I don't answer trick questions."

She started to laugh, but choked it off at the man who suddenly appeared in the kitchen doorway.

It was Matt, still in uniform, brow furrowed. "Jan said you're all bloody and—" His eyes narrowed on the blood down Amy's white tee. "What the hell happened?"

"Nothing," she said.

"Jesus Christ, Amy." He picked up the bloody towel and jerked his gaze back to her, running it over her body, stepping close.

Amy turned her back on him, on the both of them, and Matt looked at Ty. "What happened to her?"

"She's declined to say."

"A knife," Amy said over her shoulder. "No big deal. Now go away. No big, bad alpha males allowed in the kitchen."

Not even a glimmer of a smile from Matt, which was unusual. Ty hadn't any idea that Matt had something going with the pretty, prickly waitress, which was telling in itself. Usually the affable, easygoing Matt was an open book, not the type to let much get to him. But there was a whole bunch of body language going on, all of it heating up the kitchen.

Then Amy made an annoyed sound and walked to the doorway. For emphasis, she jerked her head, making her wishes perfectly clear. She wanted them out.

Matt waited a beat, just long enough for Amy to give him a little shove. She wasn't tall by any means, though her platform sneakers gave her some extra inches. Still, Matt was six feet tall and outweighed her by a good eighty pounds. She could push him around only if he allowed it, but to Ty's shock, Matt acquiesced, and with a softly muttered "fuck it," he left.

Ty followed him out, telling himself that he wasn't here to get involved. If he had been, he'd have talked himself into Mallory's bed tonight—and he could have.

Easily.

That wasn't ego, just plain fact. She wanted him. He wanted her right back, more than he could have possibly imagined. Right this minute, he could be wrapped up in her sweet, warm limbs, buried deep. "Shit."

"Yeah," Matt muttered as they strode out to the parking lot side by side. "Shit."

"What was that back there?" Ty asked him.

"I don't want to talk about it."

"Why the fuck does that work for you and not me?"

Matt ignored this to stare in appreciation at the Shelby. "You get the suspension done?"

"Yeah, but there's still a lot left to do. I've been busy on your Jimmy. Almost done, by the way."

"Good. So how's this baby running?"

"Better than any other area of my life."

Matt laughed ruefully and slid into the passenger seat of the Shelby. Apparently Ty was getting company for his late night ride tonight. Silent, brooding company, but that suited him just fine.

Chapter 11

Eat a square meal a day—a box of chocolates.

On Saturday, the doors of the HSC opened to the public. The town hadn't exactly been on board, but enough tentative support had trickled in that Mallory had been able to talk Bill into giving her the one-month trial.

Mallory knew she had Ty to thank for starting that tentative support. After the town meeting, a handful of locals had pledged money for certain programs. Ford Walker and Jax Cullen, co-owners of the local bar, had donated money for a Drink Responsibly program. Lucille was donating supplies from her art gallery for an art program. Lance, Mallory's favorite CF patient, had donated time to help counsel the chronically ill. Every day someone else called. Bill decided it was too much money and goodwill to turn away and had given Mallory approval. But things had to go smoothly or it'd be over.

For now, they'd be open five days a week for services providing crisis counseling, and education and recovery programs.

And on Saturdays, the HSC turned into a full-blown medical clinic.

They saw patients nonstop, thanks to their first attending physician, Dr. Scott. As Mallory began to close up at the end of the day, Josh came out from the back.

After a long day, Josh looked more badass ruffian than usual. His doctor's coat was wrinkled and he still had his stethoscope hanging around his neck. His dark hair was ruffled, his darker eyes lined with exhaustion. But there was a readiness to him that said he wasn't too tired to kick ass if needed. He'd worked a double shift to volunteer his time today, but Mallory knew his day wasn't over, not even close. He still had to go home to more responsibility—a young son, not to mention his own handicapped sister, both of whom he was solely responsible for.

"Nice job today," he said to Mallory.

"Thanks to you."

He lifted a shoulder, like it was no big deal. He was a big guy, over six feet and built like a bull in a china shop, which made his talent all the more impressive. He might be serious and just a little scary, but he was the most approachable doctor she'd ever met. He was also her favorite because he treated the nurses with respect. Such behavior should be automatic in doctors, but so often wasn't. This conduct also tended to land him on Lucille's *Most Wanted Single Male* list on Facebook far too often, which drove him nuts.

"I'm glad you got approval for this," he said. "You're doing something really good here."

She glowed over that as she locked up behind him. As the last staff member there, she walked each of the rooms, cleaning up a little as she went. They had two exam rooms, a very small staff kitchen, and the front reception area. There was a back walk-in closet being renovated for their drug lock-up, but for now the drugs and samples were kept in one exam room in a locked cabinet. The reception area was big enough to host groups, which was what they would likely have to do during the week.

Tomorrow night was their first scheduled AA meeting. Monday night would be Narcotics Anonymous—NA. Wednesday nights would host a series of guest speakers, all aimed at teen advocacy programs.

It was all finally happening, and it made Mallory feel useful. Helpful. Maybe she hadn't been able to help Karen, but she could reach others.

By the time she locked the front door and got to her car, yet another storm was rolling in. Night had fallen, and the lot wasn't as well-lit as she'd like. She was on the back side of the hospital, the entrance leading to a narrow side street. She made a note to get the lighting fixed tomorrow and slid into her car just as the sky started dumping rain. She inserted her key in the ignition and turned it.

Nothing, just a click. She tried again anyway and got nowhere. A dead battery, naturally. She peered out her windshield and sighed. Walking home would be a five-mile trek in the pouring rain, which she was far too tired for. Plus her feet hurt from being on them all day. With a grimace, she pulled out her phone and called Joe.

"Yo," her brother said. "Bad time."

"Bad time for me, too. I need you to come jump my car. I have a dead battery."

"You leave your lights on again?"

"No." *Maybe.* "You owe me, Joe." She had to put that one out there right away to start the negotiations. Joe was a deal maker and only dealt at all if the odds were in his favor. "I let you and your idiot friends borrow my car, remember?" she asked. "You needed more seats to get to that stupid trail party out at Peak's Landing. Maybe this is somehow your fault."

"No, the crack in the windshield is our fault. Not the battery."

She stared at the small crack in the windshield on the passenger's side and felt an eye twitch coming on. "Come on, Joe. I could really use your help tonight."

"Christ. Hang on." He covered the phone and murmured something to someone.

A muted female voice laughed, and then Joe was back. "Mal, if all you need is a jump, ask anyone around you." He lowered his voice. "I'm on a date. With *Ashley*."

She had no idea who Ashley was but she was assuming it *wasn't* his blonde. "What happened to whatshername?"

"That was so last week."

Mallory let out a disgusted sigh. "You're a man ho."

"Guilty," he said. And hung up.

Grinding her teeth, Mallory called him back.

He didn't pick up.

"Dammit." She scrolled through her contact list again. Her mother was out of the question. Ella wouldn't have a set of jumper cables, not to mention she'd want to talk about Mallory's social life. Maybe Tammy, she thought, and hit her sister's number. "Can Zach come give me a jump?"

"Honey," Tammy said. "He's a little busy jumping *me* right now."

Oh, for God's sake. Mallory hung up, her usually dormant temper beginning to steam. She would drop everything for any one of her family, and not a single one of them could help her. This depressing thought didn't change the fact that she was still wet, cold, and stranded in a dark parking lot. Again she thumbed her contacts and stopped at one in particular.

Mysterious Cute Guy, aka Ty Garrison.

She had the stuffed animals he'd won at the arcade sitting on her bed, like she was twelve and in middle school, going steady with the town bad boy.

Except would the bad boy really have stood up at a town

meeting in front of everyone and defended her? Would he have stopped and helped a stranded woman on the side of the road? Grace had told her what he'd done. And so had Amy, saying that he'd patched her up with calm efficiency.

Yeah, Ty was far more than just some mechanic, though hell if she could figure him out.

She shouldn't call him for help. For one, they'd had inappropriate sex without involvement. To compound that mistake, she'd discovered she liked him. A lot. And to compound *that* mistake, she was dreaming about sleeping with him some more.

All really good reasons not to call him.

But then there was the one really good reason *to* call him.

He would actually come. She hit his number and held her breath. He picked up on the fourth ring, his voice low and calm as always. "Garrison," he said.

"Hi. It's Mallory."

He absorbed that information for a moment, probably wondering how she'd gotten his number, a conversation she absolutely didn't want to have so she rushed on. "I'm at the HSC," she said, "and my car won't start, and I'm the only one left here, and the stupid parking lot lights aren't working and—"

"Lock your doors. I'll be right there."

"Okay, thanks—" But he was already gone. She slipped her phone into her pocket and put her head down on the steering wheel. So tired… She thought about that and how her feet hurt. She could really use a foot rub. And a body rub. She'd gotten a massage once, last year for her birthday. It'd been a present from Tammy. Her masseuse had been Chloe Traeger, who worked at the Lucky Harbor B&B where there was a lovely day spa. The massage had been fantastic but Mallory wondered what it would be like to have a man rub his hands over her body.

And not just any man, either.

She knew exactly which one she wanted. Ty. She sighed

again, picturing lying on her back on a deserted beach at sunset, Ty leaning over her in a pair of low-slung jeans and nothing else, his big hands all over her bikini-clad body.

No, scratch that.

No bikini. And Ty in board shorts. Yeah, board shorts that fell disturbingly low on his hips, his eyes creased in that way he had of showing his feelings without moving his mouth. Mmm, that was a much better image, and she sighed dreamily.

He was aroused. She could feel him when he leaned over her. Big. Hard. She smiled up at him.

Instead of smiling back, he flipped her over, face down on her towel, leaving her to gasp in shock, waiting breathlessly for him to touch her. When his lips brushed her shoulder, she wriggled for more.

"Lie still." His voice was a thrillingly rough command that she didn't obey, making him groan. He said her name in a warning whisper, running a finger down her spine, then between her legs until she was writhing with a moan of arousal.

He did it again.

And then again, until she was oscillating her hips in small, mindless circles, trying to get more of his fingers. He pushed a thigh between hers to spread her legs, and then pulled her up to her knees and entered her.

She came hard, her cries swallowed when she pressed her face to the forearm he had braced on the towel beneath her. He was right behind her, shuddering in pleasure as he collapsed on top of her—

A rap on her window had her jerking straight up and banging her head on her sun guard.

Mouth quirking, Ty waited patiently while she fumbled to roll down the window.

"Hi," she said breathlessly. "I was just..." God. *Dreaming about you making me come.*

"Sleeping?" he asked.

Or that. Which was far less embarrassing. She nodded and swiped at her sweaty temple with her arm. "Guess I'm tired."

"You look all flushed; you okay?"

She pressed her thighs together. She was more than flushed. "Yeah."

"Try starting it now."

She realized that not only had she slept through him parking next to her, he'd popped both their hoods and had hooked her car up to a set of cables.

Some nap. At least she hadn't screamed out his name. She turned the key, and her car started.

Ty turned and bent over her front end, his head buried beneath her hood. Absolutely *not* noticing how very fine his ass looked from that position, she pushed out of the car and stood next to him.

"You're going to need a new alternator sooner than later," he said.

She stared into the engine compartment, completely clueless about where the alternator might be. "Is that expensive?"

"Not for the part." He was still fiddling around. "The labor's expensive, but it shouldn't be. It's an easy thing to replace."

"So you *are* a mechanic."

He was still messing with . . . something. He pulled out her dip stick and checked the oil. "Always been pretty good with taking things apart and putting them back together again," he said.

She could vouch for that. A week ago, he'd certainly taken her apart and put her back together again. The ease with which she'd come for him in the storage attic still fueled her fantasies. She'd had sex before, even some pretty good sex, but she'd never gone off like *that*. "I don't think that was much of an answer," she said.

He looked at her. "You don't think so?"

"No."

His mouth curved. "Anyone ever tell you that you're a little—"

"Stubborn? Determined? Annoying?" She nodded. "Yep. Trust me, I've heard it all."

"You need oil. And I work for a government contractor doing the same sort of stuff I did in the military."

"Stuff?" Her inner slut drooled over the sleek back muscles bunching, stretching the material of his shirt taut as he replaced the dip stick. "Like I'd-tell-you-but-I'd-have-to-kill-you stuff?"

He actually turned his head her way and smiled, knocking off a few million of her brain cells. This wasn't good. She needed those brain cells.

"Something like that," he said.

Classified, she thought. Interesting. Disconcerting. But it certainly explained the always-ready air he had and the fact that he looked like a military recruitment poster, only better. She could see him in hot zones all over the world, working on machinery. Tanks. Subs. Missiles. Or maybe his mechanical talents were ship-oriented. He'd said Navy...Her stomach knotted at the thought of how dangerous his life must be. "You patched up Amy at the diner. That was nice of you."

This yielded her a shrug.

She waited for more information, anything, which of course was not forthcoming. "It's a good thing you look good in jeans."

Still beneath the hood, he turned his head and flashed her a quick smile.

"You're a conundrum, you know," she told him. "I mean you've got this whole hands-off thing going about you, and yet you have no problem putting your hands all over me."

"And mouth," he added helpfully. "I like my mouth on you."

Her entire body quivered. "What is it about me that you're attracted to?"

"For starters, the sexy underwear you put on beneath your clothes."

"You've only seen my underwear once."

"Twice," he said. "I looked down your top at the pier."

"You did not."

"Pink-and-white polka-dot bra."

"Oh my God."

"That's what I was thinking." He straightened out from beneath her hood. "And also, while we're on the subject, I like the noises you make when you—"

She covered his mouth with her hand.

He nipped at her fingers, and her knees wobbled. Stupid knees.

"I like your eyes," he said.

"What?"

"Yeah, I like the way they soften when you look at me."

She stared at him, wondering if he was just giving her a line, but he held her gaze evenly. "Keep going," she said slowly.

"I like the way you'd dive into a freak snowstorm to help a perfect stranger. I like how you treat everyone as if they're important, including a homeless drug addict. I like that you give one-hundred percent to every part of your life. You don't hold back, Mallory."

"You . . . you like all that about me?"

"And also that you like me." He smiled again. "I really like that."

"How about the fact that you're pretty cocky? Do you like that?"

"Mmm-hmm. And I especially like when you use the word *cock* in a sentence."

She pushed him, and he laughed, so she added another push, and of course, he didn't budge, the lout. Instead, he stepped into her, backing her to the car. "What do you like about me?" he asked.

"*Nothing.*"

He grinned. "That's not true. You like it when I—"

"Don't you say it."

"That's okay," he said. "I'm better with showing, not telling, anyway." And he covered her mouth with his. And then his hands got into the fray, and she heard a low, desperate moan.

Hers.

His big palm cupped the back of her head as he changed the kiss from sweet and friendly-like to demanding and firm and...God. *Hungry*. His hand fisted in her hair then, and he kissed her like he was starving for the connection.

Mallory was right there with him. By the time the kiss was over, neither of them were breathing steadily. "Wow," she said and shook her head to clear it. "You ought to be careful with those. A girl might forget herself."

Thoroughly challenged, he reached for her again, but she jumped back. "Oh, no," she said on a laugh. "You're lethal, you know that?"

"Am I still on your list?"

"Well, let's see. It is a list of Mr. Wrongs, and you're just biding your time until you're gone, which pretty much means you *define* Mr. Wrong." She narrowed her eyes and studied him. "But then you show up at the town meeting—after avoiding everyone for months, I might add—and stick up for me." She shook her head. "Who are you, Ty Garrison?"

Apparently he didn't have an answer for that because he was back beneath her hood. "When's the last time you had anyone look at this poor baby?"

"Uh..."

He shook his head and kept fiddling, muttering something about "the lack of respect for the vehicle, even if it *is* a piece of shit."

"Where did you learn respect for *your* vehicles?" she asked, teasing.

"My dad. He was a mechanic in the Navy."

"Ah. So it runs in the family."

"Yeah. And my mom was Air Force."

She smiled at that. "A military brat through and through, huh?"

"All I ever knew," he agreed, tightening some part or another.

"Which is why you're interested in a Vet program at the HSC," she guessed. And personal experience. And he'd made good on his promise too. She'd gotten a nice check, earmarked for what would be a damn good program by the time she was finished with it. Ty had asked her to make sure to get a good counselor involved, one who could help people like Ryan, and she would do just that. "What are they doing now, your parents?"

"My dad died in Desert Storm. My mom a couple of years ago from pneumonia."

Her heart stopped, and her smiled faded as she watched him continue to inspect . . . whatever he was inspecting. "I'm sorry," she said quietly, knowing better than most how inadequate the words were.

"Everything else looks okay for now." He straightened. "I'll follow you home to make sure."

"There you go again," she said softly, still unbearably touched by his losses. "Wanting to be on my list of Mr. Wrongs but acting like . . ." *A Mr. Right*.

"Make no mistake," he said quietly. "I'm wrong for you. All wrong."

Of that, she had no doubt.

Chapter 12

It's not that chocolate is a substitute for love.
Love is a substitute for chocolate.
Chocolate is far more reliable than a man.

On Sunday, Mallory watched with satisfaction as the citizens of Lucky Harbor lined up in the hospital's back parking lot for the car wash. The schedule had been set in advance, and as heavily advertised, every board member had agreed to put in two hours.

They were charging twenty-five bucks a pop. Big price tag but people were paying for the joy of seeing their well-known town hotshots stripped out of their usual finery and working like regular joe-schmoes.

Mallory's shift was noon to two, and she was scheduled with Matt, Josh, and Jane. Matt was out of his ranger uniform. Josh was minus his stethoscope. Both of them wore board shorts. Matt was listening to the iPod he had tucked into his shorts pocket, his head banging lightly, an easy smile on his face as he worked his line.

Without a shirt.

Mallory knew he was a gym rat, and it was time well spent. He was solid sinew wrapped in testosterone.

His line was wrapped around the block.

Josh was wearing a pale blue t-shirt, but he'd gotten wet while washing a large truck, and the thin cotton clung to him like a second skin. He spent up to sixteen hours a day at the hospital, so Mallory had no idea where *his* amazing body came from.

His line was nearly as long as Matt's.

Jane was wearing long Capri-length pants and a man's button-down shirt. The forty-year-old was tall and statuesque, and in the ER, she could wield a cold expression like a weapon, laying waste to all in her path. She was no less ferocious today.

She had no line.

"I don't understand," she said to Mallory. "People hate me. You'd think they'd *want* to line up to see me washing their car, pointing out every spot for me to hand scrub."

"Yeah," Mallory said. "Um...can I make a suggestion?"

Jane slid her a long look. "I don't know. Can you?"

Mallory ignored the Ice Queen tone. "Push up your sleeves. Oh, and tie your shirt tails at your belly button, and undo three of the top buttons."

Jane choked out an offended laugh. "Excuse me? Are you asking me to pimp myself out?"

"Yes. And roll up your pants. You're not even showing knee."

"I have knobby knees."

Mallory stared at her. "Okay, you're my boss, so I'm not going to tell you how much I hate you if *that's* your biggest body issue. But I will tell you that if you undo a few buttons and tie up your shirt, no one's going to be looking at your knees. Oh, and bend over—a lot. Your line will appear in no time."

Jane put a hand on her hip. "I am *forty* years old, Mallory."

"Exactly. You're forty, not eighty. And you have a better body than I do. When was the last time you had a date?"

Jane thought about that and grimaced. "I don't remember."

Mallory reached out and undid Jane's buttons herself. It revealed only the barest hint of cleavage, but it was really great cleavage. Then she gestured for Jane to do the rest.

Jane rolled her eyes, but tied up her shirt.

"I knew it," Mallory said on a sigh. "Great abs. Your pants."

Jane bent over to roll up the hem of her pants, and three cars got in her line.

Mallory was grinning as Jane straightened, looking a whole hell of a lot less like the uptight Director Of Nurses and more like a tousled, sexy, confident woman with attitude.

Jane looked at her line and blinked.

"You see?"

"Hmm…" Jane headed for the first car. "They'd better tip well."

Mallory went back to her own decent line. Amy was first up in an old Toyota truck that had seen better days two decades back. "Are you kidding me?" Mallory asked her. "You could have either Matt or Josh slaving over this thing, and you're in *my* line? Maybe *I* should be giving the bad girl lessons."

Amy's eyes locked in on Matt. He was washing Natalia Decker's BMW. Natalia was a CPA who ran her own accounting firm, a cute little blonde who'd dated her way through the men in Lucky Harbor with exuberant glee. She hadn't gotten her nails into Matt yet, though by the way she was hanging out her window watching him, she was working on it.

Oblivious, Matt was bent low over her bumper, scrubbing, the muscles of his back flexing with each movement. He was tan and wet, and looking pretty damn hot.

"Go get in his line," Mallory told Amy. "One of us should get an upfront, close look at him."

Amy slid dark sunglasses over her eyes and muttered something beneath her breath.

"What?" Mallory asked.

"Nothing. I don't want to talk about it. Are you going to wash my car or what?"

"Yeah, but Amy . . . he looks at you—"

"I *don't* want to talk about it."

"Okay, but this is the *first* order of business at our next Chocoholics meeting. You hear me?"

"You have other things to worry about."

"Yeah? Like what?"

"Like the fact that your Mr. Wrong is behind me."

Mallory turned to look and went still at the sight of the classic muscle car there, complete with the sexy man behind the wheel in dark glasses, dark stubble, and a darker 'tude.

Ty had been awake since before the ass-crack of dawn. He'd gone for a punishing swim and found Matt waiting on the beach. Ty had given him a long look, but Matt didn't appear to care that he wasn't welcome. He'd simply swum alongside Ty—at least until he couldn't keep the pace, and ended up waiting on the shore.

"You're doing good," Matt said when Ty walked out of the water.

It was true; he was doing good. Feeling good. He was making real progress. After the swim, Ty ran, falling only once, and only because a crab had come out of nowhere and startled the shit out of him. Then he hit the gun range, needing to push all his skills. *This* was the week he was going to get cleared. He could feel it.

The range was about thirty miles outside of Lucky Harbor. He'd been coming back into town when he'd seen Mallory amongst the car washers. She was in a T-shirt and shorts, and was wet and soapy. She looked like the Girl-Next-Door meets *Maxim* photo shoot.

Drawn in like a magnet, he'd gotten in her line. When she caught sight of him, she squinted, furtively attempting to see through the bright sun and into his windshield. He felt something loosen deep within him and wasn't sure he could have explained the feeling to save his own life.

She'd piled her hair on top of her head, but it wasn't holding. Loose strands stuck damply to her temples and cheeks, and along the back of her neck.

She was soft there, and he knew that if he put his mouth on her neck, she'd make a little sound that'd go straight through him. Crazy, he told himself. He was crazy in lust with a woman he had no business wanting. Not that *that* seemed to deter him in the slightest.

"Hey, Mysterious Cute Guy!"

Ty nearly jumped out of his skin. He hadn't even heard Lucille come up to his passenger window. She smiled knowingly. "My neighbor's got a Charger. 1970, I think. Has a front end problem. Told him you might be interested. Are you?"

A Charger was a sweet old thing. Ty wouldn't mind getting his hands on one. "Yeah. I'm interested."

Lucille smiled. "That's right nice of you."

That was him, a right nice guy.

Mallory had finished Amy's car and came up to his driver's window. "Hey," she said. "Thanks for coming."

He let a slow, suggestive smile cross his mouth. Clearly realizing what she'd said, she went bright red. "Roll up your window," she warned. "Or you'll get wet." She paused, then blushed some more. "Dammit, now *everything* I say sounds dirty!"

He was laughing when he rolled up his windows.

She got to work, looking flustered, which he loved. And maybe a little annoyed, too.

Which he also loved.

She was doing a heck of a job washing, her arms surprisingly toned and buffed as she worked the sponge. Her shirt was dark blue, a modest cut knit tee, but she was wet and it was clinging to her. Her denim shorts were snug, and she had a streak of grease on her ass. She was backing away from his car, eyeing it with close scrutiny, clearly wanting to make sure she'd gotten all the soap off, when he rolled down his window. "Watch out," he said. "Or you'll trip over the—"

Soap bucket.

Too late. She tripped and, with a little squeal of surprise, went down.

He leapt out of his car just as she hit, her fingers reflexively gripping the hose nozzle as she landed on her ass in the soapy bucket.

A steady stream of water shot out of the hose and nailed him in the chest.

"Oh God," she said, dropping the hose and trying to get out of the bucket. "I'm sorry!"

Josh and Matt, washing cars on either side of her, rushed over, but Ty got to her first. "Are you all right?" he asked, pulling her out of the bucket.

She immediately took a step back from him, her hands going to her own butt, which was now drenched with soapy water. "No worries. I have lots of padding back there."

"You sure?" Josh asked her, reaching for her arm to brace her upright while she took stock. He was frowning at her ankle. "You didn't reinjure that ankle you broke last year, did you?"

"No." She laughed a little, clearly embarrassed but resigned. "Tell me no one got a picture of that."

"Everyone's too busy staring at Jane," Matt assured her, looking over at Mallory's boss himself. "Who's . . . not her usual self today."

They all looked at Jane then, who was indeed looking *very* unlike herself. She was smiling.

Someone from Josh's line honked a horn and yelled, "*Dr. Scoottt…*"

Josh swore beneath his breath, making Mallory laugh and gently pat him on the chest. "Your women are calling, Dr. Scott. Better get back to 'em. And don't forget to give them what they want."

"A clean car?"

"Lots of views of your ass when you bend over."

He grimaced and headed back to his line. Mallory turned to Ty, gasping with shock at how wet he was. "Did I do all that?"

"You going to try telling me that it wasn't on purpose?"

"No," she said on a laugh. "It wasn't on purpose, I swear! If it had been, I'd have skipped the embarrassing bucket part, trust me."

Matt had gone back to washing a car and was busy flirting with the pretty blonde owner of said car. But Ty was extremely aware that Josh was still watching them. Josh was a good man, one of the best that Ty had ever met. But he was also on Mallory's list, and Ty wasn't evolved enough to wish him the best with her. "Mallory."

"Yeah?"

He stepped closer to her. "You can take Josh off your list."

She choked out a laugh as he pulled his now-drenched shirt away from his skin. He was still wearing his gun in a shoulder harness from the range, and he removed the wet Glock, then realized the entire parking lot had gone silent. Everyone was staring at him. Actually, not him. His gun.

Christ. "It got wet," he said. "Guns don't like to get wet."

Matt stepped away from the car he was working on and came to Ty's side, a show of solidarity. Just the supervisory forest ranger and the crazy guy.

"It's okay," Matt said. "Ty's licensed to carry." He said this with his usual easygoing smile, putting a hand on Ty's shoulder, using his other to wave at someone who pulled into the lot.

And just like that, everyone went back to what they'd been doing, giving the two men some privacy.

Matt gave Ty a look. "I keep telling you this is Lucky Harbor, not the Middle East."

Ty returned the look and said nothing.

Matt sighed. "You know that Vet program you're funding at HSC? The one you told Mallory to get a good counselor for? You ought to consider making use of it."

"I'm fine."

"Well, I'm glad to hear it. Maybe you could work on happy. You got any of that? Because you can get away with just about anything if you smile occasionally. Ought to try it sometime."

"Yeah, I'll keep that in mind," Ty said, but he didn't feel like smiling. He had no idea what he was still doing here. His leg was fine. And yet he'd stopped at the small town car wash because Mallory had been looking hot in shorts. He'd just agreed to fix someone's Charger. What the hell was he doing? He was gone, out of here, any day now, moving on as he'd done all his life.

So why the hell was he acting like he was sticking around? Why was he letting people in and making plans? It was not in the cards for him, this small town life. Ties and roots were not his thing. He paid for his car wash. He'd have said good-bye to Mallory but she was busy with another vehicle. He got into his car, but something had him looking back once more at Mallory. From across the lot she was watching him, her gaze long and thoughtful.

No regrets, she'd said.

But he thought that maybe this time, there would be at least one regret. A regret named Mallory Quinn.

That night, Mallory, Grace, and Amy sat in a corner booth at Eat Me, forks in hand, cake on a plate.

The Chocoholics were in session.

"So," Grace said, licking her fork. "The hardware store is hiring. The owner, Anderson, asked me out."

"Don't do it," both Amy and Mallory said at the same time.

Grace sighed. "He's cute. But I'd rather have the job. I filled out the application. I'm trying hard to find my happy."

"And you think counting nails is going to do it?" Amy asked.

"Is clearing dishes doing it for you?" Grace countered.

Amy shrugged. "It leaves me a lot of free time and brain cells to do what I like."

"Which is?" Mallory asked.

Amy shrugged again. "Drawing."

"You're supposed to be letting people in," Mallory reminded her. "It was your decree, remember? Drawing is a solo sport."

Amy stabbed her fork into the cake for a large bite. "I'm in training." She eyed Mallory. "You want to talk about today?"

"What about today?"

"Gee, I don't know—how about the fact that MCG is carrying?"

"MCG?"

"Mysterious Cute Guy. Ty Garrison. Hot stuff. The guy you smile dopily about every time he's mentioned."

"I do not smile dopily."

Amy looked at Grace. Grace pulled a small mirror from her purse and held it up in front of Mallory.

Mallory looked at her faint glow and—dammit—dopey smile, and did her best to wipe it off her face. "It's the chocolate cake."

Amy coughed and said "bullshit" at the same time.

Mallory sighed and set down her fork.

"Uh oh," Grace said.

"I like him," Mallory said.

"And that's a bad thing?" Grace asked. "You set out to stretch your wings, experience something new. It's happening."

"With a guy that could break her heart," Amy said softly. "Is that it, Mal? You're scared?"

"Like a little bunny rabbit," Mallory said. "Some bad girl I turned out to be."

Ty swam by moonlight, and then hit the beach for another run. He didn't fall this time, not once.

Progress.

When he was done torturing his body and his every muscle was quivering with exertion, he went to bed. Too tired for nightmares, he told himself.

Things started out good. He dreamed about the time his team had been assigned to rescue a diplomat's daughter out of Istanbul. Then the dream shifted to another mission, where they'd "commandeered" certain components from a godforsaken, forlorn corner of Iraq, components that had been waiting for another shipment, which when combined together would have been a huge terrorist threat. Then things transitioned again, to the time they'd managed to get to a bus loaded with U.S. and British journalists before their scheduled kidnapping...

All successful missions...

But then the dream changed, and everything went straight to hell in a handbasket.

He was thrown from the burning wreckage. When he opened his eyes, his ears were ringing, and although he could see the wild flames all around him, he couldn't hear a damn thing. It was a movie without sound.

His men. He belly-crawled to Kelly, but he was already gone. Ty found Tommy and Brad next and did what he could, then went after Trevor. Trevor was on the other side of the wreckage, gasping for air, his chest crushed, and all Ty could do was hold him as he faded away...

He woke up alone in bed, not on a godforsaken mountain.

"Christ," he breathed and shoved his fingers through his sweat-dampened hair. "*Christ*."

It was two in the morning but he rolled out of the bed, grabbed his jeans, and shoved his legs into them. His phone, blinking due to missed calls that were no doubt from Frances, was shoved into his pocket. Same with his empty Vicodin bottle.

He got into the Mustang and fired her up. With no idea what possessed him, he did a drive-by of Mallory's house. She wasn't the only one with recon skills, though he figured the only way she could have gotten his cell phone number was through the hospital records.

How very industrious of her.

And illegal.

He found it amusing, and in a world where nothing much amused him anymore, he was also intrigued. A deadly combination.

Distance. He needed a boatload of distance. He was working on that.

Mallory's ranch-style house was in an older neighborhood. Typical Suburbia, USA. The place was freshly painted, the yard clearly cared for, much more than the piece-of-shit car she drove.

Which was why he was here. Or so he told himself.

It took him all of six minutes to replace her alternator with the one he'd driven into Seattle to get for her.

Probably he needed to work harder on keeping his distance.

He really needed to get back to work. He needed to be fucking useful for *something* again. He put his tools back in his car and had started to get behind the wheel when he heard locks tumble. Her front door opened.

In the lit doorway, highlighted by both the porch light and a single light somewhere inside, stood Mallory. Her hair was a wild cloud around her face and shoulders, her bare feet sticking out the bottom of her robe. "Ty?"

So much for stealth.

"What are you doing?" she asked.

Funny thing about that. He had no fucking clue what he was doing. None. Not a single one. He shut his car door and walked up to her, crowding her in the open doorway.

"Ty?"

He didn't answer. If she backed up a step or told him he was crazy, or gave him the slightest sign that he wasn't welcome, he would turn on his heel and walk off.

He was good at that, and they both knew it.

And he definitely expected her to be unnerved. He'd seen her face at the car wash when he'd been holding his gun.

But she surprised him now by stepping into him, meeting him halfway. Reaching for him, her body answered his touch with a slight trembling that made him feel pretty fucking useful, and wasn't that just what he'd wished for? To be useful again?

He kept telling himself that as curious and attracted as he was to her, if Mallory hadn't started things up between them at the auction, he'd have never initiated any sort of intimacy.

He was full of shit. She'd assured him that all she'd wanted was the one night, and he'd tried like hell to believe her, but somehow they kept getting in deeper.

She was like a drug. The most addicting kind, and he had a problem—he was pretty sure that she was developing feelings for him. He no idea what to do with that, or with his own feelings, which were definitely getting in his way. This whole "no emotional attachment" thing had gone straight to shit. Because Mallory Quinn was emotionally attached to every person she ever met, and she had a way of making that contagious. He craved contact with her in a way that he wasn't experienced with.

And he liked to be experienced.

But he couldn't think about that right now because her lips were parted, her cheeks flushed, her eyes telling him that his presence affected her every bit as much as hers did him. Helpless against the pull of her, he caught her up against him and stepped over the threshold, kicking the door closed behind him.

They staggered into the entryway together, mouths fused, bumping into her umbrella stand, knocking it over as she tripped on some shoes and slammed into a coat rack.

They were both laughing as he spun her away from danger, pressing her against a little cherrywood desk and mirror. He trapped her there, and all amusement faded as she gasped, the sound full of desire.

He wanted to hear it again, needed to hear it again. Lowering his head, he kissed the sweet spot beneath her ear, along her jaw, and then the column of her neck. He spent a long moment at the hollow of her throat because, oh yeah, that's where she made the sound again, her shaky hands clutching his shoulders.

"I was dreaming about you," she said softly.

He was glad, even more so since he'd been dreaming of pure hell. He'd had no idea how much he needed this, *her*, until this very minute. "Tell me."

"We were back at the auction." Her fingers wound their way into his hair, giving him a shiver. "Working our way through all the furniture," she murmured.

"Working our way through the furniture?"

"Yeah, you know . . ." She hesitated. "Doing it on each piece," she whispered.

He drew back far enough to see her eyes. When she blushed gorgeously, he laughed softly. "After what we did that night, you can still be embarrassed to say 'doing it'?"

She pushed at him but he didn't budge. "No," he said, pulling her in tight. "I like it." Hell, she had to be able to feel the proof of that. "What piece of furniture did we do it on first?"

She turned her head away. "I'm not going to say now."

He nibbled her ear. "Tell me," he coaxed, flicking his tongue on her lobe.

She gasped. "A table."

He grinned. "I did you on a table?"

She made a sound that was only *half* embarrassment now, the other half pure arousal.

"Tell me that I spread you out for my viewing pleasure and feasted on all your sweet spots," he said.

Glowing bright red, she stared at his Adam's Apple. "No. You, um, bent me over the table and then, you know, took me from behind."

Yeah, good luck with finding distance now. He was hard as a rock. Maybe distance wasn't the way to go. Maybe they needed this, needed to just go for it, to get each other out of their systems.

Yeah, that was the story he was going with. He turned them both so that she was facing the small foyer desk. "It was just a dream," she murmured into the mirror.

"Doesn't have to be."

She stared at his reflection, watching as his hands ran down her arms to take her hands in his, drawing them up, up around his neck where they'd be out of his way.

The air crackled with electricity. And need. So much need. "What are you wearing beneath the robe?" he asked.

She nibbled on her lower lip.

"Mallory."

"Nothing."

He groaned. Her body was so close to his that a sheet of paper couldn't fit between them. He reached for the tie on her robe. "Do you want this?"

"I—" She closed her mouth.

"Yes or no, Mallory."

"*Yes*."

One tug of the tie and the robe began to loosen.

"Wait," she gasped. "I—I'm . . ." She hesitated. "I can't watch."

And yet she didn't take her hands from his neck, or her hungry gaze off the mirror, eyes glued to his fingers as they gripped the edges of her robe.

"Full access this time," he said.

"Oh, God." She nodded. "Okay, but I—" She broke off when he slowly spread the robe open, eyes riveted to her own body.

Which he already knew was the body of his dreams. "Mallory," he breathed. "You're so beautiful." He stroked his hands up her stomach to cup her breasts, his thumbs brushing her velvety nipples, wringing another gasp out of her lips. He did it again, a light teasing touch before he took his hands off her.

She whimpered.

He pulled her hands from around his neck and pushed the robe off her shoulders to puddle at their feet. Taking her hands again, he pinned them out in front of her on the table, which forced her to bend over. He gently squeezed her fingers, signaling he wanted her to stay like that.

"Ty—" she choked out, holding the position with a trusting sweetness that nearly undid him, especially when it was combined with the sexy sway of her breasts and the almost helplessly uncontrolled undulation of her hips into his crotch.

He cupped those gorgeous full breasts, teasing her nipples before skimming one hand south, between her legs.

"H—here? We really shouldn't . . ."

"No?"

"No," she whispered and then spread her legs, giving him more room.

Dipping into her folds was pure heaven, and he groaned when he found her very wet. His fingers trailed her own moisture over her, exploring every dip and crevice, until she was undulating again, her fingers white-knuckling their grip on the table, her eyes closed, her head back against his chest.

"Watch," he reminded her.

Her eyes opened and locked on the sight of her own body, naked, bent over the table, his tanned hand on her pale breast, the other slowly, languidly moving between her legs. "Oh," she breathed. "We look…"

"Hot." He slid a wet finger deep inside her, and she gave an inarticulate little cry, straining against him.

"Ty—"

"Tell me."

"In me," she gasped, breathless. "Please, in me."

"Come first."

Giving her another slow circle with his thumb, he watched as she shuddered, still holding obediently onto the desk's edges for all she was worth. He could feel her tremble as the tension gripped her and added another finger and some pressure with his thumb, nibbling along the nape of her neck to her shoulder. Strung tight, she breathed in little pants, her spine and ass braced against him, her arms taut, her face a mask of pleasure.

"*Ty.*"

"Right here with you," he assured her, and sent her skittering over the edge. She cried out as she shattered, and would have dropped to her knees if he hadn't caught her.

"*Now,*" she demanded breathlessly. "Right now."

Not one to argue with a lady, he stripped, grabbed a condom from his pocket and put it on before pushing inside her.

She cried out again. With one arm supporting her, his other hand found hers where it gripped the wood, and he linked their fingers. She was still shaking from her orgasm. Bending over her, pressing his torso to her back, brushing his mouth against her neck, he tried to give her a moment. But when she pressed her sweet ass into him, restless, he began to move, stringing them *both* up this time. She took each thrust, arching her back for more, insistent demand in her every movement.

Not so shy now, he thought with a surge of hunger and a rather shocking possessive protectiveness.

He couldn't tear his eyes from her, even as his every single nerve ending screamed at him to let go and come already. The fire she'd started in him was flashing bright, the ache for her tight and hard in his gut. He wasn't going to be able to hold on, but then it didn't matter because she went rigid and skittered over the edge again, her muscles clenching him in erotic, sensual waves.

It was not enough.

It was too much.

It was everything.

Gripping her hard, he growled out a heartfelt "oh fuck" and buried his face in her hair as he followed her over, coming so hard his legs buckled.

He managed to gain enough control to make sure his knees hit the hard wood floor and not hers. He turned her to face him and pulled her tight, nuzzling her neck. After a minute, he pulled back to look at her.

Her smile tugged a helpless one from him as well. "Good?" he asked.

She traced a finger along his lower lip. "That's a pretty weak word for what that was. I bet you could come up with something better."

He nipped gently on her finger. "I'm more of a show-not-tell kind of guy."

"Yeah?"

"Yeah."

"So..." she said, softly. "Show me."

Chapter 13

Forget love—I'd rather fall in chocolate!

Mallory didn't know what had brought Ty to her in the middle of the night, or what he'd planned on doing, but sitting in her entryway naked was a pretty damn good start.

Or finish.

She blushed as he bent in to kiss her, and he laughed softly against her lips as if he could read her mind. To distract them both, she trailed a finger down his chest, over a hip, and found an unnatural ridge. She took a look at the jagged scar that ran the length of his body from groin to knee, and she stilled in horror for what he'd suffered.

She realized that she was all comfy cozy, cuddled up against his chest. The position couldn't possibly be comfortable for him. "Is your leg okay?"

"I can't feel my leg right now."

She laughed breathlessly, relieved at the lessening of the sudden tension in his big, battle-scarred, *perfect* body. "Good," she said. "I know it gives you pain from the car crash."

"The pain's faded." He paused, then grimaced. "And it wasn't a car crash. It was a plane crash."

She controlled her instinctive gasp of horror. "You survived a plane crash?"

"That wasn't as bad as the several days that went by before rescue."

"Oh, Ty," she breathed, feeling her throat tighten in pain for him, trying to imagine it and not being able to. "How bad was it?"

"Bad enough."

"Your injuries?"

"Cracked ribs, broken wrist, collarbone fracture. Some internal injuries and the leg. That was the worst of it for me. All survivable injuries." He paused again. "Unlike everyone else."

She couldn't even imagine the horrible pain he'd suffered. *For days.* And the others… *He'd been the only one to survive.* Aching for him, she ran her fingers lightly over his chest, feeling the fine tremor of his muscles. Aftershocks of great sex, maybe.

Or memories.

"Your friends," she said softly. "The ones you've mentioned before. That's where you lost them."

"Yeah. My team."

"Were you—"

"Mallory." He shook his head. "I *really* don't want to talk about this."

"I know." She clutched the infinity charm around her neck, knowing the pain. "No one ever wants to talk about Karen either. But she was really important to me. For a long time after she was gone—after I failed to save her—I couldn't bear to remember her, much less talk about her."

He sighed, a long, shuddery exhale of breath and drew her in closer, burying his face in her hair. "How did she die?"

"She took a bottle of pills." She felt him go still. "She

was eighteen," Mallory said. "And pregnant. It was ruled an accidental OD but..." She closed her eyes and shook her head. "It wasn't. Accidental, I mean. She did it on purpose."

"Oh, Christ, Mallory." He tightened his grip on her. "Doesn't sound like you could have saved her."

"We were sisters. I knew she had a drug problem. I should have—"

"No," he said firmly, pulling back to look into her eyes. "There's nothing you can do, *nothing*, to help someone who doesn't want to be helped."

It was so regretfully true, she could barely speak. "How do you get past it?"

"You keep moving. You keep doing whatever keeps you going. You keep living." His hands were on the move again, tender and soothing...until her breath caught, and she murmured his name, hungry for him again.

His touch changed then, from tender and soothing to doggedly aggressive and doggedly determined, stealing her breath.

"Keep living," she repeated. "That's a good plan—Oh, God, Ty," she whispered when he sucked a nipple into his mouth, hard. "I thought we were talking."

"You go ahead and talk all you want," he said gently, then proceeded to not-so-gently once again take her right out of her mind, in slow, exquisite detail.

Much, much later, she lay flat on her back on the floor, completely boneless. "Good talk," she whispered hoarsely.

Ty woke up flat on his back, the wood floor stuck to his spine and ass, a warm, sated woman curled into him. He'd taken her on the floor and had the bruises on his knees to prove it. Somehow he staggered to his feet, then scooped up Mallory. He'd have to tell Josh that if his leg could hold out through marathon sex, it could hold out through anything, and see if *that* got him cleared.

"No," she muttered, the word a slur of exhaustion as she stirred in his arms. "Don't wanna get up yet."

He knew she'd been working around the clock, on her feet for twelve hours and more at a time. She worked damn hard. "Shh," he said. "Sleep."

Her muscles went taut as she woke. "Ty?"

Well, who the hell else?

"Where we going?" she asked groggily, slipping her arms around his neck.

"Bed." He was going to tuck her in and get the hell out, before he did something stupid like fall asleep with her. Sex was one thing. Sleeping together afterwards turned it into something else entirely.

You idiot, it's already something else...

At her bed, he saw the two big stuffed animals he'd won for her leaning against her pillows. An odd feeling went through him, the kind of feeling that stupid, horny teenage boys got when they had a crush. This was immediately chased by wry amusement at the both of them.

He leaned over the bed to deposit Mallory into it, but she tugged and he fell in with her. "Cold," she murmured with a shiver and tried to climb up his body.

Pulling her close—just for a minute, he told himself— he reached down and grabbed the comforter, yanking it up over the top of them. He'd share some body heat with her until she stopped shivering. Once she was asleep, he'd head out.

"Mmm," she sighed blissfully, pressing her face into his throat, tucking her cold-ass toes behind his calves. "You feel good."

"I'm not staying," he warned, not knowing which one of them he was actually telling, the woman cuddled in his arms or his own libido. So he said it again.

It didn't matter. Two minutes later, Mallory was breathing

slow and deep, the kind of sleep only the very exhausted could pull off. She was out for the count.

And all over him.

Her hair was in his face, her warm breath puffing gently against his jaw, her bare breasts flattened against his side and chest. She had one hand tucked between them, the other low on his stomach. In her sleep, her fingers twitched, and she mumbled something that sounded like "bite me, Jane."

Smiling, he ran his hand down her back. "Shh."

She immediately settled in with a deep sigh, trusting. Warm. Plastered to him like a second skin.

Christ. He didn't want to wake her, but he didn't do the sleepover thing. He never did the sleepover thing.

Ever.

But unequivocally lulled in by her soft, giving warmth, he closed his eyes. Just for a second, and fell asleep wrapped around her.

At some point, he felt the nightmare gathering, pulling him in. Luckily, he managed to wake himself up before he made a complete ass of himself. It was still dark. Too dark. Rolling off the bed, he grabbed up his jeans and was halfway out the door before he felt the hand on his arm. He nearly came out of his skin and whipped around to face Mallory.

Way to be aware of your surroundings, Soldier. Unable to help himself, he twitched free and took a step back, right into the doorknob, which jabbed him hard in the back. "Fuck, Mallory."

"I'm sorry. I didn't mean to startle you." Lit only by the slant of moonlight coming in through her bedroom blinds, she stayed where she was, a few feet away, concern pouring off her in the way that only hours before passion and need had. "You okay?"

And here was where he made his mistake. He should have

lied and said yes. He could have done it, easily. If he'd added a small smile and a kiss, she'd have bought it for sure. She'd have bought anything he tried to sell her because she trusted him.

That was who she was.

But it wasn't him. He didn't want to do this, get this close. So he shoved his feet into his running shoes and grabbed up his wallet and keys.

"Ty?"

He headed down the hallway. She came after him; he heard the pad of her bare feet. *She's going to get cold again* was his only inane thought.

She caught him at the front door. It wasn't until he felt her fingers run down his bare back that he realized he'd forgotten his shirt.

"Did you have a bad dream?"

He went still. "No," came the instant denial.

She merely stroked his back again. "That night in the storm," she said quietly. "you had a nightmare. I thought maybe it happened again here."

He dropped his head to the door. "That's not it."

"Then what happened? Things get a little too real?"

He straightened. "I have to go, Mallory."

"Without your shirt?"

He turned to face her, and she smiled.

She was wearing his shirt. "Stay," she said with a terrifying gentleness. "Sleep with me. I won't tell."

He knew she was treading softly around the crazy guy, only wanting to help. But he didn't want her help. He didn't want anyone's help. He was fine. All he needed was to be able to get back to work. And maybe to be buried deep inside her again, because there he didn't hurt. There he felt amazing. But if he took her again, he'd never leave. "Can't."

"But—"

He pulled open the door and stepped into the chilly night sans shirt, leaving before she could finish the rest of her sentence.

Mallory plopped back onto her bed and stared up at the ceiling, haunted by the expression on Ty's face as he'd left. He'd been rude and abrupt, and she should be pissed.

She wasn't.

But she couldn't put a finger on exactly *what* she was.

This, with him, was supposed to have been about fun. Just a little walk on the wild side.

But it had become so much more. Unnerving, but it was the truth. She wanted even more.

And he was so Mr. Wrong it was terrifying.

She wanted him anyway. *How was it that she wanted him anyway?*

She was good at making people feel better, at helping them heal. Or at least she liked to think she was. But this, with him...She couldn't heal what ate at him, any more than she'd been able to heal herself.

The next morning she got up and went to work. A few hours in, she was paged to the nurses' station. "What's up?" she asked Camilla, who was sitting behind the desk when she got there.

Camilla jerked her head toward the hallway. Mallory turned and found a very familiar, tall, broad-shouldered man propping up the wall. His stance was casual, his body relaxed.

But she knew better.

"I'm on break," she said to Camilla and walked toward Ty. "Hey," she said.

"Hey." His eyes never wavered from hers. "Got a minute?"

"Maybe even two."

He didn't smile. Huh. That didn't bode well. All too aware of Camilla's eyes—and ears—on them, she gestured for him to follow her. They took the stairs down to the ground floor cafeteria, and Mallory led him to a corner table.

It was too early for the lunch crowd so they had the place to themselves, except for a janitor working his way across the floor with a mop.

"Smells like a mess hall," Ty said.

"I bet the food was better at mess hall."

"I bet not."

He was sitting close, his warm thigh against hers beneath the table. He wore jeans that were battered to a velvety softness and a midnight blue button-down with the sleeves shoved up to his elbows.

He looked edible.

And she was afraid he was here to tell her his time was up, that he was leaving. "You want anything?" she asked. "Coffee? Tea? Pancakes?" *Me* . . . "They have great pancakes—"

"Nothing. Mallory—"

"A sandwich," she said desperately. "How about a sandwich? Hell, I could use a sandwich myself." She hopped up, but he grabbed her wrist.

Fine. She could handle this, whatever *this* was, and slowly sat back down, braced for a good-bye. Dammit.

He was looking at her in that way he had, steady, calm. "You okay? You seem jumpy."

"Just say it," she said. "Say good-bye already. I can't imagine it's that hard for you."

His brows went up. "You think I'm here to say good-bye? And that it wouldn't be hard for me to do?"

"Would it?"

He stared at her, his eyes fathomless, giving nothing away. "I'm not here to say good-bye. Not yet anyway."

"Oh." She nodded, knowing she should be relieved, but she wasn't. Tension had gripped her in its hard fist, and she let out a slow, purposeful breath. "I think I need a favor from you, Ty. When it *is* time to go, I want you to just do it. Don't say good-bye. Just go."

"You want me to just leave without a word."

"Yes." Her throat was tight. Her heart was tight too. "That would be best, I think." She stood and started to walk away.

"I wanted to apologize for last night," he said, catching her hand. "I was an ass."

She softened, and with a gentle squeeze of his fingers, sank back into her chair. "Well, maybe *ass* is a bit harsh. I was thinking more along the lines of a scared-y cat."

He let out a rough laugh. "Yeah. That too."

"I understand, you know."

"You shouldn't," he said.

"Why? Because I've never faced anything that haunts me?"

His gaze never left hers. "I'm sorry about Karen," he said. "And you're right. You're stronger than anyone I know. But I meant you shouldn't understand, because you deserve better from me."

Before she could respond to that, the elevator music being piped into the dining area cut off and was replaced by an authoritative male voice. "Code Red."

Mallory jumped up. Code Red meant there was a fire, and personnel were to report in immediately. Today was a scheduled drill but she'd expected it later in the day. "You're either about to be evacuated," she told Ty, "or it's going to be a few minutes before you can leave." She slapped her employee card on the table. "When the drill's over, help yourself to something to eat."

"Code Red," the voice repeated. "All personnel respond immediately. Code Red. *Repeat, Code Red.*"

Her life had great timing.

Chapter 14

When the going gets tough,
the tough eat chocolate.

With the hospital in temporary lockdown, Ty leaned back and waited. From where he sat, he could see out the cafeteria and across the reception area to the front door of the hospital. In less than four minutes, firefighters and other emergency personnel came pouring in.

A drill, he thought, since no one was being evacuated. Ten minutes later, the hospital employees reappeared, though Mallory didn't.

"You want something to eat?" the cook called out to Ty.

He realized he was starving. He stood and walked over to the cook's station and eyed all the various ingredients. A few more people came in behind him. Two women in scrubs took one look at him and began whispering between themselves.

"Quesadilla?" the cook asked. "Or maybe a grilled turkey and cheese? A burger? I have a hell of a Cobb salad today, but that's not going to fill up a big guy like you."

"Burger," Ty decided. If the plane crash hadn't killed him, or the second-story jump, then a little cholesterol couldn't touch him.

The women behind him were still murmuring. "In the Vets' Hall," one of them whispered, "where *anyone* could have seen them."

"How do you know that?" the other whispered back.

"Sheryl told Cissy who told Gail. It's really unlike her. I mean, you'd expect it of any of the other Quinns but not her..."

The cook slid Ty an apologetic glance as she flipped his burger. "Cheese?"

He nodded.

The whispers continued. "...thought she'd be more careful with her image, what with the HSC at stake and all. She's still short a lot of money and needs everyone's support."

"Do you think they did it in one of the closets *here*?"

Ty had never given a shit about image, and he didn't think Mallory did either, but this was really pissing him off. He turned to face the two nosy old bats.

They both gasped and immediately busied themselves with their trays. He stared at them long and hard, but neither of them spoke.

So he did. "Mind your own business."

They didn't make eye contact and he turned back to the cook, who handed him his plate. She gestured to the card he still held in his hand, the one Mallory had left him. "Just swipe it," she said, indicating the machine alongside the register. "Mallory's card will get you anything you want on her account. Should I add a drink? Chips?"

Mallory had given him her employee pass. She was still trying to take care of him. He wasn't used to that. Shaking his head, he pulled out cash.

"But—"

He gave the cook a look that had her quickly making his change. Extremely aware of the two women behind him boring holes in his back with their beady eyes, he took his burger and headed back to his table.

The two women bought their food and walked past him, giving him several long side glances that told him that all he'd done was make things worse.

And what the hell did he think he was doing anyway, messing around in Mallory's life? He was leaving soon but Lucky Harbor was her home, her world. He ate, feeling confused and uncertain, two entirely foreign emotions for him. He'd actually believed that *he* was the one giving here, that he was the experienced one imparting a little wildness and the dubious honor of his worldly ways. How fucking magnanimous of him.

Especially since the truth was that Mallory had done all the giving, completely schooling him in warmth, compassion, and strength. In the process, with nothing more than her soft voice and a backbone of steel, she'd wrapped him around her pinkie.

Christ, he really was such an asshole. He cleared his plate and headed out, slowing at the front entrance. There was a box there, similar to a mailbox where people could drop donations for the Health Services Clinic. He'd given money for the Vets' program, which wouldn't help if Mallory couldn't get the support for the HSC to remain open. He stared at the box and knew exactly what he was going to do to give back to the woman who'd given him so much.

On Mallory's drive home, she stopped at Eat Me. Grace had sent a text that said there was an emergency.

Mallory went running in and found Grace and Amy waiting for her with a box.

A shoe box.

"Bad girl shoes," Amy said, pushing the box toward her. "Happy birthday."

"My birthday was last month."

"Merry early Christmas."

"Oh no," Mallory said. "These meetings are always about me. It's one of you guys' turns."

"Nope," Grace said. "We can only concentrate on one of us at a time."

"Then let it be Amy," Mallory said.

"Yeah," Jan said from where she was watching TV at the other end of the counter. "She's screwed up. She's got that big, sexy, forest ranger sniffing around her, and all she does is give him dirty looks."

"Hey," Amy said. "That is none of your business."

Jan cackled.

"Not talking about it," Amy said firmly, and nudged the shoe box toward Mallory again.

Because they both looked so excited, Mallory relented and opened the box to find a beautiful pair of black, strappy, four-inch heels that were dainty and flirty and pretty much screamed sex. "Oh," she breathed and kicked off the athletic shoes she'd worked in all day, replacing them with the heels.

Two counter stools over, Mr. Wykowski put a hand to his chest and said "wow."

"Heart pains?" Mallory asked in concern, rushing over there in her scrubs and bad girl heels.

"No," he said. "Not heart pains."

"Where does it hurt?"

He was staring at her heels. "Considerably lower."

Amy snorted. Mallory went back to her stool.

Grace was grinning. "See? Use them wisely. They have the power."

"Power?"

"Bad girl power," Amy said. "Go forth and be bad."

The next day Ty brought Ryan dinner. Ryan was living in a half-way house outside of town, in a place that Mallory had arranged for him to stay in through HSC.

It was infinitely better, and safer, than living on the streets.

After they ate, Ryan asked Ty for a ride, directing him to HSC.

"What's up here tonight?" Ty asked.

"A meeting."

The sign on the front door explained what kind of meeting:

NA—Narcotics Anonymous

Someone had attached a sticky note that said: *EMPHASIS ON THE A, PEOPLE!*

Ty didn't know whether to be amused that only in Lucky Harbor would the extra note be necessary, or appalled that the town was trusted with the *anonymous* at all.

But part of the process was trusting.

He'd always sucked at that. He turned to Ryan, who'd gone still, seeming frozen on the top step. "I'm too old for this shit," Ryan muttered.

"How old are you?" Ty asked.

"Two hundred and fifty."

"Then you're in luck," Ty said. "They don't cut you off until you're three hundred."

A ghost of a smile touched Ryan's mouth. "I'm forty-three."

Only ten years older than Ty. Ryan's body was trembling. Detoxing. Not good. Ty would have paid big bucks to be anywhere else right now but he figured if anyone was interested in him as a crutch, they had to be pretty bad off. "How long has it been since your last hit?"

Ryan swiped a shaking hand over his mouth. "I ran out of Oxycontin four days ago. Doctor says I don't need it anymore. Fucking doctors."

Ty slipped his hand into his pocket and fingered the ever-present empty bottle. Two months, two weeks, and counting. He thought about saying that he'd wait outside, but that felt a little chickenshit, so he went in.

He survived the meeting, and so did Ryan. An hour later they walked out side by side. Quiet. Ty didn't know about Ryan, but he was more than a little shaken by the stories he'd heard, at the utter destruction of lives that those people in there had been trying to reboot and repair. He knew he had to be grateful because he hadn't fucked up his life. At least not completely.

He was halfway back to Ryan's place when Ryan spoke. "So are you and Mallory a thing?"

Ty had been asked this many times in the past few weeks. By the clerk at the grocery store. By the guy who'd taken his money at the gas pump. By everyone who'd crossed his path. By the very same people who—until Mallory—had been content to just stare at him.

Mallory. Mallory was the heart and soul of this town, or at least she represented what its heart and soul would look like in human form. And while maybe he'd treated her like someone he could easily walk away from, he knew different. *She* was different. Still, there was no denying the fact that while *she* was grounded here, in this place, in this life, *he* was chomping at the bit to get back to his. "No," he finally said. "We're not a thing."

Ryan scratched his scruffy jaw. "She know that?"

It'd been Mallory's idea that this be just a one-time affair, though she'd accepted his latest visit as just an addendum to the original deal. And she'd let him off the hook for being an ass.

And then asked him to leave without a good-bye. "Yeah. She knows that."

The question was, did *he*.

"Because she's a real nice lady," Ryan said. "When I was living on a bench at the park, she'd bring me food at night. She ever tell you that?"

Ty shook his head, his chest a little tight at the thought of Mallory, after a long day in the ER, seeking Ryan out to make sure he was fed.

"Yeah, she can't cook worth shit," Ryan told him with a small smile. "But I ate whatever she brought anyway. Didn't want to hurt her feelings."

Ty heard himself choke out a laugh.

Ryan nodded. "If I was…" He lifted a hand to indicate himself and trailed off. "You know, *different*," he finally said. "I'd try for her. She's something special. Way too special for the likes of me, you know?"

Ty's chest tightened even more. Yeah. He knew. He knew *exactly*. "She'd be pissed off to hear you say that."

"She's pretty when she's pissed off," Ryan said wistfully. "One time she came to the park and some kids were trying to bean me with rocks. She chased them, yelling at them at the top of her lungs. I was in a bad way then, and still I think I looked better than she did. Her hair was all over the place, and she was in her scrubs. She looked like a patient from the place I'd stayed at after I got back from my third tour."

A mental facility. Ty pictured Mallory furious and chasing the kids off. He could see it: her scrubs wrinkled after a long day of work, those ridiculous fuzzy boots, her hair looking like it had rioted around her face.

Christ, she was so fucking beautiful.

"You've seen the stuff on Facebook, right?" Ryan asked.

Ty slid him a look. "How are you getting on Facebook?"

"There's a community computer at the house." Ryan shrugged. "Facebook's the homepage. There's a pic up of you two. You two seem pretty cozy for not being a thing."

Yeah. Cozy.

Except what he'd had with Mallory had been just about the opposite of cozy. It'd been hot. Bewildering.

Staggering.

And what the hell pic was up on Facebook?

He dropped Ryan off, then went home and worked on the Jimmy for Matt until late. He showered, then eyed his blinking phone. He glanced at the missed calls, getting a little rush at the thought that maybe Mallory had called him. The last time she'd been stuck. Maybe this time she just wanted to hear his voice. He sure as hell could use the sound of her voice right about now.

But the message wasn't from Mallory. It was from Josh. Ty was expected at the radiology department at seven for scans, and then at a doctor's appointment at eight.

Ty tried to read the tone of Josh's voice to ascertain whether the news was going to be good or bad, but Josh was as good as Ty at not giving anything away.

The next morning, Ty was led to Josh's office and told to wait. He'd perfected the art of hurrying up and waiting in the military, so when Josh strode in carrying a thick file that Ty knew contained his medical history, he didn't react.

Josh was in full doctor mode today. Dark blue scrubs, a white doctor coat, a stethoscope around his neck, and his hospital ID clipped to his hip pocket. Hair rumpled, eyes tired, he dropped Ty's file on his desk, sprawled out into his chair, and put his feet up. "*Christ*."

"Long day already?"

"Is it still day?" Josh scrubbed his hands over his face. "Heard from Frances today. Or yesterday. Persistent, isn't she?"

"Among other things. What did you tell her?"

"That your prognosis was none of her goddamned business and to stop calling me."

This got a genuine smile out of Ty. "And she thanked you politely and went quietly into the night."

"Yeah," Josh said, heavy on the irony. "Or told me what she was going to do with my balls if she had to come out here to get news on you herself."

"Sounds about right." Ty looked at his closed file. "Verdict?"

"Scans show marked improvement. With another month of continued P.T., you could be back in the same lean, mean fighting shape you were. For now, I'd say you were probably up to where us normal humans are."

Another month off would fucking kill him. "So I'm good to go then."

Josh gave him a look. "Depends on your idea of go. You're not up to leaping out second-story windows."

"Yeah, but that hardly ever happens."

Josh put his feet down and leaned forward, studying Ty for a long, serious moment. "You're really going back."

"I was *always* going back."

"But you want to go back *now*."

"Hell, yeah," Ty said. "I wanted to go back the day I got here. Especially in the past few weeks, since I've been swimming and running again."

"So why didn't you? Go back?"

"I want to work," Ty said, gesturing to the file. "Need clearance."

"Yes, and that's going to come soon, but my point is that you haven't been exactly handcuffed to Lucky Harbor. You could have left."

A flash of Mallory's face came to Ty. Looking up at him while lying snuggled against him in her bed, wearing only a soft, sated smile and a slant of moonlight across her face.

It was no mystery what had kept him here.

"Mal know that you're just about out of here?" Josh asked quietly.

"This has nothing to do with her," Ty said flatly. "Sign the papers."

"You'd have to be on light duty."

"Fine. I'll push fucking papers around on a desk if I have to. Just clear me."

Josh shook his head, looking baffled. "You'd leave here for a desk job? Man, you're not a desk-job kind of guy and we both know it."

He'd deal. He needed to get close to the action, to get back to his world. He needed the adrenaline. He was wasting away here in Lucky Harbor.

"You know," Josh said with that infuriatingly calm voice, leaning on the desk, his elbows on the release papers. "Maybe we should get back to the real reason you're still here."

"Sign the papers, Josh."

Josh stared at him.

Ty stared back, holding the other man's gaze evenly. Steadily. With a shake of his head, Josh signed the papers.

Ty spent two days *not* making any plans to get back to his life. First, he told himself he needed to finish up the Jimmy. Then he told himself he had to finish up the Charger for Lucille's neighbor, and the other two cars he'd taken on as well. And people kept calling him with new car issues. He couldn't just ignore them. Plus he needed to finish the Shelby, just for himself, but the truth there was that she was running like a dream.

After that, he ran out of excuses and decided he'd give himself a day off from thinking about it.

Which turned into yet another day...

Then he woke up to a message from Josh to stop by his office at ten. Ty got up and swam. He ran, hard. He played WWE with Matt at the gym for an hour until they fell apart gasping, sweating, and equally worked over. Then Ty dragged himself to the shower and drove to Josh's office.

Josh was in dress clothes today, a white doctor's coat over his clothing, the ever-present stethoscope acting as a tie. He looked up from the mountain of paperwork on his desk and scowled at Ty. "You call The Queen yet about being cleared?"

"No."

Josh gave him a long look, then stood and shut his office door. Back in his chair, he steepled his fingers, studying Ty like a bug on a slide. "Problem?"

"No. I've just got a little pain is all." He straightened his leg and winced.

"No doubt," Josh said dryly. "I was at the gym this morning; you never even noticed me. You were too busy wiping the floor with Matt. Who, by the way, is the best street fighter I've ever met. And you kicked his ass. How much pain can you be in?"

"I pulled something."

Josh's smile faded. "Yeah?"

"Yeah."

Josh was quiet a moment. "Then maybe you should give it another week," he finally said.

Ty nodded his agreement and left. He left the back way, which meant he stood in the bright sunshine in the hospital parking lot staring at Mallory's POS car. He wondered what the hell was wrong with him, but since that was probably way too big a problem to solve in this decade, he went home. He fiddled on the Shelby until he realized it'd gotten dark. He was just getting out of his second shower of the day when he heard the knock at his door.

He'd been off the job for more than six months, and still the instinct to grab his gun before answering was second nature. But this was Lucky Harbor. The only real danger was being killed by kindness.

And nosy-ass gossip.

Shaking his head, he grabbed his Levi's up off the floor and pulled them on, then opened the door to...Mallory.

She gave him a small smile, a sweet smile. Clearly she hadn't yet heard through the cafeteria grapevine that he was single-handedly ruining her life. "Hey," he said. A chronic idiot. That was him.

"Hey yourself." Her gaze ran over his bare torso. Something went hot in her eyes as she took in the fact that all he wore were Levi's, which he hadn't yet buttoned up all the way. He did that now while she watched, and the temperature around them shot up even more.

She stepped over the threshold, and since he hadn't moved she bumped into him. He thought it was an accidental touch but then her hands came up and brushed over his chest and abs. No accident.

Nor was the fact that she was wearing a halter top, low-riding jeans and a pair of really hot heels that brought her up four point five inches and perfectly aligned their bodies. Her pulse was beating like a drum at the little dip in the base of her throat. Lifting a hand, he ran a finger over the beat, watching her pulse leap even more.

Her hand came up to join with his. "In the name of full disclosure," she murmured, "you should know that I talked to Ryan this afternoon."

Ty lifted his gaze.

"He landed in the ER," she said.

"What happened? Is he all right?"

"Someone on the highway caught sight of him wandering around and brought him in. He had a bottle of Jack and some dope he'd scored off some kids."

"*Shit.*"

"Yeah." She kept her hand on his, squeezing his fingers reassuringly. "He's fine. He's currently sleeping it off, but before that...he was talking."

"Was he?"

"You took him to NA."

That was a statement of fact so he let it sit between them.

"You...went into the meeting," she said. "You stayed."

Another statement of fact.

"Was he...unsteady?" she asked. "Did he need the assistance?"

Ah, and now he got it. She was on a fishing expedition. "He wasn't that bad off, no."

She nodded, and he waited for her expression to change but it didn't. There was no leaping to conclusions, no trial and jury, no pity, nothing.

Hell, he didn't know why that surprised him. She never did the expected. She was the warmest, most compassionate, understanding woman he'd ever met.

"Did you need something there?" she asked.

And she was also one of the most curious.

"Why don't you just ask me what you really want to know, Mallory?"

"Okay." She drew a deep breath. "Are you an addict, too?"

Unable to resist, he again stroked his thumb over that spot at the base of her neck before slipping his hand into his pocket to finger the ever-present Vicodin bottle. It was a light weight. Empty. And both those things reassured him. He'd fucked up plenty, but at least not with that. "Damn close," he said.

"Oh," she breathed, and nodded. "I see."

No, she didn't. But that was his fault. "After the plane crash, I wasn't exactly the best of patients. I was on heavy meds. A wreck, basically."

"You'd just lost your team," she said softly.

Something warm unfurled in him at that. She was defending him. To *himself*. "When I went back to work, I gave up the meds." He paused, remembering. "It sucked. Christ, it sucked bad. I liked the oblivion, too damn much."

Her eyes were on his, absorbing his words, taking it all in without judgment. So he gave her the rest. "Six months ago, I got hurt again. In the ER they got me all nice and drugged up before I could refuse the meds."

Something flickered in her eyes, and he knew she was remembering how he'd refused drugs the night of the storm.

"Then I was released," he said. "With a 'take as needed' prescription. I found myself doing exactly that and living for the clock, for the minute I could take more. That's when I stopped refilling."

"You went cold turkey?"

"I never understood that saying, cold turkey," he said with a grim smile. "It's more like *hot hell*, but yeah." He blew out a breath. "And I still crave it."

She was quiet a moment. "I think the craving part is normal. We all have our cravings. I gave up chocolate once. The cravings *sucked*."

He choked out a laugh. Christ, he liked her. A whole hell of a lot. What was he supposed to do with that? "I don't think it's exactly the same."

"True. I mean, I can't be arrested for hoarding chocolate cake," she said. "But it ruins my life. Costs money. And it makes my scrubs tight. You know how bad that is, when your drawstring pants are too tight? Pretty damn bad, Ty."

He was smiling now. He rocked back on his heels and studied her. "You're looking pretty damn good from where I'm standing."

"Because I only let myself have it once a week. Or whenever Amy calls. She's a very bad influence."

"Still crave, huh?" he asked with genuine sympathy.

"I'd give up my next breath for a piece of cake right now," she said with deep feeling. She sighed, as if with fond memories. "I think it helps to keep busy. Distracted. I know that much."

"I've been distracted plenty," he said, and her cheeks flamed. He loved that she could initiate sex in a storage room above about five hundred of her closest friends and family and *still* blush.

"Were you working on a car?" she asked. "I heard you're the new go-to mechanic guy."

"I was working before I showered."

"Show me?"

"The shower? Sure. I might have used all the hot water though."

She gave him a little laugh and a shove that took him back a step. He could have stood his ground but he liked the way she was letting her hands linger on his chest. He took one of those hands and guided her through to the kitchen and out the back door to the garage.

She looked around, taking in the cars and the slew of tools scattered across the work table. "What were you doing?"

"Brake line work on my Shelby."

"Show me," she said again.

"You want to learn how to put in new stainless steel brake lines," he said, heavy on the disbelief. "Mallory, those shoes aren't meant for working on a car."

"What are they meant for?"

"Messing with a man's head."

She smiled. "Are they working?"

"More than you can possibly imagine. Listen, this car shit, it's messy."

"So?" she asked, sounding amused, and he had to admit she had a point. She saw blood and guts and probably worse every single day. A little dirt wasn't going to bother her. Shaking his head at himself, he popped the hood. He grabbed a forgotten sweatshirt off the bench and handed it to her.

"I'm not cold."

His gaze slid to her breasts. Her nipples were poking at the material of her halter top. If she wasn't cold, then she was turned on. It would seem hard to believe since he hadn't touched her, but every time they got within five feet of each other he got a jolt to the dick, so who was he to say? "It's to keep your clothes from getting dirty." He pulled the sweatshirt over her head, unable to stop himself from touching as much of her as possible as he tugged it down her torso, only slightly mollified to hear her breathing hitch.

Yeah. They were on the same page.

The sweatshirt came to her thighs. She pushed back the hood. "It smells like you."

He felt that odd pain in his chest again, an ache that actually had nothing to do with wanting to get her naked. "And now it's going to smell like *you*," he said.

"Is that okay?"

It was so far beyond okay he didn't have words. Fucking sap. He kicked over the mechanic creeper, then his backup, and gestured her onto it. When they were both flat on their backs, she grinned at him. "Now what?"

"Under the car."

She slid herself beneath the car, and he joined her. Side by side, they looked up at the bottom of the chassis.

"What's first?" she asked.

He looked at her sweet profile. What was first? Reminding himself that he'd been cleared to leave Lucky Harbor. He handed her a roll of brake line. "You bend it to fit the contours of the frame as you go." He pointed out the route, and she began to work the brake line.

"It's peaceful," she said. "Under here."

He slid her a sideways look, and she laughed at him. No one ever laughed at him, he realized. Well, except for Matt, and Matt didn't look cute while doing it either.

"I'm serious," Mallory said, still smiling. "You don't think so?"

It was dirty, grimy, stuffy...and yeah. Peaceful. "I'm just surprised you think so."

"You don't think I can enjoy getting dirty once in awhile?" She bit her lower lip and laughed. "Okay, you know what I mean."

"Yeah. Here—" She wasn't able to put enough muscle into bending the line so he put his hands over hers and guided her. "Unravel another foot or so."

"'kay." She frowned, eyeing the space. "How long is that?"

"Like nine inches. I need twelve." He paused. "Twelve inches would be great."

He felt her gaze, and he did his best to look innocent, but she didn't buy it. "What the hell would you do with twelve inches?" she wanted to know.

He waggled a brow. "Plenty."

She shook her head. "Like you aren't lethal enough with what you have," she said, making him laugh.

They worked the brake line in companionable silence for a few moments, but Mallory didn't do silence all that well. "What do you think about under here?" she asked. "Besides your...inches?"

He smiled, but the truth was, he usually tried like hell not to think at all. "Sometimes I think about my dad."

"He was a Navy mechanic, too, right? He taught you all this stuff?"

Ty's dad had been a mechanic in the Navy, but not Ty. Yet correcting the misconception now, telling her that he'd once been a SEAL medic, wasn't something he wanted to get into. It was far easier to deny that part of himself rather than revisit it. "My dad didn't want me to learn mechanics, actually. He wanted more for me. I think he hoped that if he kept me away from anything mechanical, I'd become a lawyer or something like that."

"And . . . ?"

"And when I was fourteen, he bought a Pontiac GTO." He smiled at the memory. "A '67. God, she was sweet."

"She?" Mallory teased, turning her face to his. She was so close he reached out and stroked a rogue strand of hair from her temple, tucking it behind her ear.

"Yeah, she," he said. "Cars are always a she. And do you want to hear this story or not?"

"Very much." She nudged her shoulder to his. "Every single detail."

"I took apart the engine."

"Oh my God," she said on a shocked laugh. "Was he mad?"

"It was a classic, and it was in mint condition. *Mad* doesn't even begin to cover what he was."

She stared at him, eyes wide. "Why did you do it?"

He shrugged. "I couldn't help myself. I liked to take things apart and then put them back together again. Only I couldn't. I had no idea what I was doing." Ty could still remember the look on his father's face: utter and complete shock at the empty engine compartment, horror that his baby had been breached and violated, and then sheer fury. "I can still feel the sweat trickling down the back of my spine," he said, shaking his head. "I hadn't meant to take it so far. I'd just kept undoing and undoing . . ."

"What happened?"

"I was pretty sure he'd kick my ass."

She gasped. "He beat you?"

"Nah, he never laid a hand on me." Ty felt a smile curve his mouth. "Didn't have to. He was one scary son of a bitch. He'd talk in this low, authoritative voice that dared you to defy him. No one ever did that I know of."

"Not you?"

"*Hell* no."

She was grinning wide, and he shook his head at her. "What's so funny?"

"You," she said. "You're so big and bad. It's hard to imagine you scared of anything." She touched his jaw, cupping it in her palm and lightly running her thumb over his skin.

He hadn't shaved that morning, and he could hear the rasp of his stubble against the pad of her thumb. As she touched him, he watched the flecks in her eyes heat like gold.

"I like being under a car with you," she said.

Working on cars was his escape. Beneath a hood or a chassis was familiar ground, no matter what part of the world he was in or where he lay his head at night. It was his constant. A buffer from the shit.

And Mallory was a single-woman destruction crew, out-maneuvering him, letting herself right into his safety zone, and then into his damn heart while she was at it. Because no matter what bullshit he fed himself, he liked being here with her, too.

"You ever going to tell me what you *are* scared of?" she asked.

He let out a short laugh. "Plenty," he assured her.

Her eyes softened, and she slid her hand into the hair at the back of his neck, fisting lightly, bringing him a full-body shiver of pure pleasure.

"Such as?" she asked.

You, he nearly said.

And it would be God's truth.

"Tell me."

"I'm afraid of not living," he said. He rolled out from beneath the Shelby, then crouched beside Mallory's creeper, putting his hands on her ankles to yank her out, too.

Sitting up, she pushed her hair back and met his gaze. "Don't worry, Ty. I know."

"You know what?"

"That this isn't your real life, that you're just killing time with me until—"

He put his finger over her lips. "Mal—"

"No, it's okay," she said around his finger, wrapping her hand around his wrist. "You're not the small-town type. I know it."

And yet here he was. Free to go, but still here.

"Are we done working on the car?" she asked.

"Yeah." Her legs seemed endless in those jeans and fuck-me heels. "We're done working on the car."

"So I can teach you something about *my* work now?"

He took in her small but sexy smile and felt himself go hard. "What did you have in mind?"

"Ever play doctor?"

Chapter 15

There is nothing better than a good friend,
except maybe a good friend with chocolate.

The next morning, Mallory woke to a disgruntled *meow*. It was Sweet Pea, letting the world know it was past time for breakfast.

When Mallory ignored this, the cat batted her on the forehead with a paw.

"Shh," Mallory said.

"*Meow.*"

Mallory stretched, her body sore. She hadn't been to the gym since her membership had expired a year ago, which left only one thing to attribute the soreness to.

Ty, and his own special brand of workout.

She sighed blissfully and rolled over. She hadn't gotten home until late. Or early, depending on how you looked at it. She'd have liked to stay at Ty's all night but that would have been too much.

Not for her. For *him*.

She'd promised him that this was a simple fling. No use in telling him she'd broken that promise. Besides, she was pretty sure he was more than just physically attracted to her as well, but she wasn't sure if *he* knew it.

She loved being with him. That was the bottom line. The only line. There were no preconceived notions on how she should behave. It was freeing, exhilarating.

Amazing.

And also unsettling. She was in the big girls' sandbox when she played with Ty, and she was going to get hurt. There was nothing she could do about that so she showered. When she went to the closet for her white athletic shoes, she sniffed, then wrinkled her nose. "Oh no, you didn't," she said to Sweet Pea.

Sweet Pea was in the middle of the bed, daintily washing her face. She had no comment.

"You *poo'd in my shoe*?"

Sweet Pea gave her a look that said "see if you come home that late again" and continued with her grooming.

"Two words," Mallory told the cat. "*Glue. Factory.*"

Sweet Pea didn't look worried, and with good reason. It was an empty threat, and they both knew it. Mallory cleaned up the mess, thankful Sweet Pea hadn't used her bad girl shoes. She flashed to Ty tossing her onto his bed in the shoes and nothing else... Yeah. She was going to bronze those suckers.

She grabbed her phone off her nightstand and headed out her front door to get to work.

Joe was in her driveway, head under her opened hood. "Hey," he said. "Who did your alternator?"

"No one. What are you doing? You said you were busy."

"And now I'm not. I picked up a new alternator for you this morning, but someone beat me to it."

"What?" She stepped off the front porch and took a peek at

the thing he was pointing out, the one shiny, clean part in the whole car.

"See?" Joe said. "Brand new alternator. Maybe it was Garrison."

"Why would you think that?"

"Because he helped this guy . . . Ryan, I think . . . get a job at the welding shop. And Ryan told me you're seeing Garrison."

Ty had gotten Ryan a job. Everything in her softened at the thought of Ty caring that much, and she wondered if it was too soon to go back over there. She'd wear her heels again. And maybe a trench coat and nothing else . . .

"Hel*lo*," Joe said, irritated.

"What?"

"Are you seeing Garrison or not? Would he have done this for you?"

Mallory flashed back to finding Ty in her driveway in the middle of the night. She'd never questioned what he'd been doing here, figuring it had been about sex. She hadn't minded that; she'd wanted him, too, but she got a little warm fuzzy that it hadn't been about *just* sex.

She had no explanation for last night, which had been all her own doing. She'd have to tell Amy that she was right: bad girl shoes were awesome. Amy loved to be right.

She drove to work with the smile still on her face. She'd parked and was just getting out of the car when her phone vibrated. Odd, because she'd have sworn she'd set it to ring. Pulling it out of her pocket, she didn't even attempt to see the screen in the bright morning sun before she answered with a simple "Hello?"

There was a long beat of silence and then, "Who the hell are you and where the hell is Ty?"

Mallory blinked at the very sexy, snooty female voice sounding damn proprietary, then said, "Who is this?"

"I asked first. Oh, for fuck's sake. Just put him on the phone. *Now*."

Oh hell no, Mallory thought, feeling a proprietariness of her own, even though on some level she'd known that Ty had to have other women in his life. It made perfect sense, but that didn't mean she liked how it felt.

"Fine, have it your way," the woman snapped. "Tell him Frances called. Make sure you tell him that it's important, do you understand?"

"How did you get this number?"

"Cookie, you don't want to go there. Now listen to me. I don't care how good you suck him, I've known him longer, I know him better, and I'm the only one of us who will know him by this time next week. Give him the damn message."

Click.

Mallory stared at the phone, realizing that it wasn't her phone at all. It was an iPhone just like hers, but the background was of only the date and a clock, not the picture of the beach she'd taken last week.

She had Ty's phone.

Mallory tried calling *her* phone but it went directly to voice-mail, signaling that Ty had either turned it off or she'd run out of battery. She chewed on the situation for a minute, then punched out Amy's number. "It's me," she said. "I'm using someone else's phone. Life is getting nuts."

"Nuts is all relative on the Bad Girl scale."

"Is that right?" Mallory asked. "So where on that scale would you put getting yelled at by the ex of the guy I'm sleeping with?"

Dead silence. Then, "So the bad girl shoes worked?"

Mallory blew out a breath. "Yes. Now concentrate." She told Amy all about the call. "And really," she said. "I have no one but myself to blame. *I* wanted this one-time thing. I mean I wanted the second time too, *and* the third, but now—"

"Now you're in this, and you're worried that maybe you're in it alone."

Mallory's throat tightened. "Yeah. I mean three times. To me that's..."

"I know." Suddenly Amy wasn't sounding amused. "It's a relationship."

"And I'm pretty sure Ty's allergic to relationships."

Amy paused again. "Mallory, are you sure you haven't bitten off more than you can chew?"

Mallory choked out a laugh. "*Now*? You think to ask me this now? *You* started this. You egged me on with the list of Mr. Wrongs! Hell, yes, I've bitten off more than I can chew!"

"Okay," Amy soothed. "We can fix this. You'll just downgrade to a *less* Mr. Wrong. Someone easier to drag around by his twig and berries, you know?"

Yeah, but she didn't want just anyone's twigs and berries. "Look, I'm at work. We'll have to obsess over this later. Have cake waiting. I'm going to need it."

"Will do, babe."

Mallory clicked off and went into the hospital.

Five minutes into her shift, Jane called her into her office. "Two things," her boss said cryptically, giving nothing away. "First up." She laid a piece of paper on her desk, facing Mallory. It was a receipt for a sizeable amount.

"Anonymous donation," Jane said. "For HSC."

"My God." Mallory sank to a spare chair. "Am I looking at all those zeroes correctly?"

"Yes," Jane said. "And they're all very pretty."

Mallory's eyes jerked up to Jane's. "Did you just make a joke?"

"Tell anyone, and I'll skin you." Jane let out a rare smile but it was fleeting. "Nicely done."

"How do you know I had anything to do with this?" Mallory asked, still astonished.

Jane gave an impressive eye roll. "Mallory, without you, there would be no HSC. Even *with* you, it's barely there, and it's on tentative footing. Someone you know or talked to donated this money."

Mallory absorbed that a moment. "Someone I know? I don't *know* anyone with a spare 10K."

"Don't you?"

"You're not talking about Ty," Mallory said, but Jane's eyes said that's exactly who she was talking about. "He already donated money for the Vets' program," Mallory protested. "Besides, he doesn't have this kind of money. But truthfully, she had no idea what Ty had or didn't have. *Ten thousand dollars*... "Why would he—"

"Don't ask me that," Jane said quietly. "Because honestly, Mallory? I don't want to know why he'd give you so much money for a Health Services Clinic in a town he has no ties to, a place he apparently plans on leaving very soon."

"Not me," Mallory said. "He didn't give the money to me. He gave it to HSC. If it was even him."

"Hmm," was all Jane said to this. She paused. "I really don't like to delve into my employees' private lives, but..."

Oh boy. "But... ?"

"But since yours is being discussed over the water cooler, it's unavoidable. You're dating a man who no one knows anything about."

Well, technically, there was little "dating" involved. She was flat out boinking him. "No disrespect, Jane, but I really don't see how this affects my job."

"Whether he was the anonymous donor or not, he's been seen socializing with known drug addicts. And he yelled at two aides in the cafeteria."

Mallory's temper was usually non-existent but it flared to life at Jane's cavalier description of Ryan. "That's not quite how either of those two events went down," she said as evenly as she could. "Ty's involved in the Vets' program. He and Ryan connected because of their military backgrounds, and Ty's been helping him, giving him rides and bringing him food." Which she only knew because Lucille had told her, and thinking about it *still* melted her heart. She also knew about the hospital cafeteria incident, thanks to Lucille. "As for the radiation techs, they were just downright rude, so—"

"My point," Jane said, "is that you're not just an employee now. You're *running* the HSC. You're in a position that requires a certain public persona, and you have no one to blame but yourself for that one. You chose this, Mallory, so you have to understand that certain aspects of your life are now up for scrutiny. You have a moral and financial obligation to live up to that scrutiny."

Mallory was having a hard time swallowing this. "Are you saying I can't have a private life?"

"I'm saying that private life can't conflict with your public life. You can't date a man who might need the services HSC provides, wrong as that sounds. You just can't."

The words rang through Mallory's head for the next few hours as she dealt with her patients. She had a vomiter—oh joy— a teenager who'd let her new tattoo get infected, and an eight-months-pregnant woman who ate a jar of pickles and put herself into labor with gas pains.

Alyssa was little to no help. She was far too busy flirting with that cute new resident doctor, hoping to score a date for her night off. All of Alyssa's patients kept hailing Mallory down, until finally she physically yanked Alyssa away from the new resident and reminded her that she had actual work to do.

Mallory pretty much ran ragged until there was finally a lull. She used the rare quiet time to sit at the nurses' station and catch up on charting.

"Mallory!"

She looked up to find one of her patients, Jodi Larson, standing there beaming from ear to ear. Jodi was ten years old, a leukemia patient, and one of Mallory's all-time favorite people. She'd been in for her six-month check, and given the smile also on Jodi's mom's face behind her, the news had been good.

"Officially in remission," Jodi said proudly.

Jodi's mom's eyes were shining brilliantly as she nodded affirmation of the good news. Thrilled, Mallory hugged them both tight, and Jodi presented her with a plate of cookies. "Chocolate chip and walnut. I baked them just for you."

They hugged again, then Mallory got paged and had to go. It turned out the page was from her own mother.

"Mallory," Ella whispered, dragging her daughter into a far, quiet corner. "People are talking about how you were seen driving home at 3:20 in the morning. Why do I have a daughter coming home that late? Nothing good happens that late, Mallory. Nothing."

Oh, for the love of God. "Actually, it was only 2:30, so your source is dyslexic." And pretty damn annoying, but Mallory didn't bother to say so. Her mother had a point and she was winding up for it.

"You were with *that* man," Ella said.

Uh huh, and there it was. Mallory's left eye began to twitch. "That man has a name."

"Cute Guy."

"A *real* name."

Her mother's lips tightened. "Yes, I believe The Facebook is calling him *Mysterious* Cute Guy."

Mallory put a finger to her twitching eye. "Okay, for the last time, it's not *The* Facebook, it's just *Facebook*."

"Honey, please. It's time you came to your senses. You're going to end up as wild and crazy as Joe and Tammy, and that's not who you are."

"Mom, Joe is only twenty-four. He's not ready to settle down, so a little wild and crazy is okay. And Tammy is settled down in her own wild and crazy way. Maybe it's not what you wanted for her but she's adjusted and happy. What's wrong with being like them?"

Her mom's mouth tightened. "That's not what I mean, and you know it."

"No," Mallory agreed quietly, her chest tight. "That isn't what you mean, and I do know it. You're talking about Karen."

"No, we're not."

"Well, we should."

Her mother closed her eyes and turned away. "I have to go."

"She started dating a guy no one knew."

"I don't want to talk about this, Mallory!"

"He encouraged her to take a walk on the wild side, and—"

"*Don't*," Ella said stiffly. "Don't you—"

"And she changed. She stopped being who you thought she should be. And—"

Her mother whirled back, eyes blazing, finger pointed shakily in Mallory's face. "Don't you *dare* say it."

"Mom," Mallory said through a tight throat, suddenly *very* tired. "It's not the same this time. You know it's not the same for me. Karen was doing drugs."

"Your young man went to NA."

Mallory shook her head in disbelief. "That's *confidential*."

"It's Lucky Harbor," Ella said with a shrug that said Ty's privacy was nothing compared to her need to make sure her daughter was okay. "Remember that stormy night, when he ended up in the ER? He refused narcotics for pain. *Adamantly*."

"So?"

"Don't play dumb, Mallory. You know what I'm saying. He's an outsider, and I realize that sounds rude, but you've got to admit people are getting the wrong idea about you two."

Actually, given what she and Ty had been doing in the deep, dark of the night—and sometimes in the middle of the day— people had the exact *right* idea.

Ella took one look at Mallory's face and got a pinched look of tension. "See? It's happening. It's happening again, just like Karen with Tony."

"No," Mallory said firmly. God, no. "Tony got Karen both hooked and then pregnant, and she spiraled downward. I can't believe we're comparing my life to Karen's now, after all these years. Why not back then, when I *was* in danger of spiraling?"

Her mother looked as if Mallory had slapped her. "You...you weren't. You were our rock."

Mallory let out a breath and shook her head, feeling weary to the bone. And sad. Way too damn sad. "Forget it, Mom."

"I can't. Oh my God." She covered her face. "I thought—you were so sweet during that time. I never thought—Oh, Mallory. I'm so sorry. Are you...spiraling again?"

Mallory drew a shaky breath and stepped forward, putting her hands on her mom's arms. "No," she said gently. "I'm not spiraling again. I'm not going to kill myself, Mom." The big, fat elephant in the room. "I'm not Karen."

Ella nodded, and with tears in her eyes, hugged Mallory in tight. "I know," she whispered. Then, in the Quinn way of bucking up, she sniffed and pulled back to search her pockets, coming up with a tissue that she used to swipe her eyes. "You're really okay?"

"Really," Mallory promised.

"So can I have my sweet daughter back?"

A low laugh escaped Mallory. "I'm still sweet, Mom. I'm just not going to be amenable all the time, or compliant. And I'm not going to live my life exactly as you'd have me do."

"Are you going to keep seeing that man?"

Lucille walked by in her candy-striper uniform. "Well, I hope so," she said. "He's the hottest thing you've dated since...well, ever."

"Don't encourage her," Ella said. "This isn't just a silly thing. It's affecting her job."

"Phooey," Lucille said.

"Jane is concerned about it affecting the HSC as well."

"Phooey," Lucille said again. "And shame on you, Ella, for buying into that. It's about time our girl here stops paying for others' mistakes and regrets, don't you think?"

Ella turned and looked at Mallory for a long beat, seeming stricken by the thought of anyone thinking she wasn't fully supporting her own flesh and blood. "I never wanted you to pay for our mistakes and regrets."

"Well, she has," Lucille said, brutally honest as always, though her voice was very kind. She moved behind the nurses' desk, poured Ella some coffee, pulled a flask from her pocket, and added a dash of something that smelled 100 proof.

"Lucille!" Ella gasped. "I'm on the job!"

"You're clocking out, and it's time."

"Time for what?"

"Time for Mallory to not be the only one to stretch her wings. And speaking of wings," Lucille said to Mallory, "you're going to need wings for your next patient, and she's ready for you."

The new patient turned out to be Mrs. Burland.

"You," Mrs. B said when Mallory entered her room.

"Me," Mallory agreed and reached for the blood pressure cuff. "It says on your chart that you passed out after your bath again. Did you take your meds at the right time?"

"Well, of course I did. I'm not a complete idiot. They didn't work."

"Did you space the pills out with food, as explicitly instructed on the bottles?"

Mrs. Burland glared at her.

"I'll take that as a no," Mallory said. Mrs. B's color was off, and her blood pressure was far too low. "When was your last meal?"

"Hmph."

"Mrs. Burland." Mallory put her fingers on the woman's narrow, frail, paper-thin wrist to check her pulse. "Did you eat lunch today?"

Mrs. Burland straightened to her full four-foot-eight inches, quivering with indignity. "I know what I'm supposed to be doing."

Mallory looked into her rheumy, pissy eyes and felt her heart clench. *Dammit.* She had a feeling she knew the problem—Mrs. B didn't have any food. Probably she wasn't feeling good enough to take care of herself, and since she'd long ago scared off family and friends with her mean, petty, vicious ways, she had no one to help her. Mallory picked up the room phone and called the cafeteria. "Stella, it's Mallory. I need a full dinner tray for room three."

"Sure thing, Sweet Cheeks. Is your hunk-o-burning love going to be making any more visits my way?"

Mallory rubbed her still-twitching eye. "Not today."

When the tray came, Mallory stood over her grumpy patient. "Eat."

Mrs. Burland tried to push the tray away but Mallory was one step ahead of her, holding it still. "Oh no, you don't. You're not going to have a little tantrum and spill it, not this time."

Mrs. Burland's eyes burned bright with temper, which Mallory was happy to see because it meant her patient was already feeling better. Mallory leaned close. "I'm stronger and meaner, and *I've* eaten today."

"Well *that's* obvious." Mrs. Burland sniffed at the juice on the tray. "Hmph."

"It's apple."

"I have eyes in my head, don't I?" Mrs. Burland sipped the juice. In sixty seconds, her color was better. "You didn't used to be so mean."

"It's a newly acquired skill," Mallory said.

"I'm ready to go home now."

"You can't go home until I see you eat."

"You're making that up. This cafeteria food isn't fit for a dog," Mrs. Burland said.

Well, she had her there. Even Mallory, who'd eat just about anything, didn't like the cafeteria food, not that she'd ever say so to the cook. "Fine." Mallory went to the staff kitchen and pulled out her own lunch, which she brought back to Mrs. Burland's room. "Try my sandwich. Turkey and cheese with spinach." Which she'd only added because her mom kept asking if she was eating her vegetables. "There's a little bit of mustard and probably too much mayo but your cholesterol is the least of your problems." Mallory also tossed down a baggie of baby carrots and an apple.

Mrs. Burland took a bite of the sandwich first. "*Awful*," she said, but took another bite. And then another, until there was nothing left but a few crumbs.

"The carrot sticks and the apple too," Mallory said.

"Are they as horrid as the sandwich?"

"They're as horrid as your bad attitude. And I'll tell you this right now. You're going to eat it all if I have to shove it down your throat myself."

"*Mallory*," a voice breathed in disbelief from the doorway.

Jane. *Perfect*. Mallory turned to face her boss, but not before she saw triumph and evil glee come into Mrs. Burland's eyes.

"A moment," Jane said, face tight.

"Certainly." Mallory jabbed a finger at the carrots and apple. Mrs. Burland meekly picked up the apple.

In the hallway, Jane led Mallory just out of hearing range of Mrs. Burland. "New tactic?"

"Yes," Mallory said, refusing to defend herself. "She finish it all?"

Jane took a look over Mallory's shoulder at Mrs. B. "Every last bite. How did you do it?"

"By being a bigger bitch than she is."

"Nicely done."

By the time Mallory got in her car and left work, she was starving and exhausted. She solved the first problem by eating a handful of Jodi's cookies. Then she pulled her phone out and took a quick peek to see if she had any texts before remembering she had Ty's phone. She paused and eyed the remaining chocolate chip/walnut cookies. Fifteen minutes later, she pulled into Ty's driveway.

The garage door was open, and the man himself was flat on his back beneath his car, one long denim-clad leg straight out, the other bent. His black T-shirt had risen up. Or maybe it was his Levi's that had sunk almost indecently low on his hips. In either case, the revealed strip of his washboard abs had her mouth actually watering. She thought maybe she could stand here and just look at him all day long, but he seemed to enjoy looking at her right back and she'd had a hell of a long day and couldn't possibly be worth looking at right now.

Not that it appeared to make any difference. Ty's attraction to her was apparently based on some intangible thing she couldn't fathom. She knew she could think about that for a million years and not get used to it, to the fact that no matter what she did or what she looked like, he seemed to want her.

The feeling was far too mutual.

Chapter 16

Nothing chocolate, nothing gained.

Ty sat up on the mechanic's creeper and took in the sight of Mallory standing there. She was packing a plate of cookies, which he hoped to God were for him. He assumed she'd discovered the phone fiasco by now, but other than that, he wasn't sure what sort of mood to expect from her.

The last time he'd seen her, she'd been face down on his bed, boneless and sated right into a coma of bliss. He'd stroked a strand of damp hair from her face and she'd smiled in her sleep. His heart had constricted at the sight, his sole thought, *oh Christ, I am in trouble.* He'd been torn by the urge to tug her close, but then claustrophobia had reached up and grabbed him by the throat. Just as he'd chosen retreat, she'd awakened and gotten dressed to go.

That must have been when she'd grabbed the wrong phone, although he hadn't realized it then. He'd followed her home to make sure she got there safely, then driven back to his place and expected to crash. Instead he'd missed her.

Clearly he was losing it.

He had no idea what she was thinking, but he hadn't expected to see her smile at the sight of him, a smile that was filled with relief.

Relief, he realized, and surprise that he was still here in town. *Yeah, join my club.* He was surprised, too.

She was in pale purple scrubs and white Nikes. She had two pens sticking out of her hip pocket, one red, one black. There were correlating ink marks on her scrubs. She followed his gaze and rubbed at the stains. "I'm a mess. Don't ask."

"Not a mess," he said. "Are those cookies?"

"Yes. And I had to fight the staff to keep them for you."

"Girl-on-girl fight?" he asked hopefully. "Did you get it on video?"

"You are such a guy." She came closer and crouched at his side, holding the plate out for him. He took a big bite of a cookie and moaned in deep appreciation.

"Did you give the HSC ten thousand dollars?"

Ah, there it was, he thought, swallowing. He'd been hoping she wouldn't find out, but he supposed that was unrealistic in a town like Lucky Harbor. Taking his time, he ate cookie number two, then reached for a third.

She held the plate out of his reach. "Did you?" she asked.

He eyed her for a long moment. "Which answer will get me the rest of the cookies?"

"Oh, Ty," she breathed, looking worried as she lowered the plate. Worried for him, he realized.

"Why?" she asked. "You already gave."

"HSC needed it."

"But it's *so* much money."

"If you're asking if I can afford it, I can."

She just stared at him, so he shrugged. "The job pays well." He paused. "Really well."

She let out a breath. She was already hunkered at his side so it took little effort to lean over toward him and press a kiss to his cheek. "Thank you," she whispered, and went to kiss the other cheek, but he turned his head and caught her mouth with his. They were both gratifyingly out of breath by the time he pulled back.

"You're welcome," he said, surprised when she rose and sat on the stool at his work bench.

"Don't let me keep you from what you were doing," she said. "I'll watch."

He arched a brow, feeling amused for the first time all day. "You want me to get back under the car?"

"I just don't want you to lose any time because of me."

"Is that right?"

"Absolutely."

Humoring the both of them, he lay back down onto the mechanic's creeper and lifted his hands above his head to the edge of the car.

She nibbled on her lower lip. Watching him work turned her on. The knowledge shouldn't have surprised him—she turned him on just breathing, but he laughed softly.

She blushed. "How did you know?"

"Your nipples are hard."

She made a sound in the back of her throat and covered her breasts, making him laugh.

"It's your jeans," she said. "They're faded at your, um." She waggled a finger in the direction of his crotch. "Stress spots. And your T-shirt, it's tight on your biceps and shoulders. And when you're flat on your back under the car, you look like you know what you're doing."

"That's because I do."

"It's the whole package," she agreed miserably.

He grinned. "If it helps, my *package* likes your package. A whole hell of a lot."

"Work!" she demanded, closing her eyes.

Obliging, he rolled back beneath the car. He heard her get to her feet and walk close, peering into the opened hood above him. "So how much wrenching do you do at your work?"

She was as see-through as glass. He knew that she'd put him back beneath the car because she'd gotten him to talk beneath a car before. But she was so goddamned cute trying to outthink him that he gave her what she wanted.

Which in hindsight made her a hell of lot more dangerous than he'd thought. "I hotwired a tank once," he said. "With my team. We stole it to disable rebel insurgents."

She squatted at his side. "You've led a very different life than mine." Her hand settled on his bad thigh. It'd been only recently that he'd even gotten feeling back in it, but he was having no trouble feeling anything now. It felt like her fingers had a direct line to his groin, and things stirred to life.

"Our phones got switched," she said.

There was a new quality to her voice now, one that had him setting down his wrench and pulling himself back out from beneath the car.

She was still crouched low, and from his vantage point flat on his back, he looked up into her face. As usual, she could hide nothing from him, and for once, he wished he couldn't see her every thought. They exchanged phones but her expression didn't change. "Problem?" he asked.

"A woman called. Frances? She wants you to call her."

"She always wants me to call her."

Mallory nodded, looked down at the ground and then back into his eyes. "Are you dating her?"

"I'm not much of a dater."

"You know what I mean."

Yeah, he did. And he didn't want to go there.

"I know," she said quickly. "We agreed that this thing with you and me was...casual."

He didn't like where this was going.

"A fling," she went on. "Right? Not a relationship." She rose and turned away from him. "But I was thinking that maybe that last part isn't true. I mean, we never actually said there *wasn't* a relationship."

"I'll say it," he said. "It's not a relationship."

She went still, turning back to stare at him with those eyes he'd never once been able to resist. "Why is that?" she asked. "Why can't there be an us, if there's a you and a someone else?"

He looked into her expressive face and felt a stab of pain right in the gut. He'd survived SEAL training. He'd lived through a plane crash. He'd kept on breathing when the rest of his team, his friends, his brothers, hadn't been able to do the same. But he didn't know how to do this. "There are some things I can't tell you," he said slowly. "Things that even if I wanted to, I couldn't."

"So the reason we can't be a *we* is classified?" she asked in disbelief. "Really, Ty?"

Well, hell. Yeah, that had been pretty fucking lame. Chalk it up to the panic now residing in his hollow gut. Whatever he did here, whatever he came up with, he needed her to want to keep her distance. Except Mallory Quinn was incapable of distance when her heart was involved. That was both painfully attractive and terrifying. "Don't fall for me, Mallory. That wouldn't be good for either of us. We're too different. You said so yourself."

She sucked in a breath like he'd slapped her. "And what, you and Frances are alike? Compatible?"

"Unfortunately, yes."

Hands on hips, she narrowed her eyes. "If you're sleeping with her, then why wouldn't she just roll over and talk to you? Why is she yelling about you not returning her phone calls?"

"Frances doesn't yell."

"*Strongly* suggested then," she said with mock politeness. She paused. "You're not sleeping with her."

Gig up. "I'm not sleeping with her. And as for the why she's pissed, there are a variety of reasons. I haven't seen her in six months, for one."

She stared at him, then turned away again.

Ty rose to his feet and walked around her to see her face. "Get the rest out," he said. "Let's finish this."

A wry smile twisted her mouth. "You aren't familiar with the Quinn pattern of holding onto a good mad, I see."

"Holding onto your mad only tortures *you*," he pointed out. "If you're mad at me, let me have it."

"Are you always so logical?" With a sigh, she shook her head. "Never mind. Don't answer that." She put a finger to her eye. "Damn twitch," she muttered to herself, then looked at him, chin up. "I snooped in your phone."

"I would expect nothing less from Walking-On-The-Wild-Side Mallory."

"I thought about not telling you. But stealth isn't one of my special talents."

"You have other special talents," he said, and made her laugh.

"Dammit," she said. "I don't want to laugh with you right now."

Lifting a hand, he wrapped it around the nape of her neck and drew her in. "You need some more time to be mad at me?"

"Yes."

"Let me know when you're about done." He knew he had no right to touch her, crave her like air, but he did both. And when he put his mouth on hers, he recognized the taste of her, like she'd been made for just him. Which made him far more screwed than he'd even imagined.

But suddenly she was pulling free, shaking her head. "Ty— I can't."

"You can't kiss and be mad at me at the same time?"

"Oh, I can do that. What I can't do is this. I can't do this and keep it . . . not real."

"It's real."

"Yes, but real for you means an erection. For me, it means . . ." She rubbed her chest as if it hurt and closed her eyes. "Never mind." She took a step back and then another. "I'm sorry, this really is my fault. I shouldn't have—"

"Mallory—"

"No, it's okay. Really. But I'm going now."

He watched her get into her car and drive off. Yeah, he thought, definitely time to go back to work. Past time.

Mallory parked behind her brother's truck in her mother's driveway.

Dinner with the Quinns.

It'd been a full day since she'd left Ty standing in his garage, hot and dirty and looking a little baffled, like maybe he'd lost his copy of the rule book for their little game.

But even though she'd started the game in the first place, she no longer wanted to play. Somewhere along the way, her heart had flipped on her. She could pretend to be a bad girl all she wanted. It was only an illusion. The truth was, she needed more than just sex. And that really pissed her off about herself.

And what pissed her off even more was how much she already missed him.

Her mother was in the kitchen pulling a roasted chicken out of the oven. It looked perfect. Mallory wouldn't even know where to begin to make food that looked like that and she sniffed appreciatively.

"Did you bring the dessert?" her mother asked. "That cake you brought to Joe's birthday party was amazing. I had no idea you were so talented. Tell me you made another of those."

Mallory held out the tray of cupcakes she'd gotten from the B&B this morning. Tara had promised they were absolutely to die for. Mallory knew this to be true because she'd already inhaled two of them.

"A woman who can bake like this," her mom said, "should have kids. I wouldn't mind some grandchildren."

"Mom."

"Just sayin'."

"Well, stop just sayin'."

Joe walked in and rumpled Mallory's hair. "Hey, think you can convince that cute new LN to go out with me?"

"No, Camilla's too good for you. And how do you know her?"

"I work with her brother at the welding shop. She brought him lunch."

"Stay away from Camilla," Mallory said.

Ella was shooing everyone to the table. "Joe, put your phone away. Oh, Mal, I almost forgot. Tammy wanted me to ask if you'd take Alyssa's shift this weekend so she and Tammy can have a girl's night out."

Mallory grabbed two rolls. "Can't."

Ella took one roll back. "You'll hate yourself in the morning. And why can't you take the shift?"

"I'm working at the HSC this weekend."

"Both days?"

"No, but I need a day off."

Ella blinked. "You never say no. You're always so good about helping everyone."

Oh how she hated that adjective applied to her—*good*.

Joe grinned and took two rolls without comment from Ella, the skinny rat-fink bastard. "I don't think Mallory likes being called *good*, Mom."

"Of course she does. Why wouldn't she?"

Right. Why wouldn't she...

She escaped as soon as dinner was over. Her family was...well, her family. She loved them but they had no idea how much their opinion of her wore her down, that she yearned for so much more, that she wanted to be seen. Seen for herself.

Ty saw her for herself.

Too bad he didn't see her as someone he wanted in his life.

She was halfway home when her phone rang. She pulled over and answered Amy's call.

"You see Facebook lately?"

Mallory's heart sank. "What now?"

"Someone caught a picture of you and Ty in what looks like the hospital parking lot. He was...under your hood."

Oh boy. "Tell me you really mean that. And not as some sort of euphemism."

"The picture is hot, Mal. No one can deny that you don't look good together."

"We're *not* together. And what the hell are we doing in the picture?"

"Kissing. And he's got a hand on your ass. They've relabeled him from Mysterious Cute Guy to Good-With-His-Hands Guy."

"Oh, God."

"And Mal?"

"Yeah?"

"I think you're ready to teach your own Bad Girl Lessons now."

Mallory thunked her head on the steering wheel.

"Oh, and Chocoholics unite tomorrow. I'm getting a chocolate cake from Tara. It's got yours, Grace's, and my name on it. *You've* got a story to tell."

"So do you. I want to hear more about this thing with Matt—"

"There's no 'thing.'"

"Amy—"

"Sorry, bad connection. Must be going through a tunnel."

"You're at the diner!"

"Oh, well then it must be something I don't want to discuss." And she disconnected.

Mallory shook her head and got back on the road, hitting the gas hard. She wanted to see that Facebook pic. Two blocks from home, red and blue lights flashed in her rearview mirror.

Shit.

She pulled over, rolled down her window, and glared at Sheriff Sawyer Thompson as he ambled up to the side of her car. She and Sawyer had gone to high school together, though he'd been a couple of years ahead of her. She'd done his English papers, and he'd handled her math and science. Later, she'd patched him up several times when his wild, misspent youth had landed him on the injured list.

Then he'd settled down and become a sheriff of all things, now firmly entrenched on the right side of the law. There'd been a time when having the big, bad, sexy sheriff pull her over might have made her day. But that time wasn't now. "What?" she demanded a little crankily. "You don't have a bad guy to catch? You have to pull over people who are just trying to get home?"

"Give me a break, Mal. You were doing fifty-five in a thirty-five zone. I whooped my siren at you twice, and you never even noticed. What the hell's up with you?"

Crap. She sagged in her seat. "Nothing."

He shook his head and leaned against her car, apparently perfectly happy to take a break on her time. She sighed. "Long day?" she asked sympathetically.

"Yeah." He slid her a look. "But clearly not as long as yours."

"I'm fine."

"Is that right?" He pulled out his iPhone and thumbed his way to a page, then turned it to her.

Facebook.

A picture had indeed been posted, just as Amy had said. It was small and grainy but it was her. In Ty's arms.

With his hand on her ass.

She stared at herself. She had a dazed, dreamy smile on her face. Not Ty. His expression was possessive as he stared down at her hungrily, and she felt herself getting aroused all over again in spite of herself. This was quickly followed by a surge of her supposedly rare temper. "Are you *kidding* me?"

Sawyer slipped the phone back into his pocket.

"That's an invasion of privacy!" she said. "Arrest someone!"

"You were in a public place."

"I didn't know someone was taking pictures!"

"Obviously," Sawyer drawled, still leaning back against her car as if he had all day.

"I'm going to kick someone's ass."

His brow shot up at that. "You don't kick ass, Mal. You *save* people's asses."

"I'm over it! Give me my damn speeding ticket and get out of my way before I run your foot over."

Sawyer flashed a genuine grin now. "Are you threatening an officer?"

"My ticket, Sawyer."

"I'm not going to give you a ticket, Mallory."

"You're not?"

"Hell, no. If I gave you a ticket now, I'd get skinned alive by...well, everyone."

This was thankfully true. "That's never bothered you before." If she wasn't so mad, she might have found humor in this. "It's Chloe. Having a girlfriend has softened you up."

He grimaced. "I'm tempted to ticket you just for saying that."

She found a smile after all.

He returned it and leaned in her window, tugging on a strand of her hair. "Want some advice?"

"I want to run your foot over."

"You're not going to run me over, because then you'd have

to give me first aid and you're not in the mood." But he stepped back, proving he wasn't just all good looks. "Slow down," he warned her and tugged on her hair again. "*Everywhere*."

"What does that mean?"

"It means that I don't want to see you hurt."

Well, it was too damn late for that, wasn't it. She already hurt, thank you very much.

She blew out a breath and eased out into traffic. She was careful not to speed again, even with her phone going off every two seconds. She ignored all calls, parked in her driveway, watered Mrs. Tyler's flowers, watered her grandma's flowers, and fed Sweet Pea.

Some habits were hard to break.

She bent down to scratch the cat behind the ears and got bit for her efforts. Yeah, definitely some habits were hard to break. She walked straight through the house and out the back door. In the backyard, she headed to the sole lounge chair. Plopping down, she hit speaker on her phone and finally accessed the messages, squinting as she did, as if that would help not hear them.

"Mallory," Jane said in her Displeased Voice. "Call me."

No thank you. Clearly her boss had seen the picture. Just as clearly, she assumed that Mallory had ignored her warning. Mallory supposed she should call in and let Jane know that the picture had been taken before their "talk." Or that she was no longer seeing Ty. But tired of being the peacemaker, she hit delete.

"Wow, Mal," came the next message. Tammy. "You're one serious badass lately. If you find yourself heading to Vegas, make sure you buy the wedding package *without* the photos. You don't need any pics; this one is perfect."

Delete.

Third message. "Mallory, this is Deena. From the grocery store? Yeah, listen, I play Bunko with a group every Wednesday night, and this week we had a drawing for who could go for Cute Guy and I won. So you're going to need to back off. He's mine."

He's all yours, Deena.

Delete.

Sweet Pea bumped her head into Mallory's shin. This wasn't a show of love but a demand for more food. "You have no idea how good you have it, cat," she said with a sigh. "All you have to do is sleep for, what, eighteen hours a day? No pressure, no expectations. No Mysterious Cute Guys messing with your head, giving you mixed signals."

Except the mixed signals had been all hers. He'd been honest with her from the get-go. Well, if not exactly honest, he'd at least been up front.

Don't fall for me, Mallory. That wouldn't be good for either of us.

Right. She'd just stand firm and not fall.

Except...

Except she already had.

Chapter 17

What is the meaning of life?
All evidence to date points to chocolate.

After a sleepless night, Mallory worked a long shift, then took a detour home by Mrs. Burland's house. Last night the HSC had hosted a healthy living seminar given by Cece Martin, the local dietician, and Mrs. Burland had promised to go. Mallory had looked over the sign-in sheet from the event but Mrs. B hadn't shown up.

Mallory pulled into Mrs. B's driveway. The yard was neglected, as was the house. With a bad feeling, Mallory got out of her car, grabbed the bag of groceries she'd picked up, and knocked at the front door.

No one answered.

Mallory knocked again, knowing that Mrs. B probably wouldn't open the door to her, but something definitely felt off. She wriggled the handle, and the door opened. "Mrs. Burland?" she called out. "It's me, Mallory Quinn."

"Go away."

The voice sounded feeble and weak and somehow arrogant at the same time. Ignoring the command, Mallory walked inside the dark house and flipped on a light.

Mrs. Burland lay on the scarred wood floor at the base of a set of stairs.

Mallory dropped everything in her hands and rushed to her, setting two fingers against Mrs. B's carotid artery to search out a pulse.

Strong.

Sagging back on her knees, she let out a breath of relief. "You got dizzy and fell down the stairs?"

"No, I like to nap here," Mrs. B snapped out. "I told you to go away. You have no right to be here."

Okay, so little Miss Merry Sunshine was stringing her words together just fine, with no obvious disorientation. It was her vasovagal syncope then. Mallory ran a hand down the older woman's limbs and found nothing obviously broken. "Can you stand?"

"Sure. I just chose to be the rug today," Mrs. B snapped. "Why the hell are you here? Don't you ever get tired of saving people? *Why do you do it*?"

"Well, in your case, I do it for your charming wit and sweet nature." And anyway, there weren't enough shrinks or enough time to cover why she really did it... "Can you sit up?"

Mrs. Burland slapped Mallory's hands away but didn't move.

Well, that answered that question. Mallory sat on the floor next to her and rifled through the bag of groceries she'd brought. "What's going to float your boat today? I've got soup, a sandwich, or—"

"Just go away! I'm old. I'm alone. I'm going to die any second now. Just *let me*."

"You're not old," Mallory said. "You're just mean. And FYI, *that's* why you're alone. You could have friends if you'd stop snapping at everyone. Lucille'd take you into her posse in an instant if you were even the slightest bit less evil. She *loves* snark."

"I'm *alone*."

"Hello," Mallory said. "I'm sitting right here! You're *not* alone. You have me." She pulled out a snack-sized box of apple juice. "Your favorite."

"Not thirsty."

"Then how about some chicken soup?"

Mrs. Burland showed another sign of life as a slight spark came into her eyes. "Is it from a can?"

"No," Mallory said. "I spent all day cooking it myself. After raising the chickens and growing the carrots and celery in my garden."

Mrs. Burland sniffed. "I don't eat soup out of a can."

"Fine." Mallory pulled out a bag of prunes.

Mrs. Burland snatched the bag and opened it with shaking fingers.

Mallory smiled.

"You're enjoying my misery?"

"I knew I'd get you with the prunes."

After a minute or two, with the sugar in her system, Mrs. B glared at Mallory. "I'd have been fine without you."

"Sure. You'd be even better if you took care of yourself."

"What do you know? You're not taking care of yourself either."

"What does that mean?"

"In a storage attic?" Mrs. Burland asked snidely, then snorted at Mallory's look of shock. "Yes, I heard about your little interlude. Someone caught your Mr. Garrison coming downstairs from the auction, and then you following him a few minutes later looking all telltale mussed up. Either you were practicing for a WWE tryout or you'd been having some hanky-panky. Don't think just because I'm old that I don't know these things. I remember hormones."

Oh good Lord.

"And what kind of a woman dates a man who takes her to a storage attic?" Mrs. B wanted to know.

A red-blooded one. Ty Garrison was *seriously* potent, and Mallory defied even the most stalwart of women to be able to deny herself a Ty-induced orgasm. Just thinking it made her ache, because in spite of herself, she missed him *way* too much. She hoped he missed her too, that he wasn't planning to fill the void with...*Frances*. "Actually," she said, "it's not really an attic, but more of a storage area. And we're not dating."

"So you're giving away the milk for free?"

"First of all, I'm not a cow," Mallory said. "And second of all, we're *not* discussing this."

"You're trying to save him, right? Like you try to save everyone? Surely even you realize that a man like that isn't interested in a small town nurse, not for the long term."

The jab hit a little close to home because it happened to be true. But Mallory wasn't trying to save Ty.

She wouldn't have minded keeping him, though... "Watch it," she said mildly. "Or the prunes come with me."

"Hmph."

They sat there on the floor for a few minutes longer while Mallory checked Mrs. Burland's vitals again, which were stronger now. Then she glanced up and nearly screamed.

Jack Nicholson from *The Shining* stood in the front doorway.

Or Mr. Wykowski. He stepped inside. "Louisa," he said quietly, eyes on Mrs. B. "You all right?"

The oddest thing happened. Right before Mallory's eyes, Mrs. Burland changed. She softened. She...*smiled*. Or at least that's what Mallory thought the baring of her teeth meant.

"Of course," Mrs. B said. "I'm fine."

"Liar," Mr. Wykowski said, squatting beside her. "You get dizzy again?"

"Of course not."

"*Louisa.*"

Mrs. Burland's eyes darted away. "Maybe a little. But only for a minute."

Mr. Wykowski nodded to Mallory. "Good of you to stop by. She doesn't make it easy. She hasn't figured out that we take care of our own here in Lucky Harbor."

Mallory smiled at him, knowing she'd never be afraid of him again. "It's good to know she's not *alone*." She shot Mrs. Burland a long look.

Mrs. Burland rolled her eyes, but shockingly not a single bitchy thing crossed her lips.

There were more footsteps on the front porch and then another neighbor appeared. Lucille. She was in a neon green track suit today, which wasn't exactly flattering on a body that gravity hadn't exactly been kind to. Her wrinkled lips were in pink. Her tennis shoes were black and yellow.

You needed a pair of sunglasses to look at her.

"There you are, Teddy," Lucille said, smiling at Mr. Wykowski. "Ready for that walk around the block?"

Mrs. Burland narrowed her gaze. "He was visiting with *me*."

Lucille put her hands on her hips. "You don't even like visitors."

"Out of my house."

Lucille smiled. "Make me."

Mrs. Burland narrowed her eyes.

Lucille held out her hand. "Need help getting up first?"

Mrs. Burland struggled up by herself, glaring triumphantly at Lucille when she did it. "I could beat you around the block if I wanted."

"Yeah?" Lucille sized her up. "Prove it."

"I'll do that." Mrs. Burland moved toward the door, where Mr. Wykowski carefully drew her arm into the crook of his. Then Lucille flanked Mrs. Burland's other side.

And the three of them walked out the door and around the block.

Mallory went home. She parked, watered Mrs. Tyler's flowers, her grandma's flowers, and then unlocked her front door. She glanced at the little foyer desk—as she had every time since Ty had shown her a whole new use for it—and sighed. There was chocolate cake in her immediate future. If she wasn't going to have wild, high-calorie-burning sex, she was going to have to resort to some exercise.

"Meow."

"I hear you." She fed Sweet Pea and then changed, forcing herself to the pier for a run.

The quarter of a mile down to the end nearly killed her so she walked back, holding the stitch in her side. When she came up on the ice cream stand, she slowed even more. Lance wasn't working today but his older brother Tucker was.

"Hey Cutie," Tucker called out. "I've got a chocolate double with your name on it. Literally. We just created a new list of specials. Number one is The Good Girl Gone Bad."

She gave him a long, dark look and he laughed. "Come on," he said. "It's funny."

Maybe to someone whose name wasn't Mallory Quinn.

"Want one?"

More than her next breath. "No."

He leaned out the window, all lean, easy grace as he took in her sweaty appearance. "Wow, turning down ice cream. And you're running." His smile spread. "You're on a diet, aren't you?"

She blew out a breath. "Just trying to get some exercise and be healthy."

"You look good to me," he said.

Aw. That was nice. She was thinking maybe he'd be a nice addition to the Mr. Wrong list, but then he said, "And whatshis-face should tell you that in every attic he gets you into."

"Okay, first of all, it's a *storage area*!" And dammit. She was going to have to move. She went back to running. Without her ice cream.

It was the hardest thing she'd ever done.

She went home and glared at her foyer desk. "Somehow," she told it, "this is your fault."

The table had nothing to say in its defense.

"Fine. It's not your fault. It's Ty's." Her body ached for him, but it was more than that. Her mind ached for him, too.

Shaking her head at herself, she showered, got caught up in a *Charmed* season six marathon, and then headed over to Eat Me at the appointed time for a meeting of the Chocoholics.

As she entered Eat Me, the comforting sounds of people talking and laughing washed over her, as did scents of foods that made her stomach growl.

She'd skipped dinner. Tonight was very different from their first impromptu meeting. For one, there was no storm. It was fifty degrees outside, clear, and the air was scented with late spring.

For another, it wasn't midnight so the place wasn't deserted. She slipped onto the stool next to Grace and eyed the empty spot in front of her. "You refraining tonight?"

"Waiting on you."

Amy appeared, holding a cake and three forks.

Mallory grabbed one and dug in, guilt free since she'd run.

"No less than five customers have already tried to buy this cake," Amy said. "So you are welcome." She had to come and go at first as the diner emptied out. Then she stood on her side of the counter inhaling her third of the small cake. "God," she said on a moan. "Heaven on earth."

"Amazing," Grace admitted.

Mallory couldn't speak. She was too busy stuffing her face.

Amy swallowed and licked chocolate off her lips. "I'm calling this meeting to order. Mallory, you're first up."

"Nope. Not my turn."

"We've told you, you're first until we fix you." Grace smiled. "So spill. Tell us all."

Mallory sighed. "I'd rather talk about Amy and Sexy Forest Ranger Matt."

Grace went brows up at this and looked at Amy. "You putting out forest fires with that hot ranger who keeps coming in here for pie?"

"We have good pie," Amy said.

"There's all kinds of pie," Grace said.

Mallory nearly snorted cake out her nose, and Amy gave her a dirty look.

"This is *not* about me," she said haughtily and pointed her fork at Mallory.

Mallory stuffed in some cake.

"Uh oh," Grace said. "I'm sensing some slow down in Mission: Bad Girl."

"I wore the shoes," Mallory said. "And it was fun."

"Um, honey, from all accounts, you had more than some fun," Grace said, licking her fork.

"Accounts?"

"FB." Grace turned to Amy. "And thanks for the Facebook tip, by the way. It's a little addictive."

"You can't believe everything you read on there." Mallory sank onto her stool a little bit. "It's only a small percentage of the truth."

"Is that right?" Grace asked. "So what percentage of that picture with you and Ty looking cozy would you say is the truth?"

Mallory blew out a sigh and stabbed into the cake for another big bite. "We weren't...cozy. Then."

Grace grinned. "He's got that look. That big, sexy, I-know-how-to-please-a-woman-in-bed look."

Mallory propped up her head with her hand. With her other, she shoveled in more cake. "I don't want to talk about it."

"Yeah, but see, we *do*," Amy said.

"I broke it off," Mallory said and sighed when they gasped. "I told you, I'm not hard-wired for this bad girl stuff. Every time we were together I would find myself..." She closed her eyes. "Falling."

Grace reached for her hand and squeezed it.

Amy pushed the cake closer to Mallory.

"Thanks." Mallory shook her head. "I couldn't keep things light. He's just..." She sighed. "Too yummy."

"He was swimming the other day," Grace said. "In the ocean. I was sitting on the beach pouting after spending gas money to get to Seattle for interviews that went nowhere. Anyway, he swam for like two hours straight. Didn't know anyone but a Navy SEAL could do that. Did you know a Navy SEAL can find or hunt down anyone or anything?"

"So?" Amy said.

"So, I bet a guy like that could locate a clit without any problems."

Both Amy and Grace looked at Mallory expectantly. Mallory choked on her cake, and was still choking when someone came up behind her and patted her on the back.

She knew that touch. Intimately. Whipping around, she came face to face with Ty. Her heart clutched at the sight of him. Traitorous heart. And she couldn't help but wonder, had he been a SEAL? It made perfect sense. He'd sure had absolutely no problem finding her clit...

His gaze met hers for an unfathomably long beat, and as always, just at the sight of him, she got a little thrill. And also as always, he looked bigger than life, and a whole lot more than she could handle. But there was something different about him tonight. Tonight he seemed weary and a little rough around the edges, and her heart clenched again.

God, she'd missed him.

She didn't understand it, but he'd never looked more appealing. Or real. She wanted to take his hand in hers and kiss away his problems. Hold him.

She wanted to hold a caged lion.

It made no sense but it was the truth. She knew he was leaving, and he'd be taking a big piece of her heart along with him when he did, but that was a done deal. She also knew something else—that she wanted whatever he had to give her in the meantime. Because with him, she wasn't a caretaker. She wasn't a sister. She wasn't thinking, planning, overseeing.

She was just Mallory. And she felt...alive. So damn alive.

His eyes smiled. He touched the corner of her upper lip, then sucked on his finger. "Mmm," he said. "Chocolate."

Amy's jaw dropped open. Grace fanned herself. Ty looked at them, and they suddenly got very busy. Though Amy did give Mallory a "see, meeting interrupted *again*" look before she went off to serve a customer, and Grace remembered something she had to go do.

Which didn't stop everyone else in the diner from staring at them. "Oh good Lord," Mallory said. "Come on." She took the caged lion's hand and led him outside.

The stars were out in force tonight, like scattered diamonds on the night sky. The waves crashed up against the shore. They walked along the pier, past the dark arcade and the closed ice cream shop. Past everything until there was nothing but empty pier ahead and the black ocean. There Mallory stopped and leaned over the railing. "I'm sorry about the other day," she said quietly, facing the water. "I mean, I started this thing between us. I laid out the rules. So I had no right to change them on you without saying so, and then hold it against you."

He didn't say anything, and she turned to him, searching his impassive face, hoping to see understanding. Forgiveness. Or at the very least, a sign that he understood.

She got none of that, and her heart sank.

After a minute, he mirrored her pose, leaning on the railing to stare out at the water. "I grew up with military parents," he said. "I went into the military. And when I got out, I went to work for a private contractor to the government, doing...more military-like work. It's my job, it's my life. It's who I am."

She nodded. "I know."

"It requires things of me," he said. "Being alone, being the protector, keeping myself protected." He lifted a shoulder. "I don't know how to be anyone else."

"I don't want you to be anyone else, Ty. Ever. I like who you are."

He was quiet, absorbing that. "Frances is my boss. She's...proprietary."

To say the least. But he wasn't giving her all of it. "You've been with her. Sexually."

"Yes," he said, bluntly honest as always. "Before I worked for her, a very long time ago. It's over."

"For you," she said. "It's over for you."

He acknowledged that with a shrug. Not his problem. So it wouldn't be Mallory's either, she decided.

Turning to her, Ty ran a finger over the dainty gold chain at her neck, then beneath the infinity charm, looking at it for a moment. "After I lost my team in the plane crash, I spent the first six months recovering alone, by choice." He let out a breath and dropped his hand from her. "I couldn't...I didn't want anyone close. I still don't want anyone close."

He'd lost his parents, his friends. Everyone. She couldn't imagine how alone he must have felt.

Or maybe she could. Hadn't she, even surrounded by all the people in her life, *still* felt alone? Mallory scooped her necklace in her palm and tightened her fist on it. "Karen gave this to me right before she—" She closed her eyes for a minute, and pictured Karen's own laughing eyes. "It's the infinity sign," she told him. "Forever connected. She wore it all the time, and I always bugged her to let me borrow it. I wanted to be just like her. It used to drive her nuts. Then one day, she took the necklace off and just put it around my neck. She kissed my cheek and told me to be good, that being good would keep me out of the trouble that she'd always found herself in. She made me promise. Then she said she'd be watching me, guiding my way, making sure I was okay. I thought—I thought how sweet, but then..." Her throat tightened almost beyond bearing. "It was the last time I saw her," she said softly. "The next day she..." She let out a shuddery breath and shook her head, unable to speak.

With a low sound of empathy, Ty slid his hand to the nape of her neck, drawing her in against him. It was her undoing, and she fisted her hands in his shirt as a few tears escaped.

"I know your losses hurt," she managed. "But you're not alone, Ty." She said this fiercely, choking out the words. "You're not. I mean the pain doesn't go away, it *never* goes away, but it gets easier to remember them. And then one day, you'll remember them with a smile. I can promise you that."

He tightened his grip on her and nodded. They stood like that, locked together, a light breeze blowing her hair around. A strand of it clung to the stubble on his jaw and he left it there, bound to her, liking it...

"I thought maybe you'd left," she said.

"Not yet."

But soon... Those words, unspoken, hovered between them. When he got medically cleared, he'd be gone.

"Maybe you can't walk away from me," she said, meaning to tease, to lighten the moment.

"I can always walk away," he said. "Discipline runs deep."

Okay, so he wasn't feeling playful. Shaken, she took a step back and came up against the railing, but he put his hands on her and reeled her back in. "I need to get back to what I do," he said.

"You aren't your work."

"I am." Maintaining eye contact, he tightened his grip on her. "But I'm not ready to go yet."

"It's the sex," she said.

"It's more than sex."

"Not if it's still something that can be walked away from," she said.

He held her gaze, his own steady. Calm. So sure. "It's the way it has to be, Mallory."

She already knew that, oh how she knew it. The question was the same as always—could she live with it?

Yes.

No.

For now . . . Because the alternative was losing him right now, right this very minute, and she'd tried that. It didn't work for her. She wasn't ready to let him go.

He pressed his forehead to hers. "Your call," he said quietly. "Tell me to fuck off. Walk away from me right now and avoid any more heartbreak, I'm not worth it. Or—"

"Or," she said with soft steel. "I choose the *or*."

"Mallory." His voice was gruff. "You deserve better."

She pulled him farther down the pier, past the yacht club entrance and around the side of the building where no one who happened by could see them. There she pushed him up against the wall and kissed him. She took full advantage of his surprise, opening her mouth over his, causing a rush of heat and the melting of all the bones in her legs.

He was a soldier and knew how to turn any situation to his own advantage, and this was no exception. In less than a single heartbeat, he'd taken complete control of the kiss, stealing her breath and her heart with one sweep of his finger.

"If the decision is mine to make," she said breathing hard, her voice utterly serious, "then I'm keeping you, for as long as I can have you."

Chapter 18

*Falling in love is like eating a whole box of
chocolates—it seems like a good idea at first…*

The next day, Ty woke up in his bed with a gloriously naked
woman sprawled out over the top of him. Not that he was
opposed to such a phenomenon, but this gloriously naked woman
was all up in his space, and he'd always valued his own space.
He was a big guy and he didn't like to feel crowded. Mallory
was half his size, and as it turned out, she was a bed hog. She
was also a blanket hog and a pillow hog.

It's okay, he told himself. It was okay that they'd slept to-
gether because they both knew what this was and what it wasn't.
They'd fallen asleep together, that's all. It didn't mean anything.
Now if it happened again…well, *then* he'd panic. "Mallory."

She let out a soft snore, and he felt his heart squeeze. Fucking
heart. "Mallory. Are you working today?" He already had one
hand on her ass. Easy enough to add the other. When he squeezed,
then went exploring, a low appreciative moan escaped her lips,

and she obligingly spread her legs, giving him more room to work, murmuring something that sounded like "don't stop."

Then she froze and jerked upright. "*Whattimeisit?*"

"Seven," he said, nuzzling his face in her crazy hair.

"Seven? *Seven?* I have to be gone!" She leapt out of the bed, frantically searching for her various pieces of clothing.

Enjoying the Naked Mallory Show, he leaned back, hands behind his head.

"Where are my panties?" she demanded.

"Under the chair."

She dove under the chair, giving him a heart-stopping view that made him groan.

"They're not here!" she yelled, voice muffled from her head-down-ass-up position.

"No? Check under my jeans then," he said.

She straightened, and hair in her face—hell, hair everywhere—gave him a narrowed gaze.

He smiled.

She crawled to his jeans, another hot view, and snatched her panties. With her clothes in her arms, she vanished into his bathroom. Two minutes later she reappeared, dressed and looking thoroughly fucked. "Come here," he said, smiling.

"Oh hell no. If I come over there, you're going to kiss me."

"Yeah," he said. "I am."

"And then you'll . . . *you know*."

He laughed, feeling light-hearted and . . . happy. "I do know. I know exactly what I want to do to you. I want to put my mouth on your—"

"Oh, God." She shook her head and grabbed her keys. "*I have to go!*"

"Five minutes," he said, and thought he had her when she hesitated, biting her lower lip, looking tempted. "It'll be the best five minutes of your day," he promised.

"I usually need more like fifteen minutes."

"Not last night you didn't. Last night you only needed four before you—"

"*Bye*," she said, laughing, and shut his door.

Ty lay there smiling like an idiot for a few minutes. Then his phone beeped. Rolling out of bed, he accessed his messages. Once upon a not-so-long-ago time, there were only messages from Frances. That was no longer the case. The first message was from Ryan.

"Hey, man," the vet said. That was it, the full extent of the message. Pretty typical of Ryan, and it could mean anything from "let's have dinner" to "I'm jonesing and need someone to talk to."

Matt had called as well, looking for a sparring partner. Josh had called inquiring about his health—and Ty knew Josh meant his mental health, not his leg.

Ty stared at his phone in surprise. At some point, when he'd been busy resenting like hell this slow-paced, sleepy little town and everyone in it, something had happened.

He'd made ties, strings on the heart he wasn't even sure he had. His smile faded as he listened to his last message, which contained no words, just a seething silence.

Frances.

He should call her and check in. After all, he was cleared to go back. But he didn't call. Instead he checked up on Ryan, then he finished the last of the cars lined up for him—Matt's Jimmy.

Now he could go back.

Almost.

He showered and drove to the Health Services Clinic just as it was closing up for the day. It was Thursday, and he knew there were no activities or meetings scheduled there that night.

He'd checked.

The front room was empty, but he could hear voices so he

followed them and found Mallory in one of the small rooms, door open. She was facing a woman in her sixties. The woman was sitting in a chair, her face pinched like she'd eaten a sour apple.

Mallory was wearing purple scrubs today, and it was a good color for her. Her hair had been tied back, probably hours ago, and as usual, strands had escaped.

She wasn't good at hiding her feelings, and right now she was on edge, tired, and frustrated.

A long day, no doubt, made longer since they'd spent most of the night tearing up his sheets. He knew exactly what he'd do to relax her, but he had to remind himself that she wasn't his to take care of.

His own choice.

He was leaving, and someday, maybe someday soon, she'd stay up all night with someone else. Someone who would take care of her, help her unwind at the end of the day. Maybe someone from her list.

But if it was Anderson, Ty was going to kick his ass, just on principle. And if it was Josh, Ty'd...Jesus. It'd be whoever Mallory chose, and Ty had nothing to say about it, not even if her new Mr. Wrong used the guise of showing her how to hold a tool to kiss her. Not even if that Mr. Wrong bent her over a piece of furniture, taking her in front of a mirror, forcing her to see how gorgeous and amazing she really was. It was none of his business.

But it sucked.

"Just trust me," Mallory said to her patient, moving to a cabinet. She pulled a set of keys from her pocket and eyed the medicine samples lined up there before grabbing a box. "Take these. One a day."

"What are you poisoning me with now?" the woman asked.

"Vitamins," Mallory said.

The woman set the samples down. "Vitamins are a sham. It's the drug companies' way of making money off all us unsuspecting idiots."

Mallory put the vitamins back into the woman's hands. "Your blood work shows you're anemic. These will help. Or you can keep passing out in the bathroom and waiting until EMS finds you on the floor with your pants at your ankles again. Your choice, Mrs. Burland."

There was a long silence during which the woman glared at Mallory. "You used to be afraid of me. You used to quail and tremble like a little girl."

"Things change," Mallory said in a mild voice. No judgment, no recriminations. "Take the vitamins. Don't make me come over every night and pinch your nose and shove them down your throat."

"Well fine, if you're going to out-mean me."

"I am," Mallory said firmly.

"See, you *have* changed. You've gotten a tough skin. You've learned to hold back and keep your emotions off your sleeve for the world to see. You are very welcome."

"Oh, it wasn't *all* you," Mallory said, and Ty felt an odd tightening in his chest, because he knew who'd changed her.

Him.

He was such an asshole.

Turning from the woman, Mallory caught sight of him standing there. Her surprised smile only added to the ache in Ty's chest but he nodded to her and stepped back, leaning against the wall in the hall to wait.

Mallory looked at her patient. "I have something else for you; hold on." She came out into the hall, shutting the door behind her. She flashed Ty another smile and vanished into the next room. When she returned, she handed her patient some flyers before guiding her from the exam room and out front.

A few minutes later Mallory was back. "Hey."

"Hey. You need a lock on the front door when you're here alone," he said.

"I wasn't alone until now, and this is Lucky Harbor. I'm as safe as it gets."

"You're not safe here with the drugs."

"The meds are locked."

"Flimsy lock," he said. "Especially for someone who's desperate."

"It's only temporary. We're getting a much better set-up next week." She smiled, still not taking her safety seriously enough for him. "So what's up? What brings you here?"

"You owe me a favor," he said. "And I'm collecting."

She sputtered, then laughed. "I owe *you* a favor? Since when?"

"Since the night I pretended to be your date at the auction."

"Pretended? You were supposed to be my date all along," she reminded him.

"But I was concussed and didn't remember making the date. Which means that you owe me for that, too, taking advantage of an injured guy." He *tsk*ed. "Shame on you, Mallory Quinn. Imagine what people would say if they knew you'd done such a thing."

She narrowed her eyes, clearly amused by his playfulness, but not fully trusting him.

Smart girl. He shouldn't be trusted. Not by a long shot.

"So what exactly is this favor?" she asked. "And don't tell me it involves any storage rooms." She paused. "Okay, so we both know I'd hop into another closet with you so fast it'd make your head spin."

With a laugh, he pushed off the wall and came toward her. "It's not that," he said. "I need the same thing you needed that night."

"An orgasm?" she asked cheekily.

"Only if you ask *very* nicely. But I meant a date."

Her expression went dubious. "A date? Now?"

"Yes."

She went from dubious to blank-faced. "A *last* date?"

Well, hell. What could he say to that? It was the truth. "Actually," he said. "I don't believe we ever had a first date." He took her hand and brought it to his mouth, brushing his lips against her palm as he watched her over their joined fingers. "Say yes, Mallory."

Staring at him, she turned her hand, cupping his face, her fingers gliding across his jaw. "Always."

He felt his heart roll, exposing its underbelly. Nothing he could do about that. He was equipped to eliminate threats, protect and serve.

Not to love.

Never to love.

Mallory didn't know what to expect. Ty wouldn't tell her where they were going, but they were on the highway, heading toward Seattle. Once there, he drove to a very swank block lined with designer shops and parked.

"Um," she said.

He pulled her out of the car and into a dress shop. "Something for the orchestra," he said to the pretty sales woman who came forward. He turned to Mallory. "Whatever you want."

She was confused. "What?"

"The auction. The night on the town package."

Again, she just gaped at him. "Was that supposed to be a full explanation?"

"It's tonight," he said. "Tonight's the last night of the orchestra."

"So you what, kidnapped me to take me to it?"

"Thought you could use a night off. And you said you never got to date much." He looked endearingly baffled. "And don't women like this surprise romantic shit?"

Aw. Dammit. "What, you mean romantic '*shit*'?"

He winced, for the first time since she'd known him, looking uncomfortable in his own skin. "You're right," he said. "This was a stupid idea. It's not too late to call this whole thing off and go get a pizza and beer. Whatever you want."

The guy had grown up on military bases and then given his adult years over to the same lifestyle. Mallory knew he was far more at ease in the role of big, bad tough guy than romance guy. Certainly he'd rather have a pizza and beer over the orchestra.

And yet he'd thought of her. He wanted to give her a night off. He'd wanted to share that night off with her, and he'd brought her to a place filled with gorgeous, designer clothes to do it so that she wouldn't stress about the lack thereof in her own closet. It was a send off, a finale, a good-bye, and she knew it. But damn. Damn, she wanted this. With him. Stepping into him, she went up on tip-toe and kissed his smooth jaw. He'd shaved for her. "Thank you," she whispered.

He turned his head and claimed her mouth in one quick, hot kiss. "Take your time. I'll be waiting."

If only that was really true.

A limo pulled up front, and that's when she remembered: the package came with a limo. "Oh my God."

He leaned in close. "I'm hoping by the end of the night you'll be saying 'Oh, Ty'..." And with that, he walked out the front door toward the limo.

She stared after him. "That man is crazy."

"He's crazy *fine*," the sales clerk murmured. "And he did say whatever you wanted..." She gestured around her. "So what would you like?"

Thirty minutes later, Mallory was decked out in a silky, strappy siren-red dress that made her feel like a sex kitten. She kept trying to see the price tag but the clerk had been discreet, and firm. "He said you weren't allowed to look at the prices."

Good Lord.

By the time Mallory exited the shop, she felt like Cinderella. And her prince stepped out of the limo to greet her in a well-fitted, expensive suit that nearly made her trip over her new strappy high-heeled sandals. She'd seen him in a suit before. She'd seen him in jeans, in cargoes, and in nothing at all. He always looked mouth-wateringly gorgeous. But tonight, something felt different... "Wow."

Ignoring that, he took her hand and pulled her in. "You take my breath away," he said simply.

And that's when she realized. It was his eyes. He was looking at her differently. Heart-stoppingly differently.

Dinner was at a French restaurant and was so amazing she was starting to regret not going one size up on the dress. But the wine quickly reduced any lingering anxiety. The problem with that was, combined with a long day and almost no sleep the night before, by the time they got to the orchestra, her eyes were drooping. Still, she accepted another glass of white wine, and they found their seats. The curtain went up.

And that's the last thing Mallory remembered about the orchestra.

When she woke up, the theater was nearly empty, and Ty was leaning over her, an amused smile on his face.

"What?" she said, blinking, confused. "Where?"

His smile spread to a grin. "You snore."

"I do not!" She straightened, stared at the closed curtain on the stage and took in the fact that the few people left around them were leaving. "It's over? I missed the whole thing?"

He pulled her to her feet. "That's okay. You didn't miss the best part."

"What's the best part?"

"Wait for it." He led her back to the limo. He closed the partition between them and the driver, then pulled her onto his lap.

"Is this the best part?" she asked breathlessly when he slid his hands beneath her dress and palmed her butt cheeks, bared by her lacy thong.

"Wait for it," he whispered against her mouth, and spent the drive back to the Shelby creating a slow burn with nothing more than his mouth on hers and his hands caressing her curves.

"More," she demanded.

"*Wait for it*."

"I'm growing very tired of those three words," she said.

He drove her home, then walked her in, slowly stripping her out of her beautiful new dress and bra and panties, groaning at the sight of her in just her heels.

"So help me, if you tell me to wait for it one more time," she warned, hands on her bare hips.

"Christ, you are the most beautiful woman I've ever seen," he said. He gave her a little push, and she fell to her bed. "I know how tired you are, so feel free to just lay there and relax."

"I'm not tired," she said. "I took a very nice nap at the orchestra."

With a soft laugh, he crawled up her body, taking little nips out of her as he went. "I'm offering to do all the work here."

"I'm more of an equal opportunity type of woman."

He smiled against her mouth. "Is that right? Well, however you want to be is fine with me. But you should know, I'm ready for the best part now."

"Me too. What is it?" she asked eagerly.

He gently bit her lower lip and tugged, then let it go, soothing the ache with his tongue, making every single nerve ending on her body stand up and beg for the same treatment. "You. You're the best part."

Her heart caught. "Me?"

"Definitely you," he breathed, and then set about proving it.

Chapter 19

*I want it all. And I want it smothered in
whipped cream and chocolate!*

The next afternoon, Mallory was in the ER doing her damnedest not to dwell on the fact that Ty was probably leaving town at
any moment. She kept busy and was checking in a patient that
Sheriff Thompson had dragged in after breaking up a fight when
she took a call from Camilla.

"I'm at the HSC, just closing after the teen advocacy meeting,"
the young LVN said. "And we have a problem."

Mallory raced over there, and Camilla showed her the medicine
lock-up. "I think there's four boxes of Oxycontin missing."

Mallory's heart sank. "What?"

"A month's supply."

Mallory stared at the cabinet in complete and utter shock.
"*What?*"

"Yeah. I called Jane," Camilla said. "I didn't want it to come out later and have anyone think it happened on my watch. I never got into the lock-up today at all."

Mallory nodded. That meant it had happened yesterday, when *she'd* been in charge. She'd gone into the cabinet several times that she could remember off the top of her head. There'd been the birth control samples she'd given out to Deena and the smoker's patches she'd given Ryan. The vitamins for Mrs. Burland. Mallory recalled that one because Ty had been there. And she flashed back to him admitting he'd gotten too attached to his pain meds.

Cold turkey, he'd said with a harsh laugh. *More like hot hell*.

A tight feeling spread through her chest. Whoever had taken those samples had known what they were taking. There were only two reasons to take Oxycontin. To sell, or to use.

To use, she decided, remembering Ty's words. It was an act of desperation to steal them, and addicts were desperate.

Karen had been desperate, and Mallory had failed her. Badly.

Who else was she failing?

She went back to the ER heartsick. She was in the middle of teaching some brand new firefighter paramedics how to start IVs when she was summoned to Bill's office. She headed that way, expecting to get her hair blown back.

She didn't expect to face several board members, including Jane and her mother.

"Tell us how this could have happened," Bill said, tone stern.

Mallory drew a deep breath. "We received samples early yesterday for the weekend health clinic. I stocked the cabinet myself and locked it."

"Exactly how much is missing?"

He already knew this. He knew everything. He just wanted to hear her say it. "Four boxes," she told him. "Each was a week's supply."

"So a month. You've lost a month's supply of Oxycontin."

Mallory nodded. She was pissed, afraid, frustrated. She'd gone over the inventory a hundred times in her head, hoping she'd just miscalculated.

But she hadn't.

The meds were missing. Someone had stolen them from beneath her own nose. An anguished, distraught, frantic act, by someone she most likely knew by name.

"We'd like the list of everyone who came through the HSC yesterday," Bill said.

This was what she'd been dreading. She didn't know what she wished for the most, that Ty hadn't shown up at all, or that someone else she knew and cared about had. "Bill, we're supposed to be anonymous."

"And you were supposed to make sure something like this never happened. The list, Mallory. I want it by tomorrow morning."

"I can fix this," she said. "Let me—"

"The only way you can fix this is by trusting me to do my job," Bill told her. "And that job is the bottom line. I'm in charge of the bottom line. Do you understand?"

"Of course. But—"

"No buts, Mallory. Don't make this come down to your job being on the line as well as the HSC."

Mallory's heart lurched, and she ground her back teeth so hard she was surprised they didn't dissolve.

"And I'm sure this goes without saying," Bill said, "but until we solve this, the HSC stays closed."

A stab to the gut. "Understood." Somehow she managed to get out of there and through the rest of her shift. All she wanted was to be alone, but her mother caught up with her in the parking lot. "What aren't you telling us, Mallory?"

Mallory was good at hiding her devastation. She'd had lots of practice. "What do you mean?"

"Honey, it's me. The woman who spent thirty-six hours in labor with you. I *know* when you're hiding something."

"Mom, I have to go."

Ella looked deep into her eyes and shook her head. "Oh, no. Oh, Mallory." She cupped Mallory's jaw. "Who are you trying to save this time?"

"Mom, please. Just go back to work."

"In a minute." Ella cupped Mallory's face and kissed each cheek and then her forehead. "You can't save them all. You know that, right?"

"Yes." Mallory closed her eyes. "I don't know what happened yesterday, but whoever it was, it was my fault. Someone I know is in trouble. And it's like Karen all over again." The sob reached up and choked her, shutting off her words, and she slapped a hand over her mouth to keep it in.

Her mother's eyes filled. "Oh, honey. Honey, no. What happened to Karen wasn't your fault."

Mallory closed her eyes. "She came to me that night."

Ella gasped. "What?"

"Karen. She came into my bedroom. She said she needed me." Mallory swallowed hard. "But I'd been...I'd been needing her and she hadn't been there for me. Not once. So I lashed out at her. I said terrible things to her. And you know what she did? She gave me her necklace. She told me she loved me. She pretty much said good-bye, Mom, and I missed it."

"Mallory, you listen to me," her mother said fiercely, giving her a little shake. "You were sixteen."

"She felt like she was alone, like she had no other options. But she *wasn't* alone. There were lots of options." Mallory let out a breath. "I failed her. I have to live with that. And now I'm just trying to make sure I don't fail anyone else. I need to make sure no one else falls through the cracks."

"But at what cost?" her mother asked softly. "You're the one who said it, Mallory. There are just some things that people have to do for themselves. They have to find their own will, their own happy. Their own path."

"Yes, and this is mine."

Ella sighed and hugged her. "Oh, honey. Are you sure? Because this one's going to cost you big. It's going to cost you your job and your reputation."

"It already has. And yes, I'm sure. I have to do this, Mom. I have to figure this out and fix it."

Ella nodded her reluctant understanding, and Mallory got into her car and drove straight to Ty's house. His house, not his home. Because this was just a stop on his life's path, a destination, not the finish line.

She'd admired that about him.

Now it scared her.

Lots of things scared her. Not too long ago, she'd asked him what he was frightened of, and he'd said he was afraid of not living.

They weren't so different after all, and God, she needed verification of that fact right now.

He didn't answer her knock. The place was quiet. Empty. She put a hand to her chest, knowing damn well that last night had been a good-bye. For all she knew, he was already gone. For a minute, she panicked. After all, she had asked him not to tell her when he left. A very stupid, rash decision on her part. But when she peeked into the garage window and saw the Shelby, she sagged in relief.

Her relief was short-lived, though, because she had no idea where he might go on a night like this. None. And that didn't sit so well.

She was falling in love with a guy that she was afraid she didn't know at all.

Talk about taking a walk on the dark side . . .

Frustrated and annoyed, she went home. She didn't bother with her usual routine. Screw the flowers. Screw everything, even the cat. She simply strode through her place, intending to get into bed and pull the covers over her head and pretend the day hadn't happened.

Denial. She was thy Queen.

She'd dropped her purse in the living room. Kicked off her shoes in the hallway. She walked into her bedroom struggling with the buttons on her sweater. Giving up, she yanked the thing over her head and got her hair tangled in the buttons. "Dammit!" She was standing there arms up, face covered by the sweater, when two strong arms enveloped her.

She let out a startled scream and was immediately gathered against a warm, hard form that her body knew better than her own. "Ty," she gasped.

He pressed her back against the bedroom door. "You expecting anyone else?"

"I wasn't expecting anyone at all. Help me, I'm caught."

Instead he slid a thigh between hers.

"*Ty*." She struggled with the sweater some more and succeeded in catching her hair on a sweater button. "*Ouch*! I can't get loose."

"Hmm." His hands molded her body, everywhere. "I like you a little helpless."

She fought anew. "That's sexist."

"Sexy," he corrected, untangling her, tossing the offending sweater over his head while still holding her captive against the door. "What were you trying to do?"

"Strip." Crash. Forget. "I went looking for you."

"You found me." He tugged, and then her scrub pants were gone.

She gasped. "What are you doing?"

"Helping you strip." He slid a hand into her panties, his

eyes dark and heavy lidded with desire. "Tell me why you went looking for me."

There was something in his voice, something edgy, dark. "I wanted to see you." It was God's utter truth. She knew in her heart that he wouldn't have taken those meds. He wouldn't do anything to hurt her, ever. She knew that, just as she knew that her time with him was limited. Too limited.

She was going to be brave about that, later. "I want you," she whispered.

In the dark hallway, his eyes gleamed with heat and intent, and then his mouth was on hers, hard. She sucked his tongue into her mouth, swallowing his rough groan, savoring the taste of him. "My bed," she said. "I need you in my bed."

They staggered farther into the room and fell onto the mattress. "Hurry, Ty."

"Take everything off then," he demanded in that quiet voice that made her leap to obey. She pulled off her top and unhooked her bra. She was wriggling out of her panties when she got distracted by watching him strip. He tugged his shirt over his head, and then his hands went to his button fly, his movements quick and economical as he bared his gorgeous body. In two seconds he was naked, one hundred percent of his attention completely fixed on her. And apparently she was moving too slowly because he took over, wrapping his fingers around each of her ankles, giving a hard tug so that she fell flat on her back.

He was on her in a heartbeat. "I was working on a car, but all I could see was you, running your fingers over the brake line, holding onto the wrench. It made me hard."

She slid her hands down his sinewy, cut torso, planning on licking that same path as soon as she got a chance. "Me touching your tools makes you hard?"

"Yeah," he said silkily. "Your hands on my tool makes me *very* hard."

She laughed, and he nipped at her shoulder. "Your scent was there, too," he said almost accusingly. "In the garage, lingering like you were right there, pestering me with all your questions."

"Well—" She frowned. "*Hey.*"

His lips claimed hers in a hungry, demanding kiss. "I kept hearing your voice," he said between strokes of his tongue. "Pretending to be all sweet and warm, when really you had me pinned to the wall and were drilling me."

"Return the favor," she said breathlessly. "Pin me down and drill me, Ty."

He looked torn between laughter and determination to do just that. "You've had me in a fucking state all day, Mallory Quinn."

"How bad is this state?"

"*Bad,*" he said, grinding his hips to hers to prove it. "So bad I couldn't function."

"Mmm," she moaned at the feel of him so hard for her. "So what did you do?"

"Jacked off."

She choked out a laugh. "You did not."

"Did."

The air crackled with electricity, and he kissed her again. His hands were just as demanding as his mouth, finding her breasts, teasing her nipples, sliding a hand between her legs. Finding her already hot and wet, he groaned.

"Please, Ty. I need you. I need you so much."

"Show me," he said.

"Show you?"

"*Show me.*"

Knowing what he meant, she bit her lower lip. He'd just admitted to touching himself while thinking about her; surely she could return the favor. In the end, he helped her, entwining their fingers and dragging their joined hands up her body, positioning them on her breasts, urging her to caress her own nipples. When she did, he pulled his fingers free and watched with a low groan. Then, apparently convinced she would continue on, he slid down her body, kissing his way between her thighs. Slowly, purposefully, he sucked her into his mouth, making her writhe so much that he had to hold her down. Her toes curled, her eyes closed, her fingers abandoned her breasts and slid into his hair to hold him to that spot because God, just one more stroke of that tongue—

But he stopped. Just pulled his mouth away until she looked at him.

"Keep your eyes open," he said, and when he lowered his mouth again, she did as he'd told her, watching as he took her right to the edge again. It was the hardest thing she'd done so far with him. But nothing about Ty was in her comfort zone, not his life's experiences, not the way he made her feel, and certainly not how he got her to behave in the bedroom. It felt so absolutely wicked to keep looking at him, to be a voyeur in her own bed, but try as she might to hold on, her vision faded when he pushed her over the edge with shocking ease.

When she could open her eyes again, he easily held himself just above her, making room for himself between her thighs as he cupped her face, his own now struggling with control.

She knew he'd never intended for things to go this far. She hadn't either. But as she tugged him close and kissed him, she felt their co-mingled best intentions go right out the window.

Taking control, he slid his big hands to her bottom and pushed inside her with one hard thrust. "Oh, fuck," he said. "You feel amazing."

It was just the passion of the moment, she tried to tell herself, but she felt him to the depths of her soul. And in her heart of hearts, she knew he felt far more for her than he let on. It was in his actions, and she wrapped her arms around his broad shoulders and melted into the hard planes of his body. Emotion welled up within her, and she had to clamp her mouth closed to hold in the words that wanted to escape.

"Mallory."

Opening her eyes, she stared up into his, her heart clenching hard. His hands slid up to her hips, positioning her exactly as he wanted, and when he thrust again, she gasped as pleasure swamped her. Wrapping her legs around his waist, she whispered his name, needing him to move.

Instead, he lowered his head and traced her nipple with his tongue, causing her to arch her back and shamelessly roll her hips into his. "*Ty*."

His fingers skimmed roughly up her spine, leaving a trail of heat that she felt all the way to her toes, until his hands gripped hers on either side of her head. "I'm right here," he promised, taking her exactly where she needed to go without words. And that was it, the beginning of the point of no return for her. He was exactly what she'd wanted, what she'd never had the nerve to reach out and grasp for herself before. Ironic, really. He didn't want her to depend on him, and yet he was the one who'd given her the security to be who she was. If only he'd keep looking at her the way he was right now.

For always.

It wasn't going to happen, she knew that. She had to settle for this, for the right now. Telling herself she was stronger than she knew, that she could do it, she cupped his face and let herself go, moving with him in the age-old dance of lovers. And her release, when it came, shattered her apart and yet somehow made her whole at the same time.

At some point in the night, Ty woke up wrapped in warm woman. And it wasn't her clinging to him. Nope, that was all him. He had one hand entangled in her crazy hair, the other on her bare ass, holding her possessively and protectively to him.

Jesus.

The night of the orchestra had been a mistake, and everyone was allowed one mistake. But if he slept with her tonight, it would be mistake number two.

He didn't make mistakes, much less the same one twice. It took some doing, but he managed to get out of the bed without waking her. He gathered his things and walked out of her bedroom, quietly shutting the door behind him. Dumping everything at his feet to sort, he hesitated. In his real life, hesitating was a good way to get dead. And yet he did just that, turning back to her bedroom door, his hands up on the frame above his head. He wanted to go back in there.

Bad.

Don't do it, man. He looked down at his shit. No shirt. One sock. From his pants pocket, his phone was blinking. Frances, he knew. Because she and Josh had finally connected. The gig was up; she knew he was cleared. His last message from her had been something along the lines of *get your sorry ass back to work*. This had been accompanied by a text with a confirmation number for a one-way, first-class airplane ticket back to D.C.

He stubbed his toe on his own shoes. Swearing softly, he kicked one down the hallway, then went still when the bedroom door opened and the light came on.

Mallory stood there blinking sleepily, tousled and rumpled and wearing nothing but his shirt. "Hey," she murmured. "You okay?"

"Yeah. Sorry. Didn't mean to wake you."

"Are you leaving?"

"Yeah, I . . . Yeah, I'm leaving." He needed to. Now. Because he was starting to wonder how he was going to leave Lucky Harbor at all.

Mallory made a soft noise in the back of her throat. She was looking at his jeans still on the floor, and the two things that had spilled out of his pockets. His keys.

And the empty Vicodin bottle.

She bent and picked up the bottle, staring at it for a long time. He saw her taking in the two-month-old date of the prescription, the fact that there were refills available to him which he clearly hadn't used. Finally she handed the bottle back to him with a gentle smile. "Stay, Ty. Stay with me for tonight. Just tonight."

He couldn't. Staying would be a mistake. "Mallory—"

She covered his mouth with her fingers, then took his hand in hers, drawing him back into her bedroom and into her bed, and into her warm, soft heart.

Chapter 20

*Exercise is a dirty word. Every time I hear it
I wash my mouth out with chocolate.*

The next day Ty and Matt spent time in the gym, then Matt went home with Ty to pick up the Jimmy. Matt took one look around the cleaned-up garage. "You're leaving."

"Always was." Ty held out the Jimmy's keys but Matt didn't take them.

"The lease on this place is paid up until summer," Ty said. "Use it if you want. And I want you to take the tools."

"I'll keep them for you. You'll be back."

Ty looked at him, and Matt shook his head. "Christ," he said on a disgusted sigh. "Tell me you're not just going to vanish on her and not come back at all. You're not that big a dick, right?"

"You want to test drive this thing or what?"

"So you *are* that big a dick."

"Look, she made me promise not to say good-bye."

"And you believed her?" Matt asked. "Shit, and I thought *I* was stupid with women."

"You are." Ty tossed him the keys at him, leaving Matt no choice but to catch them.

They took the Jimmy out on a test drive. Matt drove like a guy who knew the roads intimately, down-shifting into the hairpin turns, accelerating out of them. He took them along a two-lane, narrow, curvy highway that led almost straight up. On either side were steep, unforgiving, isolated peaks, so lush—thanks to a wet spring—that they resembled a South American rainforest.

When the road ended, Matt cranked the Jimmy into four-wheel drive and kept going, making his own trail.

"You know where you're headed, City Boy?" Ty asked.

Matt sent him a long look. "What, you think you can find your way around these mountains?"

"I could find my way around on Mars," Ty assured him. "Though if you get us dead out here, I'll follow you to the depths of hell and kill you again."

"Told you, not everyone's going to die on you. I'm sure as hell not."

"See that you don't."

Matt drove on, until eventually they came to a plateau. The three-hundred-and-sixty degree vista was staggering. The jagged mountain peaks were still tipped in white. The lower ranges were covered in a thick blanket of green. And to their immediate west, the Pacific shimmered brilliantly.

"Beaut Point," Matt said.

The plateau was about the size of a football field, giving a very decent view of the ocean smashing into a valley of rocks hundreds of feet below. "Good spot," Ty said.

"I chase a lot of stupid teenagers off this ledge. They come four-wheeling up here in daddy's truck to get laid. Then the geniuses get lost, and I end up having to save their miserable asses."

"Tough job."

"Beats scooping gangbangers off the streets of Chicago any day of the week," Matt agreed. "And I imagine it's also a hell of a lot more fun than Afghanistan or Iraq this time of year."

Ty looked over at him. "Don't forget South America. My favorite."

Matt smiled. "Nothing compares to Chicago in high summer in full tactical gear."

"Pussy."

"Sure. If being a pussy means staying in Paradise over leaving for a stupid adrenaline rush in some godforsaken Third World country."

Ty shook his head and stared out at "Paradise."

"Ever climb?" Matt asked.

"Only when I have to."

Matt gestured with his chin out to a sharp outcropping at least three miles across the way. "Widow's Peak. Climbed it last weekend. It's a get-your-head-on-straight kind of spot."

"Was your head crooked?" Ty asked.

"Yeah, actually. But today I figured that was you."

"My head's on perfectly straight, thanks."

"Yeah?"

"Yeah."

"Huh," Matt said.

Ty looked at him. "Okay, let's save some time here. Why don't you just tell me whatever it is that you're fishing for?"

"All right," Matt said. "Someone stole some samples out of the Health Services Clinic from right beneath Mallory's nose."

Ty's gut tightened. "Today? Was she hurt?"

Matt was watching him carefully. "Yesterday. And no."

"What was taken?"

"Pain meds. She doesn't know when it happened, actually. She says it could have been at a couple of different points during the day."

Ty went still, remembering last night, remembering the look on Mallory's face when she'd seen the empty bottle fall out of his jeans pocket.

She'd known then, and she hadn't said a word. Had she thought he'd taken the pills? He tried to think of a reason that she wouldn't have mentioned the missing meds that didn't involve her thinking it was him. But with a grim, sinking feeling in his gut, he realized he couldn't. "Is she taking shit for it?"

"You could say that, yeah. As of right this minute, HSC is shut down, and if it gets out why, it's going to stay that way."

"She doesn't deserve the blame."

"She accepted the blame."

"How do you know all of this?"

"I'm on the hospital board. Look," he said at Ty's dark expression, "at this point only we board members know. They want her to turn in a list of who was at HSC during the hours that the meds went missing. She's objecting because it's supposed to be anonymous. That put her job in the ER at risk as well as at HSC."

Ty let out a breath and closed his eyes. "Oh, Christ."

"What?"

"I was in there yesterday afternoon." He opened his eyes and looked at Matt. "I was at HSC."

"Did you do it?" Matt asked mildly. "Did you lift the drugs?"

"Hell, no."

"Didn't figure you for being stupid," Matt said, watching as Ty pulled out his phone and hit a number. "And we don't get reception out here. No one does. Listen, this gets a little worse. Jane, her boss, rode her hard about this, and..."

"*And?*"

"Mallory walked off her job. She quit."

Ty held his hands out. "Keys."

"Excuse me?"

"I'm driving back." He needed to see Mallory. Now. *Yesterday*.

"Why are *you* driving back?" Matt wanted to know.

"Because we're in a hurry, and you drive like a girl."

Halfway back to town, Ty finally got phone reception and hit Mallory's number. While it rang in his ear, Matt *tsk*ed. "You need a blue tooth," he said. "Or you're going to get a ticket."

Ty ignored him, thinking *pick up, pick up*...but Mallory didn't. "She's probably at home, phone dead."

And he didn't have her house number.

Matt shook his head. "Nope, she's not at home."

Ty looked at him.

"Oh, did you want to know where she is?" When Ty just narrowed his eyes, Matt smiled. "Yeah, you want to know. She's at the diner. I was there earlier, heard Amy take a call from her. Something about a Chocoholic meeting."

There was something in Matt's voice when he said Amy's name, and needing a distraction, Ty slid him a glance. "So what's with you and the pretty waitress?"

"Nothing."

"There's a whole lot of tension between you two for nothing."

Matt pleaded the Fifth.

"You screw something up?"

Matt's sunglasses were mirrored, giving nothing away. He was not answering, which was the same thing as saying yeah, he'd screwed something up. "What did you do?" Ty asked.

"Jack shit."

Yeah, right. They came into town and bypassed the road to Matt's house.

"Hey," Matt said.

"Hang on, coming in hot." Ty pulled up to the diner with a screech of tires.

Matt let go of the dash and looked at him.

Ty shrugged. "Maybe misery loves company."

"You mean maybe misery loves to watch other people fuck up."

"I'm not going to fuck anything up."

"Uh huh."

Ty shook his head and went into the diner, which had been decorated for spring. There were brightly colored papier-maché flowers and animals hanging from the ceiling tiles, and streamers around the windows. It didn't much match the 50s décor but it was definitely eye-popping.

The place was full with the dinner crowd, the noise level high. Ty recognized just about everyone there, which meant he'd been here far too long. He could see Jan hustling a large tray to a table. And there was Ryan in a far corner with two guys from NA. Blue-haired Lucille was there too, with a group of other blue-haired, nosy old bats. Ty shifted past the small group of people waiting to be seated because he could see Mallory at the counter. Grace was on one side of her, with Amy on the other side of the counter.

Ty came up behind Mallory, who was staring down at a cake that said "Happy Birthday Anderson" as Amy lit the candles.

All around them were the general, noisy sounds of a diner. Dishes clanking, voices raised in conversation, laughter—each table or group involved in their own world. This particular little world, of the three women, was exclusive, and not a one of them was paying their surroundings any attention.

Mallory, the woman who'd claimed to have given up chocolate, licked her lips. "We should skip the candles," she said to Amy. "You have a full house right now. You're too busy for this."

"Oh no," Amy said. "We agreed. When bad shit happens, we meet. We eat." She lit the last candle and handed each of them a fork. "I've already called Tara and told her that Anderson's cake met a tragic demise."

"She believe you?" Grace asked.

"She's smarter than that." Amy looked at Mallory. "But she understood the emergency and is making another cake. The important thing is that we get Mallory through this situation."

Mallory sighed and thunked her forehead to the table.

Amy quickly slid the cake over a little bit, probably so Mallory's hair wouldn't catch fire. "So did you really tell Jane to stuff herself?"

"Yes." Mallory's voice was muffled, and Grace *tsk*ed sympathetically and stroked Mallory's hair.

"But that's not why I'm out of a job," Mallory said. "It's because I yelled it, and everyone heard. Bill said sometimes he wished Jane would stuff it, too, but we have to learn to not compound our errors. He was working up to firing me. He had no choice, really. And that's when I sort of lost it. I told him to stuff it, too, and left."

"Wow," Grace said. "When you decide to go bad, you go all the way."

Mallory let out a combination laugh/sob.

"What are your plans now?" Amy asked her. "Beg for your job back?"

"I'm thinking I'll end up working for some quiet little doctor's office somewhere and try to go back to behaving like myself." Mallory scooped up some cake and stuffed it into her mouth. "I don't want to talk about it."

"Tough," Ty said.

She jerked upright and whirled on her stool to face him. She had chocolate on her lips but she pointed her fork at him like she was a queen on her throne. "You need to stop doing that."

"You'd wither up and die of boredom in a quiet little doctor's office," he said.

She stared up at him, her eyes shining brilliantly. Everyone was looking at them, of course. Well, except Amy, who was looking at Matt. Matt had taken a seat at the counter to watch the circus.

Ty narrowed his eyes at everyone.

No one took the hint to give him and Mallory some privacy. Of course not. It used to be one gaze from him could terrorize people. But it hadn't worked for him in Lucky Harbor, not once. Giving up, he gestured to the candles as the little flames seemed to gather in strength. "You should blow those out," he said.

Amy blew out the candles. Grace feigned interest in a menu. Their ears were cocked.

Resigned at having an audience, Ty looked at Mallory. "Why didn't you tell me?"

"Which?" she asked.

Jesus. There was more than one thing? The candles flickered back to life on the cake, which he ignored. "Let's start with the missing drugs."

"Because I know that you didn't take them." Mallory eyed the cake. "You used trick candles?" she asked Amy.

"Yeah," she said. "They were from Lance's birthday party. His brother's idea. Tucker has a warped sense of humor. They're all I had."

"Excuse me," Lucille said, hopping off her stool and scooting close. "But I couldn't help but overhear. Missing drugs?"

"This isn't an open-to-the-public conversation, Lucille," Mallory said.

"But who would take drugs from the HSC?" the older woman asked. "A teenager? A drug dealer? One of your crazy siblings?"

Mallory pinched the bridge of her nose. "You're just as crazy as Tammy and Joe, and you know it."

Lucille blinked. "Are you sassing me?"

"Yes," Mallory said. "Apparently it's my new thing. Push me, and I'll even yell at you. Also a new thing. Now stay out of my business; I'm trying to have a private conversation here." She grimaced. "*Please*," she added politely.

Lucille blinked, then smiled. "Well, there it is. Been waiting a long time to see that."

"I *always* say please."

"Not that. Your backbone. You have one, and it looks great on you, my dear."

Mallory just stared at her, then at Ty. But he was still a little stunned at what she'd said before.

I know you didn't take them.

Somehow, in spite of his best efforts to hold back, Mallory knew him, she knew who he was, inside and out, and accepted him. As is.

And she'd believed in him, no questions asked.

This didn't help her now, he knew. Because someone *had* taken the meds under her watch. It could have been anyone. Only Mallory knew the truth, and Ty knew by just looking at her that she *did* know. She knew who it was, and she didn't want to say.

Even now she was trying to save someone.

It slayed him. *She* slayed him. "If you know I wasn't the one who took the pills," he said, "then why didn't you turn over the list of people who'd been inside the building?"

For some reason, this pissed her off. He watched as temper ignited in her eyes. Standing up, she stabbed him in the chest with her finger hard enough to make him wince. "Do you think you're the only one I care about?" she demanded.

"Uh…"

"No," she assured him. "You are not."

She was as mad as he'd ever seen her, in sky blue scrubs with a long-sleeved T-shirt beneath—*his* shirt, if he wasn't mistaken. There was a mysterious lump of things in her pockets and someone had drawn a red heart on one of her white tennis shoes. She still had chocolate on one corner of her mouth, her hair was completely out of control, and she was ready to take down anyone who got in her path.

She'd never looked more beautiful. "Mallory." He knew how much her job meant to her. How much the HSC meant. How much Lucky Harbor meant.

He was leaving, but she wasn't. Her life was here, and in that moment, he made his decision, knowing he could live with it. "I took advantage of you," he said, making sure to speak loud enough for all the eavesdroppers to hear. "Complete advantage."

Two stools over, Matt groaned. "Man, don't. Don't do it."

Mallory hadn't taken her eyes off Ty, and she was still pissed. "*What are you doing?*"

"Attempting to tell what happened," he said carefully.

"Now you all just hold it right there." Mrs. Burland was suddenly right there, pointing at Ty with her cane, almost sticking it up his nose. "Yeah, you little punk-ass," she said. "I'm talking to you."

Little punk ass? He was a foot and a half taller than her and outweighed her by at least a hundred pounds. He stared down at her in shock.

Everyone in the place sucked in a breath and did the same.

Except Matt. He grinned wide. "Little punk ass," he repeated slowly, rolling the words off his tongue in delight. "I like it."

Ty gave him a look that didn't appear to bother Matt at all. It'd been a hell of a long time since anyone had gotten in Ty's face, even longer since he'd been called a little punk ass, and by the looks of her, Mrs. Burland wasn't done with him yet.

"What the hell do you think you're doing?" she demanded.

"I'm trying to have a conversation," he said. "A *private* one."

Lucille leaned in. "There's no such thing in Lucky Harbor," she said helpfully.

Clearly tired of the interruptions, Mrs. Burland slammed her cane onto the floor three times in a row, until all eyes were back on her. She glared at Ty. "You have no right to confess to a crime you didn't commit."

Apparently, as well as being curmudgeonly and grumpy and mean as a snake, Mrs. Burland was also sharp as a tack. "Stay out of it," he said.

"You're trying to be the big hero," Mrs. Burland told him. "You think she's protecting someone, and you don't want her hurt."

Mallory turned to him. "Is that what you're doing?"

Ty opened his mouth but Mrs. Burland rose up to her full four feet eight inches and said, "It was me. *I* took the meds." She eyeballed the entire crowd. "Not a teenager. Not a drug dealer. Not any of the crazy Quinns. And not this—" She gestured toward Ty, and her mouth tightened disfavorably. "*Man*. He might be guilty of plenty, not the least of which is messing with *your* reputation, Mallory Quinn—not that you seem to mind—but he didn't take the pills. That was me."

"No." A young woman stood up from a table across the room. Ty recognized her as Deena, the clerk at the grocery store. "I was at the HSC yesterday," she said. "For birth control pills. *I* took the Oxycontin."

"That's a lie." This was from Ryan, at the far end of the counter. "We all know I have a problem. *I* took the pills."

Mallory's mouth fell open.

Nothing surprised Ty, but even he could admit to being shocked. The entire town was rallying around Mallory in the only way they knew how. He'd never seen anything like it.

Amy banged a wooden spoon on the counter to get everyone's attention. "Hey, I was there, too. I took the pills." Her eyes locked on Matt's, whose jaw bunched and ticked.

Mallory gaped at Amy. "You were not there—"

"Oh no you all don't!" Mrs. Burland yelled. "Listen you . . . you egocentric, self-absorbed, narcissistic group of *insane* people. Don't make me smack all of you!" And with that, she pulled a small box from her pocket.

A sample of Oxycontin.

"See?" she said triumphantly. "I have them. I have them all. I took them because I thought they were Probiotics for my constipation. They're the same color box. My insurance is crap, and even if it wasn't, I hate to wait in line at the pharmacy. I've spent the past decade waiting in stupid lines. A line to see the doctor. A line to wait for meds. Hell, I even had to wait in line to go to the bathroom a minute ago. I'm over it, and I'm over all of you."

"You don't need Probiotics," Lucille said. "All you need are prunes and a blender."

"*You* got Mallory fired?" Amy asked Mrs. Burland.

"No, Mallory's big mouth got her fired," Mrs. Burland said.

"I didn't get fired," Mallory said. "I quit."

Lucille tried to lean in again. "Excuse me, dear," she said to Mallory. "But—"

"*Not now*, Lucille. *Please*."

"Yes, but it's important."

"*What's more important than this*?"

"The candles."

They'd come back to life again, blazing good this time. The cake had been scooted back against the pile of menus, and several had fallen too close. The menus went up in flames just as Ty leaped toward them, grabbing Mallory's glass of water to dump it on the small fire.

The flames flickered and went out.

Except for the middle one, the largest candle. Which turned out to be not just a trick candle but some sort of bottle rocket, because it suddenly shot straight up and into the ceiling like…well, like a bottle rocket.

The fire alarm sounded, and then there was the *whoosh* of a huge pressure hose letting loose, and the sprinklers overhead came on.

And rained down on the entire diner and everyone in it.

Chapter 21

Strength is the ability to break up a solid piece of chocolate—and then eat just one of the pieces.

Mallory was shocked at how fast total chaos reigned. Instantaneously, really. As the overhead sprinklers showered down icy water, people began yelling and screaming. Everyone pushed and shoved at each other to get out.

Adding to the insanity, the decorations hanging from the ceiling soaked up the water and began to fall, pulling down ceiling tiles with them. A papier-maché elephant hit Mallory on the head, along with the attached ceiling tile. For a second she saw stars, then panicked. Someone was going to get seriously hurt. She tried to blink through the downpour to check the crowd for anyone who needed help. She could hardly see two feet in front of her but it appeared that *everyone* needed help. People were either running or down for the count. It was utter mayhem.

Mallory gulped some air and shoved her hair out of her face. Her hand came away bloody. Her cheek was bleeding, but before she could dwell on that someone grabbed her, tugged her up against his side, and began to steam-roll her toward the door.

Ty.

"Let me go," she said, banging on his chest, which was completely ineffective.

"No. I want you safe outside, *now*."

"Forget me, get Mrs. Burland and Lucille!"

"You first, goddammit." Then, still holding her tightly against him, Ty scooped up Mrs. Burland, too. Lucille was nowhere to be seen. Through the sprinklers, Mallory saw Matt grabbing Amy and Grace, shoving them out the door, and going back in for others. Ty dumped Mallory near them and went back inside.

Mallory went to leap in after him. Ty blocked her.

"I'm going in," she said. "People are hurt, Ty. I can help."

His jaw ticked but he stepped aside. The fire alarm was blaring, water from the sprinklers still pouring down. Mallory got several more people outside before she ran into Ty again. He had two of Lucille's posse by their hands but he dropped one and stopped to stroke the wet hair that wouldn't stay out of Mallory's face, ducking a little to look over her bloody cheek, then into her eyes. He was checking on her, making sure she was okay.

But he must know by now. She was always okay. Not that *that* stopped the warmth from washing through her from knowing he cared. It was in every touch, every look.

And he was going to leave.

He had a job; she got that. She'd never want to hold him back from what fueled him, whatever that might be. But she'd sort of, maybe, just a little bit, wished that *she* could be what fueled him.

By the time the fire department came, they'd gotten everyone out. Several people were injured enough to require several ambulances, which arrived right behind the fire department. Mallory was helping those lined up on the sidewalk. Near her, Matt was assisting the paramedics. Ty, too, looked just as comfortable in a position of medical authority. He had Ryan, who'd somehow gotten a nasty-looking laceration down one arm, seated at the curb. Ty was crouched at the vet's side, applying pressure to the wound, looking quite capable.

Josh pulled up to the scene and hopped out of his car. Ryan was closest to him, so he stopped beside him first.

"He's in shock," Ty said quietly.

It was true. Ryan was shaking, glassy-eyed, disoriented. Definitely in shock. Josh went back to his car and returned with an emergency kit. Ty and Josh wrapped Ryan in an emergency blanket to get him warm, then made sure he was breathing evenly and that his pulse wasn't too fast. Mallory took over then, sitting at Ryan's side, holding his hand as she watched Josh and Ty work together in perfect sync on other victims.

When the paramedics were free, they took over Ryan's care and Mallory moved toward Ty and Josh.

"The least you can do," Josh was saying to Ty, "now that you're cleared and still sitting on your ass, is hire on. You know there's that flight paramedic opening out of Seattle General. That unit runs its ass off, no shortage of adrenaline there. And hell, look at how exciting Lucky Harbor can be."

Ty ignored him and crouched at Lucille's feet. "You okay?"

"Oh, sure, honey." She patted his arm. "You're a good boy."

Ty smiled, and Mallory didn't know if that was at the idea of him being a boy, or good. Then he straightened and turned to Mallory.

She wasn't surprised that he'd known she was standing behind him. He always seemed to know where she was. "Wow," she said with what she thought was remarkable calm. "Look at you."

His eyes locked in on her cheek, and he touched the wound. With a wince, she batted his hand away.

He pulled her away from all the prying eyes and ears. "You need that taken care of," he said. "Let me help—"

"No." She needed more help than he could possibly imagine. "It can wait." She didn't know where to start, but she gave it the old college try and started at the beginning. "How is it that a mechanic knows how to treat trauma victims?"

His gaze never left hers. "I was a medic in the SEALs."

"A medic. In the SEALs." She absorbed that and shook her head. "That's funny, because I could have sworn you told me you were a mechanic. A navy mechanic, who was doing similar work now."

"No," he said. "Well, yes. I work on cars. Sometimes. But that's for me, for fun."

"For fun." She paused, but it didn't compute. "I pictured you working on ships, maybe on helicopters and tanks. Not bodies. Why didn't you tell me?"

He responded with a question of his own. "Why does it matter what I was?"

"Because it's not what you were, Ty, it's who you *are*." How could he not see that? Or hear her heart as it quietly cracked down the center? "You're going back," she said. "You're only here waiting to be cleared..." She stared at him as Josh's words sank in. "Except you already *are* cleared." Oh, God. He could leave now. Any second. "How long have you known? And why would you hide so much from me?" But she already knew the answer to that. It was because they were just fooling around.

Nothing more.

And she had no one to blame but herself. Horrified at how close she was to breaking down, she took a step backward and bumped directly into Sheriff Sawyer Thompson. He'd strode up to the soggy group and now stood there, hands on hips. "What the hell happened here?"

Everyone was still there. No one wanted to miss anything.

Every able body in the pathetic, ragtag-looking group immediately gathered ranks around Mrs. Burland, the mean old biddy who'd never done anything nice for a single one of them. In fact, she'd made their life a living hell in a hundred different ways. But they all started talking at once, each giving their story of the drug theft, and how they'd ended up being dumped on by the diner's sprinkler system.

Once again protecting one of their own.

Mrs. Burland still wasn't having any of it. She stood up, wobbled with her cane toward the sheriff and held out her wrists. "Arrest me, Copper. But don't even think about a strip search. I have rights, you know."

Sawyer assured her that he had no interest in arresting her, because then he'd have to arrest everyone else who'd confessed as well. Looking disgusted and frustrated, he started over, talking to one person at a time.

The crowd began to disperse.

Mallory sank to the curb and dropped her head to her knees, exhausted to the bone and far too close to losing it. Ty, holding so much back from her...How was that even possible? She'd given him everything she'd had.

He wasn't going to change now, and God help her, she was going to be okay with that if it killed her.

And it just might.

Two battered boots appeared in front of her, and she felt him crouch at her side.

Ty, of course. Her heart only leapt for Ty. He ran a big, warm hand down her back, made a sound of annoyance at finding her still drenched and shivering, and then she felt one of the emergency blankets from the firefighters come around her.

"I'm fine," she said.

"Yeah." He sat at her side and pulled her in against his warmth. "Extremely fine. But that's not what's in question here."

"What *is* in question?"

"You tell me."

"Fine," she said, and lifted her head. "I don't get the big secret about being a paramedic."

"It wasn't a secret."

"It feels like a secret," she said. "That day you came to the hospital to get your stitches out, you could have done that yourself."

"I wanted to see you."

Aw.

Dammit, *no* aw. "Okay, then what about what happened next?" she asked. "When that patient coded out? You got pale and shaky, almost shocky, as if you'd never seen anything like that before."

Ty was still balanced on the balls of his feet. He lowered his head and studied his shoes for a moment, then looked her right in the eyes. "Do you want to know the last thing I did as a SEAL trauma medic?" he asked, voice dangerously low. She wasn't the only one pissed off and frustrated.

"I dragged my teammates out of the burning plane," he told her. "Tommy was already dead, but the others, Brad, Kelly, and Trevor..." He closed his eyes. "I did everything I could, and they died anyway. Afterward, I couldn't do it. I tried, but I couldn't go back to being a first line trauma responder."

Her gut wrenched for him. "Oh, Ty."

"I was honorably discharged, and when I got work, it wasn't as a medic. I turned down anything like that for four years. Four years, Mallory, where I didn't so much as give out a Band-Aid."

Until he'd come to Lucky Harbor. "Amy's knife wound," she whispered.

He nodded grimly. "The first time I'd opened a first-aid kit in all that time."

And then today. Again, a situation that fell right on him, and he'd stepped into the responsibility as if into a pair of comfortable old shoes. She wondered if he realized that.

"My turn," he said. "Your job? You lost your job?"

"Not lost. *Quit*." She took a moment to study her own shoes now, until he wrapped his fingers around her ponytail and tugged.

She lifted her head and met his gaze. "Mallory," he said softly. Pained. "Why?"

Why? A million reasons, none of which she wanted to say because suddenly, it was all too much. The job, the HSC, the diner, knowing how she felt about Ty and realizing he was going to leave anyway. Her head hurt, her cheek hurt. And her heart hurt, too. When her eyes filled, he made a low sound. Hard to tell if it was male horror or empathy. But then he wrapped his arms around her, and she planted her face in the crook of his neck.

She should have known he wouldn't be uncomfortable with tears. He didn't seem to be uncomfortable with much, when it came right down to it.

Except maybe his own emotions.

How had things gotten so out of control? All she'd wanted was to stretch her wings. Live for herself instead of for others. Try new things. She'd done that, and she'd loved it.

She loved him.

And therein lay her mistake. "The whole HSC drug fiasco is *my* fault," she said into his chest. "No one else's. I screwed up there." She sucked in a breath as once again her eyes filled. "As for everything else, I always wanted to go a little crazy, but as it turns out, I'm not all that good at it," she whispered.

He made a show of looking at the utter chaos of the diner. "I don't know," he said. "I think you're better at it than you give yourself credit for."

She choked out a laugh, realizing that no matter what she did, he had her back. He'd been there for her, one hundred percent. It was in his every look, touch, kiss. "I just wanted something for myself," she said softly.

"And you deserve that," he said with absolute conviction, warming her from the inside out. From the beginning, he'd treated her like someone special, from before they'd even known each other's names. He'd shared his courage, his sense of adventure, his inner strength.

Once, she'd been a woman terribly out of balance with herself and her hopes and dreams. That had changed.

Because of him.

She was in balance now but even that wasn't enough. Loving him wasn't enough. It wasn't going to get her what she wanted. Nothing was going to get her what she wanted—which was Ty. She really needed to cut her losses now before it got worse, but God. How could she? "Ty."

He pulled back to look into her eyes, his own going very serious at the look in hers.

She cupped his face. "I've screwed up. I'm falling for you." She gently kissed his gorgeous mouth so that he couldn't say anything. "Don't worry, I know you won't let yourself do the same." She kissed him again when he went to speak, because it was in his eyes. Sorrow. "I can't do this anymore," she whispered past a throat that felt like she'd swallowed cut glass. "I'm sorry."

"Are you dumping me, Mallory?"

Was she? The truth was that *he* was the one going, and yet he hadn't. She'd have to think about that later, but for now, for right now, what she had with him wasn't enough for her. "You were never mine to dump," she said.

Something crossed his normally stoic face, but he nodded and lifted a hand to her jaw, stroking his thumb over her lips in a gentle gesture that made her ache. She started to say something, she had no idea what, but someone tapped her on the shoulder. "*Mallory Michelle Quinn.*"

Only one person ever middle-named her. Her mom; just what she needed. She swiped at her eyes and turned, considering herself lucky to be so wet that no one could possibly tell if she was crying or not. "Mom, why are you here?"

"I heard about the diner. You're hurt?"

"Now's not a good time—" Mallory brushed her mom's hand away. "*Mom.*"

"Don't you 'mom' me! You have a cut on your cheek. And you let Jane *fire* you?"

"Okay, someone give me a microphone!" Mallory said as loud as she could. "Because I wasn't fired, I *quit*. There's a difference."

Her mother stared at her for a long beat, during which Mallory did her best not to look as utterly heartbroken as she felt. Finally Ella nodded. "Well, I hope to hell you took Jane down a peg or two while you were at it."

Shock had Mallory gaping. "You're not upset?"

"She's overworked you and taken advantage of your skills. The board's already banding together to try to get you back. I suggest turning down their first offer. According to what I overheard, their second offer will be a much better deal."

Mallory choked out a shocked breath. "Overheard?"

"Fine. I put a glass to the door of Bill's office and listened in. But I'm not proud of it." Ella hesitated. "What I am proud of is you. And Sawyer sent me over here to get you. He needs one last quick word from you for his report."

Sawyer was already headed for her.

He gave her a look of frustration. "You okay?"

No. "Yes."

"Good, because so far I've heard twenty different versions of what's going on. Tell me that you're going to come up with the *right* one."

She told him the entire story the best that she could, then

turned to look for Ty and found her mom talking to him. Ella was animated, her hands moving, her mouth flapping, and Mallory's stomach sank. From the looks of things, she could be reading him the riot act, or...hell. She couldn't imagine. "I've got to go," she said to Sawyer.

Her mother saw her coming and met her halfway. "He has a way of looking at you, honey. Like you mean something to him."

Mallory shook her head. "What did you two talk about?"

"Are you asking if I accused him of destroying your reputation?" Ella looked over Mallory's shoulder and found Ty watching them. She sent him a little finger wave.

He didn't wave back but he did almost smile.

"You made it clear what you thought of my way of thinking," Ella said to Mallory. "And you were right. I've been holding the reins too tight, depending on you to be the calm in the storm of this crazy family. That was unfair, maybe even cruel, and I was wrong. I never should have done it. Just as I never should have allowed you to blame yourself for Karen. Or my divorce. Or the general insanity of our family."

"Mom—"

"Hush, honey. I told him I'd make him dinner," Ella said casually, almost as a throwaway remark, and stroked Mallory's wet hair back from her face.

"You *what*?"

"He's been good to you. I want to thank him. It's simple etiquette."

"You mean it's simple curiosity," Mallory said.

"Okay, that too."

"Mom, we're just..." God. Her heart hurt. "Friends."

"Oh, please," Ella said with a laugh. "I didn't fall for that with Tammy when she brought Zach home, and I'm not going to fall for it with you. He said yes."

"No, really," Mallory said. "We're not what you think we are. He said *yes*?"

"Sweetheart, you're drenched and still shivering. You're going to catch your death out here. Go home and take a hot shower, and put something on that cut on your cheek." Ella hugged her tight, then pushed her toward her car.

Mallory took a last look at the scene. Ty was back to helping. He was hauling things out of the wrecked diner with Matt. Two extremely fine examples of what a good use of gorgeous male muscle could do.

"Mallory." Josh gestured to Mrs. Burland, huddled on the sidewalk. "She's refusing to go to the hospital but mostly, she's just shaken up. If you're leaving, maybe you could drive her home."

Mallory ended up driving the entire senior posse home since Lucille was the only one of them still in possession of her license, and she was going into the hospital for X-rays. It took nearly an hour because each of them took forever to say their good-byes and get out of the car. When she'd finally gotten rid of them all, Mallory told herself to go home, but herself didn't listen. She drove to Ty's.

The garage was open, and he was beneath his precious Shelby.

She bet he'd never walked away from a car in his life.

Still working on adrenaline, frustration, and a pain so real it felt like maybe her heart had been split in two, she stormed up to the mechanic's creeper and nudged at his exposed calf.

Okay, maybe it was more of a kick. "You told my mother she could cook you dinner?"

He rolled out from beneath the car, and arms still braced on the chassis above him, looked up at her. He wisely didn't comment on what was surely a spectacularly bad hair day on her part. She'd been hit with the sprinklers, and then dust from the ceiling tiles, and the whole mess had dried naturally without any of her de-frizzing products that never really worked anyway.

"Problem?" he finally asked.

"Oh my God!" She tossed up her hands. "You did. You said yes. *Why*?"

"She said she'd make meatloaf. I don't think I've ever had home-cooked meatloaf. I thought it was a suburban myth."

She'd never wanted to both hug and strangle someone before. "*I'll* make you meatloaf!"

"You dumped me," he said reasonably. "And besides, you don't cook."

Dammit. Dammit, he was killing her. She pressed the heels of her hands to her eyes but she couldn't rub away the ache. Spinning on her heel, she walked out of the garage.

He caught her at her car, pulling her back against him. She felt the shaking of his chest and realized he was laughing at her.

At least until he caught sight of her face.

His smile faded then.

With a frustrated growl, she shoved him away and got into her car, but before she could shut the door, he squatted at her side, the muscles in his thighs flexing against the faded denim he wore. He blocked her escape with one hand on the door, the other on the back of her seat, his expression unreadable now. "This isn't about meatloaf," he said. "This isn't even about me. Tell me what the real problem is."

I'm in love with you . . .

"My problem," Mallory said, "is that you're blocking me from shutting the door."

"And you're shutting me out."

"That's pretty funny," she managed, throat inexplicably tight. "Coming from you. The King Of Shutting *Me* Out."

"I didn't shut you out intentionally."

"Ditto," she said, with no small amount of attitude.

He studied her for a long moment. "Tell me about the night Karen died."

She felt like he'd reached into her chest and closed his fist around her lungs. She couldn't breathe. "She's not a part of this."

"I think maybe she is. She took a walk on the dark side, and it didn't work out so well for her. She made you promise to be good, and you kept your word. Until me."

"Someone has a big mouth."

"*Many* someones," he agreed. "But then again, you love it here. You love all those someones. And they all love you."

Mallory dropped her head to the steering wheel. "Look, I'm mad at you, okay? This isn't about me. I know my painful memories are relative. My life is good. I'm lucky. This isn't about how poor little Mallory has had it so hard. I'm not falling apart or anything."

He stroked a hand down her back. "Of course you're not. You're just holding the steering wheel up with your head for a minute, that's all."

Choking out a laugh, she closed her eyes. "I'm okay."

"Yeah, you are. You're so much more okay than I've ever been. You're the strongest woman I've ever met, Mallory. Do you know that?"

"But that's just it. I'm not strong at all. I always thought I could save everyone. If I was good, I'd excel. If I was good, my family would stay together. If I was good, nothing bad could happen."

Ty's hand on her was calming. So was his voice, low and even, without judgment. And the dash of affection didn't hurt. "How did that work out for you?" he asked. "All that being good?"

Another laugh tore out of her, completely mirthless. "It didn't. All that work, all that time spent trying to please everyone, and it fell apart anyway. I failed."

"You know better than that."

"Do I?" She tightened her grip on the steering wheel. It was her only anchor in a spinning world. Nothing was working out for her. Not her job. Not the way she wanted people to see her. And not her non-relationship with Ty. "I don't want to talk about the past anymore. My sister made her choice. My family each made their own choices after that. My parents handled everything the best they could, including their divorce."

"Maybe," he said. "But it still chewed you up and spit you out."

"I'm okay."

"You don't always have to be okay."

"Well, I know that."

"Then say it. Free that sixteen-year old, Mallory. Say it wasn't her fault; not your parents' divorce, not Karen, none of it."

"Ty."

"Say it."

She gulped in some air and let it out. "It wasn't my fault."

He wrapped his hand around her hair and gently tugged until she'd lifted her head and was looking at him. "That's right," he said with terrifying gentleness. "It wasn't your fault. You did the best you could with what you had. You made the decision to progress beyond that little girl who lived to please. You stepped outside your comfort zone and went after what you wanted."

She felt the heat hit her cheeks. They both knew what she'd gone after.

Him.

Naked.

And she'd gotten him.

"Stop carrying all the responsibility for everyone," he said quietly. "Let it go, let it all go and be whoever the hell you want to be."

She gave him a little smile. "Are you going to take your own advice?"

"I'm working on it."

"You're pretty amazing, you know that?"

"Yeah." He flashed his own small smile. "Too bad you dumped my sorry ass."

She looked at him for a long beat. "I might have been too hasty on that," she whispered. "Twice now."

"Is that right?"

"Yeah. Because your ass is anything but sorry."

He gave her a smile. "Come here," he said, and then without waiting for her to move, rose to his feet and pulled her from the car.

She curled into him, wrapping her arms around his neck. "Where are we going?"

"To show you how much more amazing I can be when we're horizontal."

Chapter 22

A life without chocolate is no life at all.

Ty set Mallory down in his bathroom, and she looked around in confusion. "I'm not horizontal."

Leaning past her, he flipped on his shower and cranked the water to hot. Then he stripped. And oh good Lord, he looked so damn good without his clothes that it almost made her forget her problems, including the fact that *he* was her biggest problem. "What—"

"You're wet and frozen solid. Kick off your shoes."

While she was obeying that command, he peeled the wet clothes from her and let them hit the floor. And while she was distracted by his mouth-watering body, he checked the temperature of the shower, then pushed her in.

She sucked in a breath as the hot water hit her, and then another when he reached for the soap. He washed her with quick efficiency while she stared down at the erection brushing her stomach.

"Ignore it," he said.

She stared at it some more, and it got bigger.

He shook his head at her and washed her hair, his fingers heaven on her scalp, making her moan. Then he set her aside, soaped himself up with equally quick efficiency, which absolutely shouldn't have turned her on, but totally did.

It must have showed because his eyes went dark and hot. Turning off the water, he wrapped her up in a towel and sat her on the counter. With just a towel low on his hips, he crouched down, rooted in a drawer, and came up with a first-aid kit and a box of condoms. Both unopened. Saying nothing, he set the condoms on the counter at her hip.

She went hot looking at them.

Grabbing the first-aid kit, he straightened to his full height and pushed her wet hair from her face. He dipped his knees a little and eyed the cut over her cheek. "A few butterfly bandages will do you, I think." He disinfected the cut, and when she hissed out a pained breath, he leaned in and kissed her temple.

"Nice bedside manner," she murmured. "You patch up a lot of wet, naked women?"

"Almost never." He carefully peeled back the plastic packaging on the sterilized butterfly bandages and began to cover her wound.

"So what exactly happened that you're okay with handling this sort of thing again?" she asked.

"You happened."

"Come on."

He slid her a look. "You think you're the only one making changes in your life?" he asked. "You work your ass off, no matter how much shit you see, and you see plenty. You just want to help people, heal them. I used to be like that. I didn't realize I missed it, but I do."

"The job you're going back to," she said. "It's obviously very dangerous work."

"Not as dangerous as being a SEAL. That was about as bad as it can get."

"Like the plane crash," she said softly.

"Yeah. Like the plane crash."

"Do you have PTSD, Ty?"

"Maybe." He shrugged. "Probably, a little. Not debilitating though. Not anymore anyway."

He was still damp from the shower, his hair pushed back from his face. He concentrated on his task, leaving her free to stare at him. His mouth was somehow both stern and generous at the same time, his jaw square and rough with a day's worth of scruff that she knew would feel deliciously sensual against her skin. He had a scar along one side of his jaw and another on his temple. His chest was broad, his abs ridged with muscle.

He was beautiful.

"You really miss it," she said softly. "The action."

"Once an adrenaline junkie, always one, I guess." He finished with the cut on her face and lifted her hand, turning it over to gently probe her swollen and already bruised wrist. She had no idea how he'd noticed it.

"It's not broken," she said.

He nodded in agreement, then lifted it to his mouth and brushed a kiss to her skin.

While she melted, he expertly wrapped it in an Ace bandage, then looked at her shin.

Bleeding.

She hadn't even realized.

He dropped to his knees and attended to that with the same concentration and professionalism he'd given everything else. His head was level with the counter she was sitting on, and his hands were on her bare leg. And all she could think was if he shifted her leg an inch more to the left, her towel would gape, and he'd be eye level with her bare crotch.

It was a suggestive, erotic thought that led to others, and she squirmed, wondering how she could get her towel to drop without being obvious about it.

"You okay?" he asked.

"Why didn't you leave when you were cleared?"

He looked up into her face. "I think you know why."

"Me."

"You," he agreed.

There were some advantages to changing her life around, to living for herself instead of for others' expectations, she decided. For one thing, it had given her new confidence. So she accessed some of that and unwrapped the towel, letting it fall to the counter at her hips.

Ty went still, and a sensual thrill rushed through her.

He let out a breath and slid his hands up her legs, applying gentle pressure until she opened them for him. He groaned at his new-found view and pressed a kiss to first one inner thigh, and then the other.

And then in between.

His hands were on her, rough and strong but tender at the same time, and her body quivered, rejoicing in the rightness of his touch. He murmured something against her skin and though she couldn't hear him, she urged him on, clutching at his shoulders until her toes curled, until she cried out his name, until there were no more thoughts.

She opened her eyes and found him rising to his feet, eyes hot, mouth wet, as he helped her off the counter. Then she was staring at him as he turned and walked out of the bathroom. "What are you—"

Since he was gone, she followed him into his bedroom, watching as he quickly dropped his towel, but instead of finishing the horizontal lessons, he pulled on black knit boxers that barely fit over his massive erection. "What are you doing?"

"Someone's at the door." He slid his long legs into jeans and grimaced when he tried to button them up.

Still in her orgasmic glow, she was thinking that she'd like to trace the cords of every one of his muscles, starting with his chest and working her way down. It'd take a while but she thought it would be time well spent. Then what he'd said sank in. "Someone's at your door? I didn't hear anything."

A small smile escaped him. "That's because you were making more noise than the doorbell."

"I was not—" God. She covered her hot cheeks. "Who is it?"

"Your mother."

She squeaked. "*What*?"

"I caught sight of her walking up to the door from the bathroom window." He glanced down at his hard-on. "You're going to have to get it." He eyed her body from head to toe and groaned. "And probably you should get dressed."

"*Why is my mother here?*"

"Meatloaf."

She'd forgotten about the meatloaf. Panicked, she turned in a circle. "My scrubs are wet and in a pile on your bathroom floor!"

"Hydrogen, helium, lithium—"

She stared at him. "What are you doing now?"

"Listing the chemical elements so I can answer the door without a boner."

"And knowing my mother is on your porch isn't taking care of that?"

"Good point." He threw her a pair of sweats that had been lying on a chair and left the room.

In the end, she tossed dignity and wore his sweats instead of her wet scrubs, but by the time she got to the living room, it was empty.

She found Ty in the big kitchen setting down a large bag. "She didn't stay," he said. "She said she figured I had my hands full making sure you were okay. She said she'd water your flowers and feed the cat for you, that you were to just sit your tired patoot down and relax, and I was to make sure you did just that."

"My mother, the Master Manipulator."

"Is your patoot tired?" he asked, sounding amused though his eyes were very serious.

"No. Are you hungry?"

His eyes roamed hungrily over her features. "Yes, but not for food. You?"

"I'll have whatever you're having."

Ty had been wanting to get his hands on Mallory since he'd heard from Matt about the missing drugs. Hell, he'd been wanting to put his hands on her since... always. He *always* wanted to put his hands on her. His hands, his mouth. *Everything.*

He stood her by the bed, making short work of the sweats she'd pulled on. When he dropped to his knees before her, he found her still warm and wet, already making those noises he loved, and when he slid a finger inside her, she gasped and opened her legs even wider for him.

A woman who knew what she wanted.

He loved that about her.

Her fingers were in his hair, holding him to her as if she was afraid he'd stop too soon.

Not a chance.

He wanted to hear her cry out his name again, wanted to feel her fly apart for him, so he worked her slow and easy, driving her right to the edge before backing off. She'd tightened her hands in his hair, doing her best to make him bald. He smiled against her and finally took her to the end. She was still shuddering when he surged to his feet and tossed her to the bed. She lay back, arms stretched out at her sides and gave him a little smile.

Sweet.

Hot.

"Why are you still dressed?" she wanted to know.

It was a good question. He stripped, grabbed a condom and rolled it on. When he had, he pushed inside her, just one long, slick slide that had them both sucking in a harsh breath of sheer, unadulterated pleasure.

Nothing had ever felt so good as being buried deep inside her. Nothing.

"Ty?"

He drowned in her eyes. "Yeah?"

"This is far more than I thought it would be."

He knew that. He knew it to the depths of his soul. With one hand in her hair, holding her for a hard, deep kiss, the other cupping her sweet ass, he began to move, thrusting into her slow and steady, and for the first time all day—hell, all damn *week*— his world started to make sense.

He'd been a military brat who'd never landed in one place for long, then a soldier himself. There'd been next to no softness in his life. He'd taken the time for the occasional relationship, although none of them were serious; none stuck long enough to affect him deeply. Certainly no previous relationship had managed to fit what his idea of love was.

Mallory was different.

In his heart of hearts, he knew that much. Hell, from that first stormy night, his tie to her had been undeniable. It'd happened in an instant and only strengthened with time, and he wanted to be with her. Talking, touching, kissing, fucking—whatever he could get, because she beat back the darkness inside him. But being with her was a double-edged sword, because every minute he spent with her absolutely changed his definitions of . . . *everything*.

She made him yearn for things he'd never yearned for before:

home, family, love. And Christ if that didn't stump him. What did he know about any of those things?

All he did know was that this—her mouth open on his, her body warm and soft and welcoming, her hands sliding up his chest and around his neck—felt right. *Real.* "Careful," he murmured, kissing her swollen cheek, then her wrapped wrist. "Don't let me hurt you."

"You healed me," she murmured. "Now let me heal you." Her hands slid down his back and then up again, and that felt so good he nearly purred. She melted into him and he warned himself that she'd had a rough time of it, that he needed to go slowly, but then she wrapped her legs around his waist and he sank in even further. With a moan, she arched beneath him, head back, eyes closed, hunger and desire etched on her face. "Oh, Ty..."

He nuzzled her exposed throat, then sucked a patch of skin into his mouth, making her gasp and tighten her grip on him.

Everywhere.

It set him on fire.

She did it again, and he let it roll over him: the feel of her heat gripping him like a vise, her scent, the scent of them together, the sound of her ragged breathing combined with wordless entreaties. Yeah. This. *This* was what he'd needed, her body hot and trembling against his, everything connecting. She was rocking into each thrust, her cries echoing in his mouth as he drove deeper, then deeper still. She was saying his name over and over now, straining against him, and then she was coming, shuddering in his arms as she went straight over the edge, taking him right along with her.

It was so good. That was his only thought as he let himself go. So good, so damn good...

Her hair was in his face, but he didn't breathe because he didn't want to disturb her. Her body, still overheated and damp, was plastered to his. She had one leg thrown over him, her cheek stuck to his pec, her hand on his favorite body part as if she owned it.

She did own it. She owned his heart and soul as well.

Jesus. It had started out so innocuously. Innocent, even.

Okay, not innocent. They'd had sex that first night in an attic. Some pretty fan-fucking-tastic sex.

He'd not been in a good place then. He hadn't felt good enough for his own life, much less anyone else's.

Certainly not good enough for a woman like Mallory, who'd give a perfect stranger the very shirt off her back.

But watching her, being with her, made him feel good.

Worthy.

It was unbelievable to him that one little woman could do that, but she had.

And where did that leave him? He'd never intended to be anything to Mallory other than a good time, but best laid plans...

Maybe he should have run hard and fast that very first night, but there'd been something about her, something that had drawn him in.

Even when he'd cost her, with her job, with her relationships with her family, she'd never hesitated. She'd given him everything she had. And in return, she'd only asked one thing of him. Just one.

Don't say good-bye. Just go.

His arms involuntarily tightened on her, and although she gave a soft sigh and cuddled deeper into him, she didn't waken. Nor did she stir when he finally forced himself to let go of her and slip out of the bed.

Mallory came awake slowly, thinking about all that had happened the day before. The HSC being shut down, her quitting, the diner's destruction... Ty making it all okay. It was subtle, he was subtle, but last night he'd given her just what she'd needed. Responsive but not smothering, encouraging her to talk when she'd needed to, and letting her be quiet when it'd counted.

She stretched, feeling her muscles ache in a very delicious way. He'd worshipped her body until nearly dawn.

Not just sex.

In truth, it hadn't been just sex for her since their first time, but she hadn't been sure how Ty felt.

Until last night.

Last night, the way he'd touched her, how he'd looked while deep in the throes, shuddering against her, claiming her body and giving her his...that had been lovemaking at its finest. Smiling at the memory, she rolled over and reached for him, but he wasn't in the bed. His pillow was cold.

And something inside her went cold as well.

She grabbed her buzzing phone off the nightstand. She put it there before falling asleep, as was her habit. She thought it might be Ty, but it was a text from Jane:

Bill refused your resignation. Also, due to a new donation earmarked specifically for HSC, the place has been granted a stay of execution for the next six months. On top of that, you are no longer pro bono for your hours there. Your next shift is tomorrow at eight. Be there, Mallory.

A new donation... *What had Ty done now?* Wrapping herself in his sheet, she walked through his house, her glow quickly subsiding. There'd never been much of him anywhere in the place to begin with, but the few traces of his existence were gone. His clothes, his duffle bag on the chair, his iPhone.

Gone.

Running now, she got to the garage and flipped on the light. The Shelby was still there, pretty and shiny.

Finished.

Confused, she went back through the house and into the bedroom. There she found the note that must have been on his pillow but had slipped to the floor, weighted down by a single key. A car key. The note read:

Mallory,

It was far more than I thought it would be, too.

I left you the Shelby. Sell it, it's worth enough that you can take your time deciding on the job thing. Matt'll get what it's worth for you. If you keep it, don't park it on the street.

No regrets.

Love, Ty

She stared at the note for a good ten minutes. He'd left her his baby? Given her permission to sell it so she wouldn't have to worry about money?

And then signed the note *Love, Ty*?

She let out a laugh, then clapped her hand over her mouth when it was followed by a soft sob.

He loved her.

The fool.

Or maybe that was her. *She* was the fool, because she loved him, too. Oh, how she loved him. "No regrets," she whispered, and wrapped her fingers around the key.

Chapter 23

Life is like a box of chocolates—full of nuts.

Mallory sat in Bill's office staring at him in disbelief. "Wait," she said, shaking her head. "Tell me that last part again. Ty tried to give you another donation, and you turned him down?"

"Yes," Bill said. "He's done enough for HSC, and I mean that in the best possible way."

Mallory swallowed hard. It was true. He'd done a lot for her, too. And even as he'd gone back to his life, he'd tried to make sure she'd be taken care of. She wished he was still here so she could smack him.

And then hug him.

"You turned down money?" she asked. "You never turn down money."

"It's not always about the bottom line." He smiled briefly but warmly. "See, even an old dog can learn new tricks."

"But Jane told me there was a donation."

"Yes. Another donation did come in. Mrs. Burland donated one hundred thousand dollars and—"

Mallory gasped and Bill held up a hand. "And she wanted it to be clear that everyone know she was the donor. She said, and I quote, '*I want it yelled from the rooftops that I was the one to save HSC.*'"

Mallory just stared. "Mrs. Burland," she repeated. "The woman who hates all of us, especially me?"

"Yes," Bill said. "Although I don't think she hates you as much as the rest of us. I believe Jane told you, there's a special condition on her donation."

"Me."

"Yeah. Consider your new salary for HSC a raise since I don't have it in the budget to offer you one for your RN position in the ER."

"But I quit."

"So un-quit. Take the knowledge that HSC is now secure, and so is your job, and get out of my office and back to work."

She thought about that for all of two seconds. "Yes, sir." She got up and moved to the door.

"Oh, and Mallory?"

She turned back.

"Don't ever quit again. My voice mail and e-mail box is overloaded with just about everyone in town demanding I'd best not lose you. Your mother has been hounding my ass since you walked out. Hell, *my* mother is hounding me. Understand?"

For the first time since she'd woken alone that morning, Mallory managed a smile. "I understand."

One week later, Mallory's life looked good—on paper. She had her job back, the future of HSC was secured, and the town was behind her.

What she didn't have was Ty.

Get used to it, she told herself, but on Saturday she rolled out of bed with a decided lack of enthusiasm. She'd done as she'd wanted. She'd stepped out of her comfort zone. She'd been selfish and lived her life the way she wanted, and it'd been more exciting than she could have imagined.

But how did she go back to being herself?

You don't, she decided. She'd put her heart on the line for the first time in her life but she'd made the choice to do it.

No regrets.

That was the day she got the delivery—a plain padded envelope, the return address too blurry and smeared to make out. She opened it up and a carefully wrapped package fell out. Opening the tissue paper, she stared down at the beautiful charm bracelet she'd coveted from the charity auction all those weeks ago.

There was no note, but none was necessary. She knew who'd sent it, and she pressed her hand to her aching heart at what it meant.

Ty, of course. He'd understood her as no other man ever had. He got that she was vested in this town, maybe in the same way he'd yearned to be, that the bracelet meant something to her. He'd added a charm, a '68 Shelby. She had no idea where he could have gotten it from, or what it'd cost him.

What did it mean?

It meant he cared about her, she told herself. Deeply. It meant she was on his mind, maybe even that he missed her.

She missed him, too, so very much.

Throat tight, she put the bracelet on, swallowed her tears, and shored up her determination to continue stretching her wings.

Two weeks later, Ty was on a flight back to the U.S. after an assignment that had involved escorting diplomats to a Somalian peace treaty.

The team he'd been with were all well-trained, seasoned men with the exception of one, who was fresh out of the military.

Their first night, there'd been a kidnapping attempt, but they'd shut it down with no problem.

There'd been no injuries on Ty's team unless he counted the newbie, who'd gotten so nervous when it was over that he'd thrown up and needed an IV fluid replacement. Ty had done the honors.

"Sorry," the kid muttered to Ty that night, embarrassed as he watched Ty pull the IV. "I lost it."

Ty shook his head. "Happens."

"But not to you, right?"

On Ty's first mission, and on every assignment up to the plane crash, he'd thrived on what he'd been doing. He'd believed in it with every fiber of his soul, understood that he'd belonged out there doing what he could to save lives.

After the crash, he hadn't just lost four friends. He'd also lost something of himself. His ability to connect. To get attached.

Until Lucky Harbor. Until the nosy, pestering people of Lucky Harbor, who cared about everyone and everything in their path. Including him.

And Mallory. God, Mallory. She'd been the last piece of his shattered soul fitting back into place. "Hell yeah, it happens to me."

The kid looked surprised to hear Ty admit such a thing but he nodded in appreciation. "I can do this," he told Ty. "I'm ready for whatever comes our way."

But nothing did.

They spent two entire weeks doing nothing more than cooling their heels in the African bush, where the most exciting thing to happen was watching through the long-range scope of a rifle as an elephant gave birth in the distance.

Ty had come back to this because he thought he'd needed the rush of the job to be happy.

So where in the holy hell was his happy?

He knew the answer to that. It was thousands and thousands

of miles away, with a woman who'd decimated the carefully constructed wall around his heart. And that's when it hit him between the eyes: It wasn't the job that fueled him, that kept him sane.

It was Mallory.

She was his team. She and Lucky Harbor. When he was there with her, she filled him up. Made him whole.

Made him everything.

Christ, he was slow. Too slow. It was probably far too late for such realizations. He'd been a fool and walked away from the best thing to ever happen to him, and Mallory didn't suffer fools well.

He looked out the airplane window as they finally circled D.C. Normally, at this point he'd be thinking about his priorities: sleeping for two days, fueling up on good food, and maybe finding a warm, willing woman.

He could get behind the sleep and the food, but there was only one woman he could think of, only one woman he wanted.

He'd left Lucky Harbor certain this had been his future, the nomadic, dangerous work he'd given his life to. He'd told himself it was the right thing to do, that he had to do this to make his team's deaths mean something. Plus, he could never give Mallory the kind of life she wanted. It just wasn't for him.

He'd been wrong on all counts. He knew it now. Brad, Tommy, Kelly, and Trevor's deaths would *always* mean something. And *his* life meant something, too. Probably he'd always known that, but he hadn't had his head screwed on right for a long time. He had it on tight now.

Debriefing took far too long. Frances was waiting for him. A tall, stacked blonde, she had mile-long legs that looked so good in a power suit she was her boss' sole weapon for recruiting.

Once upon a time, she'd recruited the hell out of Ty.

Now there was nothing between them but an odd mix of

hostility and affection. She looked him over from head to toe and then back again. "You look like shit."

"Aw. Thanks."

She didn't offer him a smile, just another long gaze, giving nothing away. "You're not staying," she guessed.

"I'm not staying." He tossed her his security pass and walked.

"Do you really think a place like Lucky Harbor has anything to offer you?" she called after him.

He knew it did. He had connections there, real ones.

"Dammit, Ty," she said to his back when he kept walking. "At some point, you have to stop running."

"That's exactly what I'm doing."

Ty caught a red-eye flight into Seattle, and as he landed he brought up Lucky Harbor's Facebook. He'd resisted until now, but as the page loaded, he felt a smile curve his mouth at the latest note posted on the wall:

By now, you've all heard about Mrs. Burland's $100,000 donation to HSC, and how she single-handedly saved the clinic, brought back Mallory Quinn, AND created peace on earth.

Okay, maybe not quite peace on earth, but we do worship the ground she walks on. (Did I get that right, Louisa?)

ANYWAY, last week's raffle raised an additional $5K for the hospital. Thanks to our own Mallory Quinn for her tireless efforts. The grand prize—a date with Hospital Administrator Bill Lawson—was won by Jane Miller, Director of Nurses. Rumor has it that there was a good-night kiss. Wonder if Bill put out? Sources say yes. Look for a summer wedding . . .

Dawn hit the eastern sky as Ty drove a rental car into Lucky Harbor. He wondered if Mallory was still asleep in her bed, warm and soft.

Alone.

Christ, he hoped so. It'd only been two weeks but he'd left abruptly. Cruelly. He had no right to be back, no right at all to ask her to forgive him.

But that's exactly what he was going to do.

The ocean was still an inky purple as he drove past the pier, then hit the brakes.

The Shelby was in the lot at the diner.

Heart pounding, he parked and entered. The place smelled like fresh paint. The floors looked new and yet seemed to be made of the same timeless linoleum as they'd been before the sprinkler situation. He found Amy, Grace, and Mallory seated at the counter eating chocolate chip pancakes.

Or they had been eating, until he entered.

Three forks went still in the air.

Grace's and Amy's gazes slid to Mallory, but she was paying them no attention whatsoever. She was staring at Ty, her fork halfway to her mouth.

He'd walked through fire fights with less nerves, but he took hope from the sight of the charm bracelet glinting on her wrist.

"This is a private meeting," Grace told him. "Locals only."

"Grace," Mallory said quietly, her eyes never leaving Ty, but for once not giving anything of herself away, either. Ty had absolutely no idea what she was thinking; her face was carefully blank.

A lesson she'd probably learned from him.

Chapter 24

In the cookies of life,
friends and lovers are the chocolate chips.

Mallory stared at Ty and got light-headed, which turned out to be because she wasn't breathing.

"I thought you Chocoholics met over cake," Ty said.

Two weeks. It'd been two weeks since she'd seen him, and he wanted to discuss cake. She hungrily drank in the sight of him. He wore battered Levi's and a white button-down, looking as good as ever. But he'd lost some weight, and his eyes were guarded.

"We've been banned from cake," Grace said. "On account of the candles."

Amy pointed at Ty with her fork. "You planning on walking in and out of her life again?"

"Just in," he said, his gaze never leaving Mallory's. "We need to talk."

"So talk," Grace said.

Amy nodded.

Heart pounding, Mallory stood up and gave both of her friends a shake of her head. "You know what he's asking. Give us a minute."

"Okay, but this is his third time interrupting us," Amy pointed out. "And—"

"*Please*," Mallory said to her friends.

Amy looked at Ty, using her first two fingers to point at him, going back and forth between his eyes and hers, silently giving him notice that she was watching him and not to even *think* about misbehaving.

Grace dragged her away.

Mallory waited until they were out of earshot to look at Ty. Her entire being went warm as she drank him in. She had no idea why he was back but she hoped like hell she was part of the reason.

"You still trying to save me, Mallory?" Ty asked quietly.

Her heart was hammering so loud she couldn't hear herself talk. "I can't seem to help myself."

"I don't need saving."

No. No, he sure didn't. He was strong and capable, and more than able to take care of himself. "What *do* you need?"

"You," he said simply. "Only you."

"Oh," Grace breathed softly from behind them. "Oh, that's good."

Both Mallory and Ty turned to find that Amy and Grace had scooted close enough to eavesdrop. Grace winced and held up an apologetic hand. "Sorry. Continue."

Mallory turned back to Ty, who took her hand in his big, warm one to entwine their fingers, bringing them up to his chest. His heartbeat was a reassuring steady thump. "I know you've looked for Mr. Right," he said. "And then Mr. Wrong. I was thinking maybe you'd be interested in a Mr. . . . . Regular."

Her throat went tight. "That'd be great," she managed. "But I don't see any regular guys standing in front of me."

The corner of his mouth tipped up and melted her but she wasn't going to be distracted by his hotness right now. "Your job," she said.

"Yeah, I thought that's what drove me, gave me what I needed. I was wrong, Mallory. It's you. *You* fulfill me, like no job or no person ever has. You make me whole."

There was a sniffle behind them. Two sniffles. Mallory ignored them, even as she felt like sniffling herself. "Won't you go crazy here?"

"There's an opening in Seattle for a trauma flight paramedic. Also, I was thinking I want to work with veterans at HSC. I think I could help. And if I get bored and need some real action, there's always the arcade."

Mallory was absorbing this with what felt like a huge bucket of hope sitting on her chest. "And me," she whispered. "I could show you some action. You know, once in awhile."

"Mallory," he said, sounding raw and staggered and touched beyond words. "God, I was so stupid. So slow. I didn't know what to do with you. I tried to keep my distance but my world doesn't work without you in it."

She melted. Given the twin sighs behind her, she wasn't the only one. "But is a trauma paramedic job enough for you?"

"There's more important things to me than an adrenaline rush. There's more important things than *any* job. But there's nothing more important than you," he said. "Mallory, I lo—"

"*Wait!*" This was from Amy, and she looked at Mallory. "I'm sorry, but don't you think you should tell him about the car before he finishes that sentence?"

"*No,*" Mallory said, giving Amy the evil eye. She wanted the rest of Ty's sentence, dammit!

Ty frowned. "What's wrong with the Shelby?"

"*Nothing*," Mallory said quickly.

"Nothing," Amy agreed. "Except for the dinged door where she parked too close to the mailbox."

"Oh my God," Mallory said to her. "What are you, the car police?"

"The *classic* car police," Amy said smugly.

"You parked the Shelby on the street?" Ty asked Mallory incredulously.

She went brows-up.

"Okay," he said, lifting his hands. "It's okay. Never mind about the car."

"I've got this one," Grace said, wrapping an arm around Amy, covering the waitress's mouth while she was at it. "Go on."

Mallory turned back to Ty, who pulled her off her stool and touched the small scar on her cheek before leaning in to kiss her. "I love you, Mallory," he said very quietly, very seriously. "So damn much."

Warmth and affection and need and so much more rushed her. "I know."

"You know?"

"Yes."

"Well, hell," he said with a small smile and a shake of his head. "You might have told me and saved me a lot of time."

"How about I tell you something else?" she said. "I love you, too."

The rest of the wariness he'd arrived with drained from him. "Tell me what you need from me for there to be an us," he said.

Hope blossomed, full and bright. "You want an us?"

"I want an us. Tell me, Mallory."

"I like what we had," she said. "Being together after a long day, maybe dinner out sometimes. That was nice. We could skip the orchestra, though."

"Mallory," he said on a short laugh. "Tell me you want more from me than that."

She bit her lower lip, but the naughty grin escaped anyway. "Well, maybe a little bit more."

He laughed softly, his eyes going dark. He pulled her in and kissed her hard, threading his hands in her hair. "How do you feel about sealing the deal with a ring?" he murmured against her lips.

All three women gasped.

"What?" Mallory squeaked. "You mean an engagement ring? To be *married*?"

"Yes," he said. "You're it for me, Mallory. You're everything."

He was serious. And suddenly, so was she. "I'd like that," she said softly.

"Good," he said. "Anything else we need to work out?"

Only a hundred things. Where was he going to live? *With her*, she thought possessively. She wanted him with her. Wait—Did that mean that she'd have to learn to cook? Because that might be a stretch. And she didn't have any room in her closet to share. And the cat. What if Sweet Pea pooped in his boots?

Ty cupped her face and made her look at him, deep into his eyes, and it was there she found the truth. All these worries were inconsequential. They didn't matter. Nothing mattered but this.

Him.

Besides, she had time to make room for him in her closet. The cat had time to get used to him. They had all the time they needed, because he'd told her he was hers, and he was a man of his word. "I've got all I need," she told him.

He leaned down and kissed her again, then stroked a finger over her temple, tucking a loose strand of hair behind her ear. "I want you to know," he said. "That you're the best choice I ever made."

"No regrets?"

"No regrets."

Heart full to bursting, she tugged him down and kissed the man she was going to spend the rest of her life with.

THE CHOCOHOLICS' WICKEDLY AWESOME
CHOCOLATE CAKE

Cake

- 1 8-ounce bag of dark chocolate chips
- ½ cup and 3 extra tablespoons butter
- 1 ¼ cups cake flour
- ½ cup cocoa
- 1 box of instant chocolate pudding mix
- ½ teaspoon salt
- ½ teaspoon baking powder
- ¼ teaspoon baking soda
- 4 large eggs
- ¼ cup vegetable oil
- ½ cup white sugar
- ⅓ cup dark brown sugar
- 1 ½ teaspoon vanilla extract
- ⅔ cup milk

Melt the chocolate chips in a microwave-safe bowl by combining the chocolate chips and 3 tablespoons of butter and microwaving on power level 3 for 2 minutes. Take the bowl out of the oven, stir, and put back in the microwave for 2 more minutes. Take it out, stir, and put back in the microwave for 2 final minutes. Stir until the melted chocolate is fully incorporated with the butter.

Mix the dry ingredients together in a medium bowl: cake flour, cocoa, pudding mix, salt, baking powder, and baking soda.

In a large bowl, using an electric mixer, beat the eggs, oil, and sugars together until it thickens, approximately five minutes. Reduce mixer to low speed then add in vanilla and milk. Gradually add in the dry ingredients and beat together.

After it's fully mixed, pour batter into a greased 8-inch square cake pan. Bake at 350 degrees until you can put a toothpick in the middle and it comes out clean, approximately 35 to 45 minutes.

Frosting

- ½ cup powdered sugar
- ¾ cup cocoa
- 2 tablespoons butter (softened)
- 1 8-ounce package of cream cheese (softened)
- 1 teaspoon vanilla
- ¼ cup milk

Mix the powdered sugar and cocoa together.

In a separate bowl, using an electric mixer, beat the butter and cream cheese together. Add vanilla and mix it in. Slowly start incorporating some of the sugar-cocoa mixture. When it starts to firm up, slowly mix in some of the milk. Alternate sugar-cocoa mix and milk until you have the right frosting consistency.

Frost the cooled cake and then…yum!

About the Author

New York Times bestselling author **Jill Shalvis** lives in a small town in the Sierras full of quirky characters. Any resemblance to the quirky characters in her books is mostly coincidental. Look for Jill's bestselling, award-winning books wherever romances are sold and visit her website for a complete book list and daily blog detailing her city-girl-living-in-the-mountains adventures.

You can learn more at:

JillShalvis.com
Twitter @JillShalvis
Facebook.com/JillShalvis

Want more charming small towns?
Fall in love with these Forever contemporary romances!

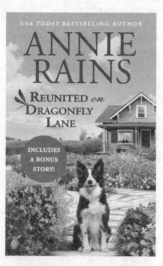

REUNITED ON DRAGONFLY LANE
by Annie Rains

Boutique owner Sophie Daniels certainly wasn't looking to adopt a rambunctious puppy with a broken leg. Yet somehow handsome veterinarian—and her high school sweetheart—Chase Lewis convinced her to take in Comet. But house calls from Chase soon force them to face the past and their unresolved feelings. Can Sophie open up her heart again to see that first love is even better the second time around? Includes the bonus story *A Wedding on Lavender Hill*!

DREAM A LITTLE DREAM
by Melinda Curtis

Darcy Jones Harper is thrilled to have finally shed her reputation as the girl from the wrong side of the tracks. The people of Sunshine Valley have to respect her now that she's the new town judge. But when the guy who broke her heart back in high school shows up in her courtroom, she realizes maybe things haven't changed so much after all...because her pulse still races at the sight of bad-boy bull rider Jason Petrie.

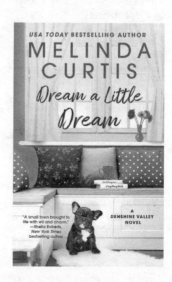

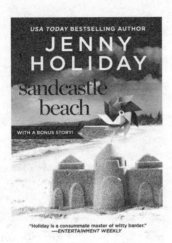

"Holiday is a consummate master of witty banter."
—*ENTERTAINMENT WEEKLY*

SANDCASTLE BEACH
by Jenny Holiday

What Maya Mehta really needs to save her beloved community theater is Matchmaker Bay's new business grant. She's got some serious competition, though: Benjamin Lawson, local bar owner, Jerk Extraordinaire, and Maya's annoyingly hot arch nemesis. Turns out there's a thin line between hate and irresistible desire, and Maya and Law are really good at crossing it. But when things heat up, will they allow their long-standing feud to get in the way of their growing feelings? Includes the bonus story *Once Upon a Bride*, for the first time in print!

A WEDDING ON LILAC LANE
by Hope Ramsay

After returning home from her country music career, Ella McMillan is shocked to find her mother is engaged. Worse, she asks Ella to plan the event with her fiancé's straitlaced son, Dr. Dylan Killough. While Ella wants to create the perfect day, Dylan is determined the two shouldn't get married at all. Somehow amid all their arguing, sparks start flying. And soon everyone in Magnolia Harbor is wondering if Dylan and Ella will be joining their parents in a trip down the aisle.

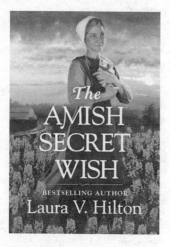

THE AMISH SECRET WISH
by Laura V. Hilton

Waitress Hallie Brunstetter has a secret: She writes a popular column for her local Amish paper under the pen name GHB. When Hallie receives a letter from a reader asking to become her pen pal, Hallie reluctantly agrees. She can't help but be drawn to the compassionate stranger, never expecting him to show up in Hidden Springs looking for GHB...nor for him to be quite so handsome in real life. But after losing her beau in a tragic accident, Hallie can't risk her heart—or her secrets—again.

HER AMISH WEDDING QUILT
by Winnie Griggs

When the man she thought she would wed chooses another woman, Greta Eicher pours her energy into crafting beautiful quilts at her shop and helping widower Noah Stoll care for his adorable young children. But when her feelings for Noah grow into something even deeper, will she be able to convince him to have enough faith to give love another chance?

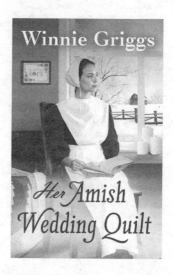

Discover bonus content and more on
read-forever.com

ONE LUCKY DAY
(2-IN-1 EDITION)
by Jill Shalvis

Have double the fun with these two novels from the bestselling Lucky Harbor series! Can a rebel find a way to keep the peace with a straitlaced sheriff? Or will Chloe Traeger's past keep her from a love that lasts in *Head Over Heels*? When a just-for-fun fling with Ty Garrison, the mysterious new guy in town, becomes something more, will Mallory Quinn quit playing it safe—and play for keeps instead—in *Lucky in Love*?

FOREVER FRIENDS
by Sarah Mackenzie

With her daughter away at college, single mom Renee isn't sure who she is anymore. What she *is* sure of is that she shouldn't be crushing on her new boss, Dr. Dan Hanlon. But when Renee comes to the rescue of her neighbor Sadie, the two unexpectedly hatch a plan to open her dream bakery. As Renee finds friendship with Sadie and summons the courage to explore her attraction to Dr. Dan, is it possible Renee can have the life she's always imagined?

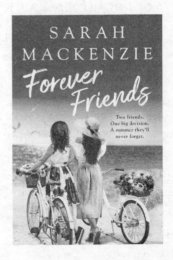